Danger at Every Turn

Danger at Every Turn

Devon Vaughn Archer

www.urbanbooks.net

Urban Books, LLC
78 East Industry Court
Deer Park, NY 11729

Danger at Every Turn Copyright © 2012
Devon Vaughn Archer

ISBN 13: 978-1-60162-342-3
ISBN 10: 1-60162-342-9

First Trade Paperback Printing April 2012
Printed in the United States of America

10 9 8 7 6 5 4 3 2 1

This is a work of fiction. Any references or similarities to actual events, real people, living, or dead, or to real locales are intended to give the novel a sense of reality. Any similarity in other names, characters, places, and incidents is entirely coincidental.

Distributed by Kensington Publishing Corp.
Submit Wholesale Orders to:
Kensington Publishing Corp.
C/O Penguin Group (USA) Inc.
Attention: Order Processing
405 Murray Hill Parkway
East Rutherford, NJ 07073-2316
Phone: 1-800-526-0275
Fax: 1-800-227-9604

Danger at Every Turn

by

Devon Vaughn Archer

Other Devon Vaughn Archer Titles

The Secrets of Paradise Bay

The Hitman's Woman

Dedication

To the Maui Mermaid, the love of my life, and all the fans who have devotedly supported my writings over the years.

Also for my loving mother, Marjah Aljean, who got me on the right track way back when as a college student, dreaming of someday becoming a successful writer.

PROLOGUE

"It's time." He spoke softly, yet with a firmness that underscored his intentions.

The urge hit him like a cold slap in the face. Even if he'd wanted to look the other way, there was no stopping what had to be done. The dark forces within propelled him to kill and kill again. The best he—and his victims—could hope for was to try to control his robust appetite for killing as much as possible so there was no a target on his back for the police to take out sooner or later.

Right now, it was time to pounce upon his latest prey like any good bloodthirsty hunter. And there was nothing she or anyone else could do to stop him.

Nothing at all.

He moved across the green grass wet with dew and onto one of the trails that zigzagged through Pelle Park like a maze. Effortlessly, he passed between a cluster of aging red cedar trees dying a slow death much like he intended for his target to suffer. He kept his steps deliberate and mind focused on the task at hand.

His gaze sharpened like a razor on to the female jogger whom he had been following ever since watching friends drop her off at the park for what, unbeknownst to her, would be the last run. Like the others, she was African American and pretty enough with long, dark, braided hair. She was wearing a sports bra and shorts. He admired her long, lean legs in stride and imagined them wrapped high around his waist.

All in good time.

He continued to shadow her like her worst nightmare, keeping his distance according to plan, until the last possible moment. There were other runners crisscrossing paths, each seemingly caught up in their own world. Too busy to notice a killer hidden in plain view.

Just the way he liked it.

He watched as the object of his attention picked up her speed, separating herself from the crowd like she couldn't be bothered with them, as she ran between rows of fir trees and out of site.

Almost.

Good girl. He smiled. *I was counting on that.*

He took a short cut and risked losing site of her to shorten the distance. If his timing was right, he knew exactly where they would rendezvous and when.

Along with what would happen from that point on.

Kendre Potter's long dookie braids bounced across her shoulders and back as she broke into a full stride across the dirt trail. She loved jogging in this park, one of the friendliest in town for runners. It gave her time to think about work, boyfriend headaches, and her plans to buy a new condo in a waterfront development this summer. But, most of all, she loved breathing in the springtime air of the Pacific Northwest, working on her calves, and feeling free as a bird in flight.

She took measured breaths and moved smoothly along the tree-lined path, expecting to come to a clearing on the other side with more trails and nature to appreciate in this forest wonderland.

She never considered that someone had been watching her every move and had devilish intentions in mind.

***

As it turned out, he had reached the point with a few seconds to spare. He spied a bird overhead that momentarily captured his attention, flying in the direction of the jogger as if to warn her of impending danger. But she was apparently too focused on her routine to notice or care.

He positioned himself behind a thick tree so that she would not see him 'til it was too late.

As she rounded the corner, he stepped out and they came face to face, startling her. He could tell that she didn't feel threatened by him, and probably thought he was just another runner she only needed to jog past so they didn't collide.

Yet when she tried this, he was quicker, blocking her path with his muscular body. Before she could react to what she now realized was imminent danger, his fist connected flush with her jaw. He could tell he'd broken it and she fell to the ground like a rag doll, knocked out stone cold.

He quickly dragged her limp body into the woods and away from prying eyes. His heart was racing with anticipation at what was about to happen. He quickly removed her clothing, ignoring the blood spilling from her mouth and nose.

Soon she would awaken and wish she hadn't. The excruciating facial pain would be the least of her problems. By the time he was through with her, she would welcome death a thousand times over. Make that a million.

And he would gladly answer her prayers to be put out of her misery as surely as one day turned to the next.

But first things first. . . .

ONE

Spencer Berry took his German shepherd named Sky out for their usual afternoon run in the park. They lived in Sinclair Heights, Oregon, dubbed the "City of Parks," for its many parks peppered throughout the city, some forty miles from Portland. Pelle Park was not too far from Spencer's home or Sinclair Heights College, where he taught psychology. He enjoyed running in the park as well as using it as a place for relaxation and contemplation. Spencer was sure that Sky liked these outings even more than he did, since he could do something besides tear up his backyard or lie around the house all day.

Spencer felt the dog yank on the leash, longing to roam freely. But the leash laws in the city were strictly enforced and he had no desire to test them. "Sorry, boy, no can do."

Sky settled down and seemed to acquiescence to a leisurely, controlled run.

Spencer sucked in a calculated breath and thought about the tragic twists and turns his life had taken. A decade ago his mother died, leaving his father a widower much too soon. Then last year, his twin brother, Wesley, was killed when his boat capsized during a lone outing at sea. Being a great swimmer was not enough to save him from the undercurrent in the lake that muggy day, his body forever buried in the depths of the murky water. At thirty-one, Wesley had his whole life ahead of him. Now Spencer had nothing left of his brother but memories.

One memory was that it was Wesley who had been the first one to date and fall for Spencer's ex-wife, Fiona. But, at the time, Fiona chose to marry Spencer instead as the more secure, practical, and successful one who worked as a criminal psychologist for the FBI's Portland office.

For his part, Spencer had gone with his heart and soul when he married the woman he wanted to spend a lifetime with. They had a little girl named Charity, and he'd hoped that would be enough to bond them in ways they might never have otherwise. Instead, it seemed to have the opposite effect, drawing them further apart in spite of their shared love for their daughter.

Now he had to wonder if Fiona ever truly loved him the way a man needed to be loved, or if he had just been a poor substitute for Wesley, whom she had clearly been unable to get out of her system.

Either way, the breakup of their marriage a few weeks after his brother's death had soured Spencer on women—certainly Fiona—insofar as serious commitments. Not to mention love. This had left more than one woman with ill feelings toward him after the romance ended. But he couldn't make himself feel what wasn't there, any more than Fiona had been able to do during much of their marriage. She had made it all too clear, in actions if not words, that what they had was largely a marriage of convenience, with love as a very small part of the equation.

So I guess I'll just have to get used to being alone. Not exactly something to look forward to when I have so much affection to offer.

Sky's raucous barking snapped Spencer from his reverie.

"What is it, boy?" The dog was trying to break free and didn't seem to want to take no for an answer.

Spencer spotted a group of young men getting up in each other's faces.

"That ain't my problem, man," a short male with an Afro and baggy clothing argued.

"I'm making it your problem!" said a tall, thin male with micro braids.

It was obvious to Spencer by their body language that they were rival gang members, no doubt battling over turf or a misunderstanding that was threatening to get out of hand. Having worked with gang members when he was with the FBI's Gang Unit, he recognized their characteristics and was well aware of their propensity to commit violence at even the slightest pretext.

No sooner had the thought crossed his mind than Spencer watched the one with micro braids pull out a gun and fire it at point-blank range at the other, hitting him in the chest. The victim went down immediately.

"Hey," Spencer yelled, getting the youths' attention.

Those on their feet saw him and scattered like flies. Spencer noted that the shooter had darted off in a direction all by himself, as if to ditch the gun somewhere to keep from being connected with it. Instinctively, Spencer went to aid the one shot. His six-foot-four frame with long, strapping legs served him well, as he quickly narrowed the distance. In the process, the leash slipped from his hand and Sky ran off in hot pursuit of the shooter.

"Sky, no! Come back!" Spencer ordered, but the dog, normally mild mannered, seemed to have a mind of his own and was not to be denied his hopes of nabbing the man.

Dammit! The last thing Spencer wanted was for his dog to be shot by this asshole. But, since no one else seemed in a hurry to help the victim, it was up to him. He could only hope that Sky did not come face to face with a desperate and frightened shooter before he got rid of the gun.

The victim was lying on the grass, blood oozing from his chest. He looked all of fifteen or sixteen, if that. Any anger he had in his face was mitigated by the anguish in his eyes.

"Just hang on," Spencer told him. He took out his cell phone and called 911, giving his location and the situation. He turned back to the victim who was weaving in and out of consciousness. "Help's on the way."

The teenager moaned something indecipherable and tried to get up, but Spencer held him down. "You're in no condition to get up. Wait for the paramedics."

"I don't wanna die, man," he gasped in a frightened voice.

Maybe you should have thought of that before you joined a gang. "You won't," Spencer tried to reassure him. He looked up and saw a forty-something woman standing over them.

"Can I help?" she asked. "I'm a nurse."

"Your timing couldn't be better," Spencer said. "He's been shot. My dog's gone after the shooter."

"Go find your dog," she said, and started tending to the victim 'til the paramedics arrived.

"I'll do that." Spencer was confident the young man would survive this. He wasn't as confident the same could be said for Sky. After all, if the shooter was willing to kill another human being, he'd have no problem killing his dog.

Spencer followed the sound of Sky's ferocious barks off the trail through thick trees and shrubbery, moving deeper into the woods. After several minutes of searching, Spencer had yet to spot the dog. Or the shooter.

"Where are you, boy?" Spencer called out when the barking suddenly stopped. He feared his dog had been wounded by the cowardly gang member. Or worse. When Spencer called out Sky's name again, the dog responded with a steady series of barks interspersed with whimpers.

Spencer continued to move in the direction of Sky's barks. He was at the northern edge of Pelle Park close to a stretch of large, old Victorian homes. He climbed through thick shrubs and trampled over wildflowers 'til he finally spotted his dog.

"There you are, boy." The dog ran up to him, jumping up and down wildly, as if pleased to be in familiar company. Spencer was just as happy to see him, relieved that the dog did not appear to be hurt. He saw no sign of the shooter. "Calm down, Sky. Where's the punk who shot the kid? Did he get away?"

Sky suddenly broke for the nearby creek, barking almost hysterically and seemingly urging Spencer to follow him.

"What is it?"

He followed the dog, expecting to find the shooter injured, courtesy of Sky's sharp bite. The dog stopped at the edge of the creek that was almost obscured by overgrown ferns.

Spencer took two steps forward before spotting what looked to be a bare leg and foot sticking out of the ferns. He moved closer and quickly realized that it wasn't the shooter's body parts he was looking at.

Lying face up in the shallow water was the naked body of a young African American woman. Her face was discolored and badly swollen on one side. Though her eyes were wide open, she was motionless. Spencer didn't need to be a medical examiner to know that the woman was dead.

Or look twice to realize that he knew her. Rebecca London was a psychology professor at Sinclair Heights College. She was also a runner, making good use of Pelle Park every chance she got to exercise her legs.

Spencer's stomach churned. It appeared as if the so-called Park Killer had struck again. Over the past year, six women had been badly beaten, sexually assaulted, and strangled in or around one of the city's parks. Every one of them had been someone Spencer was acquainted with in some manner, bizarre as it was to him. Now he had to add to the list a fellow professor who had only been at the college for three months.

The police had attributed the killings to a serial killer who seemed as elusive as Jack the Ripper. And was every bit as diabolical, unpredictable, and lethal.

Spencer attached the leash to Sky's collar, pulling the dog away from the horrific scene that so fascinated him. "Back away, boy. I don't think there's anything either of us can do for her now. And I can't let you taint the crime scene any more than you already have. Never mind that you let the gangbanger get away."

Spencer had to notify the authorities. He got out his cell phone and quickly realized the damn battery had died. Glancing at the back of a house that wasn't too far away, he decided he would use their phone to report the crime. Or get them to do so.

TWO

Deidre Lawrence watched in horror from the passenger seat as the man holding a gun opened the car door just as her husband, Marshall, was about to start the engine. Their six-year-old son, Adam, had already been secured in the child seat in back.

"What the . . . ?" spurted from Marshall's lips as he looked toward the carjacker.

He was a Latino male in his early twenties with a buzz cut, dark hair, slender build, and a scowl that looked like a permanent fixture on his long face.

"Get out of the damn car!" he demanded, pointing the barrel of the gun at Marshall's head.

Deidre expected her husband to do the smart thing and obey the man. After all, the car wasn't worth losing their lives over. Even if it was a brand new BMW that was Marshall's pride and joy. Instead, he chose to resist the carjacker, grabbing on to the barrel of the gun with both hands.

"Like hell I will!" Marshall spat defiantly as the two struggled for control of the weapon.

"Stop it, Marshall!" Deidre screamed. She glanced over her shoulder at their son, who started to cry. "Let him have the car, please!"

"I'll give him something all right," her husband growled angrily. "I'll make this gutless bastard wish he'd never been born."

Marshall, an ex-player for the Philadelphia Eagles, was used to being in control and able to intimidate others by looks alone. He was not afraid to use his imposing size to his advantage. Apparently, he thought this was one of those times. Deidre sat frozen as her husband took one hand off the gun to hit the carjacker squarely on the left side of his face. However, instead of going down for the count as might be expected, the man shrugged it off, seeming just as determined to get what he was after.

In the ensuing struggle for possession of the gun, a shot rang out, followed by another. For a moment, everything seemed to happen in slow motion and Deidre caught her breath with uncertainty. When she realized that Marshall had been shot in the chest, it never occurred to her that the same bullet had somehow ended up grazing her arm. Or that the second bullet had gone through the seat and hit Adam.

Clearly panicked that it had come down to this, the would-be carjacker, who was unharmed in the exchange other than having a sore jaw, abandoned his mission of stealing the car, and ran off like a jackrabbit.

Deidre heard herself weeping when she woke up. Opening her teary eyes to the afternoon sunlight streaming through the wooden blinds in her bedroom, she realized it was only a dream that had terrified her so.

In fact, she knew it was far more than that.

It was a nightmare Deidre had lived three years ago, and relived many times since. While her life had been spared that awful day with only a flesh wound, Deidre's husband and son were not so fortunate, both dying before they reached the emergency room. Having gotten a good look at the man responsible for their deaths, Deidre had described him to a tee. He was apprehended shortly thereafter and convicted of attempted carjacking and two counts of second-degree murder, getting hard time.

At the tender age of twenty-nine, Deidre had been left a widow and childless, effectively ending the life she'd known and wanted desperately to cling to as though there were no such thing as new beginnings. She blamed Marshall as much as the carjacker for the tragedy that occurred. If only he hadn't been so damned bullheaded, trying to take on an armed carjacker at risk to himself and his family.

Deidre knew that the carjacker probably would have killed them all no matter what, so they couldn't identify him, had things worked out a different way. Maybe she would be dead now too, if Marshall hadn't taken matters into his own hands.

Or maybe we'd all still be alive and I wouldn't have to wake up alone every day in this big, empty house.

Deidre dragged herself out of bed. For the longest time, she'd wondered if it would have been better if she'd joined her husband and son in heaven. At least there she would have no more pain in their absence.

It was only after she decided to stop feeling sorry for herself and do something productive with her life that Deidre abandoned such thoughts, recognizing that it wasn't her time to go. She had to carry on for Marshall and Adam. Isn't that what they would have wanted?

Deidre's bare feet padded across the cold hardwood floor of the Victorian home her grandparents had lived in for four decades 'til they passed away within two years of one another. Deidre's mother had inherited the house upon her grandfather's death last year.

As of one month ago, Deidre called it home. The architectural elegance, antique furnishings, family heirlooms, and sense of familiarity brought her back to her childhood memories of summer vacations at the house. She'd left Philadelphia and the dark memories behind for a fresh start in Sinclair Heights, Oregon—a predominantly African American up-and-coming Northwest town with a down-to-earth cost of living.

To supplement her income as a freelance artist, Deidre worked part time for the Sinclair Heights Police Bureau as a civilian police spokesperson, putting to use her bachelor's degree in communications and her dual major of graphic design. Though it was difficult reporting criminality and investigations to the media, Deidre considered it a catharsis of sorts in facing her fears as a crime victim by speaking on behalf of the police as they dealt with other crimes. So far, she'd received high marks from her employers.

After throwing on some jeans and a sweater, Deidre went into the remodeled gourmet kitchen and made herself a cup of coffee. Before she could take a sip, her cell phone rang. Grabbing it off the granite countertop, she saw that the caller was her mother, Lucille.

No doubt checking on me once again in her overburdening, yet well-meaning, way.

Deidre groaned. "Hello, Momma."

"Hello, honey. Just calling to make sure you're all right there?"

"Yes, I'm fine," she said with an exaggerated sigh. "Just like yesterday and two days before that. . . ."

Deidre could almost see the color deepen in her mother's face.

"I don't mean to be a pest, Deidre," she claimed.

"You're not," Deidre lied. "I know you're just concerned about me living alone in Granddad's house, even though I seem to remember it was *your* idea in the first place that I move here."

"I know, and it was a good idea," Lucille said. "Someone needed to put life back into that old house and keep it going as part of the family's heritage. Still, without Marshall there and—"

"But that's the whole point," Deidre said, cutting her off. "Marshall and Adam are *not* here or there. I have to live for myself now and I'm doing just that. I like my job well enough and I'm starting to make friends."

"And you don't need your mother trying to micromanage your life from Philadelphia," she said. "I get that. I'll try to remember that you're blessed with an independent spirit I can only dream about."

"Dream about?" Deidre rolled her eyes. "Who do you think I got it from, Momma? Certainly not Daddy." Actually, Deidre felt she had inherited the best and worst of her character from both of them, but was trying to make her mother feel better. Or maybe herself.

The doorbell rang, giving Deidre a good excuse to cut this short. "There's someone at the door," she said. "Have to go. I'll call you soon."

"You better." Her mother sighed and said, "I love you, sweetheart."

"You too. Tell Daddy I said hello."

Deidre hung up. She took a sip of her coffee and set the mug down. She wondered who had decided to pay her a visit on this Saturday afternoon. Maybe it was her boss, Hal Iverson, who, she believed, had a crush on her. Or was that just her imagination? He happened to live in the neighborhood and wasn't afraid to drop by from time to time to see if she needed anything, which Deidre in no way encouraged.

I'm not interested in mixing police business with intimate pleasure.

Perhaps it was her friend Agatha Huston, who worked in the records department at the police bureau and was the local queen of gab.

Wonder what juicy tidbits she has to tell me this time?

Last, but certainly not least, Deidre suspected the visitor could be her neighbor and fellow artist, Sabrina Murray, who often ran at this time of day and had no qualms about trying to get Deidre to take up the exercise routine.

Thanks, but I think I'll spare my knees the wear and tear and stick to working out at the gym.

Peering through the woven wood shades covering the small window on the door, Deidre saw that she was wrong on all counts. Standing there was a tall, oak-skinned, bald man in casual attire with a German shepherd at his side. What did they want? She didn't figure him to be a salesman. But, then again, what did a salesman look like? And who said he couldn't come with his pet? Maybe he used the dog to scare people into buying whatever he was selling.

Deidre tried to assess if the dog was truly dangerous, noting that he had a firm grip on its leash.

Maybe I should be more concerned about the man than the dog. Or maybe I'm just letting paranoia get the better of me.

Opening the door a crack with the chain still in place, Deidre said in a deliberately cold voice, "Yes?"

The man seemed cool, calm, and collected, while saying in a smooth baritone voice, "Sorry to disturb you, but I just thought you'd like to know there's a dead woman in your backyard. . . ."

"What?" Deidre batted her lashes as she focused her bold ebony eyes at him, as if she had misheard.

Spencer could see she was taken aback, still hiding behind the door. He would be too, had the situation been reversed. Unfortunately, there was no easy way to say what he'd discovered.

"Sky found her," he explained, glancing at his dog. "Look, I hate to put this on you, but my cell phone died and someone needs to report this. Since your house was the closest—"

"Are you serious?" Deidre said, though there was no indication from the hard contours of his face that he was lying.

"Dead serious, no pun intended." Spencer paused, studying the attractive lady's caramel-toned face, bordered by sable hair that was stylishly cut above her shoulders. Her nose was dainty and her lips full. She reminded him a lot of Beyoncé. And maybe a bit of Halle Berry and Sanaa Lathan thrown in for good measure. "From the looks of the corpse, I'd say she was murdered. . . ."

Deidre gulped. "Murdered?" Her eyes grew large. "By who—you?"

Spencer frowned. "No, definitely not. As I said, my dog found her body." He decided to spare her the part about the gangbanger Sky had hoped to take a bite out of. And describing the murder victim as the work of a serial killer was probably not a good idea either. At least not 'til she had reported the crime and come to realize he was only the messenger.

Deidre was aware that a serial killer was on the loose in the city, targeting attractive African American women. From what she gathered, his attacks usually took place in the evening or nighttime hours rather than in broad daylight. But that didn't mean he couldn't change his MO.

She studied the man at her door, still unsure if he was on the level or if this was somehow just a clever ploy to get her to open the door. After all, wasn't that what killers did, talked smoothly to gain your confidence? If so, she'd fallen for it. Deidre's instincts told her that this handsome man meant her no harm. Certainly not like the woman he'd described. She hoped the same could be said for his dog, who was large enough to probably do some damage if he had a mind to.

Spencer sensed her fear. Maybe he would be wary too, were the shoe on the other foot. But he was the one who had discovered the dead woman—one day after last seeing her alive. And now the woman before him was privy to it as well. Soon others would also have to deal with the victim, how she died, and how she ended up in the creek.

Spencer backed off a bit. "Look, I'm going to go now, before Sky and I scare *you* to death. After we've left, you can check out the gruesome scene for yourself. I have a feeling the victim's not going to be leaving on her own. Then you can give the police a buzz, assuming I haven't gotten home to call them myself by then."

Deidre reacted. *I can't let him leave.* If there really was a dead body out there, the police would definitely want to talk to him.

"Hold on," Deidre uttered. "If you could just wait here for a moment, I'll report it and, uh, you can show me exactly where the body is."

"No problem. Sky and I have nowhere to go right now." Not that this was how Spencer had planned to spend his Saturday afternoon. Not by a long shot. But it could be worse, much worse, like it was for the poor dead woman in the creek.

Spencer noted that there was only one car in the driveway—a blue Subaru Legacy. Did that mean she lived in this big house alone? He couldn't imagine someone so striking being on her own. Never mind the fact that he was alone too, and liked it that way for now.

Maybe she felt the same way.

Sky tugged on the leash, obviously getting restless.

"I know, boy," Spencer said sympathetically.

"Shouldn't be too much longer before we're home and you can eat and run free in the backyard to your heart's content." *Too much longer being a relative term.* Spencer suspected he would need to give a statement to the police. Make that two statements, as he now had a gang shooting and a female homicide to report as part of his civic duty and desire to see Sinclair Heights kept as crime free as possible.

THREE

Deidre reported the alleged crime to a homicide lieutenant she knew with the police bureau. Then she quickly texted her friend Sabrina to let her know what was going on. Satisfied that the wheels were in motion and help was on the way, Deidre unchained the door and opened it so she was fully face to face with the man on the other side. She decided he could give Denzel Washington a real run for his money in the looks department. His gray-brown eyes were deep and alluring beneath thick black brows. His broad nose was slightly crooked, as though it had been broken once. Below his wide mouth was a faint half moon–shaped scar on his chin, perhaps the result of nicking it with a razor some time ago.

"The police are on their way," she told him.

"Good."

Deidre looked at the dog tentatively. "He doesn't bite, does he?"

"Only people who rub him the wrong way." Spencer looked at Deidre with a crooked grin. "That usually doesn't include pretty women."

Yeah, right. She stepped cautiously onto the wraparound porch. The dog, still attached to the leash, immediately began licking her hand. Deidre flinched, but did not back away.

Don't you dare make a liar out of me, Spencer warned Sky with a tug on the leash. He seemed to get the message and behaved himself. In the meantime, Spencer couldn't help but be taken by the lady of the house, who looked even better when the door wasn't blocking much of her. She had a nice figure that exuded sexuality. He only wished they were meeting under less difficult circumstances where she wasn't on guard as though he was the enemy.

Deidre steeled her nerves, petting the dog gently. He seemed more fascinated by her than anything and had not attacked. She held her cell phone out of the dog's reach.

"So where is this body?" Deidre lifted her eyes to meet the man's probing gaze.

"Over there." Spencer tilted his head toward the creek. "Are you sure you want to see her? It's not a pretty picture."

Deidre didn't suppose it would be. But after experiencing death firsthand and as a police spokesperson, she had built somewhat of a wall to shield her from the powerful effects of a corpse. "Yes, I want to see her."

"Very well," he said. "Sky will lead the way, won't you, boy?"

The dog barked as if he and his owner spoke the same language. He pulled the man around the side of the house gamely. Deidre walked alongside him, very much aware of his manly presence in ways that surprised her, even as she tried to keep her thoughts on the notion that there was a dead woman behind her house.

They had moved beyond the alder trees that surrounded Deidre's property and now stood near the creek that ran through it. Deidre gasped when she saw the disfigured face and nude body of a female. The dog barked raucously as if he also knew the woman was gone, but had suffered terribly before being killed.

Deidre turned pale and Spencer thought she was going to faint. He prepared himself to catch her, should it become necessary. "Sorry, but I told you she was in pretty bad shape."

Deidre didn't argue, shaken to the core. But seeing was believing. It brought back vivid memories of her husband and son who died before her very eyes from the carjacker's bullets. She'd done everything in her power to try to save them, using her knowledge from first aid classes and survival instincts. But the damage had been too extensive and irrevocable.

This woman had surely died an awful death, Deidre decided sorrowfully as she looked at the traumatized body. And the killer was still out there somewhere . . . waiting to strike again. . . .

She regarded the man who had apparently discovered the remains, knowing they needed to preserve the crime scene as much as possible. "Why don't we wait by the house? The police should be here shortly."

Spencer nodded. "Good idea."

The wooded area behind Deidre's house was crawling with police and crime scene technicians within minutes of the time she phoned in the grisly discovery. The telltale signs seemed to indicate that the Park Killer had struck again. The fact that the victim had been killed or dumped so close to her home unnerved Deidre more than anytime since she had moved to Sinclair Heights. She could just as easily have been the victim.

Or her friend Sabrina.

Almost as unsettling was being in the spotlight as the homeowner, when she operated far better behind the scenes of a crime as a police spokesperson. But at least she shared the burden with the handsome stranger and his dog, neither of whom seemed particularly interested in being in the limelight.

"By the way, my name's Spencer Berry." Spencer thought it was time to get past the awkwardness of being brought together by the unexpected. "And you already know that this is Sky."

Deidre wasn't sure if she should volunteer her name, but decided that if there was any harm to come, knowing her name wouldn't make much difference. Besides, something told her that even though he was a stranger, he was not a dangerous man—at least where it concerned criminal behavior. Deidre had seen a killer up close and personal when he murdered her family. And Spencer Berry didn't seem to be made of the same fiber. Yet she suspected that he could be very dangerous when it pertained to matters of the heart, body, and soul, were a woman to let her defenses down.

"Deidre Lawrence."

He nodded. "Not exactly the ideal meeting circumstances, but at least we're both on our feet. Unlike that poor woman—"

"I agree," Deidre said. How could she not? No one wanted to die so young when they had so much life ahead of them. Especially at the hands of a killer. Nor was she happy that the victim had been killed so close to her property. Should she be concerned?

She eyed Spencer, wondering how he and his dog had happened to find the body. It wasn't exactly located amid one of the many park pathways. Or dog areas. "How did you and your dog discover the body?"

Spencer considered the question. He didn't want to spook her, but decided it was best to tell her the whole story. "Well, we witnessed a gang shooting in the park and Sky broke loose to go after the shooter, who ran this way. When I finally caught up to him, I got a hell of a lot more than either of us bargained for."

"I'll bet." Deidre knew that there was a gang presence in the area and they seemed to be getting more and more violent. Now they had a serial killer to deal with. Maybe Sinclair Heights wasn't the safe haven she'd thought it was when she moved there. "I appreciate you telling me about it, even if it's something no one should ever have to see or experience."

"I would've wanted to be told, had the situation been reversed," Spencer said, knowing a dead cell phone was the driving force behind him invading her life. "Let's just hope the police get the son of a bitch."

"Yeah, sooner than later," Deidre said, gazing at his dog. She looked up and saw a police lieutenant associate indicating he would like to talk to her. She turned to Spencer, who was close enough that she could feel the heat emanating from his body. "Could you excuse me for a minute?"

Spencer watched thoughtfully as Deidre headed straight for the man who seemed to be in charge of the investigation.

"So he and his dog just *happened* to stumble upon the body?" Lieutenant Hal Iverson of the Sinclair Heights Police Bureau asked Deidre. He narrowed his eyes at Spencer, who was talking to an officer several feet away.

Deidre shrugged. "Isn't that how *most* serial killers' victims are discovered?" Not that she wanted or needed to defend Spencer Berry. He looked like he was more than capable of defending his own actions.

They were standing on her front porch. Deidre thought about inviting Hal in, but didn't want to give him the wrong idea that it was anything resembling a social invitation. Especially when the focus should be on the investigation, not her. Or them.

"I suppose," Hal allowed, and tugged at the jacket of his dark blue suit.

Deidre reiterated the part about a gang member being shot.

"Yeah, you told me. We know about that and we're looking into it as well." Hal gave her a skeptical look. "In reality, many killers like to get involved in their own crimes by pretending to be *poor* innocents caught up in something else purely by accident. On top of that, a witness reported seeing a man fleeing the scene after the park shooting. Someone fitting *your* Mr. Berry's description."

"He's not *my* Mr. Berry," Deidre stressed. "I only met him this morning, for heaven's sake."

Hal almost looked relieved, as if he had some claim to her. He didn't. They both happened to work for the police department and live in the same neighborhood. And, although she found him handsome, he wasn't her type.

"Either way, we'll need to get a *lot* more answers from him before this is over," Hal told her. "In the meantime, if you like, I can have a detective park outside your house for a while. Whether it's Spencer Berry or someone else you need to be worried about, it may not be safe staying here all alone."

Deidre had considered that, but quickly dismissed the notion. The old house didn't have a security system and, because it was at the end of the block, was closest to the creek where the body was found. However, she didn't believe she was in imminent danger. Her grandfather had installed double bolt locks on the exterior doors and had reinforced the windows, apparently to keep out local burglars. She also had a Glock pistol that Marshall had bought for protection, in addition to more than one can of pepper Mace, as well as any number of other household items that could be turned into a weapon if need be. The last thing Deidre wanted was to become a prisoner in her own home. Similar to the way she had felt in Philadelphia for the longest time after Marshall and Adam were killed.

"I'll be fine, Hal," she tried to reassure him. "I seriously doubt the killer will show his face around here anytime soon, knowing the police will be on the lookout. Besides, my neighbors are mostly a friendly bunch and we try to keep an eye on each other."

In fact, Deidre had yet to really get to know anyone very well in the neighborhood other than Sabrina and Hal. And, in his case, theirs was more of a professional than personal relationship, though he seemed to want it to go further than that. She wasn't going to let what happened to that poor woman compromise her life and sense of security, as long as she believed she wasn't putting herself directly in harm's way.

Hal frowned at her. "Well, the offer is open-ended in case you change your mind."

"I'll remember that," she said and flashed him a gracious smile.

"Guess I'd better go have a talk with Mr. Berry. So, I'll see you later. . . ."

That was a given, since she was scheduled to work today at the police bureau and they would certainly want to issue a statement related to this homicide and the park shooting. Though she was still feeling a bit shaken by all of this, she could think of no good reason for not showing up at work.

She watched for a moment as Hal walked up to Spencer. Aside from hanging out at the park with his dog, witnessing gang members trying to kill each other, and finding a dead woman in the creek, what was his story? He must not have lived very far from the park. She tried to picture him in a home setting, but needed to fill in the blanks. Was he married? She hadn't noticed a ring on his finger, but who knew these days?

Only recently had Deidre stopped wearing her wedding ring, realizing that Marshall was not coming back and she needed to move on without the constant painful reminder of what they once shared and had lost forever.

She found herself wondering if Spencer Berry had any children. She somehow pictured him being as gentle with kids as he was with his dog. He was likely even gentler with a woman.

And why do I even care about his gentle nature? Or his willingness to help where it concerns criminality?

Deidre tried to push the thoughts out of her mind. It wasn't very likely that she would ever see the man again. Or was it? After all, she spent time in the park too. But that didn't mean she was looking to make an intimate connection with Spencer. The last thing she wanted or needed was romance and sex in her life right now.

Who am I kidding? Those are the very things I would love to share with the right man to fill the void in my heart and my longing to feel the touch of a man again.

But Deidre seriously doubted that such a man existed who could captivate her in this way. That included the handsome and somewhat intriguing dog owner named Spencer Berry.

FOUR

Hal Iverson wasn't sure if his bad feelings about Spencer Berry arose from plain old gut instincts, his considerable experience in law enforcement, or because he had a thing for Deidre Lawrence as a beautiful, sexy woman who could light his fire anytime she wanted—and he didn't want some other dude to get in the way of that. Whatever way he sliced it, he had to play it cool and check Berry out, Hal knew, as a cop on the job and not as someone who feared the competition in his pursuit of Deidre. She had said that she'd never even met Berry before today when he supposedly discovered the body. So what was the big deal? The man posed no threat to him where it concerned Deidre, at least not in the romance department, if he had anything to say about it.

But that didn't mean Berry wasn't a threat to the women in the community as a rapist or murderer. Or even to young gang members as some sort of damned vigilante out to get them.

Hal approached Spencer Berry and the officer who had been talking to him. It was time to get some answers.

"If anything else comes to mind, I'll definitely let the police know," Spencer said following a few routine questions from the young officer, even while observing Deidre talking to the cop in the cheap blue suit. For some reason, a twinge of jealousy crept over Spencer like a scorned lover as he stood near a squad car.

He hardly knew the woman but, for some reason, he doubted she would be attracted to the beefy cop. Somehow, he just didn't seem like her type.

But was *he* her type? Spencer wasn't too confident of that at this point. *How do I even know what she likes in a man—in or out of bed? Or if she hasn't already found that with someone who is perhaps sharing that big old house with her?*

Spencer watched as the man finished talking to Deidre and approached him and Sky. His dog had shown remarkable calmness under the circumstances and had to be hungry. Or maybe Spencer was thinking about himself and his growling stomach.

After excusing the officer, the man looked Spencer in the eye. "I'm Lieutenant Iverson, Mr. Berry," he said in an even voice and stuck out a large hand.

"Feel free to call me Spencer." He clasped the lieutenant's hand in a firm shake. "And this is Sky."

Hal tried to pet the dog, but Sky backed away and growled, surprising Spencer.

"He's not here to hurt you, boy." *At least I don't think so.*

Hal turned his attention to Spencer, who was two inches taller and much more solid in build. "So I understand you were the one who found the body?"

Spencer glanced at Sky. "Actually, it was my dog."

"The first *human* to find her," Hal said irritably.

"As far as I know. Wish it had been someone else, though."

"And why is that?" Hal asked suspiciously.

Spencer thought that sounded more like an accusation than a routine question, but kept his cool. "Not exactly the way one wants to spend time in the park, Lieutenant, trust me."

"No, I don't suppose it is."

"Especially when I knew the victim," Spencer volunteered.

Hal cocked a brow and checked his notes, as though he had overlooked this information. "Oh, really?"

Spencer had not come forward to connect the dots with the previous victims for the obvious reasons of wanting to stay out of the investigation and not draw the wrong conclusions. He had nothing to hide, but sure as hell wasn't going to do the police bureau's job for them. He wasn't eager to become a suspect in the Park Killer investigation simply because he happened to have known the dead women in one respect or another. But discovering the victim's body changed the dynamics in this case. Rather than wait for the police to come calling, it seemed wise to be up front about their association.

"As I told the others I spoke with, the victim—Rebecca London—taught in the psychology department at Sinclair Heights College where I'm also a professor."

Hal gazed at him intently. "That's too bad—for her. And when did you last see Ms. London alive?"

"Yesterday at a staff meeting."

"I see." He jotted this down and looked up. "Were you and the victim romantically involved?"

Spencer expected the question. He got along well enough with Rebecca and even found her attractive. But it never went beyond that.

"No romance between us whatsoever," he stated resolutely.

"Just checking." Hal touched his broad nose. "Is there anything else you'd like to add about what you saw or . . . ?"

Spencer mentally went over his statement and came up with nothing new. "I doubt I could tell you much more than I already told the officer and the one before him."

"Maybe so, maybe no." Hal paused deliberately. "There was a shooting in the park this afternoon. Wouldn't happen to know anything about that, would you, Berry?"

By the look in the lieutenant's eyes, Spencer could tell that he thought the shooter might be him.

"Yes, I would know something about that," he answered. "I witnessed the whole thing—"

Hal nodded as if pleased with himself for solving a crime. Or landing a suspect. "Seems like you have a knack for being in the wrong place at the wrong time."

"Only if you consider hanging out at the park with my dog and trying to break up a gang confrontation, then finding Rebecca's body, wrong timing," Spencer said evenly. "And, by the way, I was the one who called 911 to report the park shooting. Unfortunately, my cell phone battery died before I could call in to report Rebecca's death. I got Deidre to do that."

"Yeah, I'm the one she called," Hal said, unsmiling.

Spencer could see that there was some acquaintance between Deidre and him, having watched them conversing earlier. So she had a pipeline to the lieutenant, which turned out to be a good thing in this instance, Spencer supposed, though calling 911 would have been just as effective. But whatever was going on between them, it wasn't any of his business.

"Then you know everything there is to know," Spencer told him.

"Yeah, pretty much, I guess." Hal put his pad away. "Still, would you mind coming downtown to answer a few more questions? It might be helpful to the dual investigations." He looked over his shoulder to where Deidre had been standing on her porch.

Both men saw that she was gone.

Spencer might have told the cop that he didn't want to go downtown. And that it sure as hell wouldn't help his cause to be essentially interrogated like a common criminal instead of someone who wanted only to cooperate voluntarily. However, he suspected that would only get him in more hot water with Lieutenant Iverson, as if this had become personal to him.

Or perhaps it was Deidre in whom the man had a personal interest.

"Not a problem," he said levelly. "I'll just need to take my dog home and feed him. And, in case you're wondering, I have no intention of making a run for it."

Spencer flashed an unenthusiastic smile and watched as the lieutenant tried to decide if he was truly trustworthy and innocent. Or if he just might be Public Enemy Number One in Sinclair Heights.

After a long moment, Hal said, "That's good to know. I'll be waiting to speak further with you about this. In the meantime, why don't you give your address and phone number to the officer."

"Sure." Spencer decided it would be a good idea to get ahead of the game here. "And just for the record, I'm an ex–FBI agent." He had worked for the agency for nearly seven years before calling it quits after his brother's tragic death.

"Really?" Hal gave him a look of surprise. "In Portland?"

"For a while."

"Retired or—"

"I wasn't canned," Spencer made clear, "if that's what you were thinking."

"Thanks for letting me know," Hal said and paused. "So I'll see you downtown a little later then?"

"I'll be there." Spencer hadn't necessarily expected a free pass as an ex–FBI psychologist. As it was, he wanted to help if he could in the investigations. Rebecca's murder needed to be solved and the gang shooter was still on the loose.

And maybe this whole thing could even earn him the right to visit Deidre Lawrence again, feeling a strong pull toward her, in spite of the unusual circumstances that brought them together. Or maybe because of. Who knew what could become of it if they were able to spend more time together without criminality clouding things.

Hal glared at Sky. The dog bared his teeth, but wisely did not attack as the lieutenant walked away.

Glancing at the house once more, Spencer thought he saw someone move away from the blinds in an upstairs window. Meaning that either Deidre had been watching him or she had company. He found himself much more preferring the former.

Deidre quickly stepped away from the bedroom window when she saw Spencer look up. She certainly wasn't trying to be a snoop or anything. But she did wonder if Hal had been satisfied with Spencer's responses. And if Spencer had second thoughts about being a Good Samaritan, as it seemed to have resulted in a bad situation for him. Not that the discovery of a dead woman just feet away from her house made Deidre feel any better after the fact.

Maybe someday she and Spencer would meet again under better circumstances. Deidre doubted it. After all, there would be no reason for them to come into contact now that the official police investigation was in full swing. Still, she could imagine them bumping into each other at the park. Or maybe at the grocery store.

Dream on. He probably has better things to do. Or someone in his life to do them with.

The phone rang, saving Deidre from further reverie.

"I just heard some of the guys coming in say that a woman was found dead in the creek—behind *your* house!" Deidre's work friend, Agatha Huston, voiced with consternation. "Tell me it's not true."

"I wish I could say you misheard." Deidre groaned. "But you didn't. I saw her myself. It was awful." That was putting it mildly.

"This is really starting to freak me out, girl! A serial killer who seems able to pick out victims without missing a beat anywhere in this damned city."

"Then you can imagine how I feel." Deidre sat on her bed and tried to imagine the last moments before the woman in the creek met her violent death. Could the killer have been a copycat or someone other than the Park Killer? Or was it truly the same man killing all these women as though all in a day's macabre work?

Not that it made Deidre feel any better or safer. How could any attractive African American young woman living in Sinclair Heights feel anything but scared out of her wits?

"What about the man who discovered the body?" Agatha asked.

Deidre blinked, thinking about Spencer and his dog. "What about him?"

"Do the police consider him a suspect?"

"The police consider *every* man to be a suspect, Agatha." Hal did anyhow, with the possible exception of himself. Or was he pointing the finger at Spencer for reasons that had nothing to do with the crimes at issue? "But it's not like Spencer is the Park Killer."

Did I just say that? Can I be so sure after only a brief assessment and exchange with the man?

Yes, I think I know enough about human nature to go with my feelings here. Spencer is no more of a serial killer than I am.

Deidre also dismissed Hal's suggestion that Spencer
fit the description of the park shooter, choosing to believe Spencer's account of what happened. Had he not
intervened when he did, who knew what might have
happened with the out-of-control rival gang members.

"Spencer, huh?" Agatha made a humming sound.
"So you two are *already* on a first-name basis?"

"Don't go drawing any conclusions, especially the
wrong ones," Deidre warned.

"Who's drawing conclusions? I'm just asking."

"Yeah, right, Ms. *Matchmaker*. As long as he's not
a killer or shooter . . . and is tall, dark, and extremely
good-looking." All of which Deidre had to admit fit the
man to perfection.

"Then you've already scoped him out?"

Deidre chuckled. "Hardly. Spenc . . . he came to
my door to tell me what he and his dog found. We
exchanged names at some point between here, there,
and showing me the dead woman's body. All strictly
perfunctory, I assure you." *Not to mention ghastly.*

Agatha didn't press for more. "Well, I'm glad you
weren't hurt—instead of that poor woman. Do you
want me to come over later so we can talk about it?"

"I have to work today, so I'll probably see you there
in a couple of hours."

"Cool. I'll try to catch up with you before my mani-
pedi appointment at five."

"Sounds divine," Deidre said, trying to remember
the last time she'd been pampered.

She hung up and went to the window, peeking through
the blinds. The sidewalk in front of her house was empty,
though there was still a police presence. A crime scene
van was parked on the street as investigators probed the
area for evidence. She wondered again if she had seen
the last of Spencer Berry and Sky.

She found the thought disconcerting.

FIVE

Spencer lived in a Cape Cod–style home in the West Hills section of Sinclair Heights. He'd purchased the two-story residence not far from the college shortly after his divorce was finalized six months ago. He'd gotten his hands dirty remodeling the place mostly by himself, replacing carpeting with stone flooring and renovating the space between the living room and kitchen to make a great room. But it was the former den converted into an airy workout and rec room that Spencer was most proud of, and where he spent much of his time at home working on his upper and lower body strength.

He fed Sky and then grabbed a bite to eat—some leftover chicken and rice—before freshening up. Spencer was almost positive that someone from the police bureau had followed them home, albeit discreetly. He could only imagine what it must have been like to be a real criminal tailed by those who wanted nothing more than to put you away for life.

Spencer had seen it all too many times while working for the FBI. They used every damned trick in the book to go after suspects, then made their lives a living hell 'til they got what they wanted or found someone else to pursue. Maybe that was partly why he had called it quits, surprising nearly everyone he worked with. He'd played a major role in psychoanalyzing suspects—some innocent, some guilty as sin. And he didn't always feel good about himself afterward. Stepping away from the stress-

ful, all-consuming, and, at times, thankless profession
was probably the best thing he had ever done, even if it
didn't always feel that way. Yes, sometimes he missed
the action and the feeling that he'd made a difference,
but not enough to go back in spite of attempts by his
former employer to do just that.

"Oh, hell!" Spencer glanced at his watch and realized
that he was due to pick up his daughter in less than an
hour. He had custody of Charity every other weekend,
an arrangement that Spencer had allowed more for his
ex-wife's benefit than his own. She seemed to think
that he was incapable of being a good father to a seven-
year-old, teach psychology, and be an active, available
single man at the same time. This couldn't be further
from the truth, as he loved Charity more than life itself
and would always make time for his little angel. But he
also wanted to keep the peace with Fiona for the sake of
their daughter and, as such, made no waves that might
threaten that.

Spencer grabbed the landline phone in the kitchen
and held it for a moment without making the call.
Though he usually preferred that Charity answered the
phone, in this case Spencer actually found himself hoping Fiona would answer. He hated the thought of hearing the letdown in his daughter's voice after having her
heart set on taking in a movie this afternoon, followed
by shopping and dinner at her favorite fast food restaurant: Burger King. There was always tomorrow for
that. Tonight they could stay up a little past Charity's
bedtime to play games, talk, and eat pizza. What Spencer called father and daughter bonding time.

He hoped Fiona hadn't made any special plans for
today that he would have to ask her to delay if they
didn't include Charity. As far as Spencer knew, his ex
wasn't dating anyone in particular. But what went on

in Fiona's personal life wasn't really any of his business anymore. Aside from Charity. He didn't want to see her tossed back and forth emotionally between them like a Ping-Pong ball as they tried to get their lives in order. Charity wasn't responsible for their breakup and shouldn't have to shoulder any of the burden beyond the norm.

He pushed the button to automatically dial Fiona's number.

"Please don't tell me you're going to be late *again* . . . ?" Fiona moaned without so much as a hello. "Because Charity's practically waiting by the door with her bag packed."

Spencer felt the anguish in the pit of his stomach picturing that scene with Charity eager to have the time with her daddy. He suspected Fiona would not be all that broken up about his spending less time with his daughter, meaning she got to spend more time with her. In spite of their differences, Spencer had no doubt that Fiona loved Charity as much as he did and, in her own way, may have been afraid that he might someday go to court and try to change the custody arrangement. He wasn't ruling it out altogether as, at some point before Charity reached adulthood, he just might want to share equal custody of her.

But, at the moment, he sensed that neither Fiona nor Charity would be happy with his excuses for being late in picking up his daughter, no matter how valid the reason.

"Something's come up," he said with a catch to his voice.

"What's that supposed to mean?"

Spencer sighed. "It means I'm going to be tied up for a while," he said reluctantly. "I'm not sure when I'll be able to pick Charity up. If you could keep her preoccupied 'til I get there, it would be great."

"Why does *everything* have to revolve around what's right for *you,* Spencer?" Fiona snorted.

He expected the bitching. "This isn't about right or wrong, Fiona."

"Don't even start with me," she snapped. "If you have some *hot* date who's more important than your own daughter, just say so!"

Can't say what's not true, though a hot date sounds pretty good about now. Especially if her name happens to be Deidre Lawrence. He could envision making love to her and would be willing to bet that she was all that in bed, too.

"I have a date, if you wish to call it that, with the Sinclair Heights Police Bureau." Spencer pursed his lips while wondering if his ex could actually be jealous at a point in their lives where neither had a claim to the other and hadn't for a long time now. It had been her choice to end their marriage, not his. Was she having second thoughts now? "And, no, I haven't committed a crime. But I did witness a shooting between gang members and then Sky found a dead woman." He saw no reason to get into the specifics about the victim. "So I have to answer a few questions to that effect. . . ."

"I don't even want to know how you and Sky get into these situations," Fiona said dramatically.

"Neither do I," Spencer said.

Fiona sighed. "Anyway, it's probably a good idea that you don't subject *my* daughter to criminals," she said.

He frowned. "I'd never do that."

"Whatever you say. Hopefully by the time you get here, you can give Charity a *normal* piece of your time."

"Yeah, hopefully," Spencer retorted, resisting any notion of responding harshly. He'd always tried to make things as normal as possible for a child who was already the product of a broken home and had lost an uncle whom she adored. But what was normal these days? Spencer would settle for loving and caring for his daughter, while doing the best damned job he could as a father.

"Do you want me to tell Charity you're *not* on your way?" Fiona asked as though it would be her pleasure. "Or would you like to?"

It sounded almost like a challenge to Spencer and one he had to step up to the plate for, like it or not. "I'll tell her."

"Hold on. Charity!" he heard Fiona yell. "Your daddy's on the phone."

While waiting, Spencer thought about what he would say to ease a seven-year-old's pain of expectation turned to disappointment.

A moment later, Charity said enthusiastically, "Hi, Daddy! I'm all ready to go."

"Hi there, sweetheart." Spencer swallowed, wishing he hadn't succumbed to the lieutenant's demands. "Look, Charity, I ran into some trouble this afternoon that requires my attention. Since I'm not exactly sure when I'll be able to come and get you, your mom and I agreed that I would pick you up later on today—just as soon as I can get there."

"What kind of trouble, Daddy?"

"Some bad things happened today at the park," he explained as generically as possible. "Sky and I were witnesses. Now the police need my help to tell them what I saw, so they can catch the bad guys. Do you understand?"

She paused. "Yeah . . . I guess."

Spencer heard the discontent in his daughter's voice, but also the desire to give him the benefit of the doubt.

"I promise I'll make it up to you," he said. "Okay?"

Another pause. "Okay."

Spencer took a deep breath. "I love you, honey."

"Love you too, Daddy."

Spencer was grateful he had the unconditional love of his daughter, offering the same in return. He hoped to someday find that with a woman who really wanted him and not just as a substitute for someone else.

Spencer let Sky out into the large fenced backyard and was off to tell the police once again what he knew about the park shooting and what he didn't know about the murder of Rebecca London.

SIX

Deidre sat on the train reading the current issue of *Essence* magazine. She preferred taking light rail whenever possible to enjoy the sights and sounds of Sinclair Heights, and save on gas and car wear and tear at the same time. She glanced up at some of the other passengers and found herself wondering what their stories were. Had they had difficult lives? Or lost loved ones? Were they eternal optimists? Or extreme pessimists? Were they using the rapid transit system because of convenience or out of necessity?

Deidre honed in on one man in particular who was sitting across from her. She believed he was trying to be inconspicuous for some reason. He was African American, tall, and wearing baggy clothes with a hood over his head, obscuring part of his face. The part of his face she did see had a thin, uneven beard, as if he didn't know the meaning of shaving. He had dark and foreboding eyes. The kind of eyes that could bore deep into your soul if you let them.

Deidre turned away when he suddenly looked at her. *Hope I didn't trigger some impulse in him to go on the attack.* She assumed he was homeless—like others she'd seen on the train who lived on the streets in her neighborhood—and only rode the light rail because it was warm and a chance to get off the streets for a while.

When her stop came, Deidre was only too happy to exit the train since the man was starting to give her the creeps. She looked over her shoulder twice to see if he had followed her, but thankfully did not see him. Maybe she was just letting her imagination run away with itself. But who could blame her? After all, a dead woman had been found just a few feet from her house that very day. She had a right to be on guard, especially when she had to fend for herself these days with Marshall no longer in the picture as her ultimate protector.

Deidre stepped up her pace on the sidewalk 'til she arrived at the Sinclair Heights Police Bureau's downtown headquarters. Only then did she breathe a sigh of relief while hurrying inside.

The man watched as the woman and the homeless man got off the train. He had been watching her watch the bearded man at length, as if she had some reason to fear him.

Think again.

She'd chosen the wrong man to escape from, which played right into his large hands.

At the last possible moment, he exited through a rear door, believing that she had relaxed somewhat in her trepidation of being followed on the busy sidewalk.

But he had misread her. She moved briskly, as if to err on the side of caution. He deliberately kept his distance, not wanting to feed her paranoia. Not yet. His secret life hinged on outthinking his prey as the predator.

He wondered who she was. She looked vaguely familiar, though they all began to look the same after a while. He could smell the faint, but sweet, scent of the perfume she wore. It was invigorating to his nostrils and made him envision her lying naked beneath him, doing whatever he damn well wanted to her body.

Perhaps that time would come. He watched as she turned to enter the police bureau building.

Could she be a cop?

No, he didn't sense that. He also doubted that she was going there to report some homeless man spying on her. Had there been an offense committed on that basis, she would have been as guilty as he was, if not more. Last he knew, staring at a nice-looking woman, no matter how creepy it may have seemed to her, was not a crime.

Especially if the lady wasn't even the wiser.

So she must work for the cops in some other capacity, he decided. Interesting and unnerving at the same time. That type of heat he didn't really need. However, when he wasn't targeting particular women, he was game for a challenge. This one seemed like she just might fit the bill.

He walked past police headquarters like he was just another city resident out for a leisurely stroll. Who would consider that the person in the runner's suit and athletic shoes was the one they called the Park Killer? The one who had assaulted, raped, and murdered practically more women than he could count. He doubted his own mother would recognize the hardened man he had become, were she still alive to disapprove. He was glad she wasn't.

Better that way. There was no room in his life for regrets. Well, maybe a few, but there wasn't a damned thing he could do about them now.

Other than exactly what he was doing to the bitches on his hunting list.

He hoped to run into the pretty woman from the train again. Next time, she might not be so lucky to walk away unscathed.

He crossed the street and was surprised when he saw a man approaching, looking directly at him as if they were long-lost buddies or something. His first instinct was to turn away, as if he would be recognized for the killing machine that he had become.

But his second instinct prevailed, which was to lock gazes with the man and see what happened.

"Excuse me," Spencer apologized after nearly bull-dozing a homeless man—or so he assumed by his dirty clothing, unkempt appearance, and stench—as he crossed the street.

"Ain't no big deal," the man said in a raspy voice. He was on his way before Spencer could utter another word.

Since the man probably didn't even know where his next meal was coming from, much less his next drink, Spencer wondered why the hell he was in such a big hurry. Maybe to get away from the police bureau as fast as he could, just in case they wanted to throw his ass in jail as a vagrant badly in need of a bath. Or maybe he planned to raid a Dumpster before the garbage truck came and emptied it.

Spencer watched as the man slipped between some cars and disappeared around a corner. It pained him that in a city as prosperous as Sinclair Heights there were still some people who managed to fall between the cracks. And there seemingly wasn't anything that could be done about it, short of locking them away somewhere and pretending they didn't exist.

Oh, well, I've got my own problems. Like meeting with a police lieutenant when he'd much rather be spending time with his daughter.

Spencer went inside and hoped this wouldn't take very long. He had better things to do today.

Making his way through the usual police personnel and suspects coming and going, Spencer reached the desk of the officer on duty. He was balding, overweight, and chewing gum as if it was a tobacco substitute.

"How can I help you?" he asked disinterestedly.

"Name's Spencer Berry. I'm here to see Lieutenant Iverson."

"Oh, yeah, he's expecting you."

I'll bet he is.

Spencer figured that if Iverson had his way, he'd just as soon charge him with shooting the kid *and* killing Rebecca London, if only to clear both cases from the books in one fell swoop. Never mind the fact that he was innocent on both counts.

A few minutes later, Spencer was sitting in an interview room. It was small, windowless, and stuffy. He felt just slightly claustrophobic, though no stranger to this. As an FBI psychologist, he'd often been on the other side of the fence, so to speak, interviewing felons and trying to get inside their heads. He had quit the job soon after his brother's death, unsure if it was due to burnout or guilt for not being able to use his skills to help Wesley. He knew that his brother had been despondent on a variety of fronts, including having recently lost his job as a store manager and witnessing his latest girlfriend take her life after dealing with substance abuse problems. Spencer feared that what had been ruled an accident in the water had really been suicide, though he would never be able to prove it.

Maybe I could've done something that might have made a difference in Wesley's fate. Got into his head as a psychologist and concerned brother to try to better help him to deal with his problems in a constructive way. Never mind the fact that Wesley had resisted his help, preferring to internalize everything.

But it was too late to go back.

Not that he had any desire to turn back the hands of time, enjoying the relatively stress-free life of a psychology professor at Sinclair Heights College. With any luck and continued proper investments, it wouldn't be long before he could retire and maybe start writing psychological thrillers if he ever got bored with his life.

The door opened and Spencer watched Lieutenant Hal Iverson walk in with another man. He was Latino and in his thirties with short black hair, wearing a brown suit that looked too large for his slender frame.

"Sorry to keep you waiting," Hal said in an unapologetic tone.

Yeah, right. Spencer felt just slightly warm under the collar.

"This is Detective Zack Hernandez. He's working the Park Killer case."

"Thanks for coming in," Hernandez said. He stuck out a small hand.

Spencer shook it, thinking it felt cold and clammy. "Anything to help."

"I understand you were with the FBI."

"That's right," Spencer said.

"A buddy of mine, Ulysses Bernstein, works at Quantico," Hernandez said, taking a seat.

Am I supposed to be impressed? Or is this a test? "I know Ulysses," Spencer said truthfully. "Good man."

"Yeah, he is." Hernandez glanced at Hal who was sitting on the edge of the table. "So let's talk about the woman you found this afternoon in the creek, Rebecca London—"

"What do you want to know?" Spencer asked, as if he couldn't guess.

"Did you have the hots for her?"

"As I told the lieutenant here, there was no romance between us."

"So you say," Hernandez said.

Spencer stiffened. "I have no reason to lie, Detective. Moreover, I fail to see what this has to do with—"

"Did she ever talk to you about being stalked by someone?" Hernandez broke in. "Or that she was in an abusive relationship?"

"Never," Spencer responded. "But we weren't that close."

Hernandez paused, removing a notepad. He flipped through it casually. "In looking over the case file on the Park Killer, it seems like one name that has come up just below the radar in interviews with family, friends, and associates of the victims as someone who knew each of them is Spencer Berry—or you. Obviously, that now includes Rebecca London. What do you have to say about that?"

Spencer took a moment to contemplate the question. In truth, he wondered what had taken them so long to make the association. The last thing he needed was to be considered a *serious* suspect in a serial killer case. But to deny what they had obviously put together would only complicate matters.

"Yes, I was acquainted with the victims," he confessed. "I don't think that's a crime in and of itself."

The two men looked at each other before Hal said testily, "Maybe not, but it sure as hell gives one pause when the one man who just happens to discover Ms. London's remains not only knew her, but all the women believed to have been killed by some psychopath."

Spencer narrowed his eyes. "I don't think I like the way this is headed," he told them candidly. "I already told you that I found Rebecca purely by chance, thanks to my dog going after a dude who shot a rival gang member. The fact that I happened to know her is beside the point. I wasn't at the scene of any of the other so-called Park Killings."

"Not that we know of," the lieutenant suggested skeptically.

Spencer didn't flinch. "Let's be honest here—if either of you really thought for one moment that I had anything to do with their murders, then you would have already come to me rather than the other way around. As it is, I can account for my whereabouts in every instance and want nothing more than to see the killer apprehended."

He watched as the two digested his words and, for a moment, seemed to no longer view him as the possible answer to their problems.

Hernandez said, "Could be we're on the same side of the track here, Berry. Time will tell. . . ."

"I've got plenty of that," Spencer said while thinking of much better ways to spend it than being interrogated by police.

Hal eyed him sharply. "I have some questions about the shooting at the park."

"Go right ahead," Spencer said.

"You said earlier that you saw the victim get shot and the shooter run away?"

"That's right."

"Well, now, see, here's the problem," Hal began. "The victim isn't talking—though he's awake. And the only other person said to have been running away from the scene is *you*. . . ."

Spencer straightened his shoulders. "Are you really that surprised the kid is tightlipped about this?" he challenged. "Gang members are notorious for their code of silence, all the while planning their revenge. There were at least ten kids there at the time, facing off on each other. They scattered liked windblown sand when the shot was fired. The shooter ran off on his own and my dog went after him. I followed. You know the rest."

"Yeah, I know what you've said." Hal's brows knitted. "Why would you send your dog after someone with a loaded weapon?"

It was a good question. "I didn't," he responded. "His leash slipped from my grasp when my attention was diverted to the kid who was shot." Spencer felt fortunate that hadn't cost Sky his life. "There was another witness to the gang warfare—a nurse. She stayed with the victim 'til the paramedics arrived."

"Yeah, we spoke to her," Hal said tonelessly. "Didn't have much to offer. So it's still on you to give us something to work with."

Spencer lowered his brows. "You mean me and the kid who was shot," he said. "Oh, that's right, he's suddenly developed a case of amnesia." He recalled how afraid the kid was that he might die. Apparently that was more preferable than ratting out the person who shot him.

"Look, we know there's been gang activity at the park," Hal conceded. "And the victim has been identified as a gang member."

"So what's the problem?" Spencer dared to ask.

"Problem is we don't want some vigilante out there going after these kids."

Spencer met his eyes in disbelief. "You think that's what this is about?"

"You tell me."

"I already have. The shooter was a gang member."

"How can you be so sure?" Hal asked.

"I have eyes," Spencer said sarcastically. He then spoke briefly about his work with the FBI's Gang Unit.

"All right, all right," Hal said, seemingly satisfied. "This is all just routine. I'm sure you understand?"

"Not really, but I can live with it." Spencer glanced at his watch, thinking about the time lost with his daughter. "If we're done here . . ."

"Just about. If it's okay with you, I'd like to get a sketch artist in here, so you can give him something to go on for this shooter. It won't take long."

Spencer sighed, starting to feel frustrated that this was being stretched out longer than he wanted and unappreciated by those who seemed to be fishing for something that wasn't there. He would make it up to Charity for being late in spending their precious time together. "Fine."

"Thanks for your cooperation," Hal told him. "We want to get this guy, if he's out there."

"If . . . ?" Spencer's eyes grew. "Gang shootings are pretty routine these days, even in Sinclair Heights. Why would this be any different?"

"It isn't," he responded tartly. "What's different is that we also happen to have a serial killer on our hands. Juggling the two is no big deal, per se. The fact that an ex–FBI agent had a front-row seat to both crimes could prove invaluable at the end of the day."

Or not. Spencer wasn't sure if he was considered a suspect in either case, or was simply made to feel that way. Though he had retired from active participation in criminality, he would be happy to do his part to help solve these cases. As long as it didn't take any further time away from what little time he had to spend with Charity.

"I'll do what I can to help you," Spencer told the two men.

SEVEN

Deidre stood at the podium in the media room, having conferred with investigators and her superiors before reading a prepared statement for the press. She recalled her shyness as a teenager in speaking in the front of the class. Slowly over the years she had overcome that, though she still got an occasional case of butterflies. Such as now, when talking about something that had become more personal with the victim being found within a stone's throw of her house.

"This afternoon at three o'clock, the body of a twenty-seven-year-old woman was found in Swanson's Creek," she said evenly. "Early indications are that she was murdered. The victim's name is being withheld pending notification of next of kin. At this point, it appears as though this is the work of the Park Killer. . . ."

Deidre also mentioned the shooting of a fifteen-year-old at Pelle Park, not releasing his name as a minor, and the search for the shooter. The victim was listed in stable condition. She took no questions, per her directives, leaving that to Hal and detectives working the cases.

After exiting the room, she went down the hall, hoping that both cases would be resolved quickly. Especially the one that had all the makings of the Park Killer signature. Deidre prayed she never came face to face with that monster, feeling deeply for those women who had.

She watched as sketch artist Roland Vesper walked out of an interrogation room. He was followed by a taller man, whom Deidre was surprised to see was Spencer Berry.

He met her eyes. "I see they dragged you down here too."

She smiled. "Actually, I work for the police department as a spokesperson."

Spencer cocked a brow. That threw him for a loop. "I see."

"You two know each other?" Roland asked rhetorically.

"Spencer found the body of Rebecca London not far from my house," Deidre explained, not going into details.

"You all right?" Roland asked in a fatherly way, as he was around sixty.

"I'm fine," she assured him, even if the thought of that poor woman lying there dead and battered was pretty creepy, to say the least.

He nodded and turned to Spencer. "We'll get the image of the shooter out there and see if we can bring him in before the other side retaliates."

"Good idea," Spencer said, knowing how easily gang problems could get out of hand.

"Nice to know you're doing your part to try to get some criminals off the street," Deidre remarked after Roland left.

"Well, I didn't really have much choice," Spencer told her.

"Didn't you?" She looked at his face. "Not everyone chooses to get involved when a crime—or two—is committed."

"Good point." He smiled at her, wishing they were anywhere but the police department right now. At least it gave them a chance to talk again. Perhaps it was as good a time as any to make a little confession, assuming she wasn't already privy to it. "Regarding Rebecca London, I knew her."

"You did?"

Spencer nodded. "We both teach at Sinclair Heights College."

"Why didn't you mention it before?"

"Probably for the same reason I didn't tell you that I also happened to know the other women believed to be victims of the Park Killer. I didn't want to freak you out any more than you already were."

Deidre wondered what to make of this revelation, admittedly feeling a bit unnerved, yet safe considering where they were. She assumed Hal already knew about it and had questioned him to that effect. Were they former girlfriends? Or otherwise closely associated?

"You're probably right—it may have only added to the anxiety of the moment," she conceded.

"My thoughts exactly," he said.

Deidre met his eyes. "What are the odds that you would know all these women?"

"Probably not as high as you might think," Spencer said, keeping his voice level. "Sinclair Heights is not exactly New York City. Or even Portland for that matter. It's not that difficult to meet people here and there in the city. But I had nothing to do with any of their deaths," he added, in case she was leaning in that direction.

Deidre had no real reason to doubt him. After all, the man had shown up at her door with his dog to announce he'd found Rebecca's body. No killer she had ever heard of would have much interest in setting himself up for obvious scrutiny from the police by voluntarily tracking not one, but two crimes.

Still, it made her wonder if being in Spencer's company was a smart idea for any woman, all things considered.

"I believe you," she told him.

Spencer smiled. For some reason, it meant a lot to him that she did. "Thanks."

Deidre thought about the dead woman in the creek. "I'm sorry you had to find someone you actually knew personally dead like that." It brought back vivid images of her late husband and child being murdered.

"So am I. But Rebecca and I were only professionally acquainted," Spencer stressed. "The other women were also either just friends or casual acquaintances. But it doesn't make their deaths any less hard to swallow."

"Mr. Berry, it's not necessary to—" Deidre started, though feeling better knowing he wasn't intimately involved with any of the women.

Spencer cut her off. "I know, but I wanted us to get off on the right foot here." Or avoid staying on the wrong foot, given the circumstances in which they met. "On that note, you can also feel free to call me Spencer and maybe I can call you Deidre, if you don't mind. Less formal that way, don't you think? After all, we are neighbors to some extent."

Was he trying to flirt with her? Deidre mused about them being neighbors, even though he lived blocks away from her. Somehow she decided she liked having him and his dog as neighbors, trying to put aside the fact that being friendly with Spencer Berry could be hazardous to her health.

"First names are fine," she said. "So I suppose your dog is tied up in front of the building waiting on you, probably starving to death?"

Spencer twisted his lips into a grin. "I wouldn't do that to Sky, not even for my duty as a Sinclair Heights resident and witness to criminal activity. Or, for that matter, as an ex–FBI psychologist who has always treated animals with the same respect as humans. He's at home soaking up what little sun there is in my back-yard, which is full of tall, very old oak trees. And he has been fed."

"Good." Deidre loved animals, though she didn't cur-rently have a pet. Maybe at some point she would adopt a stray. She thought about him being a former FBI agent. She could imagine that somehow. "So you were with the FBI?"

"Yes, but don't hold that against me," he said lightly.

"I'll try not to." Deidre smiled. She held all law en-forcement personnel in high esteem for their hard work and putting their lives on the line. "How did you go from FBI agent to professor, if you don't mind my asking?"

"I don't, but it's a long story. I'll tell you about it someday when we have more time."

"Or not," Deidre said, realizing she was intruding on what may have been very personal reasons. "And, you're right, I'm sure we're both busy, so . . ."

"Do you have any kids?" Spencer asked suddenly, though not sure why. This usually didn't come until the second date. And they hadn't exactly had a first one yet. But she seemed like a mother. If so, was there a father in the picture too?

"Excuse me?" Deidre had heard exactly what he'd asked, but wasn't sure it was a question she felt comfort-able answering, giving the dark memories it evoked.

Spencer could tell he'd hit a sore spot. "I wondered if there were any children running around in that big house of yours," he said. "Just curious, but if I've stepped on your toes—"

"No, I don't," she said tersely. *Not anymore.* "Why do you ask?"

"Only because I have a daughter—a seven-year-old little angel—who I've given up spending precious time with to be here."

"Sorry about that," Deidre offered genuinely. She assumed he was involved with his daughter's mother. *Too bad.* Or maybe not, since she wasn't exactly looking for Mr. Right. She'd already been blessed to find him once in her life. Expecting it to happen again seemed highly unlikely—like lightning striking twice in the same place. Especially with this man, who was apparently already spoken for and may not have been a good candidate for dating anyway, given his unsettling predicament. "I won't keep you from your daughter, Mr. Ber . . . Spencer."

"I didn't mean to suggest you were," Spencer said, finding that he enjoyed the company of this beautiful woman, even if he could do without the setting. "I get my daughter every other weekend from my ex-wife. She was nice enough to keep Charity a bit longer today to accommodate this unscheduled turn of events."

So he's divorced. Deidre got a warm feeling at the thought. *And lives with his dog and has custody of his daughter every other week. Interesting.*

"I'm sure the department appreciates your cooperation," she told him, smiling.

Spencer wondered if that was true, since Iverson and Hernandez hadn't exactly gone out of their way to make him seem like a welcome ally. Not that he could totally blame them, considering. But, gazing at the lovely face of Deidre, it had been worth his time and distraction to make a detour from his plans for the day.

He smiled back. "And I appreciate yours after I landed on your porch with such news."

"It was something you had to do," she said, aware that even if his cell phone had worked, she still would have learned about Rebecca London's body being found where it was. "Well, I suppose I'd better get back to work. Have fun with your daughter—and dog."

"I intend to," Spencer assured her, wishing she could join them, but not wanting to jump the gun too soon in pursuing the lady. "See you later. . . ."

"Bye." Deidre walked away, hopeful that it would be *sooner* than later.

She ran into Agatha Gray from records.

"Hey, girl," Agatha said, sporting a wide grin on her fudge-toned face.

"What?" Deidre looked at her, wondering what she was grinning about.

"Who was that hunk I just saw you talking to?"

Deidre batted her lashes innocently. "Oh him . . ."

"Yeah, him," Agatha said.

Deidre looked over her shoulder, expecting Spencer would still be visible, but he was gone. "He's the man whose dog inadvertently found the body behind my house."

"I see." Agatha rested a hand on her wide hip. "Looked to me like a mutual admiration society."

"We were *just* talking," Deidre said, even though she felt the same way. She was aware that Spencer was checking her out as much as she was him. Wasn't that what single people did when they were attracted to each other?

"Don't get all defensive on me," Agatha said. "There's nothing wrong with being beguiled by a good-looking guy who has a dog."

"I don't know about being beguiled," Deidre said with a laugh, "but he does seem like an interesting man."

"Then I say go for it and see what else your interesting man has going for him."

Deidre blushed. The idea was tempting. It had certainly been a long time since she had been involved with anyone. But the truth was that even if Spencer seemed like a potential good catch, she didn't know if he had a girlfriend. She knew that some men liked playing the field and juggling more than one woman. Spencer didn't seem like the type, but one never knew these days.

"Right now, I'd just like to catch up on some reports I need to write." She gave Agatha a friendly smile. "If there's romance in my future, I won't try to rush it."

"Who's says you're rushing into something?" Agatha uttered. "These things happen when they're meant to."

"We'll see." Deidre wished she could be as confident as Agatha, who seemed to have no problem chasing men she was interested in, when they weren't chasing her. Being much more conservative, Deidre preferred to be romanced by the man, but only after a suitable time once they'd gotten to know each other. She felt the same way regarding Spencer, assuming they moved in that direction and he wasn't truly a person who brought bad luck to the women he knew.

Just who the hell does Spencer Berry think he is? Hal's brow furrowed while he sat at his desk. He had watched as Spencer damned near made himself at home chatting with Deidre as if they were on a date rather than at police headquarters. When he invited Spencer to come down here, he hadn't anticipated that he and Deidre might actually run into each other. Or that Deidre just might take a liking to the good-looking former FBI agent who happened to be caught up in the middle of two ongoing police investigations. Or at least that was how it seemed to him. And it was more or less supported by Agatha Huston, who seemed only two happy to contend that they were a match in the making.

The man was definitely starting to get on his nerves. Nerves that were already frayed—mainly due to the serial killer case that had the community in a state of terror. It still didn't sit particularly well with Hal that Spencer Berry knew the seven women who were now dead, presumably at the hands of the Park Killer. Maybe it really was just coincidence or a case of bad karma.

Or maybe I'm just allowing my personal feelings for Deidre to cloud my judgment where it concerns Berry, who seems like he's also got his eye on her.

Hal fumbled with a pencil. Though thus far Deidre hadn't reciprocated his clear interest in her, he still wanted to keep her out of harm's way if he could. There were never any guarantees, though. Especially when there was a cold-blooded killer in the city who, until apprehended, could go after any attractive woman at any time.

Including Deidre.

Hal frowned. The truth was, with much of the force working this serial killer case and no evidence that Deidre had been specifically targeted, he couldn't justify to the top brass the need to put anyone on her part time, much less full time. But he could certainly try to keep an eye on her himself—if she let him.

In the meantime, there was still the purported gang-related shooting that needed to be resolved. It was important that they nip what seemed to be a growing gang problem in Sinclair Heights in the bud, before it turned into all-out warfare. It was no secret to local authorities that the East Side Gang and West Side Gang, both comprised of African American and Latino youth, were battling for control of turf, respect, drugs, and whatever the hell else they could think of. Maybe the victim was ready to help his own cause by identifying his attacker. Or was that too much to ask of someone bound by the street code of silence, even if on the receiving end of a bullet?

Hal hoped Spencer Berry's description of the alleged shooter helped. He still hadn't ruled out the possibility that someone other than a rival gang member had shot the kid. Right now, it all came back to Berry and his word on what happened. He gave the man the benefit of the doubt, given his background with the FBI and his willingness to offer information.

Still, it might not be a bad idea to get more info on him.

Hal picked up the phone, intending to do just that. "Get me the FBI's Portland office."

EIGHT

It was after six when Spencer arrived at the house in Northeast Sinclair Heights that he once shared with his ex-wife. It was a two-story home that was brand new when they moved in, but grew old quickly when their marriage failed the test of love and commitment. Fiona's black Honda Accord was in the driveway.

Spencer had hoped that honking the horn once would be enough to send Charity out and spare everyone the drama that seemed to come whenever he and Fiona got together, even briefly. But when there was no indication that would happen, he went up to the door and rang the bell.

Moments later, Fiona opened the door with pursed lips. "Thought you'd forgotten about Charity what with you're running around and all."

Spencer frowned at his ex-wife, forgetting for the moment that she was still damned good-looking. Tall and shapely at thirty-three, she wore her brown hair in a layered, feathered style and there was a natural glow to her butterscotch complexion.

"I'd *never* forget my daughter," he said irritably at the mere suggestion. "I came as soon as I could."

"Well it wasn't soon enough. She's asleep. And I really don't want to wake her."

Spencer sighed. "Why don't you cut me some slack here, Fiona. I'm doing my best. You think I don't want to spend every moment I can with Charity?"

Fiona fluttered her lashes. "You tell me."

"All right, I'm telling you. Yes, I love the time I have with our daughter." He met her eyes squarely. "Now will you please go and get her? We'll be out of your hair until it's time to bring her back."

"Fine," Fiona said. "I'll wake her up."

See, was that so hard? "Thank you."

"You want to come in?" she asked unenthusiastically.

Not particularly. "Yeah, why not. . . ."

Spencer stood in the sunken living room, admiring the furnishings that had once belonged to him as well. Now he felt like a stranger there, as if totally out of place. Probably better that way. He had no desire to feel comfortable in a home where he was no longer wanted.

"*Daddeeee!*" The word floated to Spencer's ears.

He watched as Charity came bounding down the stairs, her thick black pigtails flopping on her shoulders. She was tall for her age, but thin, and looked more like her mother than him.

She ran into his arms and gave him big hug.

He kissed her cheek. "Hi, precious!"

"I thought you changed your mind and weren't going to come." Her big black eyes looked up at him dourly.

"Well, you thought wrong!" He tickled her stomach and she giggled. "It took a little longer than I thought to finish what I was doing. But now I'm all yours. Are you ready to go?"

"Yes," she answered sprightly.

Fiona came down the stairs carrying Charity's overnight bag. "What time will you bring her back on Sunday?"

Spencer took the bag from her. "The usual . . . around eight. Why?"

She paused. "I have a date that afternoon," she said. "Just want to make sure our schedules are coordinated."

"I'll have her here at eight on the nose," Spencer said flatly. "Or is that too early?"

"Eight is fine."

"So be it."

Spencer was mildly curious about Fiona's date, but wouldn't let her know that in case she got the wrong idea. She deserved to have romance—even love—in her life just as he did. Apparently, she was one up on him in at least one of those departments at the moment.

Fiona hugged Charity. "Have fun."

"I *always* have fun when I'm with Daddy."

Spencer felt good hearing that and almost detected a little envy in Fiona's eyes.

"Enjoy your date," he told her as they walked out the door, and meant it. As long as he always had access to his daughter, and any man Fiona dated treated Charity right, Spencer had no desire to stand in her way. Just like he expected to have her full cooperation if and when he met someone who could fill that void in his life.

Fiona Berry listened as Spencer's car drove off. It seemed like only yesterday that they had walked down the aisle, promising to make a good, long life together. It was a promise she wished she'd never made. At least not with Spencer. The truth was she had chosen the wrong Berry brother to marry. She'd turned her back on Wesley and the love they'd shared to marry Spencer, who offered her better financial security and stability. Wesley had been heartbroken and it made it hard for them to be friends afterward.

When she got pregnant with Charity, Fiona found herself wishing it had been Wesley's child, so a part of him would always belong to her. But she had remained true to Spencer and gave him a daughter instead. For a time, it seemed like their baby girl would be enough to make the marriage survive. Instead, Charity only made Fiona realize what a big mistake she'd made in marrying a man she didn't love for what turned out to be the wrong reasons.

The relationship between the two brothers had suffered as well, with Wesley barely on speaking terms with Spencer for the longest time. It wasn't until Wesley met someone else to romance that things between him and Spencer began to finally get back to something resembling a kinship.

Then tragedy struck as Wesley lost his girlfriend to drugs, seemingly sending him on a downward spiral. When he died at sea, Fiona was devastated, blaming herself to some degree for turning her back on him earlier. She didn't know if it had truly been accidental or if he'd just become fed up with life and some bad choices.

Fiona had made her own bad choices. She got out from under one by divorcing Spencer, feeling it was the right thing to do for both of them. Now she had met someone new who offered her hope of finding true love again after losing it when she let Wesley go. But there would always be a bond between her and Spencer, thanks to Charity. Even if things had soured in their marital relationship, she would never deliberately prevent him from seeing his daughter, though Fiona worried if she would be in a safe environment when Spencer seemed unable to let the ex–FBI agent in him go.

***

"So who's the lucky man your mother is going on a date with?" Spencer asked Charity casually, glancing at the rearview mirror. He was merely curious, given that Fiona had seemingly been too preoccupied with work and home life for a new romance. But then, what did he know?

"His name is Clint. He works with Mommy."

Fiona was an analyst at a brokerage house. Spencer recalled that his ex once had a rule about never dating on the job. *Guess rules are made to be broken.* He should know, having broken more than a few in his dating life since their divorce.

Spencer wondered if it was serious with Clint. The thought of his daughter having a stepfather to vie for her affections was somewhat unsettling in spite of his pledge to stay out of Fiona's love life. Probably because it seemed like he'd never find a stepmother for Charity. Having been hurt by one marriage, he was in no hurry to marry again. Of course, if a serious candidate loomed over the horizon, he might be singing a different tune. Spencer could imagine someone like Deidre potentially being good marriage material. Of course, he wouldn't know for sure until when and if they became better acquainted.

Sky greeted Charity when they arrived at Spencer's house by licking her face. "Hi, Sky," she giggled, wiping the wetness from her cheek.

"Easy, boy," Spencer admonished the dog. "Charity knows you love her. You don't have to lick her to death."

The dog backed off, as if he understood the need to exercise restraint.

After Charity took her things to her room and returned, Spencer asked, "Are you hungry?" He assumed she'd already had a snack.

"Yeah," she drawled.

"How about burgers and fries, kiddo?"

"Yummeeeee!"

He smiled. "Well, since I know that Sky will eat just about anything, burgers and fries it is!"

The following day, Spencer took Charity to the Cinco de Mayo Fiesta at Waterway Park. He was happy to bring her to this wonderful annual event that celebrated Latino culture and demonstrated the racial diversity in Sinclair Heights. They went on the Ferris wheel—twice—and Charity squealed with delight as they rode the horses up and down on the carousel. Spencer laughed as he watched the performers in the children's plaza entertain Charity with a puppet show. They walked hand in hand on the sidewalk, enjoying the various booths full of colorful displays and wares.

Soon, Spencer was dragged along by his daughter to have her picture drawn by the pretty lady at the booth up ahead.

It wasn't 'til he honed in on her face that Spencer realized the artist was none other than Deidre Lawrence. She was talking on a cell phone, but seemed as acutely aware of him as he was of her.

He couldn't help but overhear her say to someone, "Val's Deli, Friday at noon. Got it!"

Deidre had participated in the Cinco de Mayo celebration in Philadelphia for years, where she'd given drawing lessons and sketched faces. She had been prompted to get involved more in the Latino community by her father, who was half-Mexican. She was only too happy to continue to use her talents in Sinclair Heights to help bring joy to others.

After taking a phone call from her friend Sabrina during a lag in activity, Deidre cut short the chat when she saw Spencer Berry approaching her table. He was holding hands with a girl she guessed to be six or seven. His daughter. Deidre could see some resemblance if she looked hard enough.

If she hadn't known better, Deidre would think Spencer was following her around like a smitten puppy. Realistically, it appeared as though fate had found yet another way to bring them together. As if they hadn't already run into each other enough times lately. She wasn't sure if this was a good thing or a bad thing. Yet. If she was honest about it, she had to admit she was happy to see the handsome man again.

"So we meet again." Spencer kept his voice on a serious level, for it was anything but a joke to him the way they seemed to keep meeting as if a magnet were pulling them together. Could fate be at work here?

"Looks like it." Deidre flashed him a soft smile.

"You're an artist as well as spokesperson for the police bureau?" Spencer asked, impressed.

"Yes," she admitted. "Helps pay the bills in a tough economy."

"I can relate to that." In spite of his investment portfolio and early retirement dreams, he wasn't there yet. He'd supplemented his teaching salary by writing articles for psychology and criminology journals.

Deidre willed her nerves to remain calm under the heat of his incredible eyes. She averted her eyes to the girl. "And who might this be?"

"My name's Charity."

"Hi, Charity. I'm Deidre."

"Do you know my daddy?"

Deidre looked at Spencer, who grinned boyishly, seemingly curious as to how she would respond.

"Yes, we've met a couple of times before," she told her.

"Do you like him?" Charity was wide-eyed with interest.

Deidre colored. "Well, I haven't really gotten to know him, but your dad seems like a nice man."

And was very nice-looking as well. Deidre needed more time to determine if she liked Spencer in a romantic way. Or even as friends. Or was she jumping the gun there?

Charity looked up at her father, giggling as if Deidre's words had much broader implications than she meant.

"Can you draw a picture of me?" Charity asked.

"I can certainly try," Deidre said. "Assuming I have your father's permission."

"You do." Spencer was more than willing to watch her brighten his daughter's face. And his own at the same time.

There was no question in Spencer's mind that Deidre Lawrence was a woman who was capturing his attention in ways few women could. He wondered what else was there to discover beyond the attractive exterior, police spokeswoman, and impressive not-so-hidden talent.

If he played his cards right, maybe he'd get to find out.

The woman watched Spencer and Charity with interest as they stood at the artist's booth. They seemed to be engaged in an animated conversation with the artist while she did a sketch of the girl. This infuriated the woman, though she had little to fear from the artist who was just doing what she was being paid for, even if she was striking. She suspected Spencer Berry was attracted to the artist. He had a sharp eye for the ladies, which could prove to be his undoing if he wasn't careful.

I'm a hell of a lot prettier than her. And he's already given himself to me, just as I've given myself to him . . . completely and satisfyingly. Nothing and no one could ever change that.

Not if she had anything to do with it.

Spencer glanced her way, but she was hidden behind a display that made it look like she was simply admiring the goods, rather than using it as a means to keep an eye on her man without him being the wiser. It was better that way. *For now. Let him have some fun with his daughter.* As long as he didn't overstep his boundaries with the artist.

Or any other woman for that matter.

When Spencer and his daughter walked away, she noted that the artist watched them thoughtfully, as if she were wishing they might meet again under more romantic circumstances.

Don't even think about it, bitch! The woman felt her temperature rise tenfold. *Spencer is off-limits to you and everyone else. If you know what's good for you, you'll turn your attention to someone other than my man!*

The woman followed as Spencer and Charity went to watch some Latino performers sing and dance. She fantasized that they might become a real family someday. If only Spencer would follow his heart as much as he once had her body.

Yes, time was very much on her side and she had plenty of it.

NINE

Two days later, Spencer drove to Sinclair Heights General Hospital where he had heard the park shooting victim, identified as sixteen-year-old Marcus Hobson, was recovering in the intensive care unit. From what he gathered, the boy was still mum on who shot him. Spencer had no illusions he could get through to him, given the tightlipped silence among gang members who preferred to respond through give-and-take violence. And the cycle of gang warfare continued from generation to generation, even in such smaller cities as Sinclair Heights, where gangs had cropped up over the years and become a force to be reckoned with.

Spencer made his way to the victim's room, where he spotted a forty-something woman by the bedside. When she saw Spencer, he motioned for her to come out. She kissed Marcus, who was awake, on the forehead and stood up.

"How's he doing?" Spencer asked.

She looked weary and had been crying. "Looks like he'll pull through."

"That's good." Spencer paused. "My name's Spencer Berry. I was at the park when he was shot."

She met his eyes. "You saw who shot my boy?"

"Yeah, I did," Spencer admitted. "I've told the police everything I know, but it's not enough. They need some help from your son. . . ."

She frowned. "I warned him to stay out of gangs. But the pressure on him was coming from all sides. He just wasn't strong enough to resist."

Spencer felt for her in what must have seemed like a losing battle. "Can I talk to him?"

"He's weak and in pain."

"I know. I promise I won't take long."

She nodded slowly and accompanied him into the room.

When Spencer walked up to the bed, the boy looked at him suspiciously. "What's he doin' here?" he asked his mother.

"He just wants to help you."

Marcus frowned. "Yeah? How you gonna help me?"

It was a good question and Spencer wasn't sure how to answer it without further alienating himself as an outsider. "By doing my part to get a shooter off the streets. But that won't happen if you don't name any names."

"Why should I tell you anythin'?" Marcus demanded. "You don't care what happens to me."

"I do care. That's why I'm here," Spencer said. "I can't say I've been where you are now, but I've worked with youth in gangs and I know that there's basically two ways to go. You either end up in prison or *dead*. Unless you're brave enough to speak up after being shot in the chest, things will just continue to escalate and the next kid won't be so lucky. His mother will be at his gravesite instead of the ICU. Just give me a name and I'll make sure the police get the guy who tried to kill you. Then you can focus on your recovery and getting out of gang life."

Marcus looked away as if he had nothing to say.

"I think you'd better go now," the boy's mother told Spencer.

Guess I wasted my time. "All right," he muttered and eyed the victim. "Sorry I bothered you."

Spencer was nearly out of the room when he heard Marcus say, "Rodney Rochester."

Spencer smiled. *Thanks, kid.*

In the lobby, he phoned the police bureau and asked to speak to Lieutenant Iverson.

"Yeah, Iverson," he said a few moments later. "How can I help you, Berry?"

"I'm not the one who needs help right now," Spencer said. "I think the kid who was shot does. He just gave me the name of the shooter."

"Is that right?" Hal Iverson asked skeptically. "What's the name?"

Spencer told him, not expecting any thanks for doing his job, but feeling good about it nevertheless. "You might want to get someone down here to guard the kid in case his would-be killer decides to try to finish the job."

"I'll see what I can do," he said. "Anything else?"

"Yeah, while we're at it," Spencer responded thoughtfully, "I think you should keep a patrol car in the area around Deidre Lawrence's house."

"You're not in law enforcement anymore, Berry, and certainly not part of this force, so lay off playing cop. Unless you know more about the Park Killer than you've let on. . . ."

Spencer stiffened. "I know only what I've heard on the news and from you," he said. "And I wasn't playing anything. I'm just concerned for the lady's welfare, that's all." He was also concerned about the mere possibility the killer might return to the spot where he dumped Rebecca London's body. Spencer couldn't bear to see another woman he knew end up dead without having a clue as to whether it was random or much more than coincidental.

"Well, I don't need you telling me how to do my job," Hal said resentfully. "But, for the record, we always take care of our own."

"That's good enough for me," Spencer said. He felt some solace that she would apparently be safe from harm at home. He wasn't quite sure what it was about her that made him feel protective and captivated at the same time. The last part spoke for itself, as she was gorgeous and sexy as hell. As for the first part, it was only natural that he would want no harm to come to her as someone with whom he saw the possibility of sparks flying between them, and potentially much more.

Deidre met her friend Sabrina Murray for lunch at a downtown deli. They sat at a corner table by the window and ordered sandwiches, chips, and coffee.

Sabrina had hazel eyes, was slender, and wore her long dark hair in a two-strand twist. She seemingly had a new man in her life every week and wasn't afraid to admit it and enjoy it for as long as the man could hold her interest. But her major focus was her art. She painted beautiful sea- and landscapes that Deidre could only dream of doing; though her own talent for painting and drawing portraits, objects, and abstracts was something she was quite proud of.

"The art exhibit Saturday night is going to be huge," Sabrina said.

Deidre agreed. "Yes, should be a packed house. No pressure, right? How can it not be when we, along with some other local artists, are showing some of our best stuff for others to appreciate and hopefully want as part of their art collection?"

"Maybe just a tad." Sabrina grinned. "But I didn't want to leave expectations to chance, so I invited everyone I know and told them I'd never speak to them again if they didn't show up."

Deidre laughed. "Well, with that type of ultimatum, I'd say we can't lose."

"Who said anything about losing?" Sabina said, lifting her sandwich. "Do you see any losers sitting at this table?"

"Not a one," Deidre declared.

"That's what I'm talking about," Sabrina said. "We've both made pretty damned good lives for ourselves that others would die for."

Though grateful for the kind words, Deidre couldn't help but say, "Sometimes I wonder just what type of life I have made for myself—or haven't." She was a thirty-two-year-old widow, living alone, while using work and art to keep from thinking too much about the cruel past that still haunted her.

Sabrina reached over and touched her hand. "Yes, you were dealt a bad hand at such a young age and you're allowed to have some extended grief after losing your loved ones. But having such a wonderful house to live in, mortgage free, is a real blessing, even if you have no one to share it with at the moment. You know your grandparents would be happy that you're living there, keeping it in the family. As for working to keep busy, we all do that, girl. Even if some of us do manage to squeeze in a bit of romance between paintings."

Deidre chuckled, feeling better hearing her sensible words. "Just a bit of romance?"

Sabrina laughed. "Okay, so I love to date hot men. A lot! But only the ones who really bring something special to the table."

"You mean besides food?" Deidre winked playfully.

"Maybe it's time you taste the entrée yourself," Sabrina suggested. "I'd be happy to introduce you to some pretty good prospects."

Though tempted, Deidre squelched the notion. "No, thanks. I'll take a rain check on that."

"If you say so." Sabrina frowned. "My collection of rain checks will just continue to grow."

Deidre had resisted numerous attempts by Sabrina and Agatha to set her up. She wasn't sure if it was due to fear that she might forget Marshall. Or if she wanted things to occur naturally in starting a new romance without the pressures of blind dates or trying to please others.

For some reason, Spencer Berry came to mind. He was certainly a good candidate in the looks department, and charming in a mysterious way. But that hardly made him the ideal mate in ways that counted most. Deidre wanted someone she could trust first and foremost, with respect a very close second. It remained to be seen if Spencer was that type of man. Or if falling for him would be a big mistake for any woman, all things considered.

Still, Deidre couldn't help but wonder if there was someone special in Spencer's life other than his daughter. Charity was a real cutie and obviously the center of Spencer's world. The girl had lit up when Deidre sketched her face five days ago at the Cinco de Mayo Fiesta. Her father had seemed quite pleased too.

That helped make Deidre feel that it was worthwhile using her skills for the benefit of others. Especially children, who seemed to appreciate being her subjects the most while showing much more patience than most adults gave them credit for.

Making me completely happy will take a lot more, of course. But she had learned through tragedy to take

one day at a time and hope for the best while not necessarily expecting the worst.

"Who on earth is that hottie who just walked through
the door?" Sabrina asked, looking across the deli.

Deidre turned and saw Spencer Berry step up to
the counter. Her chest heaved involuntarily and she
wondered if this was merely another chance meeting
or what. They seemed to have a knack for being at the
same place at the same time. Or was there something
more to it?

Maybe he wouldn't even notice her.

That wasn't happening, as his eyes latched on to her
face.

TEN

Spencer spotted Deidre practically the moment he entered the deli. She seemed to shrink into her chair, as if that would somehow make her less visible to him. Little chance of that, since she stood out much more than most women he knew.

His presence there was no accident this time. Nor some serendipitous twist of fate. After overhearing Deidre confirming lunch with someone on the phone at the Cinco de Mayo Fiesta, Spencer couldn't resist showing up for another opportunity to see the lady in a setting that wouldn't seem threatening to her.

Or him, for that matter.

Now Spencer wondered if he should simply ignore the strong sexual vibes he sensed between them—or were they even more powerful than that?—and be on his way with the takeout food he'd ordered. Maybe Deidre had no interest in becoming involved romantically or otherwise, especially if there was already someone in her life.

But since her companion seemed to spot Spencer before Deidre did, alerting her to his presence, it would be impolite to not at least go over and say hello.

It had been several days since Marcus Hobson had identified his shooter by name. But so far the perpetrator had remained at large. Spencer suspected he was being hidden by fellow gang members who viewed his actions as heroic and one-upmanship over the rival gang.

Though it seemed like an unwinnable battle, Spencer believed if but a few gang members decided to take a stand against violence, it could make all the difference in the world in stopping the madness and needless loss of life or a future.

There had also been little on the investigation into the murder of Rebecca London, which frustrated Spencer. Apart from positively identifying her and concluding that her death was the work of the Park Killer, the authorities were remaining tightlipped. Spencer wondered if the string of deaths of women he knew would be broken one way or the other. Or was any woman he associated with at risk for no reason that he knew of other than the random bad luck of the draw?

Spencer picked up his order and walked over to the two women, casting his eyes squarely on Deidre. "So we meet again."

"Again? . . ." Sabrina looked at her friend quizzically. "You two know each other?"

"Sort of," Deidre said. "Spencer and his dog found the body behind my house last weekend." She felt the intensity of his stare. "He also witnessed a shooting at the park."

"Oh, I see." Sabrina hummed reflectively, her gaze moving from one to the other.

Since Deidre was slow with introductions, Spencer took the liberty. He stretched out a hand. "Spencer Berry."

Sabrina put her hand in his and shook it. "Sabrina Murray. Nice to meet you, Spencer."

"Same here." He looked at Deidre. "Seems as if Deidre and I have already become good friends."

"I'm not sure I'd go that far," Deidre felt compelled to say. They seemed to keep running into each other through no fault of their own. "I'd say we're more like acquaintances."

Spencer flashed a devilish smile. "That's a good start."

"Won't you join us?" volunteered Sabrina, pulling out a chair.

Deidre wanted to immediately object to this presumptuous get-together, not sure it was such a great idea, but Spencer beat her to the punch.

"Actually, I wouldn't want to intrude," he forced himself to say, sensing it was probably not the best way to get to know Deidre better in spite of her friend's desires to the contrary. "Besides, I've got to get home and work on some papers, along with feeding my dog. He's a big fan of corned beef."

"Are you a writer?" Sabrina asked.

"Not exactly, though I have written an article or two in my time. I'm a psychology professor and most of my writing these days consists of grading papers."

Deidre recalled him mentioning his occupation at the police station after revealing that he knew the woman whose body was dumped behind her house. Both had taken Deidre by surprise, though she tried not to pass judgment prematurely. She hadn't taken Spencer for the professor type, though she didn't doubt for one moment that there was intelligence about the man that intrigued her, almost as much as his handsome features and hard body.

"Well, good luck with your papers," Deidre said.

"I can always use plenty of luck when I'm trying to understand what goes on in the heads of some of these twenty-first-century students."

"Are they any different from those of the last century?" Deidre couldn't help but ask.

Spencer grinned. "Probably not, though I suspect they've become a little more spoiled by today's technology and a little less independent thinkers."

"Are you by chance an art lover, Spencer?" Sabrina asked, taking a furtive peek at Deidre and back.

"I am," he said, wondering what she had in mind. "I have a few decent pieces in my collection, but always enjoy seeing what else is out there."

Sabrina smiled and pulled out a card, handing it to him. "Well, in that case, you're invited to come to our showing on Saturday at eight. That is, if you're not doing anything better?"

Spencer met Deidre's eyes. "Showing? So your art talents go beyond sketching bright-eyed little girls?"

Deidre smiled. "Yes, a bit," she said, downplaying it.

"I'm sure it's much more than that." He had a feeling that she wasn't exactly on board with him coming, as though afraid to open herself up to the possibilities. But why? Was it because of the circumstances under which they'd met? He felt it was up to him to show her that he was not a threat or someone to turn away from. Not to mention he felt an urge to explore the chemistry that seemed to be building between them like steam in an engine. "As a matter of fact, I don't have anything going on Saturday night," he told Sabrina. "So, yes, I'd be happy to come to your showing. If that's all right with you, Deidre? . . ."

She batted her lashes at him, feeling put on the spot thanks to her overzealous friend. "Why wouldn't it be?"

"Good. Then I'll see you on Saturday." Spencer nodded with a slight grin and left them alone to debate the issue, certain that they would.

"Don't hate me," Sabrina said after Spencer had left the deli.

"Now why would I hate you?" Deidre set her jaw. "You can invite *anyone* you want to the exhibition."

Sabrina sighed. "Well, aside from the fact that Spencer's cute as a button and fit like a runner, he's also another body to fill space and maybe even *buy* a Deidre Lawrence or Sabrina Murray painting to add to his collection. If that fails, there's always the possibility that you might even find yourself interested in the man, heaven forbid." Sabrina winked at her mischievously.

Deidre sneered. *I just might at that.* This unnerved her, and not so much for the fact that Spencer was acquainted with at least seven women who were now dead at the hands of a serial killer. She trusted her instincts and didn't believe for one minute that he was anything but innocent regarding the murders.

So what was the big hang-up then? It wasn't as if she had no attraction to the man. Quite the opposite. Who wouldn't be physically attracted to *him?*

Perhaps it was because there hadn't been a man in her life since Marshall's death.

Or maybe there was just something about Spencer Berry that made her feel she ought to be very wary of the powerful effect he could have on any woman who fell for him.

Deidre decided not to allow fears to get the better of her. Or jump to the wrong conclusions about Spencer before making sure there was ample reason to.

After all, the man could very well have no interest in her at all, other than as a friendly neighbor needing help with a dead body. Or to show off to his daughter. Or even someone who could appreciate art and the artist.

Something told Deidre it went beyond that, and it worked both ways.

Spencer drove home amid a steady stream of lunch hour downtown traffic. All the while he found himself thinking about Deidre and how lovely she looked this afternoon. He might have thought that he'd run out of ways to see her, by chance or design, had her friend not invited him to their art exhibit. Maybe she knew something that Deidre was unwilling to admit to herself—there was definite physical chemistry between them that didn't necessarily have to go to waste. Maybe it wouldn't have to when all was said and done. . . .

Sky greeted Spencer at the door like he'd been gone for years.

"Missed me after only a few hours, did you, boy?" He rubbed the dog's head. "Well, I feel the same way. Brought some chow back with me. You're welcome to share, or I'll get you your own."

Sky barked and then ran off toward the kitchen, as though he couldn't wait.

Before heading to the kitchen, Spencer turned on his cell phone and listened to his four voice mail messages.

"Hi, Daddy. It's Charity . . . Mommy's about to take me to school now, but thought I'd sneak in a call to you. Can't wait to see you again. Bye."

Spencer smiled as the next message came on. All he could hear was some static, as though communication were being attempted from another planet. Strange.

"Yeah, this is your dad." Spencer heard the third message. "Just callin' to chat, nothin' special. Talk to you later."

There was a pause, before a woman's voice on the fourth message uttered peevishly, "If you're there, Spencer, please pick up. I *really* need to talk to you. Don't ignore me! This is *so* unfair." She waited a beat and then snorted. "I'll try again later. . . ."

Spencer groaned. *Don't do me any favors. Please.*

The last caller was Gayle Kincaid. She was a twenty-six-year-old graduate student he had made the mistake of getting involved with briefly. Though he told her it was over, Spencer couldn't seem to get rid of her. He could only hope that his silence spoke volumes and she would back off.

Spencer went into the kitchen where a hungry Sky was ready to eat. So was he.

Gayle Kincaid gazed up at Spencer's bedroom window, remembering when she had been in that room, sharing his bed and body. It seemed like a lifetime ago even if only three weeks had passed since he tried to break off their relationship after stealing her heart and taking her body. She would not be tossed away by him or any man like yesterday's garbage.

No way in hell.

She knew he was in there. Why hadn't he called her back? Did he think she would give up that easily?

Gayle pushed the redial on her cell phone. He picked up on the third ring.

"Hi, Spencer," she said sweetly.

"Hey, Gayle. Look, now's not a good time."

"Then when? I really want to sit down and talk for a while."

"I don't think there's much more for us to say."

Anger boiled inside her and threatened to blow up all over him. "There's a lot for us to say, baby. If you just give it a chance, I know we can—"

"Don't make this any more difficult than it has to be, Gayle," Spencer cut in sternly. "We had a good time together, but it's over."

"It's *not* over," she said. "Please, don't say that."

"Someone has to." He sighed. "I've really got to go now. I have to take Sky out for some fresh air. Bye."

Once again, Spencer was trying to shut her out of his life like she no longer had a place in it. But it wasn't going to happen.

Not today. Not tomorrow. Not *ever*.

She thought about when she'd seen him at the Cinco de Mayo Fiesta, wanting desperately to be on his arm while they took in the festivities. Instead, it appeared that her man may have been smitten by an artist. Or was it the other way around?

Didn't matter. Gayle would never give him up. Or allow some other bitch to step into her shoes as his lover. She'd rather see Spencer dead than with someone else.

Gayle found herself imagining that very scenario in vivid detail.

ELEVEN

Later that day, Spencer drove to his father's house, still shaken by his eerie phone conversation with Gayle. The last thing he needed in his life right now was an embittered woman who wouldn't let go of a dead relationship. In his mind, the best remedy was simply to keep his distance and hope she'd go away for good. That said, he felt sorry for the next guy Gayle would set her sights on. She was definitely bad news. Her neediness and apparent inability to leave well enough alone was a big turnoff.

Spencer's thoughts turned to his father's cryptic voice mail message. He didn't feel there was any sense of urgency, but since his father rarely called these days, a visit to check on him seemed like a good idea.

Evan Berry still lived in the Craftsman-style bungalow where Spencer grew up. It had been the place where his parents were supposed to enjoy their golden years. But then his mother died of cancer ten years ago and Wesley nine years later, destroying the dream forever.

This left his father an embittered and broken man at the relatively young age of sixty-three. And he had, in many respects, turned his back on Spencer when he needed him most. Though he'd tried to be understanding, Spencer had trouble with that, feeling the divide between them had never been greater, only deepening since Wesley's death.

Spencer felt as badly as anyone did over the loss of his twin brother. But he was still alive and his father had to respect that. Convincing him of such was a different story altogether.

Spencer pulled into the driveway behind a black Ford Bronco.

"Come on, boy." He urged Sky out of the car. "Let's go see Pops, for better or worse."

The front door opened before they got to the porch. Evan Berry stood there, still as imposing as ever to Spencer, in spite of the fact that his once hefty frame had been reduced to frailty by age and arthritis. He had retired a year ago from his job as a foreman for a construction company.

"You're not here because of that damn message I left earlier, are you?" Evan asked in a gruff voice.

Instead of saying what was expected, Spencer decided to take a different approach. Especially since his father showed no indication that he was physically ill, over and beyond his normal aches and pains.

"No, you said it was no big deal," he replied. "I just had some free time on my hands and Sky and I thought we'd come over to hang out for a while."

As if on cue, Sky ran up to Evan and started to lick his hands. Evan seemed to warm to the dog's affections, petting Sky's back. "Nice to see you, too, old boy." He looked at his son. "Let's go inside."

Spencer grabbed a couple of beers from the refrigerator and found his father sitting in a rocking chair in the den. The television was on a sports network and the stale odor of cigar smoke permeated the air. Spencer had a feeling of déjà vu as he could almost see the whole family sitting around, talking and laughing like old times. But then he came back to reality, knowing that those days were gone forever.

He handed his father a bottle, then sat on a well-worn leather sofa. Spencer figured if he waited long enough, he'd find out what was on his father's mind. In the meantime, he took the lead. "Guess you probably heard that the Park Killer has been at it again?"

"Yeah, I heard." Evan gulped down beer. "Hope the son of a bitch is caught soon."

"Don't we all." Spencer had not told his father he knew the victims, since it would serve no purpose other than to make him fearful that the press would somehow latch on to it and draw attention away from the search for the killer. "Well, it was Sky who found the latest victim's body."

Spencer doubted his father was privy to these details, given his general distaste for the news media ever since Wesley's death. Evan had convinced himself that if the media had remained interested in the case beyond the first week, it would have kept the pressure on the authorities to continue to search for his body that was never found. But when an infant was abducted from her house in the middle of the night and found in a shallow grave a week later, the media turned its attention to that and never looked back.

Evan regarded him with surprise. "Yeah? How'd he manage to do that?"

Spencer related the whole story, including how they ended up at Deidre Lawrence's door; and that Deidre turned out to be a police spokeswoman.

His father scratched his thinning gray-white hair. "Maybe you shouldn't have quit the FBI. Looks like you've got a real knack for gettin' caught up in crimes, whether you want to or not."

"I was a forensic psychologist and never in the field," Spencer reminded him. In fact, he had been at more than one crime scene in his job of attempting to profile some fugitive criminals. "I'm happy being a college professor and would prefer not to witness a shooting at the park or happen upon a dead body."

The one thing Spencer didn't regret for one second was meeting Deidre Lawrence. It wasn't every day that he came across a woman so damned good-looking and with such powerful sex appeal that he doubted she was even aware of it. Maybe they could turn misfortune into pure magic at some point.

"There's more to life than doin' what you're doin'," Evan said brusquely.

Spencer gazed at him. "Meaning?"

"You say you're happy teachin'. But at what cost? You gave up a job that meant somethin' to you, and you let a good woman like Fiona get away."

Spencer felt the hairs stand up on the back of his neck. "The job was too stressful and I got a lot less out if it than I put in," he said defensively. "As for Fiona, she left me, not the other way around."

"Whatever," his father grumbled.

"Actually it's more than that," Spencer shot back. "I don't think she ever really loved me." It was a painful thing to admit, but the pieces seemed to fit the more he thought about in replaying their lives over the years.

"Maybe not," Evan allowed, sipping beer. "But you got a little girl to think about. What do you think it's doin' to her being constantly shuffled back and forth between the two of you?"

"Believe it or not, Charity's a well-adjusted girl who understands that these things happen when married people no longer love each other and get divorced." Spencer wondered why this was being brought up in his face now. It wasn't as if their marriage had just ended yesterday.

Evan picked up a half-used cigar from an ashtray and lit up. He inhaled nicotine and blew out smoke through his mouth and nose thoughtfully. "If only Wesley hadn't died so young. There were so many things he had left to do."

Spencer tasted the beer and peered at his father. Though he agreed with him about Wesley, he had to ask, "Where is this coming from, Pops?"

Evan met his gaze with hard eyes. "I don't know," he muttered. "Guess I've just been thinkin' about him lately and what a damned stupid waste his life turned out to be."

"Excuse me?" Spencer wasn't sure he'd heard correctly what sounded like a slap in his dead brother's face.

"That boy had every opportunity just like you. But he chose to take a different route—one that probably cost him his life."

"It was a boating accident, Dad. It had nothing to do with his personal choices."

"Had *everything* to do with his personal choices," Evan insisted. "If your brother hadn't been so damned depressed about losing his job and then seein' that gal he was with blow her brains out, Wesley might never have . . ."

Committed suicide. The idea had crossed Spencer's mind on more than one occasion. He had seen this as a strong possibility too, but no one ever wanted to talk about it, as if that would somehow make it true. He hadn't realized it had weighed so heavily on his father's mind. Or perhaps it was just starting to as he faced his own mortality.

"We don't know what happened out there," Spencer told him. "We may never know."

"Yeah, maybe not." Evan finished off his beer.

"What matters now is that Wesley's with Mom in heaven."

"I know."

"We're all we've got left, Pops. Let's try to make the best of it." Spencer waited for a response, but got none. He stood, not wanting to rock the boat between them any further. "I'll go see what's Sky's gotten himself into."

At 4:00 P.M., Deidre stood on the lawn of a home in a newer subdivision across town. She could feel the tension in the air as the press waited for her to speak. The butterflies she felt were nothing compared to the terror she imagined the parents were experiencing for their abducted child.

On cue, Deidre began her statement as the police spokeswoman. "Good afternoon. At three-thirty this afternoon, an Amber Alert was issued for an eight-year-old girl named Keaare Sanchez, who was abducted in broad daylight in front of her home by a man described as being either African American or dark-skinned Hispanic, stocky, and of medium build, with short, dark hair. The alleged abductor is believed to have been driving a black or dark blue van. Keaare is described as being African American, four foot seven, and slender with black pigtails and black eyes. If anyone sees her or someone fitting her description, you are urged to call 911 immediately. Thank you."

Deidre directed a few questions to the detective who was in charge of the investigation. Later, she would give another statement at police headquarters when she had more information to work with.

She headed for the house where the frantic single mother and an older sister, the only witness to the abduction, were being interviewed by a detective.

"Way too many of these creeps out there," said Roland Vesper, the sketch artist, who caught up to her.

"Tell me about it," she agreed. "Seems like if it isn't one thing, it's another."

"Nature of the beast, I'm afraid. As long as there are people to be victimized, there will be perps happy to oblige."

The thought made Deidre sick. She could only imagine how she would feel if it had been her child taken away by a stranger, which was still the assumption at this point. Having her child harmed in any way by a sexual predator would be more than she could bear. Though losing a child to gun violence was every bit as painful.

Two hours later, Deidre was at police headquarters where she ran into Lieutenant Hal Iverson.

"We'll find her," he said positively.

"I certainly hope so," she replied, not wishing that on any mother. Even then, she understood that with each hour they did not locate the girl, chances for her survival grew smaller.

Hal looked at her thoughtfully. "How are you doing?"

Deidre assumed he was referring to the job. "I'm okay."

"Ready for your big showing?"

Honestly, she had forgotten she'd mentioned it to him. "I think so."

"It'll be nice to finally see some of your work," Hal said.

She had resisted his requests to check out her art room. "I hope you like it."

"I like the artist, so there's a pretty good chance that I'll like the paintings."

Deidre forced a smile. "We'll see."

Hal studied her. "You haven't seen any bad guys lurking around your place lately, have you?" he asked.

Deidre met his eyes and couldn't help but wonder if he was referring to Spencer Berry. More likely, she decided, he meant anyone who could be doubling as a serial killer still very much on the loose.

"No, I haven't," she responded. "It's been pretty quiet on the home front lately." She had tried hard not to get too paranoid when she spotted someone she didn't recognize, given that the neighboring park attracted new—and sometimes weird-looking or acting—people all the time.

Hal gave her a deadpan look. "Let's hope it stays that way. Maybe our psycho serial killer has moved off in another direction. If you do happen to see anyone acting suspicious at any time, don't hesitate to call me here or on my cell, day or night. I mean it."

"Thanks, Hal." Deidre appreciated his concern, but didn't want any special treatment from him, fearful it might be construed as something other than a professional relationship. She hoped she was just imagining his romantic interest in her.

TWELVE

After work, Deidre took the light rail train home. She noted the same bearded, unkempt man she had seen last week. This time, he was seated across from her and seemed intent on staring directly at her with those ominously dark eyes, as if to frighten her to death. She pretended not to notice, but felt very uncomfortable. Her first thought was to find another seat. However, since the train was full, it wasn't really an option.

He obviously has nothing better to do than ride the free downtown light rail day and night—and gawk at women for some sort of thrill.

But did that mean he was dangerous? Or was he merely to be pitied as someone with no real life outside of that on the streets, which she knew could be difficult for even the most hardened people.

Deidre wondered if she should take Hal up on his offer to call him to report any suspicious-looking characters. That notion was quickly shot down. After all, he was clearly talking about someone who might be lurking around outside her house. Not a weird man on the train, whose only crime thus far had been sitting there peering at her, as if women were specimens for his eyes to dissect.

Instead, Deidre tried to concentrate on her novel and shut him out. When she came to her stop, she got off with a number of other passengers.

Unsure if the man had exited too, Deidre quickly moved across the lot where she'd parked her car to catch the train. Reaching the vehicle, she fumbled with her purse, trying to find her key fob to unlock the door. She heard footsteps behind her that were getting closer.

Deidre's heart thumped wildly as she imagined being accosted in the light of day and left for dead. She finally got the door open and practically dove inside the car, slamming the door shut and locking in it one swift motion. Only then did she breathe again and allow herself to look out the window. She saw people passing by innocently, heading to their cars. There was no sign of the man from the train.

False alarm. The man, strange as he was, probably hadn't even gotten off the train. There would be no attempted carjacking. No sexual assault. Or murder.

Deidre closed her eyes for a moment, remembering that fateful day three years ago that had altered her future forever. She had been a little on edge ever since and accepted that, given the stakes.

She started the car and drove home.

He watched stealthily from behind a van as the woman from the train drove off in a blue Subaru. Just like the last time, when he'd followed her 'til she disappeared into the police station, he was certain that she was clueless about him.

Instead, her focus had once again been on the same homeless man who, no doubt, rode the train just for the hell of it and likely posed no threat to her.

But let her think otherwise. That'll play right into my hands quite nicely.

And make her wish she had chosen the right man to fear.

There was something about the woman that captured his attention and brought out the worst in him. Much like the other women whose jaws he had broken before he had his way with them and then strangled their lives away effortlessly.

But somehow he sensed that this one would not be as easy, as if she had a built-in defense mechanism that he would have to break to get to her.

He was more than willing to go for it. She would be well worth the risk, given the reward of having her as his sex slave before killing her.

All in good time.

He was in no hurry. Especially when there were other things going on in his life to keep him busy in the interim.

He walked away from the parking lot, attracting little attention as he headed down the street, whistling.

"Your father went to see his doctor this afternoon," Deidre's mother said to her over the phone.

"What's wrong with Daddy?" Deidre asked nervously, clutching the phone tightly as she sat on a stool in her breakfast nook.

"Oh, there's nothing to worry about, dear," her mother said calmly. "Other than high blood pressure and borderline high cholesterol, he's fine."

Deidre's heart settled down a bit. Her father had generally been in good health over the years, but that was just the type of person to worry about. Wasn't it?

"Maybe Daddy needs to slow down," she suggested. He was a postal employee and had a small flea market business on the side selling Persian and Oriental rugs. When he wasn't working, her father spent hours fixing things around the house. Or trying to.

"I agree," her mother said, "but convincing him of that is a different matter. You know how stubborn your father can be."

Too stubborn for his own good. "Talk to him anyway, Momma. Or I can. I'd hate to see Daddy work himself to death. After losing Marshall and Adam, I'm just not sure I could take losing either of you anytime soon."

"We're not going anywhere 'til the good Lord is ready for us," her mother said confidently. "And I expect that won't be for years to come. So don't worry about us, honey. I'd much rather you focused on being happy with your life in Sinclair Heights."

"I am," Deidre insisted. Or as happy as one could expect to be living there for just over a month and trying to acclimate to her surroundings. She didn't bother mentioning the dead body found in the creek that the authorities believed was the work of a serial killer. Her mother would have freaked out and probably demanded that she leave Sinclair Heights immediately and return to the relatively safe confines of Philadelphia, totally discounting the fact that her husband and son had fallen prey to a criminal there.

"Have you started dating again?" her mother asked.

Why is everyone suddenly so interested in my love life?

Deidre was mildly surprised at the question, considering the source. For all her meddling, her mother had not attempted to cross the line into the romance department since Marshall's death, giving Deidre the space she needed. So what had changed?

"Not yet."

Deidre found herself once again thinking about Spencer Berry. They were hardly at the point of dating, if it ever happened. But the man did seem to be an eligible and very good-looking bachelor, and they certainly had a knack for running into each other all over the city. Maybe that meant something. Or not. Either way, there was no need to get her mother all excited by even hinting at such.

"And why not?" her mother probed.

"I'm just too busy right now," Deidre said. She decided it wouldn't hurt to pacify her mother a little bit. "But I am open to dating again, as soon as I'm a little more settled in."

Her mother's tone perked up. "Well, that's good to hear. You're way too young to be alone, Deidre, and Marshall wouldn't have wanted that."

"I know, Momma."

The reality was that Marshall had been a selfish man, though loving in his own way. As such, Deidre was not sure that he would have wanted her to find another man to share her life and body with. But Marshall had given up that right to determine her future when he had rather foolishly tried to disarm a man wielding a loaded weapon with fatal consequences. Deidre knew she had to control her own destiny now, no matter where it led her.

Or with whom.

When the phone indicated she had another caller, Deidre quickly said her good-byes. She promised to speak to her father next time, assuming he was home and not too busy for his daughter.

"Hi, Sabrina." Deidre stood up and went into the living room, where sunlight filtered through the blinds.

"Only seven hours 'til show time and I just had to call someone to try to calm my nerves," Sabrina said.

"What's there to be nervous about, girl? Isn't this what we've both been dreaming about?" Truthfully, Deidre was just as jittery with her artwork on public display for the first time at a gallery in Sinclair Heights.

"But what if no one likes our stuff?" Sabrina asked. "Or the critics trash our work?"

"I don't see that happening on either score," Deidre told her, keeping a positive outlook. "We both have great talent and it shows up in our paintings. My advice is to just chill and get ready for our coming out party."

Sabrina chuckled. "Consider me chilled," she said. "I feel much better now that we've talked. I'm so glad that we met, Deidre."

"Me, too," Deidre said. "We artists have to stick together, no matter what."

"Amen to that. So do you think Spencer will really show up? Or is he all hot air and no fire?"

"Since I really don't know the man all that well, your guess is as good as mine," Deidre admitted. She was hardly qualified as an expert on reading men's minds. Especially a man like Spencer Berry, who had not been very easy to figure out thus far. What little had come to the surface gave her pause. "Either way, the show will go on with or without him."

"Agreed."

Deidre suddenly decided that the show would be better with him, if only to make the event that much more interesting over and beyond her desire to wow local art collectors with some of her best work on display. The next step lay squarely on Spencer.

THIRTEEN

For the show, Deidre chose to wear a black silk dress and matching slingback shoes. She put her hair up in a chignon and added some simple pearls around her neck for effect.

"Wow! You look fantastic," declared Sabrina.

"So do you," Deidre said, admiring her friend in a strapless red gown and high-heeled pumps. "Of course, what's more important is that our paintings are a hit— and they are."

Sabrina beamed. "That's what everyone's saying so far, knock on wood. Everything seems to be coming together quite nicely."

"I never doubted it, girlfriend. We deserve to have our paintings seen and appreciated."

"You'll get no argument from me there."

Deidre smiled, keeping her fingers crossed that the evening went as she envisioned. Though she enjoyed being a police spokesperson, art was her true passion in life and a great coping mechanism when things were rough.

Sabrina took her hand. "Come with me and I'll introduce you to some of the people I know."

"Lead the way," Deidre said, realizing she was still pretty new to the art crowd in town. As such, she had only invited a few people and wasn't sure if they would show. She looked around for the man she had not personally invited, but seemed intent on coming: Spencer

Berry. He was nowhere to be seen, which disappointed her a little. But Deidre refused to get too worked up over whether he showed. After all, there was still a lot she didn't know about the man. And vice versa. *No need to put the cart ahead of the horse, so to speak.*

A half hour later, Deidre had grown pretty comfortable at the gallery. Sabrina had used her connections and somehow managed to convince the gallery owner to agree to show their collection. Deidre tried to fit in here, hoping to become as much a part of the art world in Sinclair Heights as she had in Philadelphia. She did her best to entertain Hal and Agatha, who came together but made it clear they were not a couple. As if Deidre needed to be convinced, knowing the two were about as different as night and day.

"You've definitely got it going on," Hal marveled, eyeing a portrait of two schoolchildren that she'd done early in the year.

"Thank you," she said, blushing.

"Maybe I'll commission you to paint me one day," he suggested.

"You probably couldn't afford her fees," quipped Agatha.

Deidre laughed. "Oh, I'm sure we could work something out, Hal." As long as it was only a painting and nothing more. "Will you excuse me?" she said to them as an excuse to mingle with others.

There was still no sign of Spencer Berry, and Deidre wondered if he had changed his mind, deciding that this wasn't really his thing.

Or perhaps that she wasn't.

It was probably better all the way around if he didn't show. That way, neither of them would be disappointed for expecting too much and getting too little.

Just as Deidre had managed to put the man out of her mind, she spotted Spencer entering the gallery. Sabrina saw him too, and quickly made her way over to Deidre as the owner of the gallery began talking to Spencer.

"Looks like Paul might be giving Spencer the third degree," hummed Sabrina. "Do you want to rescue him, or shall I?"

Deidre considered the choices. Did she want Spencer to think she was coming on to him or otherwise misread her intervention as something else? Or did she want to see him become part of Sabrina's revolving door of men?

In the end, Deidre decided that there was no harm in greeting Spencer and leaving Sabrina to dazzle the other guests while showing off her amazing talent.

"I'll give it a go," she told her friend.

Sabrina curved her glossy lips into a smile. "I thought so. Good luck!"

Spencer showed up at the Chestnut Art Gallery at a quarter to nine. He figured that by then things would be in full swing and he could easily blend right in. The gallery was located in the Wellington District, where there were a number of galleries, bookstores, boutiques, and coffeehouses.

For an instant, Spencer wondered about the wisdom of accepting the invitation under the guise of wanting to see paintings. Though he did appreciate such talent, his real interests went beyond the artwork. What he truly wanted most of all was to be in the company of Deidre Lawrence again any way he could. He had no intention of backing out now.

As he entered the gallery, he half expected—or hoped—
to run right into Deidre and have her all to himself. But
that wasn't the case, at least not yet. Instead, he saw a
large crowd of art lovers milling around almost aimlessly
amid framed oil-based paintings that included portraits,
scenery, and objects.

Spencer made his way into the mix, grabbing a flute
of champagne and a chocolate truffle from a tray.

"Welcome," he heard the accented voice say. Turning, Spencer saw a forty-something, well-dressed man
with greased back graying hair approaching. "Are you
here for the showing?"

Spencer nodded. "From the looks of things, I'd say I
found it."

"Indeed. I'm Paul Duvalier, the owner of the gallery."
They shook hands.

"Spencer Berry."

"Nice meeting you, Spencer. Are you a friend of . . . ?"

"Deidre," Spencer said, adding, "and Sabrina."

"Spencer, you came. . . ." Deidre suddenly appeared
in front of him, to his surprise.

He met her eyes. "Wouldn't have missed it." *Or you,
in particular.*

She looked at Paul. "He's with me—us. Sabrina personally invited Spencer."

This seemed to have left an impression on the gallery
owner, though Spencer was far more impressed with
Deidre, who looked the part of an artist, notwithstanding her stunning beauty.

"Wonderful," Paul said. "Make yourself right at home,
Spencer."

"I intend to." Spencer watched as Paul greeted other
newcomers, then he turned his attention to Deidre. He
was quite pleased with what he saw from head to toe.

Maybe too much.

"It's nice to know that I'm here with you," he said, amused, but not at all displeased.

"I was just trying to help you out, since this is an invitation-only event," Deidre stammered, trying to explain her choice of words, though knowing how lame it sounded. "Paul can be a bit too overzealous sometimes and his greeting can seem more like an interrogation."

"I understand." Spencer grinned. "I think I liked it better that we were an item. At least tonight."

Deidre flushed as she looked at him favorably in a perfectly fitting dark brown suit. Before he got too carried away with himself, or she did, she thought it best to set things straight. "Before two people can become an item, they should probably get to know each other first. Don't you think?"

"I couldn't agree more," he said smoothly. "I think we already have a head start. We know each other's profession and have shared the experience of discovering a dead body, bumping heads at the police station, hanging out at the Cinco de Mayo Fiesta, running into each other at a deli, and now I get to see your artwork. Where should we go from here in getting to know each other better?"

Deidre smiled crookedly, accepting his humor for what it was. What she really wanted to know about was his relationship status. It seemed a safe bet that there was no one in his life. But looks could be deceiving.

"You can tell me if there's anyone else in the picture right now, besides your daughter," she said boldly.

He raised a brow. "You mean as in a woman?"

She met his eyes. "Yes."

Spencer thought about some of the women he'd been involved with in the past, including the last one, and knew that they were all out of his system. And at just the right time.

108 Devon Vaughn Archer

He held Deidre's gaze and gave her a straight answer. "At the moment, I'm totally single . . . and unattached." This seemed to please her. "How about you? Is there a man in the picture, who's crazy as hell about you?" Spencer assumed this wasn't the case, but why not start whatever they were starting on an even playing field.

Deidre was aware that Hal probably had a thing for her, but it was hardly in the crazy-about-you category, and was entirely one-sided. And she'd been given the eye by more than her fair share of men since arriving in Sinclair Heights, no doubt like most attractive young women, but didn't put much stock into it. The reality was there was no one she'd been even remotely attracted to since Marshall died.

Until now. . . .

"There's no one in the picture. I'm a widow." Deidre trembled slightly, but was sure Spencer didn't notice. "My husband and son were killed by a carjacker three years ago."

Spencer's brow furrowed in surprise that she was also a victim of tragedy of the worst kind. "I'm really sorry to hear that."

"Everyone is, but unfortunately it can't bring them back." Deidre didn't mean to sound cold. Just giving a statement of fact.

"Yeah, I know," he said dolefully. "I lost my twin brother last year in a boating accident."

Deidre felt the pain from someone who had suffered in his own way as much as she had. "I'm sorry for your loss. Looks as though misfortune has hit us both hard."

Spencer agreed and wished it had been different. But neither of them could rewrite history. And there was no reason to put a damper on the evening. Or possibly the future, where perhaps both of their fortunes could take a turn for the better.

"Maybe in some ways it has made us stronger and taught us to not take things for granted like so many people do," he contended.

Deidre nodded thoughtfully, feeling as if Spencer truly understood where she was coming from. But understanding her as a woman would take longer. And certainly could not be accomplished at a showing in an art gallery. If at all. Her protective defenses kicked in and she felt herself withdrawing from what seemed like something that could be promising the more she got to know this man.

"Why don't I show you around?" she offered. "I would not want Sabrina to think you came for all the wrong reasons."

"No, we wouldn't want that, would we?" Spencer said with a wry grin. "I'd love to see your paintings." *I'd rather go somewhere for a drink—just the two of us—if I had my way.*

Or maybe an even more intimate setting.

But why risk ruining a potentially good thing? Time was on their side to get to know one another well beyond how they made their living.

Wasn't it?

FOURTEEN

"What the hell are you doing here?" Hal asked snidely when he spotted Spencer standing all by his lonesome in front of one of Deidre's paintings.

Spencer turned, surprised to see the lieutenant there as well. The man didn't strike him as an art connoisseur, which meant he was likely there to support the artist and police spokeswoman. Or was there more to it than that?

"I'm sure that I'm here for the same reason you are," he answered curtly.

Hal's brows knitted over his suspicious eyes. "Deidre invited you?"

"Actually, it was her friend Sabrina. Have I violated any laws by taking her up on the kind offer, Lieutenant?"

"Not that I know of," Hal admitted, wishing he could haul his ass off to jail for trespassing. "Just curious, that's all."

"Is that why you're here?" Spencer asked. "Are you curious about what Deidre does with her time when she's not working for the police bureau?"

Hal had no desire to debate his reasons for being there and who he'd come for, though it was obvious they both had the hots for Deidre. He couldn't do much about that, other than hope she preferred someone with thicker skin and a willingness to stay the course when the going got tough. Which wasn't the case for the former FBI agent.

"Deidre invited me," Hal said simply.

Spencer left it at that, not seeing him as serious competition in romancing Deidre. Though he suspected the lieutenant didn't see it that way. "So have you gotten any closer to nabbing the shooter?"

"We're closing in on him," was all that Hal was at liberty to say. The truth was that the gang member had managed to elude capture thus far, but he was sure it was only a matter of time before they took his sorry ass into custody. Hal wasn't thrilled that Berry had been the one to get the victim to identify his attacker, but it admittedly made the job of solving this case a little easier.

"That's good," Spencer said and sipped his champagne. "What about the Park Killer?"

"I can't talk about that investigation with you," Hal told him in no uncertain terms.

Spencer frowned. "Come on, Lieutenant. Remember who discovered the last victim. It's not like I'm asking you to divulge any classified information."

"True, but your connection with all of the victims of the so-called Park Killer still makes me a little uneasy, I won't lie about it."

"I thought we'd gone over all that."

"We have. But it doesn't mean you're off the hook entirely," Hal said, even if he didn't truly believe he was their serial killer. But maybe he knew who was. "Until this case is solved, what the police know about it stays with the police. Understand?"

"Perfectly," Spencer said, wishing he'd just kept his mouth shut. Not that he was too worried about the authorities coming after him. He trusted that they were smart enough, when looking at things squarely, to know what was a complete waste of their time and what wasn't. If not, he would just have to cross that bridge when he came to it.

"I hope you two are enjoying the showing," Deidre said as she approached the men. She had a feeling that their exchange had little to do with art. She hoped it didn't have to do with some sort of manly competition with her being the prize. As it was, she only had interest in one of them and believed the feeling was mutual.

"What's not to enjoy?" Spencer said, grinning. "Between you and Sabrina, I'd say you've cornered the local market on exquisite art."

"I couldn't agree more," Hal said.

Deidre smiled at the compliment as both men raised their champagne glasses in salute.

Gayle Kincaid had followed Spencer from his home to the art gallery. She wanted to know everywhere he was going and who he was seeing, as if to be a part of his life even without him being aware of it. She was sure that their differences could be resolved at the end of the day and they would be together again.

She went inside and charmed a man at the door into letting her in without an invitation by insisting that she'd accidentally left her invite at home, but was here with her boyfriend who had just come in. Once past that obstacle, Gayle immediately made herself fit right in at the art exhibit. It was easy for her to put on a good front while pursuing her true intent—finding her man.

Where are you, Spencer? Gayle repeated the words in her head several times. Even then, she was not necessarily in any hurry to confront Spencer. Not with all these witnesses around to make it seem like she was crazy or something.

Obsessed, yes, but still very much in control. All she needed was Spencer in her life to make things right again.

"Nice works of art, don't you think?" The voice with a thick Jamaican accent startled Gayle.

She looked at the man behind the voice, batting her lashes. "Excuse me? . . ."

He smiled broadly. "I was saying that our artists are quite talented, don't you think?"

It suddenly dawned on Gayle that she was supposed to be admiring the artwork, which to this point had barely registered in her consciousness.

She grinned. "Yes, very much."

"My name's Paul Duvalier, by the way. I own the place."

Big deal. Am I supposed to be impressed? "Cool. It's a great gallery."

"The gallery is only as good as the paintings," he said with a chuckle. "Are you here with someone?"

No, but I'd sure like to be. Gayle strained her eyes, trying to look past the crowd to spot Spencer. When she seemed to be getting nowhere, she glared at the man pestering her.

"Actually, I was supposed to meet someone here, but I don't see him. . . ."

She watched an expression of disappointment crease Paul's dark face. "Does your friend have a name?"

Should I or shouldn't I? Gayle decided that giving him too much information might be a bad thing. "It doesn't matter. He probably never showed."

Paul's face lit up. "That would be his misfortune. But I would be more than happy to show you around."

"That's sweet," she said in a sugary tone. "Would you mind getting me a glass of that champagne I thought I saw being passed around?"

"It would be my pleasure."

Her eyes crinkled as she put on a fake smile. "I'll just mingle around and catch up with you."

He nodded eagerly and Gayle watched him walk off. *Asshole.* She hurriedly went in the opposite direction.

Gayle had just about decided that Spencer must have been on to her and had given her the slip, when she spotted him. He was chatting with two women. At first glance she thought Spencer was just conversing with some other guests.

It was only when she moved to get a better angle that Gayle recognized one of the women. It was that sketch artist from the Cinco de Mayo Fiesta.

What the hell was she doing here?

And why is she flirting shamelessly with my man?

Gayle's fury caused her nostrils to swell. She would be damned if she'd let some other woman steal the love of her life. But to go over and make a scene now would only do more harm than good. She couldn't give Spencer an excuse to further distance himself from her.

No, she would have to patiently bide her time 'til she could deal with the situation.

And that conniving little bitch!

Swiveling around perfectly, Gayle marched toward the door. She had hoped to avoid Paul Duvalier, but had no such luck. He blocked her path with two champagne flutes in hand.

"Don't tell me you're leaving so soon? . . ."

Gayle sucked in a deep breath and resisted telling him what she really thought of some too thin, unattractive man trying to come on to her. "Look, Paul, you seem like a nice man, but you're not really my type. Sorry."

"No more than I am." His face sagged. "Have some champagne anyway." He held the glass out to her.

For an instant, Gayle considered taking it—if only to drown her sorrows—but she was seething too much inside knowing that Spencer was socializing with everyone but her. She needed to get out of there fast before she did something she would truly regret.

"I can't," she said abruptly, and pushed past him out the door.

Only when the cool air hit her face did Gayle manage to regain control. But with that came a greater resolve to prove to Spencer just how much she loved him. And that no other woman could ever take her place.

She wouldn't allow it.

FIFTEEN

Why in the world did I freeze up and seek the com-fort of the art exhibit over Spencer Berry's company?

Deidre could only wonder about the answer to that as she relaxed in a bubble bath. She'd passed up on the chance to spend more time with Spencer, opting instead to continue circulating among the crowd over and beyond what was called for. *What am I afraid of? Finding someone who might actually make me forget the pain of losing my family and help me remember what it's like to want a man and be desired by him?*

Deidre was sure it was desire that she'd seen in Spencer's wondrous eyes, even though he'd tried to hide it from her. She was equally certain that she was beginning to develop feelings for him that she hadn't expected to feel. She wanted to cultivate these feelings and see what happened. It was time to get involved again with someone who was interesting, good-looking, and had more than his share of sex appeal.

Spencer definitely fit the bill to perfection. She also saw a sensitive side to him as a man who, like her, had experienced grief firsthand with the death of his brother; and also indirectly through the murders of women he knew. He seemed to cope by putting up a brave front and not letting his emotions show much.

I like Spencer Berry and want to pursue this some-how.

But had she blown it by clearly using the art show as an excuse to cut their conversation short? Maybe Spencer had given up his pursuit of her, if in fact that's what it was. And she'd have no one to blame but herself.

The thought was slightly depressing to Deidre as she rinsed the soap off her body, got out of the tub, dried off, and slipped into a nightshirt. She dabbed some moisturizer on her face and had a glass of wine before going to bed.

Deidre prayed that the nightmare she had been unable to escape since Marshall and Adam died would not return this night. More welcome would be to dream about Spencer Berry and rediscovering the magic of passion and romance.

Spencer sat on the bench in his workout room lifting weights.

Did I blow it by not seizing the moment in getting closer to Deidre, even when she seemed to back away before we could cross some proverbial line?

Maybe he was just as hesitant, fearful of getting involved in a real relationship, after having been burned once and still having the scars of disillusion to prove it. It seemed easier to try a different flavor of the month than to be with someone of substance who made his blood race and challenged his mind in a way that made him long for much more.

Spencer wondered if easy was no longer the answer for what and whom he wanted in his life. Maybe it was time to put himself out there and find a woman who truly meant something to him beyond a quick and sweet escapade.

Someone like Deidre Lawrence.

Had he let the chance slip through his fingers at the art exhibit? He and Deidre had gone their separate ways after it ended with no promises of a repeat engagement. Instead they'd only given each other a hint of cordiality, seemingly primarily for the benefit of Sabrina, whom Deidre had left with.

Spencer increased his speed while raising and lowering the weights. He felt his heart rate rise and wondered if his thoughts about Deidre had more to do with that than the workout. He fully intended to find out, casting aside any second thoughts and past regrets.

He did pushups routinely, counting backward from two hundred. Even during this ritual, he was still able to think about the striking woman he'd seen on the train. He imagined having her under him instead of a hardwood floor, being inside that tight body while she writhed for him; then hearing her gasp her last breath as he strangled her to death.

The thoughts got him highly aroused and a devilish smile spread across his face. It quickly turned into a scowl as he realized that his wishes were far from reality at the moment.

First he needed to find out who the woman was and where she lived, and then plot his strategy. Just like all the others. Afterward, it would just be a mere formality to do what needed to be done.

By the time he finished his workout, he was drenched with sweat and could feel his heart racing. He sucked in a deep breath and stepped out onto the balcony.

It was a full moon, and more stars seemed to come out, too. Behind the façade of his normal life was a man who still had something to prove, if not to himself then to others. He was more than up to the challenge.

He thought again about the woman from the train and envisioned her probably sleeping peacefully tonight, just like the others had slept before her.

Unaware that danger was right around the corner. And death a stone's throw away.

Spencer took Sky out for some much-needed exercise on Sunday. Instead of their normal route, they ended up crossing the park and heading for Deidre's house, for better or worse.

He stood in front of the Victorian with his dog. Now what? He didn't exactly have an invitation. What if Deidre liked to sleep late? Or had company?

He decided that the gains definitely outweighed the risks, so he went for it and trusted his instincts about the lady.

If the doorbell ringing didn't do the trick, Sky's barking did. The door opened and Deidre stood there in an oversized sweatshirt and jeans.

"Hi," Spencer said sheepishly.

"Hi, yourself." Deidre was surprised to see the twosome, but not displeased in the slightest. Then she suddenly recalled the last time they had shown up at her door. She frowned. "Please don't tell me you've found another dead body . . . ?"

Spencer chuckled humorlessly. "We found nothing of the sort," he assured her.

Deidre gave a sigh of relief. "Well, I just had to be sure." She thought back to the art gallery and how their private time had ended all too soon. This was a chance to maybe start over and see what happened. "Would you like to come in? I was just playing around with my sketch pad."

"Must be a pretty slow day," Spencer joked, knowing that practice always made perfect, though he couldn't imagine the woman before him being any more perfect.

"Yeah, I guess you could say that." She smoothed a thin eyebrow and smiled unevenly.

"Actually, we were hoping you'd like to come out for some fresh air," he prodded. "I wouldn't want Sky to track dirt and such into your house. We were about to take a walk in the park. Care to join us?"

It was an offer Deidre found hard to refuse, considering that she could use a break. She also liked the man, and his dog was also starting to grow on her.

"All right, just give me two minutes."

"Not one second longer," Spencer joked. "Otherwise Sky and I just might have to come in and get you."

Deidre laughed, enjoying his dry sense of humor. "Be right back."

Spencer watched her vanish behind the door. *So far, so good.* Maybe they finally were going to be able to spend some quality time together. And who knew where it could lead them? He certainly saw no reason why this couldn't blossom into something meaningful. He refused to believe that some women he'd known being murdered somehow made him responsible for their deaths. Or that any woman whom he associated with was cursed. In Deidre's case, she had already had her fair share of bad luck. He'd be damned if any more misfortune came her way simply because they had met and were perhaps ready to start a relationship.

SIXTEEN

To Spencer, they seemed like a perfect couple walking in the park, minus holding hands and conjuring up some sinfully erotic plans for the evening. But he would take it one step at a time, if that was what it took to win her over.

"So, it looks like the show was a real success," he tossed out thoughtfully.

"Yes, Sabrina and I, along with some other local artists, were pretty excited about it." Deidre wondered if she might have been even more excited at the time had she not been so preoccupied with the man beside her.

"When you're not hanging out at art galleries or the police station, what do you like to do?" Spencer asked as he gazed at her profile.

Feeling his eyes on her, Deidre faced him. "Oh, lots of things."

"Such as . . . ?"

In truth, Deidre had done few of the things she had enjoyed in Philadelphia since moving to Sinclair Heights. Maybe that would change now, especially if the right person were there to partner with.

"Well, I like playing tennis, though I'm a long way from being Serena or Venus Williams," she told him. "And I enjoy dancing, reading mystery novels, going to fairs and ethnic festivals, movies, musicals, and concerts, and, of course, shopping."

Spencer chuckled. "What woman doesn't like to shop?"

"True. We have to look great and keep up with the latest styles."

"Of course." He imagined that she would look fantastic in a potato sack. Or in nothing at all. "Sounds as if you like a bit of everything."

"That's true," she admitted. She'd always kept an open mind regarding exploring what was out there, but it had been squelched somewhat after losing her family. "How about you?"

Deidre could envision him shooting some hoops or bowling strikes. Maybe even fishing. Playing golf. Or participating in a triathlon.

Spencer continued to surprise her when he said, "I like listening to old standards sung by such great jazz artists as Sarah Vaughan, Billie Holiday, and Ella Fitzgerald. I also enjoy playing the piano, hanging out with my daughter, and reading history, World War II, contemporary, and sci-fi books."

"Wonderful and varied," she told him.

Spencer felt just as taken with Deidre and the versatility of her interests. He could only imagine what other ways she could leave a favorable impression on him.

"Oh, and I'm a big fan of the Philadelphia Phillies and Indianapolis Colts," he added, wondering if she was into professional sports.

"I'm from Philly," she told him.

"Really?" He glanced at her. "You're a long ways from home."

"I know." Deidre thought about the changes in her life, some good, some bad. "My late husband played for the Eagles."

"No kidding?" Spencer hadn't expected that one. "What's his name?"

"Marshall Lawrence."

"I remember him," Spencer said, flashing back as a longtime football fan. "He was good."

"Yes, he was," Deidre agreed proudly.

Spencer wondered if he could compete with a football legend in his own rite in pursuing her. "How long have you been in Sinclair Heights?"

"Not long," she told him. "I take it you've lived here for a while?"

"Yeah, like basically most of my life. I've had my ups and downs here but, for the most part, it's been a nice place to live."

"Not for those women murdered by a serial killer," Deidre pointed out sadly.

"You're right," Spencer said, not wanting her to think for a moment that he didn't care about what happened to them. "But crime on the whole here is low compared to most cities of a similar size."

Deidre knew he was trying to make her feel better, and he had to some degree. She certainly felt safe in his presence, though the thought that she had moved somewhere with a serial killer on the loose and some gang violence was more than a little alarming.

"That's good to know," she told him.

"And since you work for the police, I'm sure you also know that they take crime seriously here and are dedicated to keeping the streets as safe as possible."

"Yes, I do," she said. Hal certainly seemed to take every case personally and insisted that those under his command do the same.

Spencer hoped he had managed to defuse a potentially awkward moment. Though his association with the police bureau had been rocky at best, that wasn't always the case. On the whole, he was sure that they would do everything in their power to catch the Park Killer, as well as deal with any other criminality in town.

Sky's sudden loud barks drew their attention. The dog bared his teeth threateningly.

"What is it, boy?" Spencer held on to the leash tightly as the dog sought to break loose.

Deidre looked around to see what had gotten Sky so riled up. She spotted a man across the park rummaging through the trash.

Spencer also noted the all-too-familiar man: Rodney Rochester, the one who shot Marcus Hobson in the park and had managed to stay out of police custody. Spencer's first instinct was to let Sky at him. But, fearing the shooter might still have a gun, he thought better of it.

I'll go after him myself this time.

"It's the guy who shot the kid in the park," he whispered to Deidre.

She tensed. "What are we going to do?"

"Can you hold Sky's leash?" Spencer asked.

Deidre took it, but was concerned. "Are you going to call the police?"

"Yes, but not 'til I take him down."

"You shouldn't take any chances," she warned, thinking back to Marshall and Adam being shot.

"I won't do anything foolish," he promised, not including accosting a potentially armed and obviously dangerous gang member. "Be right back."

He sprinted across the grass. Sky's barking would surely alert the shooter, if it hadn't already, putting Spencer on the defensive. But he decided it was worth the risk, as he'd had about enough of gang violence and wanted to take a stand that hopefully others would follow by taking back the streets.

"Hey, Rodney," Spencer shouted at him.

Rodney Rochester turned. "Leave me alone, man—"

"Wish I could, but the police want to talk to you about a shooting. Why don't we go in together and no one else has to get hurt."

Spencer half expected him to pull out his gun, but he didn't. Apparently he had been smart enough to ditch it, but too dumb to know when he'd reached the end of the line. He took off running.

Rodney darted through the trees and demonstrated his skills at evasion that he had previously used to successfully elude Sky and a police search for him.

But Spencer was determined not to let him get away again only to be involved in another gang shooting. With long legs and plenty of determination, he closed the gap between them, and quickly tackled the gang member. Spencer immediately subdued him, twisting one hand behind his back.

"You're not going anywhere, Rodney, except to jail."

Rodney yelled an expletive at him, but showed little fight when he didn't have a gun.

Spencer looked up and saw Deidre and Sky approaching.

"Are you all right?" Deidre asked. She felt that, like Marshall, he had been a bit too brash in risking bodily harm by going after someone who could have been armed, but apparently was not. She also realized that, unlike Marshall, as a former FBI agent Spencer had been trained to deal with potentially volatile situations, giving her some peace of mind.

"You're asking the wrong person that," Spencer responded as he continued to hold down the suspect. "But thanks for your concern."

"The police should be here any minute now," she said as Sky continued to bark nonstop.

"Great," he said. "Sky, calm down!" Spencer ordered the dog. "The situation is under control."

"Thanks to you." If Deidre hadn't known better, she would have thought he'd planned this whole thing just to impress her. Well, she was impressed that he had proven to be so calm under fire. She imagined Hal would love to have Spencer on the police force. However, she wasn't too crazy about the prospect of dating anyone in law enforcement. Not with the long and odd hours and inherent risks of the job. So, in that case, she was happy that Spencer was now in a less dangerous job as a college professor.

"No thanks necessary," Spencer said humbly, though he knew he'd gained some brownie points for his heroics. "Just being neighborly. We should all feel safe in this park. At least we'll have one less criminal to contend with now. Maybe somehow, someway, the gang members will come together and find a new more constructive way to challenge each other." He knew that was an uphill battle, if not impossible, but believed that if someone were to take the lead, others might follow.

"Why not?" Deidre said, holding Sky's leash tightly to keep him away from the shooter. "I've seen it work in Philadelphia. It could work here too."

"I agree. Maybe you should pass that along to Lieutenant Iverson and others at the police bureau. I'm sure they'd be interested in what you have to say."

She laughed. "I'm not so sure about that. I'm just a civilian employee."

Yes, but you obviously have some pull with Iverson, whether you know it or not. "But you care, just like me," Spencer said. "That should mean something in and of itself."

"It clearly does," Deidre concurred, as she watched him keep his weight on the culprit, determined to score one victory for the good guys in what could be a very long battle. The selfish part of her feared that this surge of masculinity couldn't have come at a worse time, as they were just starting to make some progress getting to know each other beyond the surface. She hoped they would be able to pick up where they left off another day.

SEVENTEEN

This wasn't Rodney Rochester's first brush with the law. The twenty-two-year-old had been in trouble for nearly half his life, in and out of the gang, for offenses ranging from drug dealing to assault. The latest charge of attempted murder would likely put him away for a long, long time.

Spencer watched from the one-way window as Detective Zack Hernandez questioned the suspect as a person of interest in the Park Killer investigation.

"Looks like you got lucky, Berry," Hal said tonelessly, standing beside him. "That gangbanger could've put you six feet under."

"Is that what you call it, Lieutenant?" Spencer asked sardonically. "I'd say it was more like *his* luck ran out."

"Yeah, that too." Hal narrowed his eyes at Spencer and frowned. "Now run this by me one more time. Exactly how did you *just happen* to be in the park with Deidre and spot the suspect?"

Spencer could tell that he was pissed Deidre seemed to be more interested in him than in the lieutenant. But how that translated into some notion that he was in the park for any other reason, like criminal activity, was beyond him.

He looked at the lieutenant, who always seemed like he was having a bad day even though he had Rochester in custody. Spencer had no desire to cause unnecessary friction between them. But he wasn't about to back away from trying to get something going with Deidre either just to make the cop happy.

"As I told you before, Sky and I were taking our usual walk in the park, this time accompanied by Deidre. That's when we saw Rodney Rochester digging in the trash. Since I knew he was a wanted man and didn't want to see him get away a second time, I did my civic duty, like any good citizen, and held him 'til the police arrived."

Hal ran a hand across the length of his stiff jaw line. He didn't bother to ask him how he ended up with Deidre. It was obvious that she had gone to the park with him willingly. As a result, she had once again put herself in harm's way, which seemed to be the case whenever Berry was around. "I just wanted to get the record straight," he told him.

Spencer was tempted to say something snide, but refrained.

"Truth is, you did us a favor," Hal admitted, though he wished they had been able to get to the shooter first. "One less gangbanging asshole on the streets—at least for now."

Spencer grinned. "Why, Lieutenant, that almost sounds like a sincere note of gratitude."

Hal did not return the smile. "Don't get too excited about it. We would've gotten him sooner or later, with or without your help."

"Maybe," Spencer allowed. "But how many more young people would've gotten shot or killed by then?"

"I'm not in the business of predicting things," Hal said stiffly.

"Neither am I," Spencer said, preferring to focus more on prevention, though he could only do so much now that he was out of law enforcement. He shifted his attention back to the suspect being interrogated. "You don't *really* think he's the Park Killer, do you?"

Hal sighed. "Doesn't matter what I think. We're not excluding *anyone* at this point, especially someone with a penchant for violence who was also spotted in the same area where we found the last victim. You know as well as I do that while there's a serial killer out there, we've got to look closely at everyone—including a gangbanger." Hal paused and looked directly at Spencer. "Unless, of course, *you've* got some pertinent information on the Park Killer that would make me look in different direction."

"Not if you're asking if I'm ready to confess," Spencer said, tongue-in-cheek, with the lieutenant's hard eyes still glued on him. "If so, that won't be happening anytime soon."

Hal grunted. "Didn't think so. But if there's anything else you'd care to share, I'm listening. . . ."

"Nothing in particular," Spencer said carefully. He had no interest in doing the cop's job for him or suggesting that he had any special insight into the case, though perhaps he did as a result of his FBI background. "I'm just using common sense here. Rochester is definitely your man as a gangbanger who shot another gangbanger in their turf war. And he deserves everything he's got coming to him. But raping, brutalizing, and strangling women to death—I just don't buy it, if his rap sheet is accurate."

"So maybe we missed something in his character and crimes," Hal speculated. "Or am I really just missing something about *you*, Berry?" *Why is Deidre throwing away her chance to be with me for him?*

Spencer absorbed the intensity of his glare, but didn't let it faze him. "I don't think so. I'm just a college professor—nothing more, nothing less—who sometimes finds himself not minding his own business, to the detriment of others." *Including a gangbanger.*

"Yeah, whatever. . . ." Hal mumbled.

Before the debate could go any further, Detective Hernandez stepped out of the interrogation room, looking weary.

"What did you come up with?" Hal asked him curiously.

"Not enough to convince me that Rochester is our man," he responded, grim faced. "Just the opposite. I'd have to say that we're pretty much back to square one in identifying the park serial killer son of a bitch. Unless Berry here can help us connect the dots. . . ."

Spencer frowned at Hernandez. "I've already told you everything I know, Detective. Believe me, I want this killer caught, even more than getting that gang member in there for shooting a kid he happened to have a disagreement with. But I'm afraid it's up to you guys to solve this case."

"So what else is new?" Hernandez muttered.

"I think we'll do just that, Berry," Hal added, "no matter how long it takes and who we have to go after."

Sensing that the tension in the air was getting thick enough to cut, Spencer left it alone, only too happy to be an innocent bystander on this one. Still, he knew that no one in the city was going to get any rest 'til this killer was captured. Or killed.

That included him.

And Deidre.

The last thing Spencer wanted was for her to become a target of someone who obviously got off on violating and humiliating women before killing them. She'd already had enough sorrow in her life to last a lifetime. Even though they were still just getting to know each other, he cared for her and had a strong suspicion it worked both ways. And there was nothing Hal Iverson could do about it, except be a man and stay out of the way.

Something told Spencer he couldn't count on that philosophy.

Once again, Deidre was caught in a recurring nightmare that was all too real.

When the carjacker pointed his gun at her husband, ordering them out of the car, she knew instinctively that Marshall would resist.

"Like hell I will." He snorted angrily.

The two began to fight for control of the firearm. Even as she glanced in the backseat at their frightened child, Deidre sensed that something was different this time. When she turned back to the confrontation, instead of Marshall behind the wheel, it was Spencer Berry battling the carjacker.

Deidre watched in speechless horror, trying to make sense of what she instinctively knew was out of whack. But that thought gave way to the immediate danger from a man who was willing to kill to get the car.

"Stop it!" she cried out to Spencer, not willing to risk their lives.

Her words seemed to resonate with him and Spencer let down his guard, releasing the hold on the gun's barrel. The carjacker seized the moment, regaining control of the gun. He fired it at Spencer, hitting him in the chest. Deidre felt instant pain in her arm, even as another shot went off inadvertently and through the seat. She screamed as she looked at her son, who had a bullet wound in his forehead with blood pouring from it.

Just as she turned to Spencer, Deidre could hear the carjacker running away. In an instant, she found herself transported to another place.

But where?

Then recognition set in. It was Pelle Park. Deidre watched as Spencer sat on top of a man, hitting him with his fists. When she got closer, she saw that it was the carjacker who was on the receiving end of the heavy blows. Then his face underwent a transformation, and it was suddenly Marshall being attacked by Spencer.

Deidre screamed and everything seemed to go black.

The scream woke Deidre up. It had been the same nightmare that had plagued her ever since Marshall's and Adam's deaths. Only this time there was a new and unsettling twist to it. Spencer Berry had somehow become interspersed in her dream—as both a hero and a villain. Was this merely a weird manifestation of being shaken more than she realized by Spencer nailing the park shooter? Or was it really about her real life ordeal with a carjacker that somehow got mixed up with another much more recent crime in her subconscious?

Deidre feared it was probably a little of both. She sat up and realized that her nightgown was drenched from sweat.

Guess Spencer Berry is getting to me more than I realized. He's even finding his way into my dreams.

Deidre wasn't sure if that was a good omen or a bad one. Only time would tell. She hoped that time was on her side regarding how things progressed between her and Spencer over the course of it.

EIGHTEEN

On Monday, Spencer found himself thinking about Deidre Lawrence. He imagined what it would be like to make love to her and had no doubt that it would be totally hot and all consuming. For both of them. Hard as it was, he managed to push the lascivious thoughts aside and focused on the students before him in class.

He enjoyed teaching social psychology, even if admittedly a small part of him missed his work with the FBI. At least as a college professor, he was helping to educate people who could actually learn something worthwhile from him. And he didn't have his dead brother's shadow hanging over him like a dark cloud, as was the case when Spencer was still with the Bureau. The tragic and questionable circumstances of Wesley's death was forever a reminder that he'd never truly understood him. Now he never would with his brother gone for good, almost as though he'd never been an important part of his life, which Spencer regretted not having expressed more often when he'd had the chance.

After class, Spencer left the building. He planned to head over to the International Center for a bite to eat before his afternoon class. He was halfway there when he was practically accosted by someone he hoped to never see again.

Gayle flashed him a casual smile. "Hey, Spencer."

He could smell her perfume, which nearly overpowering, and not in a good way. "What do you want, Gayle?"

She frowned, tossing back her braids. "Is that really any way to greet your lover, baby?"

"We are *not* lovers, Gayle, and haven't been for weeks now."

"And *whose* fault is that?" She placed a hand on her hip. "I'm *always* ready and willing."

Spencer's brows twitched. "I thought I made it perfectly clear that you and I are finished," he said sternly. He tried to control his irritation, not wanting to make a scene, which he suspected was what she'd hoped to accomplish.

Gayle, who stood about five six and was in good shape, moved closer. Batting her long lashes, she said, "We will *never* be finished, Spencer! We belong together."

"We do not," he countered. "We never did!"

"I never heard you say that when we were having sex almost every time we were together," she challenged him. "And in every way imaginable."

"That was a mistake," Spencer said quickly. He knew that now more than ever and wished to hell that he could have seen it before he got involved with her.

"No, baby, the mistake is what you're making if you think you can just use me, abuse me, and then toss me aside," Gayle said, shaking her head. "It ain't happening."

Meeting Gayle's hardened gaze, Spencer hoped to reason with her and not attract undue attention at the same time. "Look, Gayle," he said gently as though speaking to a child, "we had fun together, but that was all. I'm sorry if I gave you the wrong idea about a future for us, but you can't make me feel what I don't feel for you."

"But I can if you'll let me," she insisted, and ran a hand across his cheek. "All I ask is that you just give me a chance to show you what we can be like as a couple. Maybe even as man *and* wife—"

Spencer's eyes ballooned. *So much for the gentle approach.* "Have you lost your damned mind?" He hoped that wasn't the case. "Don't go there, Gayle. It's *over* between us and the sooner you get that through your head, the better. Now, if you'll excuse me, I'm late for lunch."

He attempted to walk past her, but Gayle was quicker and blocked his path.

"She can't have you!" Gayle said sharply.

Spencer's head snapped back as though he'd been slapped. "Excuse me?"

Gayle glared at him with piercing eyes. "You heard me. That stupid artist bitch can't take what belongs to me. I saw you talking to her at the Cinco de Mayo *and* at the art gallery—"

"Whoa now, wait a minute . . ." Spencer said. He could barely believe what he'd just heard. She was starting to scare him. "Are you saying you've been following me?"

She twisted her lips into a nasty smirk. "Why shouldn't I? You're my man, like it or not!"

He narrowed his eyes in disgust. *She really is crazy.* "You need help, Gayle. And I don't mean from me. Stalking is a crime, in case you didn't know."

If he thought his words would intimidate her, they seemed to have the opposite effect.

She jutted her chin at him. "Yeah? Well so is *murder!*"

"Are you threatening me?" Spencer felt his blood pressure rising.

"Alls I'm sayin' is that you don't want to mess with me, Spencer!" Gayle warned. "Tell that stupid little bitch you're mine. You got that?"

She poked him hard in the chest as she said those last three words. Having made her point, she stormed away, leaving Spencer frustrated and unsure of himself.

Gayle had more or less threatened him and Deidre with bodily harm. Yet there wasn't a damned thing he could do about it at this point. Except hope that she was merely letting off steam from a relationship, if you could call it such, that had come to a grinding halt sooner than she would have liked. Spencer certainly wasn't going to allow her to dictate who he saw and who he didn't see.

The one thing Gayle had ensured was that she would never be in his life again.

Deidre was another thing altogether. But could he risk putting her in harm's way by asking her out and angering Gayle even more, possibly causing her to do something rash?

Not to mention the fact that a serial killer was still running amok in town, seemingly targeting women Spencer had recently been associated with in one way or another.

Between that and Gayle's apparent volatility, Spencer's head was spinning. Nevertheless, he convinced himself that the serial killer's victims had nothing to do with him. And, as such, he shouldn't be overly concerned that Deidre was in any more danger if she was involved with him than not.

As for Gayle, Spencer had to believe she had her limits, in spite of her unstable personality that he hadn't seen coming even though it was staring him right in the face. Though hurt and vindictive, she was an attractive woman and should have had no problem finding someone else to fall for. At least Spencer was banking on that as he made plans to move full steam ahead in trying to establish a relationship with Deidre.

Hal was in attendance at the Park Killer task force meeting. The task force consisted of detectives from several police departments in Oregon and Washington as well as agents from the local FBI field office. They were once again reviewing the perpetrator's MO, proximity of the crimes, and clues he'd left behind, which were few. They had what was believed to be the killer's DNA, but no one on file who matched it. Further complicating their efforts was the fact that they didn't even have a definitive description of this psycho.

Hal slumped down in his chair with frustration. The plain truth of the matter was their mysterious serial killer remained as elusive as ever. This despite the fact that all of the killings had taken place within a fifteen-mile radius, indicating the killer was most likely a local or someone who spent a lot of time in the area and was familiar with his surroundings. The members of the task force disagreed about many things in their investigation, but what they all agreed about was that they were dealing with a person who would most certainly batter, rape, and murder young women again and again until he was caught.

Or killed.

But how the hell many more women would be victimized until then?

Hal's mind drifted to the gangbanger they had in custody. It hadn't taken too much investigating to link him to a number of armed robberies. The asshole had apparently been busy working on the side even while acting on behalf of his gang when he shot the rival gang member. With all of his offenses, he wasn't going to taste freedom again anytime soon. *Stupid bastard.*

Unfortunately, one thing he wouldn't be doing time for was being a serial killer. As much as they wanted to pin the Park Killer murders on him, it just didn't add up in any way, shape, or form. So they had officially removed him from their list of suspects.

Apparently, Spencer Berry wasn't their man either. Hal had already come to terms with this. Though he had been linked to all the victims, Berry's alibis had checked out for every murder. And they had nothing else on Berry to indicate he had anything to do with the crimes. On a personal level, Hal would have loved to be the one to nail his ass to the wall, which would have gotten the prick out of Deidre's life for good. But that wasn't going to happen.

When he looked at the situation squarely, Hal had to admit that the man was too damned smooth and self-assured to be a cold-blooded killer. Still, Berry was far from perfect and had a few skeletons in his closet, which Hal had discovered from his background check and in talking to the FBI. He'd been surprised to learn that Spencer Berry wasn't just a former agent; he was once a prominent forensic psychologist for the FBI. He had retired prematurely, and took a teaching job at Sinclair Heights College after his twin brother drowned under suspicious circumstances. Suicide was listed as the official cause of death, but questions still remained as to whether there was more to the story.

Hal couldn't help but wonder why the hell he had really quit the agency. Was it out of guilt? Bitterness? Denial? Maybe he wasn't as solid on the inside as he appeared on the outside. Hal couldn't help but wonder if Spencer Berry had ever tried applying his psychology mumbo jumbo to himself and the weight of cracking under the pressure of losing a loved one.

Hal figured the man had probably done the FBI a favor. If Spencer Berry couldn't handle the job, walking away was best for everyone. Hal had been there himself under very different circumstances. He'd left the Sacramento Police Department two years ago after bumping heads one time too many with his superiors, hindering his ability to perform his duties even to his own high standards. But things were much different in Sinclair Heights, where the lines of communication were always open and feedback was encouraged.

That notwithstanding, Hal felt that this spirit of cooperation was being severely tested these days. As long as a ruthless killer continued to terrorize the community, everyone's ass was on the line, including his. Something he wasn't likely to forget while doing his job as best he could under the weight of pressure to solve this case.

NINETEEN

After work, Deidre and Agatha went for a drink at Bert's Place, a favorite watering hole for police bureau employees. It wasn't very crowded, so they had no problem finding a table.

"Wish it was like this more often," Agatha said. "There's nothing like having some breathing room when you're enjoying a drink or two. I hate it when you can't even turn around without bumping into someone and spilling your drink!"

Deidre chuckled. "I'd have to agree." In truth, she wasn't really into bars. But she wanted to make an effort to be sociable with her few friends and colleagues in town.

They ordered cocktails and Deidre listened as Agatha droned on and on about her social life, or lack thereof. "Girl, I'm telling you that they're too tall or too short, too light or too dark, and they don't have enough money, or they're too damn cheap to spend what they have. You hear what I'm saying?"

"Loud and clear," Deidre said with a laugh. "You're looking for someone who doesn't exist."

"Right. And you aren't?" Agatha asked with a raised brow. "And please, girl, don't say it's because he's already dead."

Deidre tasted her drink thoughtfully. "I wasn't going to," she said. "The man I'm looking for does exist." And he was clearly in the market and looking solidly at her, too.

"Of course," Agatha said. "The psychology professor with the lovable dog, right?"

"I don't know yet just how lovable his dog is," Deidre admitted. "But the man does offer some interesting possibilities."

"I'll bet." Agatha lifted her drink. "Well, here's to interesting possibilities and wherever they make take you."

Deidre raised her glass. "Ditto."

"I'll try to keep my options open, in case an interesting guy drops on my lap and . . ." Agatha stopped mid-sentence and her eyes grew wide. "Uh-oh, look who's coming. . . ."

Deidre turned to see Hal headed their way. "You had me worried for a minute there," Deidre said, as the thought of the Park Killer entered her head.

Agatha made a face. "Maybe you should be worried, girlfriend. You know Hal has the hots for you. . . ."

"I think Hal has the hots for *any* woman who's thin, pretty, and single," Deidre said with a nervous chuckle. Deep down inside, she knew it went further than that. Without saying it in so many words, he'd made it clear that he was open to a romantic involvement if she was interested. She wasn't interested, so she tried avoid the subject altogether.

"Well, that leaves me out on two of the three," Agatha said, looking down at her medium frame. "In fact, make that three for three, since I'm not really *single* in the true sense of the word. Even though Darren does still legally belong to another woman."

"I didn't mean that the way it came out," Deidre said, certain that her face had colored a darker shade of brown. In fact, Agatha was a good-looking woman with enough spunk for the two of them. Deidre considered it a good thing that Agatha had broken up for the time being with her married lover and, in the meantime, was looking for someone better.

"I know. It's okay," Agatha said. "Hal isn't my type anyway."

"We're on the same page there," Deidre agreed. "But we still have to work with the man, so—"

"Hey, ladies." Hal stood before them with a broad smile playing on his lips "What's up?"

"Just chilling," Agatha said.

"Mind if I chill with you?"

Agatha glanced at Deidre, as if needing her permission. She gave no objection. "Suit yourself."

"Don't mind if I do," Hal said with a grin.

Agatha stood up. "I have to go to the ladies' room. Try not to miss me too much while I'm gone." She winked at Deidre.

Deidre sneered at her friend, wondering if she was just being mischievous at her expense by leaving her alone with Hal. She forced herself to smile as he sat down in Agatha's chair.

"Hope it wasn't something I said," he joked.

"It wasn't," she assured him.

Deidre hoped to make the best of the situation, even if she could think of a certain other man she'd have rather been sitting with right now.

Hal ordered a malt liquor. He looked at Deidre and said thoughtfully, "I take it you haven't had any problems near your place since that body turned up in your creek?"

"None to speak of."

"That's good to know. Sometimes serial killers like to taunt the police by dumping the bodies of victims in the same place time after the time—daring us to catch them."

Deidre shuddered at the thought that another woman might end up dead in her backyard. "Has the Park Killer done that with any of the other women?"

Hal touched the silver cuff on his ear. "Nope. But he can change the pattern anytime his warped mind wants to for his own sick gratification or to throw us off guard."

"Scary," Deidre said, shuddering again.

"Yeah, for all of us."

After the waitress brought Hal his drink, Deidre asked, "So are you any closer to finding the serial killer?" She had heard rumors and innuendoes inside the police bureau, but nothing concrete. Other than that Spencer happened to have been associated with all of the victims, but not in a way that made him a suspect in their deaths.

Hal gulped down some malt liquor and frowned. "Wish I could say we're closing in on him, but as of this moment, we still don't have any solid leads to speak of."

"Meaning he'll keep killing 'til he makes a mistake?"

Hal furrowed his brow. "Well I wouldn't quite put it that way. The killer's obviously clever. But he's also been damned lucky. Sooner or later—preferably the former—he will either slip up or someone will see something and we'll nail his ass to the ground. Hopefully before anyone else is murdered."

Deidre knew that the police did not take this lightly by any stretch of the imagination and were doing all they possibly could to solve the case before another woman was killed. But they had come up empty thus far, in spite of their best efforts. She couldn't help but wonder just how many more women would not live to see the next week, month, or year because of this one man?

She spotted Agatha talking to another woman at the bar, whom Deidre recognized as a fellow employee at the police bureau.

"So have we run into our Mr. Berry lately . . . ?" Hal said, getting her attention.

She smiled, slightly amused. *At first, he was "your Mr. Berry" and now he's "ours"?* From where Deidre sat, Spencer Berry belonged to no one but himself.

Indeed, they had spent time together in the park last week, before their outing was cut short. But they had hardly become an item. Deidre couldn't help but think that she'd always been attracted to strong men. Men like Spencer and his singlehandedly taking down a gang member, even when it made her seem weaker than she truly was.

She met Hal's steady gaze. "As a matter of fact, I have run into Spencer once or twice. Why do you ask?"

Hal shrugged and wiped his mouth with the back of his hand. "Just wondering, that's all." Hal looked around the bar. "The man seems to be everywhere these days."

"I suppose." She couldn't really argue the point, considering. Was that a bad thing, though?

"Unfortunately, he can't seem to stay put professionally."

She batted her eyes. "Meaning what?"

"He used to be an FBI forensic psychologist, 'til his brother died last year. Now he sits before a class of underachievers, playing babysitter. Guess it was all just too much for him to deal with."

Deidre cocked a brow with irritation. "You mean you actually dug into his background?"

Hal tasted his drink, seeing no reason to deny it. "Hey, don't look so surprised. It's my job to check out *everyone* who's associated with a criminal investigation or two."

"He was a witness to a shooting in the park—and his dog found a body," she said hotly, knowing it wasn't quite that simple. "Since when does that make someone a suspect?"

"Now you're defending the man?" Hal asked, narrowing his eyes at her. He wished she would show that same interest in him.

Was she defending him? "No, I'm not defending Spencer," Deidre said, having made up her mind. "I just wondered if it was normal police procedure to go after someone and dig around in their past when it seems to me that he's trying to do his civic duty. In fact, I think he's gone over and beyond his civic duty to help the police."

"Look, Deidre, I'm not on a witch hunt here just trying to dig up anything I can on Berry, if that's what you're thinking," Hal said. "But let's face it, some women he's known have ended up dead for reasons beyond the obvious. And while it seems like he has nothing to do with their misfortune, it certainly does give one pause for thought." Hal drew a breath. "I just like to know who I'm dealing with in any case I'm working on, no matter how helpful or innocent the person may be."

Maybe she had jumped the gun a bit by questioning his motives. Deidre felt a little foolish as a result. No matter how she viewed Spencer, he was not above the law as either a suspect or a citizen. And she certainly couldn't expect the Sinclair Heights Police Bureau to turn a blind eye to his connection to the murdered women, no matter how inconsequential it may have appeared.

Unless, of course, Hal has his own self-serving agenda, which has more to do with me than police work.

Deidre found herself wondering if his brother's death had been the reason behind Spencer leaving the FBI. Was he so psychologically wounded that he'd retreated from what had been too painful by association, similar to the reasons she had left Philadelphia after losing Marshall and Adam?

Is it even any of my business? Or had it become her business by virtue of the fact that she and Spencer did seem to be developing into something other than mere acquaintances. In which case, she'd want to know as much about him and his past as possible.

"Oh, don't mind me," she tried to apologize to Hal. "You know your job much better than I do. I'm just a police spokeswoman and an artist. I have a bad habit of saying what's on my mind a little more than I should."

"Yes, but I like that about you, Deidre." Hal tasted the malt liquor and licked his lips. "Next thing I know, you'll be telling me that Berry's your type—say, more than I am. Is he your type?"

Deidre felt a trifle uneasy about where this conversation was going and the loaded question, but tried not to show it. "I don't have a certain type of man I look for," she lied.

In reality, she could very much imagine being with someone like Spencer, even if delving into a full-fledged relationship again—no matter whom it was with—scared Deidre half to death. But that didn't mean she wasn't open to seeing if could find the same type of emotional, physical, and sexual connection that she'd had with Marshall, as long as it was with someone who wanted it just as much as she did.

Hal raised a brow. "Oh? So does that mean you're totally open-minded about the men you date?" Hal peered at her, figuring this might be a good opportunity to make a play for her.

"Only up to a point," Deidre said. She forced her eyes to look at his. "What I do have is a policy against going out with the men I work with."

That seemed like a good way to put it without coming right out and saying he wasn't the right man for her. But maybe Spencer was. Assuming they were ever in the same place long enough to see if there was really something to the undeniable chemistry that existed between them on more than one level.

"So that means I'd be wasting my time if I asked you out on a date?" Hal's face sagged disappointingly as if he already knew the answer.

Deidre chuckled nervously. "What I meant is that you're my boss—or my superior with the police department—and you're a friend. I just think it's best all the way around if we don't rock that boat. Can you understand where I'm coming from?"

"Yeah," he said after a moment or two. "I may not like it a hell of a lot, but I do understand. And I value your talent on the job as well as your friendship outside the job."

Deidre smiled warmly at Hal. She felt as though she had dodged a bullet of sorts and had actually brought about a greater understanding between them.

She wondered if it would be as simple with Spencer. Would they be able to sort out just what it was that seemed to have them on the same wavelength? Or would outside forces stand in the way of whatever might come out of this connection they clearly had?

TWENTY

Spencer was playing around with Sky when the phone rang. "Sorry, boy, have to get that." He untangled himself from the dog and got to his feet.

Grabbing the cell phone from the table, Spencer saw that the caller was Deidre Lawrence. Joy surged through him in that instant, viewing the call as something that could only be positive.

He took a breath and answered. "Well, hello there. . . ."

"Hi, Spencer," she said. "Hope I didn't catch you at a bad time?"

"Not at all. I was just trying to beat Sky at his own game and not doing a very good job at it." Spencer paused, thinking about the last time they saw each other at the park and regretting that it had been cut way too short. "Is everything all right?" He hoped she hadn't stumbled upon any more corpses.

Now it was Deidre's turn to pause for a moment of contemplation. She was out of practice when it came to inviting men to do anything remotely close to romantic. What if he turned her down? Then what would she do? Would she go back into her shell? Be thoroughly humiliated forever? Would she wonder what she'd ever seen in him in the first place?

Deidre decided she just had to put it all out there and go for it. She would deal with the consequences, if there were any, later.

Well, here goes nothing. . . .

"Actually, I was just wondering if you'd like to come over for dinner?" she asked unevenly.

As enthusiastic as Spencer felt at the invite, another part of him couldn't help but think about Gayle and her not-so-thinly veiled warning. Was she serious? Would dating Deidre be a trigger for Gayle to do something crazy?

In his heart of hearts, Spencer still clung to the firm belief that she would get over him in time—perhaps sooner than later. And lay off on the stalking and threats. But what if things only went from bad to worse? He certainly didn't want to jeopardize Deidre's safety—or any other woman's, for that matter.

In the end, Spencer decided he wasn't going to allow a jilted ex-lover to dictate his life. At least where it pertained to having dinner with a new, and very attractive, sexy friend.

"When?" he asked with keen interest.

"Tonight." Deidre was afraid that if she were to wait 'til another day, she might lose her nerve. But if he had to ask when, maybe he was reluctant to take up her offer. "If you had some—"

"I'd love to come over for dinner," Spencer said reassuringly, before she found an excuse to change her mind. "I'll even bring the wine."

She let out a quiet breath. "Great."

"What time?"

"Seven o'clock."

"I'll be there," he promised.

For an instant, Deidre nearly gave him directions; then she remembered that he had already been to her house twice before. "I'll see you then."

"Count on it." Spencer hung up and Sky ambled over to him, ready to get back to where they'd left off with their play. "Sorry, boy, no time for that right now. I've got myself a date with a gorgeous and intriguing lady. You remember Deidre, don't you?"

The dog barked as though he did at that.

Spencer laughed. "Yeah, I thought you would. And since she didn't invite you this time, you're on your own 'til I get back."

Deidre had butterflies swirling around her stomach as she prepared a dinner of roast beef, brown rice, collard greens, yams, and homemade biscuits. It was her first time cooking a real meal for anyone other than herself since she had moved to Sinclair Heights. She just hoped her skills had not diminished too much with Marshall and Adam no longer around to feed. Or maybe Spencer pretty much liked anything he put in his mouth that was edible. The thought was somehow heartening to her.

By the time the clock struck seven, Deidre had showered and put on one of her favorite dresses—a light blue wraparound silk dress—combed her hair, and dabbed a little bit of Eternity perfume behind each ear. Not that she was trying to entice the man or anything. She just wanted to present herself as a nice host who smelled good.

Deidre was in the kitchen checking the food when she heard the doorbell ring. She felt a little jittery with Spencer's arrival, but pushed it away. There was no turning back now. She checked herself one last time in the hallway mirror and then made her way to the door, all the while wondering what the evening had in store for them.

Spencer stood there, well dressed in a casual way with a dark gray blazer over a black mesh polo shirt and khaki twills. A handsome smile was spread across his face.

"Not too early, am I?"

She smiled back, impressed. "You're right on time," Deidre said. *Guess he couldn't wait to see me.* Or maybe it was the other way around.

Spencer almost felt like this was his first date in high school. Then again, that was something he would just as soon forget. Whereas this was something he definitely wanted to remember for a long time to come.

She looks great tonight. And she smells good, too.

"I hope red is all right?" Spencer handed the bottle of wine to Deidre.

"It's perfect." *And so are you.* At least it seemed that way to her regarding his appearance and personality. The rest would be determined over time.

"Can I help with anything?" Spencer asked politely.

Deidre could tell that he was serious, which was a good thing. But, as the host, she just wanted him to relax and enjoy being a guest in her home.

"I have it all under control," she said. "Make yourself at home. Dinner will be served shortly."

Spencer took her up on the offer to feel at home, walking around the first floor and admiring the antique furniture and splendid architecture these old houses had. He noticed a photograph on the mantel of Deidre with a muscular man and a little boy. Obviously, it was her late husband and son. Spencer had to admit a bit enviously that they made a nice-looking family. Too bad they were taken away from Deidre by circumstances beyond her control.

Whereas Spencer's family had broken up due to circumstances that were not quite as cut and dry as that. He wished things could have worked out differently between him and Fiona. But fate had another idea. Life went on and he was not going to look back. Certainly not now, when it suddenly seemed like he had something—or someone—to look forward to developing a relationship with.

Deidre found Spencer in the living room. She could tell that he was deep in thought while looking at the picture of her, Marshall, and Adam. She wondered if he was thinking about his daughter and ex-wife. Did he regret getting a divorce? Did he still love her?

Those thoughts caused Deidre to muse about her late husband and son and the terrible circumstances that had taken them away way too soon. Had things been different, they would still be together. Instead, here she was living on the other side of the country entertaining another man. But there was nothing she could do about what happened any more than Spencer could have done when his marriage ended or when he lost his twin brother. All they could do now was move on and try to be happy with whatever life had to offer. She was sure that was precisely what Marshall and Adam would have wanted her to do.

"I hope you're hungry," Deidre said, getting Spencer's attention.

He turned to her and grinned. "I'm famished!" *And I'm not just talking about food.* Spencer admired her again and liked everything he saw from head to toe.

Maybe too damned much.

"Well, good!" She flashed her teeth. "Because there's plenty to eat."

"Then let's dig in!"

"Yes, let's," Deidre said, already pondering just what might be in store for this date beyond the meal.

TWENTY-ONE

"Mmmm, this is delicious," Spencer declared for the third time as he savored the mouth-watering, tender roast and all the trimmings.

Deidre was pleased. "I'm glad you're enjoying it. I was afraid I might be a bit out of practice."

"No way," he mumbled with food in his mouth.

"I can see that," she said with a little giggle.

It was really nice to hear a man compliment her cooking and practically drool over it. *Guess I haven't lost my touch after all. At least not in the kitchen.*

"So how long have you been an artist?" Spencer asked between bites.

Deidre sipped her wine before responding. "As far as making money at it, I'd say probably six or seven years. But I've being doing one type of art or another my whole life."

"Then it's obviously in your blood," Spencer said and dabbed a napkin to his lips.

"I suppose it is."

"Well, I'm glad you've found ways to use your talent and earn income at the same time."

Deidre smiled. "I do feel blessed in that regard." She considered his multiple talents that extended from the FBI to teaching at the college level to showing courage in taking on gang members. Then there was the part of him that was a daddy and a dog lover, traits that were even more admirable.

"I know you're from Philadelphia," Spencer said, "but have you lived anywhere else other than here?"

"I was actually born in Mississippi," Deidre told him. "My parents left there shortly after I was born and moved to Philly, where my father had a job waiting."

"Mississippi, huh?" Spencer leaned back in the chair. "A onetime friend of mine with the FBI used to live in Clarksdale, Mississippi." That was before Jeremy Haskell joined the agency and went from Quantico to the Sinclair Heights FBI field office. They only kept in touch every so often now since Spencer retired from the FBI. It was unfortunate, but that's how it was when you became an outsider. It was as if you were no longer relevant if you weren't part of the team. He had learned to deal with it, as though he had a choice short of staying on at a job that had lost its appeal to him.

"Small world it seems," Deidre said as she buttered a biscuit. She wondered why they were onetime friends. Or did he no longer communicate with fellow FBI agents now that he was no longer one of them?

"So how did you end up in Sinclair Heights?" Spencer asked curiously. He guessed it probably had something to do with the tragedy she'd experienced.

"After my husband and son's death, there was really nothing left for me in Philly," she said sadly, "aside from my parents and some sad memories. When I was offered the opportunity to live in my grandfather's house, courtesy of an inheritance left to my mother, I decided to take her up on it as a new beginning."

"Well, I'd say that was a very good move on your part," Spencer said, sipping his wine. He could certainly relate to a person needing to get past haunting memories. "These turn of the last century Victorians are great to live in if you get the opportunity."

Deidre curled her lips into a soft smile. "Well, I'm not so sure all people would agree with that. They can be a lot of work to restore and maintain compared to newer homes."

"True, but that's half the charm of old homes," he countered. "It gives you something to do that's worthwhile to make the house all your own."

"Sounds like you're speaking with the voice of experience?"

"You could say that. My place is not as old as this, but I did do a lot of the remodeling myself and wouldn't change it for anything."

"I'm impressed," Deidre said, though she had yet to see what he'd done with his house. "Somehow you don't strike me as the remodeling, get your hands dirty type of guy."

Spencer laughed. "And exactly what type of guy do I seem like?" Or did he really want to know?

Deidre hadn't meant to put herself on the spot. "I don't know." She shrugged. "I guess someone who likes dogs, but not necessarily home refurbishment."

Spencer leaned toward her. "I guess you've still got a *lot* to learn about me." And there was just as much for him to learn about her. He looked forward to the latter in particular.

They took their wine glasses and the bottle into the living room.

Deidre decided this was as good a time as any to mention what she did know about him, as she was naturally curious too. "I'd love to hear more about your work as a forensic psychologist with the FBI."

Spencer lifted a brow. "Would you now?"

"Yes, if you wouldn't mind."

He tasted his wine. "I did a lot of profiling and psychoanalyzing of the criminals we were tracking," he said. "It was pretty routine stuff, but, at the same time, there was never a dull moment."

"I'm sure." She could picture him doing his thing in getting the bad guys, just as he had at the park, only in a more official capacity and making a different use of his background in psychology.

"It was an important part of my life at the time and I'm glad I put in my years with the FBI."

"Hal ran an occupation background check on you," Deidre admitted, feeling a bit guilty, as though she'd put him up to it.

"I wouldn't have expected anything less," Spencer told her, even though he wasn't thrilled to hear it.

"Guess he just wanted to be sure you weren't a—"

"Killer disguised as a professor or former FBI psychologist," Spencer finished.

She offered a weak smile. "Yes, something like that."

For one of the few times that he could remember, Spencer was tongue-tied. Whether he liked it or not, his acquaintance with women who wound up becoming murder victims had cast a dark shadow over him, even as an innocent man. Being civic-minded and approachable had proven to be more of a negative than a positive as it related to keeping him out of the fray.

He fixed his eyes on Deidre's face, wanting to comfort her, lest she have any doubts about him. "I can promise you that I'm not a killer," he said. "Not even close. I value life too much, including animals."

Deidre held his gaze. "I believe you, Spencer." She supposed she had known he was innocent from the very first time they met, reading into his character and soul before really getting to know the man himself. If she'd had any uncertainties on this score, inviting him to dinner would've been the last thing on her mind.

Spencer was relieved to hear that. Whatever else, he didn't want Deidre to fear him. Even though, for some reason, her boss seemed determined to stay on his case. He suspected the cop was looking at it as one sweet package. But it was Lieutenant Hal Iverson's problem if he wanted what he couldn't have.

My problem is trying to control my own growing desire to be with this woman like I've never felt before.

He strongly sensed that it wasn't just a one-way street either, and was eager to put that to the test.

Deidre tried to read what was going on inside Spencer's head at the moment. Did he view Hal as a threat either as a police lieutenant or on a personal level? She hoped not. Now that she had cleared the air with Hal and told him she was not interested in anything beyond friendship, Deidre expected him to back off a bit. That would allow her to more comfortably pursue the man who did capture her fancy in a way no one had since Marshall's death. But was that enough at this stage of her life?

Deidre managed to shut her mind off from the strong physical attraction to the man beside her and go back to the unfinished thoughts and questions she had.

"So did your brother's death have anything to do with your leaving the FBI?" she asked.

Spencer stared at the question. He wasn't totally comfortable talking about Wesley and his premature death. But he also knew as a psychologist that bottling it up inside wasn't good either, particularly when he wanted the lady of the house to open up as well.

He slowly sipped some wine and looked at Deidre pensively. "I think it had to do with a lot of things, and that was one of them. My brother's life was spinning out of control when he died. Part of me blamed myself for my failure to see that he was hurting and not trying hard enough to help him. I think I also felt like my own life was going in the wrong direction and I needed to try something different for my livelihood. Something that wasn't so consuming and emotionally draining."

"Like teaching?"

"Yeah. I can't say that it isn't an emotional challenge at times, but I kind of feel like I'm making a contribution of sorts to young people who want to learn, without the built-in stresses of being on the FBI's payroll."

"I agree. With your background, you must be making a real contribution to developing the minds of students," Deidre said over her wine glass. She felt like she could really empathize with him in having experienced a great loss and its life-altering impact in her world that would never quite be the same again.

Deidre was becoming more and more attracted to Spencer as a very good-looking, intelligent, and sexy man. She was sure this feeling had nothing to do with finishing off a bottle of wine, but was more a response to the undeniable physical and sexual energy between them and her mind accepting this as something she could no more control than he could.

Surprising herself, Deidre leaned over and kissed Spencer lightly on the mouth. She savored the softness of his lips for a moment before pulling away, embarrassed at being so forward. "Sorry about that."

"Don't be," he said smoothly. "I'm not."

She looked into his eyes. "You sure?"

Spencer didn't blink. "Are you kidding me? I've been wanting to kiss you from the moment I first laid eyes on you." He paused. "Or at least once we got past the circumstances under which we came to meet."

Deidre was flattered to hear that, even though at the time kissing him was the last thing on her mind. But that was then and this was now. She'd enjoyed the taste of her mouth on his.

"So what's stopping you now?" she dared ask.

His gaze swept over her face, settling on her full lips. "Not a damned thing."

Spencer tilted his head and kissed her passionately. He hesitated ever so slightly when he remembered Gayle's implied threat against Deidre, fearing the ramifications should things go any further. Just as quickly, Spencer buried these thoughts. He wouldn't let Gayle hurt Deidre. Not if he could help it.

For now, he just wanted to experience the raw pleasure and sheer passion of the moment.

TWENTY-TWO

One thing led to another and Deidre knew she had no desire to stop this from happening. Quite the contrary, it was something she wanted more than anything she could remember since Marshall died and, with him, seemingly her libido. Spencer had managed to single-handedly bring her back to life, and with a purpose.

Between kisses they had managed to undress right there on the couch—or undress each other was more like it—'til they were both completely naked. Any shame Deidre had in exposing her body to a man other than her late husband quickly gave way to how Spencer made her feel: comfortable and wanted her as badly as she wanted him.

With a sense of urgency that threatened to explode at any moment, Spencer put on a condom, slid between Deidre's legs, and drove purposefully into her waiting body. Deidre clutched his buttocks, pulling him deeper inside, needing and wanting the feel of his erection and the closeness of his hard frame.

Deidre climaxed almost instantly, so strong was her need to be appeased. He followed shortly thereafter. She clung to Spencer while his body trembled against hers, until they both settled down.

As soon as her breathing returned to normal, Deidre said with a soft, embarrassed chuckle, "It looks like neither of us had any staying power at all."

Spencer gazed at her salaciously. "It's called pure lust that needed a very quick fix."

"I suppose," she admitted. She actually felt relieved that he hadn't been able to hold back either.

"Now that we've gotten that out of the way, what do you say we make *love*?" Spencer asked while peppering her body with light kisses.

Deidre's eyes widened as body tingled. "Are you sure you're up for it?"

He laughed and looked down at his still full erection. "No problem there."

"Then no problem here," she declared. Her body was already anticipating more passion and ready to give back just as much.

Deidre stood up and grabbed Spencer's hand, wanting them to use the bed this time, even as she was afraid to look beyond the here and now.

"I could kiss you forever," Spencer said, even as their mouths moved in harmony. "But I'd rather save some of those kisses and enjoy the rest of you. . . ."

"Be my guest," Deidre cooed.

Spencer pulled away from her lips and began kissing Deidre's neckline and down to her smallish but firm breasts, holding each in his hand like a melon. He teased one nipple, then the other, and Deidre gasped, enjoying the sensations from his mouth and tongue.

"Hmm . . ." she heard herself say as a wave of pleasure swept over her.

Spencer bit back his need to be inside Deidre again, trailing kisses down her belly, 'til he reached the dense, dark, curly triangle of hair. He met his lover's eyes for an instant, detecting her slight embarrassment that excited him even more, before spreading her legs and kissing the insides of her thighs. He made his way to her most sensitive spot and, tasting her, found it utterly delightful and wanted more.

Deidre tensed and tried to hide her unease at this type of intimacy. Marshall, as good a lover as he was, had never taken her to this height of ecstasy and she wasn't quite sure how to react to it. Other than to simply enjoy it as Spencer obviously wanted her to.

It took a couple of minutes before he brought her to orgasm again, causing Deidre's breath to quicken, and her body to quaver with excitement. She expected Spencer to read her mind and enter her at that moment, but he seemed to have a mind of his own and continued to pleasure her, sending waves of bliss throughout her body.

Only after he was satisfied that Deidre was ready for him, Spencer rose up, his throbbing manhood ready to explode at any moment. He quickly slipped on another condom and sandwiched himself between her splayed legs. Moving easily inside her, his thrusts burned with urgency like a man possessed.

Deidre readjusted to Spencer's fullness inside her as if for the very first time. Only better. Oh, so much better. She arched her back and met him halfway, contracting around him, as they pounded against each other seeking mutual fulfillment.

She urged Spencer's face down 'til she could take hold of his lips with hers. They kissed passionately and Deidre felt a sudden surge of desire build inside her for what was about to happen again. Only this time she sensed it would be much more intense. All the heartache and pain she had experienced in the past seemed lost to the moment at hand.

After holding out as long as he could, wanting to extend their lovemaking well into the night, Spencer felt his release coming with a fury.

Deidre did too, and clung to him for dear life as his body quivered wildly.

Slick with perspiration, they both gasped and grunted and reached a powerful climax simultaneously.

Spencer gave Deidre a final lingering kiss, before rolling off her spent body one very, very contented man.

"You were incredible," he told her, and meant every word. Yes, there had been others, including his ex-wife and Gayle. But Spencer honestly could not remember a time when it had meant so much. Or when he had been left with such a sense of satisfaction that he wanted to experience over and over again with Deidre. He hoped she felt the same way.

"So were you," she responded in a dreamy voice, still very much caught up in the afterglow. Was this what she'd been missing, but had somehow forgotten? She found the thought both frightening and enlightening.

Spencer smiled, feeling good about this and her. While a part of him would have liked nothing better than to go another round, he couldn't help but think about the unstable Gayle and her threats. Spencer feared that were he to stay the night, he might put Deidre directly in Gayle's line of fire. And that was unacceptable, regardless of his powerful attraction to the lady.

"As much as I hate to leave, I'd better get home and feed Sky," he said sourly.

Deidre almost said, *I can go with you.* But common sense prevailed. No matter what had just happened, they still barely knew each other and had their own lives.

She managed a smile. "I understand. I have some things to do too." *Like thinking about where this relationship is going at the end of the day. If anywhere.*

Deidre watched Spencer get up, and followed, slipping into her robe. He remained naked since his clothes were strewn across the living room floor, meaning she got to admire *all* of the man once more, causing her body to react favorably while longing for more of his.

After Spencer had dressed, Deidre walked him to the door. "Say hello to Sky for me," she said dryly.

Spencer's lips formed a crooked grin. "Yeah, I'll do that." He kissed her and gazed steadily into her eyes. "I want to see you again."

I want to see you even more. Deidre decided it was best to show at least a little restraint. She gave him her cell phone number. "Call me."

"I will," he promised.

They kissed again, and then Deidre locked the door as soon as Spencer left. She touched her lips that were still swollen from his passionate kisses, and could only hope that it was just the start of many more such wonderful experiences between them.

TWENTY-THREE

Gayle had followed Spencer, careful to keep from being spotted, as he drove to the house on Foothills Lane. She watched as a woman answered the door. The bitch greeted him like she thought she was his lady or something, as he handed her a bottle of wine. Gayle recognized the woman as the one Spencer had talked to at the Cinco de Mayo Fiesta, and then at the art gallery.

That little cunt was trying to steal her man, as if he were hers for the taking.

Like hell she would.

Gayle seethed in her car as she imagined just what Spencer and the woman were doing inside that house. It should have been her that he was with, making passionate love to her as they had done more times than Gayle cared to count. She'd be damned if someone else took her place in his eyes.

After waiting for over two hours, Gayle felt a little relieved when Spencer finally emerged from the house. Alone. He got in his car and she ducked her head down while he drove past.

Now that he was gone, she could deal with the woman who threatened to come between them.

She sucked in a deep breath and left the car, heading in a straight line toward the house on a hill.

Deidre put the leftover food in the refrigerator and loaded the dishwasher. Her mind was still very much occupied with the surprising, but ultra satisfying, events of the night, while wondering if it was truly a sign of things to come or if it was just a one-night stand between two needy people, when she heard the knock on the door.

Guess someone else was wondering the same thing. Deidre imagined that Spencer had missed her so much already that he'd fed his dog and come back to appease his powerful sexual appetite once again.

And hers.

When she looked through the door window, Deidre saw that the person standing there was not Spencer, but a tall and pretty African American woman with long braids. She looked vaguely familiar, but not in a way that Deidre felt she knew her. Perhaps she was a neighbor or a relative of one. Still, it was kind of late to be knocking on someone's door.

Seeing no one else there on the porch, Deidre felt it was reasonably safe to see what the woman wanted.

She opened the door a crack. "Yes? . . ."

"Hi." The woman gave her a bright smile. "My car broke down over there." She pointed to the vehicle. "And my cell phone's dead. Can you believe that? I guess I forgot to charge it or something. Anyway, do you mind if I use your phone to call my man?"

The car—a brown Chevrolet—didn't look like it was disabled to Deidre. It looked like it was parked at a slight angle as if positioned to leave in a hurry. But what did she know about cars? Practically nothing.

Deidre recalled when Spencer had shown up a week and a half ago wanting to use the phone. She had turned him down flat after he'd told her he discovered a dead woman's body outside.

But this woman is very much alive. And apparently in need of assistance.

She certainly looked harmless enough.

"Come on in."

The woman smiled gratefully.

"You can use my cell phone." Deidre led her halfway to the phone sitting on the coffee table.

The woman crinkled her dark eyes at Deidre and walked to the phone, picking it up and studying it as though it were a foreign object. Suddenly Deidre watched the woman's face contort with rage. She flung the phone against the wall and approached Deidre with such swiftness that she hardly had time to react.

"I want you to leave *him* alone!" The woman exposed her teeth like a rabid animal.

"What? . . ." Deidre was sure the woman was about to attack her as she tried to make sense of her words.

"You heard me, you conniving little bitch!"

"Wait a minute," Deidre said, assuming the lady had her mixed up with someone else. "Who are we talking about here?"

"You know damned well who—*Spencer Berry*," the woman proclaimed.

"Spencer?" Deidre was confused. "Leave him alone. I don't understand . . .?"

"Don't play dumb with me," she hissed. "I know you have the hots for Spencer—and his body too. I'm sure you used both to your advantage tonight when you seduced him. Well, he's mine!"

Deidre blinked twice. She was starting to get the picture and didn't like what she saw on the canvas. "Are you saying that you're . . . *dating* Spencer?"

The woman narrowed her eyes. "Yeah, that's exactly what I'm saying. He's *my* man and I'm not about to give him up for you or anyone else. Do you hear me?"

Deidre caught her breath and forced herself to look at the woman. "Yes, I get the message loud and clear. Spencer is *your* man. I'll remember that."

She only wished he had told her this himself. *Before* they slept together. And she'd presumed that it meant something to Spencer, too, other than just another sexual conquest of a gullible victim. Apparently at the expense of his girlfriend.

The woman's lips parted into a sneer as she got up in Deidre's face. "You'd damned well better get the message, if you know what's good for you! If I ever catch you with him again, there will be hell to pay for you and him both!"

On that note, she stormed out the door, not bothering to close it.

Once she stopped shaking, Deidre hurriedly closed and locked the door. She wondered how she could have been so wrong about Spencer. What had she gotten herself into?

More importantly, how on earth was she going to get out of it in one emotional and safe piece?

TWENTY-FOUR

It was a quiet night with not much traffic and few people out and about. This would make his plans that much easier to complete.

He walked unassumingly down the street, hands in his deep pockets. For a moment, he thought of the well-dressed woman he'd seen more than once on the light rail and fantasized about how killing her would be extra special—after he was finished with her.

But right now his focus had to be on someone more accessible. One who had walked right into his trap without ever knowing it 'til it was much too late to do anything about.

When he spotted the woman coming out of the tavern staggering, he could barely contain his enthusiasm. He had expected her to follow the same pattern on the same night. And she had. Like clockwork.

She was young and attractive, tall and slender. Just the way he liked them.

He walked right past her, never giving any indication that he gave a damn about her presence.

Not 'til he had her right where he wanted her.

He doubled back when she headed to the small lot behind the tavern. There were only three cars back there, and hers—a red Toyota—was parked in a dimly lit corner all by its lonesome.

She stumbled up to the car and began to fumble with her keys. Sensing the kill, literally, he took long, looping strides toward her, knowing that the element of surprise was his best offense to make for her worse defense.

She'd had too much to drink and probably shouldn't drive home. But since she had come alone, she didn't trust any creep in the tavern to do the honors while expecting nothing in return. So she'd just take her chances and hope she didn't run into any other drunks on the road.

Or on the sidewalk, for that matter. Like the man she passed outside the tavern. Maybe he wasn't drunk, but there was something about him that rubbed her the wrong way. Even if he tried to pretend she didn't exist.

But that was his problem, not hers. She only wanted to get home and sleep it off before another day of work stress frayed her nerves.

She groped in her purse for her keys, wishing she didn't have so much damn crap in her purse. When she heard a sound behind her, she thought nothing of it. Then something inside her sensed danger and she turned around.

Standing there was the man who had pretended not to notice her, but apparently had.

He could plainly see that she was taken aback and fearful at the same time. Neither would do her any good at this point.

She tried to dart away from him and scream at once. But anticipating her every move, he rammed a fist hard into the side of her face, hearing the bone crack in two places. The force of the blow knocked her out and he caught before she hit the ground.

He grabbed the keys to her car and unlocked it before pulling his captive inside. This was going to be a long night and one in which she would wish she'd never been born.

Deidre tried hard to forget about what happened between her and Spencer, though it wasn't easy. She was not that desperate to give herself to someone who was already seeing another woman. And a crazy one at that.

I'm totally single . . . and unattached. The words from Spencer replayed in Deidre's mind.

Obviously, he forgot to tell his girlfriend that. So what else was new? How many men lied through their teeth just to take a woman to bed?

But that didn't make it right. And it certainly didn't make Deidre feel any better.

That's what I get for taking chances. I was better off living with my tender and loving memories than opening myself up to someone new only to be humiliated and irritated by him.

The more she tried to sleep, the more Deidre tossed and turned. She suspected that would not change 'til she spoke to Spencer and gave him a piece of her mind.

Finally, when she could stand it no more, Deidre grabbed her cell phone, surprised it was still in one piece after that bitch used to vent her anger. She pushed redial for the last number she'd called. The clock said it was nearly 5:00 A.M. Any slight bit of guilt Deidre felt for waking Spencer—assuming he wasn't already awake with his psycho girlfriend—was overcome by the deep sense of betrayal she felt.

Spencer's eyes popped open when the phone jingle jarred him out of a deep stupor. He looked down on the floor and saw that Sky hadn't even budged. He hated to think that the dog might be totally useless if there were ever a break-in or fire.

He yawned, wondering who the hell was calling this early in the morning.

Lifting the phone just before his voice mail picked up, Spencer smiled when he realized who the caller was.

"I missed you too, Deidre," he said sleepily, thinking back to hours earlier when they were naked, hot, sweaty, and heavily into each other every step of the way.

"Did you miss your *girlfriend* as well?" Deidre asked cynically.

"Girlfriend? . . ."

"Yeah. She showed up here right after you left, threatening to hurt me—and you—if I didn't leave you alone."

"What did she look like?" Spencer asked, as if he hadn't a clue. In fact, he knew exactly who it was and it angered him more than he could say.

Deidre was in no mood to play games. But on the mere chance that this woman really was a lunatic who had no claim to him, she went along with his request. "Tall, attractive, long braids . . ."

"Dammit," muttered Spencer under his breath. Gayle had made good on her threat to intimidate Deidre, leaving him to try to explain and hope it wasn't too late. "I know her, but—"

"Save it for someone who gives a damn!" Deidre snapped. "You're just like every other man out there— saying anything you think will work to get into a girl's pants."

"It wasn't like that, baby."

"Like hell it wasn't. And don't call me baby! If there was someone else in your life, you should have been man enough to admit it instead of taking me to bed and letting that crazy bitch connive her way into my house, only to give me a clear warning to stay away from you. Or else. Well, you know what, Spencer? I *get* the message loud and clear!"

"But it's the *wrong* message, Deidre," Spencer said. "I'd like to try and—"

She cut him off. "I'm too tired and pissed to want to talk about this anymore. Just leave me alone and go back to your girlfriend—if you weren't with her all along."

He heard the phone disconnect and Spencer knew that Deidre had hung up on him, essentially casting him out of her life for good. He sure as hell wasn't about to let her get away that easy. Not before she heard him out and he gave it his best shot to try to explain . . . and hopefully come to an understanding.

Hal got the call at a quarter to six that a woman was found dead in Pelle Park. All the signs indicated that the serial killer had struck again. Hal cursed the thought of it while getting dressed and racing to the scene.

Zack Hernandez met him there, greeting Hal just as he made his way past the crime scene tape.

"Hell of a way to get the day started," Hernandez groaned.

"Yeah, tell me about it." Hal tried to hide the sleepiness in his voice. "What have we got?" As if he didn't already know. He could smell forced sex and death in the air he breathed.

Hernandez frowned. "Same old, same old. Pretty young woman—or at least she used to be before he violated her—appears to have had her jaw broken, was raped, and then strangled."

Hal shook his head disgustedly. "Where is she?"

"Over here." They began to walk. Hernandez pointed to the covered corpse on the asphalt. "The body was in that Toyota—the victim's car."

Hal looked at the car, which was being worked over by crime scene technicians. "So you're telling me that she just happened to have been here late into the night, maybe doing drugs or selling sex, when the killer surprised her?"

Hernandez shook his head. "I don't think so. My guess is the killer surprised her somewhere else, abducted her, and then drove here where he finished her off."

"We got a name on the victim?"

"Yeah." Hernandez lifted a notepad from his pocket. "According to her driver's license, her name is Judith Carpenter, age thirty."

Hal furrowed his brow. "Wonder if she's a friend of Spencer Berry?" he tossed out, thoughtful. "Or maybe we should already be making that assumption, if history is any indication."

Hernandez rubbed his nose. "Yeah, probably. Not sure there's anything to it, though. We've checked the man out pretty damned thoroughly and he's clean as far as we've been able to determine. Berry may be as much a victim of bizarre circumstances and bad luck as these women. Who's to say? No reason to believe he's the key to this. I think it's more likely some son of a bitch is simply taking out his frustrations on any woman who happens to be within range whenever the urge hits him."

Hal chewed on those thoughts, unable to refute them, given what they knew. It was what they didn't know that had him tied up in knots and nearly at his wits' end.

He glanced at the covered body. "What a waste. And for what reason? To feed this bastard's perverted mind." Hal regarded the detective. "I don't suppose anyone saw anything?"

"As a matter of fact, we may have a witness," Hernandez said. He angled his head at a middle-aged woman who was standing near a uniformed officer.

"Could be the break we've been looking for," Hal said, even if he was less than convinced. "Let's see what she has to say. . . ."

TWENTY-FIVE

Deidre knew it would be all but impossible to go to sleep now. She put on her robe and went downstairs to make coffee. For a moment, she stood frozen in the living room, remembering the confrontation last night. It still gave her a chill that she had been accosted by the woman she had allowed in her home under very false pretenses.

Even more disturbing to Deidre was falling for a man who hadn't been straight with her about his current love life, putting her in a dangerous situation. At least she'd told him off and where to go. Not that it made her feel any better than had she never laid eyes on Spencer Berry.

I probably should have listened to Hal regarding his bad vibes on Spencer. Too late now to turn back the clock. I just have to find a way to put it all behind me.

Before this latest turn of events, Deidre had believed that Spencer deserved a fair chance, rather than prejudging him on things that were largely outside of his control. Now she wondered if she had made one of the biggest mistakes of her life where it concerned an area that was well within Spencer's control.

Deidre heard a car drive up. She went to the window to peek out, fearing that the woman might have come back for more terrorizing. Instead, she saw Spencer moving briskly up the walkway. She trembled involuntarily.

Did he really think all he had to do was come over, say a few sweet words, and all the mistrust and deception would just vanish?

The bell rang and she heard him say rather loudly, "Open the door, Deidre. We need to talk about this."

Deidre wanted to ignore him, but suspected he would not go away 'til she at least acknowledged his presence.

"There's nothing more to talk about," she yelled through the door. "Go home, Spencer!"

"Not until we talk—face to face." Spencer felt his blood pressure rise. He expected Deidre to play hardball. Could he blame her? Especially after Gayle had probably scared the hell out of her.

"I'm not interested in anything you have to say," Deidre insisted.

Spencer was growing more frustrated by the second. "Just give me five minutes and I'll go—if that's what you want. You owe me that much. Please . . ."

Deidre could barely believe this man. She didn't owe him anything—certainly not her dignity—and what audacity of him to suggest otherwise.

All she really wanted was to be left alone. But since he seemed just as determined to say what he had to, Deidre relented and opened the door. She glared at the man she'd made passionate love to a few hours earlier. A man who had brought her sexual desires back to life and made Deidre forget what loneliness felt like. At least for a short while.

"You have five minutes," she said, but wasn't expecting it to make much difference in the scheme of things.

Spencer walked past her. *I'd much rather be here for carnal reasons than trying to dig myself out of the deep damned hole Gayle put me in.* The reality of the matter was quite a bit different. He had to make every word count. Otherwise, Deidre would probably banish him from her life for good.

Spencer sighed and looked Deidre in the eye. "Her name is Gayle Kincaid. She's a graduate student at Sinclair Heights College. We dated for a very short time and I ended it a few weeks ago. She's sort of been stalking me ever since."

Deidre held his gaze. "Didn't you think I just might want to know that your ex-girlfriend was *still* in the picture?"

He set his jaw. "Don't you see, that's just it—she wasn't in the picture anymore as far as I was concerned. And she was never my girlfriend."

"But you slept with her, right?" Deidre asked, as if she needed to know who else he had made love to in recent memory.

Even if Spencer wanted to deny it, the answer was obvious. "Yes," he answered. "But that doesn't change the fact that it was over and done with between us, Deidre. I swear it. I never expected her to *really* come after you—"

Deidre batted her lashes in disbelief. "You're telling me that you *knew* this crazy woman might practically break into my house and threaten me with bodily harm—and you never bothered to say anything? . . ."

Spencer lowered his head with regret and lifted it again. "It was stupid, I know. But I didn't think she'd go that far. And I didn't want the past to derail whatever was going on with us." He closed the distance between them 'til he could feel the heat emanating from Deidre's body. "I'm truly sorry about what happened with Gayle, and for not telling you about her. I'll deal with Gayle. I just don't want that situation to stop us from seeing each other."

"I don't see how it can't," Deidre said. She ignored her strong desire to be with him even in the face of a stalker, whom she wasn't convinced Spencer could appease, other than to give into her demands that they be together. Even if he—or she—were to get a restraining order against Gayle, it might not be enough. Most stalkers couldn't care less about a piece of paper if they were determined to do what they had set out to.

Deidre could feel Spencer's warm breath on her cheeks when he said, "Gayle means absolutely nothing to me, Deidre. You do. Let's not allow her to drive a wedge between us. That's what she wants. This can still work if you just give us a chance."

Deidre wanted to believe that more than anything, as her body had reacted to him like possibly no other, including Marshall. Maybe they could somehow get past this and still have something to look forward to.

Finding it all but impossible to resist tasting those pouty lips, Spencer angled his head and moved within an inch of Deidre's mouth. When she made no attempt to stop him, he kissed her heartily and enjoyed it. But did she?

He pulled away, gazed down at her eyes, and pressed their lips together again, feeling the friction between them melt away like snow on a warm spring day that was getting hotter by the second.

Deidre tried to move, but realized her feet were planted and unwilling to move as though they were stuck in cement. She'd wanted Spencer's kiss and to kiss him back. She imagined him being inside her again, and her body tingled at the prospect.

The ringing of the phone brought her face away from his and reality back into the picture. Deidre read the disappointment in Spencer's eyes, but actually welcomed the call as a way to keep a proper perspective.

"Excuse me," she told him, and walked to the cell phone.

It was Hal. "Didn't wake you, did I?"

"No, you didn't." Deidre looked at Spencer, who stared back. "What's up, Hal?"

"Sorry to say this, but it looks like the Park Killer has struck again. We've got a possible witness to the crime. You need to come down to the station and give a pre-pared statement to the press. . . ."

Deidre's heart sank to her stomach at the thought of another woman dying a horrible death at the hands of a demented serial killer. "I'll be there as soon as I can."

Spencer could tell by her expression that the call was not good.

"What is it?" he asked after she had hung up.

Deidre regarded him with a blank stare. "There's been another woman murdered. . . ."

He suspected as much and immediately wondered if it was again someone he knew. Was there no end to this madness? He hated to think that it could have been Deidre brutalized by the killer.

"Where?" he asked, as though it made one damned bit of difference. Certainly not to the victim, given the end result.

"I don't know," she responded tonelessly. "I have to go get ready for work."

"I'll go with you."

"I'd rather you didn't." She feared that being around him right now would only complicate things between them that much more.

"So we'll go separately," Spencer said. "I need to know if the victim was again someone I'm acquainted with. If so, maybe I can help somehow." He doubted this was the case, considering he hadn't known any of the previous victims well enough to be able to provide the authorities with much of anything useful. But he wanted to give it his best shot.

More importantly, he wanted to stay as close to Deidre as she would allow him to.

That aside, Spencer knew he would have to deal with Gayle sooner or later—something he wasn't particularly looking forward to, given her unbalanced state of mind. But he couldn't allow her antics to go any further.

Her personal feelings aside, Deidre realized that Spencer had every right to want to go and see if he knew the victim and, if so, to what extent. Hal and Zack would certainly want to take his statement to this effect, even if Deidre was sure that Spencer was not involved with the crime. Completely exonerating him where it concerned his relationship with Gayle was another story altogether and still up in the air.

She raised her eyes to meet his. "Separate is better."

Spencer nodded. At least that was a step in the right direction. "Then I guess I'll see you there."

"Fine." Deidre's thoughts meandered back and forth among their situation, Gayle, and the latest victim of a serial killer.

TWENTY-SIX

Spencer arranged to meet Detective Hernandez at the morgue to look at the latest victim of the Park Killer. He would have preferred to avoid this, had he not taken an even more personal interest in the case now that he had developed a romance with Deidre—though it was currently in a state of flux, thanks to Gayle. Apart from that, it seemed like something he was obliged to do in possibly identifying the victim right away rather than waiting 'til her face and name were revealed to the public.

"Glad you called, Berry," Hernandez said wearily to him.

Spencer nodded. "Yeah, thought it was probably a good idea."

"I agree. Must give you nightmares to know that someone out there is knocking off good-looking women you know left and right—at least that was the case before he got through working them over."

"It would've been much worse if I'd known them better." *Or intimately,* Spencer thought, as his mind drifted to Deidre by way of example. "But, yes, who wouldn't be bothered by something like this?"

"I doubt the killer is losing a hell of a lot of sleep over it," Hernandez said cynically.

Spencer knew he'd walked right into that one. All he could do now was hope that the latest life lost was not a woman he had been connected with in some way. "Let's get this over with. . . ."

Moments later, Hernandez ordered the attendant to open the drawer.

Spencer held his breath as he studied the face of an African American woman. Her skin was discolored and the right side of her face was badly swollen. Dark red Bantu knots bordered it haphazardly. He closed his eyes for an instant, thinking that hours earlier she had been a living, breathing person . . . before being taken down by a killer.

"Well, do you know her or not?" Hernandez asked impatiently.

Spencer gazed at the corpse again, and his heart went out to the woman's family. "Yes and no."

"What's that supposed to mean? . . ."

Spencer sighed. "Her name's Judith, which I assume you already know. She works—or worked—as a cashier at a supermarket in the neighborhood. We've spoken every now and then, but it was only small talk and never outside the store."

"Well someone made sure she'd never speak to you or anyone else ever again," Hernandez said flatly.

Spencer furrowed his brow. "Yeah, I can see that," he muttered, wishing that weren't the case.

Hernandez stared hard at him. "And you have no idea who this killer might be?"

Spencer shrugged. "No more than you, Detective. I'm out of the business of probing killers' minds. Sorry. All I can tell you is that he's probably someone who's been stalking these women and victimizing them on his schedule, not theirs."

"Too damned bad for them." Hernandez looked down at the woman. "Wish you could open your mouth one last time and tell us who did this to you."

Spencer shared that wish more than he could say.

***

At the police station, Spencer briefed Deidre on his visit to the morgue, as he was certain that Hernandez was giving the details to Lieutenant Iverson.

Spencer hated to admit that, once again, he knew the victim, though not personally. He could only hope that this wouldn't put a further strain on their relationship, as unrealistic as that was.

"I'm sorry," Deidre said genuinely. What was it about women he knew that was causing them to die? Did he even have a clue?

"So am I, but not sorry for me," he said. "I'm sorry that these lives have been lost so senselessly and violently and that the killer is somehow always able to stay one step ahead of the law."

"Maybe that can change," she said on a wing and a prayer. "With any luck, the witness will give our sketch artist enough to work with so we can get his likeness plastered throughout the state and on the Internet."

"That would be great—for everyone." Spencer's eyes latched on to hers and his thoughts shifted to where they had left off before Deidre got the phone call. He wanted nothing more than to hold her in his arms right now and forget everything else. If only. "So what about us . . . ?" he asked hesitantly.

Deidre had wondered the same thing, but was too confused to have an answer. Especially not now, between his crazy ex and an even crazier killer on the loose. "I'm not sure," she told him honestly. "Maybe you need to sort things out with Gayle first and we can go from there."

While he found himself wanting to sidestep the issue of Gayle and work directly on their relationship, Spencer knew she was right. He had to get his own house in order—if he was going to spend more time in hers.

"Guess we should lie low for a little while then—'til I can get Gayle off my back for good."

"I think that's probably the best thing all the way around," agreed Deidre, even if it killed her to think that they would have to keep their distance until such time. But it seemed to be the only sensible way to go, under the circumstances.

Not to mention, Deidre could hardly ignore the equally pressing matter of keeping the local press and community informed in her capacity as police spokeswoman on the latest tragic news of another woman falling victim to a serial killer with seemingly no end in sight.

The victim was last seen alive at the Walnut Tavern, where her killer was apparently waiting for her. He abducted her in her own car. Then he beat, raped, and strangled her. Deidre closed her eyes for a moment, imagining the horror Judith Carpenter must have surely endured before she met her Maker.

"Are you going to be all right?" Hal asked her from the other side of his desk. Seated next to Deidre was Detective Hernandez.

What if I say no? Then what?

"I'll be fine," she said quietly. "Guess this case is just starting to get to me a little—no, make that a lot."

It was probably getting to *every* woman in Sinclair Heights, whether they happened to be acquainted with Spencer or not. The mere thought caused a chill to run down Deidre's spine.

"Believe me, it's not easy for anyone in the police bureau, Deidre," he stressed. "That's why we need to find this son of a bitch before he turns this whole city into a graveyard full of women."

She was not about to argue the point, listening with her notepad in hand as the two men updated her on information about the crime and alleged witness to it.

Hal spoke first, the lines on his brow deepening, as this case was causing everyone in the police department to grow increasingly stressed. When Hal finished his piece, he deferred to the detective in charge of the murder investigation.

Hernandez ran a hand through his hair. "She's a homeless woman who spends a lot of time at Pelle Park, where the victim's car was found with her in it. According to the possible witness, a man she's seen in the park from time to time was hanging around the car, then, as she put it, 'just disappeared into the woods.' We'd like to talk to this man—if he's out there at all—and find out if he was just looking for something to eat or steal. Or if, in fact, he was walking away from a murder he'd just committed. Then there's also the possibility that if he's innocent, he may've seen the real killer—"

"So, in other words, Deidre, we need you to put this out there and let's see what happens." Hal had a desperate tone to his voice. "It'll either point us in the right direction . . . or just be another dead end. Hopefully, the former."

"I'll do my best," she promised, aware that was all that was ever asked of her. Only, in this case, the stakes were higher than ever. Failing to convey the right words or message was not an option, for it could make the difference between identifying a ruthless killer and waiting for him to strike again.

TWENTY-SEVEN

Spencer knocked hard on the apartment door, ignoring the pain to his knuckles. It was almost eight A.M. and he was in no mood to respect the fact that Gayle might be sleeping, remembering that was one of her favorite pastimes. This whole stalking thing had gone far enough. He would be damned if he allowed her to not only try to make his life miserable, but frighten Deidre into turning away from what they had.

He banged on the door again and, for an instant, had second thoughts as to whether or not this was the right way to handle the situation.

Then the door opened and he saw Gayle, sleepy-eyed, peek out.

"You could have called first," she moaned.

"What I wanted to say couldn't be said on the phone." Spencer pushed the door open farther and strode past her. Rounding on Gayle, he noticed that she was only wearing an oversized shirt. His eyes locked in on her face. "Just who the hell do you think you are anyway?"

Gayle moseyed over to him. "You tell me, baby. Who knows me better than you?"

She tried to reach in for a kiss, but Spencer grabbed her shoulders and held her at arm's length. He was definitely in no mood for games—certainly not with her.

"I'm not sure I ever knew you, Gayle. But what I do know is that going after Deidre was a really dumb move on your part."

Gayle flashed her big eyes at him. "I have no idea what you're talking about."

"Like hell you don't. She described you to a tee."

"And probably half of the other African American women in this city." She snorted. "Why don't I fix us a drink and we can talk about it."

"I'm done talking with you," Spencer grunted, still gripping her shoulders. "Now I'm warning you—stay the hell away from Deidre and stay the hell away from me!"

"Or what?" She gave him an icy look. "You're going to beat me up, Spencer? Show the world what a big man you are by hitting your woman? Go ahead—do it. It might even turn me on."

Only then did Spencer realize that she was somehow getting off on this. And he was falling right into her trap. *Damn.* He released his hold on her and backed off, as though he was in the presence of a monster.

He sucked in a deep breath. "I'm not going to spar with you, Gayle, even if I'd like nothing better than to try to knock some sense into you. Obviously, that would only backfire."

She licked her lips and stepped toward him. "So why don't we make peace and just forget about some bitch who's trying to take my man away from me."

Spencer took an involuntary step backward. "I'm not your man," he reiterated. "I was never your man. We had a brief thing and that was it." Maybe he could still reason with her. Or was that even possible at this point? He softened his tone. "Look, Gayle, you're an attractive, intelligent young woman, and any other man in town would be happy to have you. So why not be smart and move on with your life."

Gayle sneered. "Because I don't *want* any other man. I want *you!* No one has ever made me feel so special, baby. And no one ever will." She extended her arms and wrapped them around his neck before Spencer could react, bringing their faces within kissing distance. "Get rid of that bitch and let's go back to the way things were between us."

Gayle tried to kiss Spencer, but he averted his lips at the last moment. *She's really gone off the deep end.* How the hell had he not seen this in her psychological makeup when they first met? Or had he simply not wanted to see what was painfully clear now?

He had missed the boat, just like he had with his brother. Again, it made Spencer wonder if all of his education and experience as a psychologist had done him one damned bit of good.

He grabbed Gayle's arms and removed them from his neck before releasing them. "Things are never going back to the way they were. The sooner you realize that, the better it'll be for everyone. Stalking is not a game, Gayle, and neither is threatening people with bodily harm. I'll tell you here and now that I won't let you harass Deidre anymore, and you can take that any way you want."

Gayle's mouth tightened. "It doesn't have to be this way, baby."

"Oh yes, it does, *ba-by,*" Spencer retorted. "I intend to get a restraining order to keep you away from me—and Deidre. If you violate it, you're going to jail. Simple as that. Which means no more freedom, higher education, or acting crazy—not in public anyway. Think about it!"

On that note, Spencer walked out the door without looking back, satisfied that he'd at least gotten Gayle to realize that he was dead serious. He sincerely hoped she took that for what it was worth.

Now Spencer had to see if he could patch things up with Deidre and try to put this behind them, even in the midst of yet another murder attributed to the ruthless Park Killer.

Gayle felt anger welling inside her like never before. She picked up a vase and flung it against the wall, watching it shatter into pieces. Her whole world seemed to be crumbling down around her like a sandcastle and it didn't appear as though there was much she could do to change things. Whatever charms she had used to get Spencer into her bed before were no longer working.

And it was all because of that stupid bitch he was now attracted to and obviously sleeping with. Gayle had tried to scare her off, but instead Spencer had come to the rescue as her black knight in shining armor.

Now both of them would pay . . . and pay dearly.

She would not allow Spencer to just dump her and go elsewhere. No way. Not on his life. Or that stupid, conniving little bitch's life.

"This isn't over, baby," Gayle said through clenched teeth as she watched Spencer get into his car. "It'll never be over between us. . . ."

The woman's hair was unkempt and she wore tattered, baggy clothing. Deidre, who sat in while Roland prepared to draw a sketch of the possible killer, suppressed a need to gag from the stench emanating from Marina Elkins due to her life on the streets as a drunk and apparently not having bathed in some time. She hated to think that there were so many women out there like Marina—women who had either given up on the world or that the world had given up on.

Maybe this could be a turning point for her, to give life another chance. But Deidre wasn't counting on that by any means, knowing it was a cruel reality that some of the homeless people were right where they wanted to be.

"Why don't you describe the man you saw, Marina?" Roland spoke evenly.

Marina fidgeted. "No problem. Ain't like I never seen him before. He's about forty—or just looks that old—tall, got dark skin, and kinda muscular, I think, even though I never seen much of his body under all them clothes."

Deidre took mental notes for work and her personal knowledge of what this serial killer might look like. "What did his face look like? Any distinguishing marks?"

Marina pulled on her nose that looked like it had been broken. "Never 'ave seen much of his face. He's got a lot of hair on it. You know, a mustache, beard, the whole works. Guess it's good for livin' outside during the cold months. Keeps you warm. Maybe it does jus' the opposite when it get hot."

Roland started sketching. "Does he have hair on his head? Bald?"

"He's got them dreadlocks."

"What about his eyes?"

"Real creepy, they was." The mere mental image seemed to frighten Marina. "Dark and deep, like they wanted to pop out at you if you was lookin' at him the wrong way."

Roland added this to his sketch. "What type of nose did he have?"

"Dunno." Marina shrugged. "Wide with big nostrils," she said as if with sudden clarity.

Deidre pictured this, getting a portrait of the man with her mind's eye.

"Anything else you can think of to describe the man?" Roland asked.

Marina coughed noisily. "Nuh-uh. I didn't study his face or body too much. Peoples who hang out in the park tend to mind they own business. Me included, mosta the time."

Except for the ones who like to get into other people's business like gangbangers, muggers and murderers. Deidre winced at the thought, believing that the woman might well have seen the killer and lived to tell about it.

"Does this look like him?" Roland showed the sketch to Marina.

She studied it. "Yeah, you done good. Looks like 'im to me."

"You're sure?"

She paused for further examination. "Yeah."

"Did he see you?" Deidre asked curiously as she leaned over to look at the sketch.

As if the thought just occurred to her and was unnerving, Marina stammered, "Uhh, I . . . I, uh, I don't think so."

Deidre had a feeling that this was more wishful thinking than anything on her part. Which meant that if this man was the killer, Marina's life could be in danger.

"Do you have anywhere you can go?" she asked her.

Marina's brows lifted. "Like where?"

"I don't know. Family? Friends?"

"Ain't got no family. No friends. All on my own— 'cept for the peoples I be knowin' on the streets."

Deidre felt for her and anyone who was more at home outside of a home than inside. "I don't think it's safe for you to be on the streets right now. At least not while a killer is on the loose who may come after you."

Marina's weathered face softened. "Don't you go worryin' 'bout me none, honey. I can take care of myself."

"That's probably what Judith Carpenter thought," Deidre said sadly. "And look what happened to her. And a number of other women in recent memory who came face to face with this monster."

Marina's forehead creased worriedly. "Guess I could try a shelter. If they got any room for me."

Deidre felt comforted somehow by that, as though she were looking at her own mother. Or what could have become of her if she'd been dealt a bad hand in life. Deidre knew of a shelter not far from her house and vowed to call them personally and plead that they make room for this woman. And maybe they could try to help get Marina back on her feet instead of sending her back out on the streets.

She resisted giving Marina money, knowing it was a policy the police bureau frowned upon, especially where it concerned witnesses. Furthermore, Deidre suspected it would only do more harm than good in paying for alcohol and its consequences.

Roland smiled at the woman. "Thanks for coming in. You've been a big help."

Marina hunched a shoulder. "Just told what I seen. Everybody's kinda jumpy these days with these killings all around us."

After the witness left, Deidre studied the sketch of the suspect again. Specifically, she focused on the eyes as described by Marina. They were eyes that Deidre was sure she had seen before. That, coupled with the facial hair and brooding look, and she suddenly knew where.

"What is it?" Roland asked her.

"I'm not sure, but I think this might be the man I've seen riding on the light rail," she said unsteadily. "The same man I could swear followed me off the train twice, but I just chalked it up to paranoia."

Deidre's heart skipped a beat. Had she been right all along?

Were he and the man in the sketch one and the same: the Park Killer?

TWENTY-EIGHT

Detective Hernandez peered at the sketch skeptically. "You really think this is the same man you've seen riding the train?" he asked.

Deidre was not positive based on the drawing alone, and the less-than-reliable memory of a witness with a penchant for cheap wine and homeless living. "I wouldn't stake my life on it, Zack, but if I had described that man to someone else, this is the person I would see in my mind—minus the dreadlocks, since I only saw him with a hood over his head."

"Well, that's good enough for me," Hal said, looking at the sketch over her shoulder. "Between the homeless woman and you, a far more credible source of information, this could be the break we've been waiting for."

"Yeah, I think I've heard that before," Hernandez muttered. "For all we know, this man, whether he rides the train or not, was doing nothing more than looking over the victim's car the way people look at zoo animals while wondering where his next meal was coming from. Doesn't make him the Park Killer."

"Maybe not," Hal allowed. "But right now he's the closest thing we've got to a suspect, 'til proven otherwise."

Hernandez nodded thoughtfully. "Can't disagree with you there."

"I didn't think so. Get copies of this sketch out to the media and other law enforcement statewide. In the meantime, let's see if we can find a match to anyone who's already in the system."

"I'm already on top of it," Hernandez said.

Hal rubbed his chin. "Good. Maybe we'll get lucky and put a name to him right away and go from there."

Deidre cringed at the thought that someone she had seen and had seen her as well could be the serial killer. "What if I see him again on the train?" she asked with dread.

Hal looked at her, concerned that she might be in danger. His first thought was to insist that she no longer take light rail. But, knowing her, he was sure Deidre would reject the idea, wanting to maintain her independence as a civilian, in spite of having seen firsthand how violent criminals operate.

"Just pretend you don't notice and call it in," Hal told her. "Don't do anything foolish to tip him off that you may be on to him. If this is our man, we need to stop him in his tracks, so to speak, before someone else dies."

You mean like me. Deidre bit her lip fearfully. "I'll be careful," she promised, while wondering if she could ever be careful enough to stay out of harm's way from a determined and hard-to-apprehend killer.

By five o'clock, Deidre had put in a full day's work, releasing statements about other crimes that had occurred. But it was the sketch that could be the face of a serial killer who liked to ride the rails that left Deidre still shaken.

"Now you know why I don't take light rail," said Agatha, who had offered to give Deidre a ride to her car. "Too many creeps on it. Now you can add to that possible sicko killers."

Deidre dismissed the words and her fears in the process. "Those same creeps are in cars, on the streets, and everywhere," she said realistically. "Same with killers. It's not the train you have to worry about, it's bad people, period."

"Yeah, tell that to someone who hasn't seen the reports on what this man did to those women. Nasty," Agatha said with an exaggerated shiver.

Deidre shivered, too. Hal and Hernandez had pretty much given her all the gory details of what the victims of the Park Killer had been put through, making death seem all too welcome. It was an ordeal Deidre prayed she would never have to go through. Or anyone else she knew, for that matter.

She gazed at Agatha behind the wheel. "We all need to be careful, wherever we are. I don't think any of the victims of the Park Killer have been targeted riding the train, per se." Unless the homeless bearded man really was stalking her with the intention of physically assaulting, raping, and killing her.

"There's always a first time," Agatha said with a catch to her voice. "My advice to you is to drive to work in your car for a while. Maybe we can carpool on days that you work eight hours."

"Maybe," Deidre said. "Either that, or I can simply take a leave of absence from the Sinclair Heights Police Bureau 'til they catch this guy."

"Hey, if you can afford it, I say go for it!"

Though she was only kidding, Deidre was sure her mother would want her to do that very thing if she were aware of what was going on in the supposedly peaceful city of Sinclair Heights. Deidre refused to allow herself to become paralyzed again with the type of irrational fear she'd tried to bury with her husband and son. But could she realistically do that any more than Agatha or any other vulnerable woman in town?

They pulled up to Deidre's car in the free parking lot for light rail riders.

"Thanks for the lift."

Agatha smiled. "Sure. Anytime. So what's up for the rest of your day?"

Deidre hadn't thought about it—happy to have just gotten through what had been a trying last day and a half, beginning with the unwanted company of Spencer's stalker ex.

"Not much," she said when nothing in particular came to mind. "Think I'll just chill."

"Sounds boring."

"It can be, at times," Deidre admitted. "But I'll get over it. Beats some of the alternatives."

"Girl, you need a man in your life," Agatha said bluntly. "I do too, but that's another story. You need someone who can take your mind off all this crap. . . ."

Deidre immediately thought of Spencer. And last night when he was all man, and then some. Now their relationship was at a standstill with no guarantee that anything more would come out of their intimate experience. She wondered if he'd made any headway in confronting his ex-girlfriend—or whatever he chose to call her. Or would Gayle continue to threaten anyone who tried to come into Spencer's life?

"There may be some light at the end of the tunnel in that regard," Deidre hinted.

"Oh, really? . . ." Agatha's brows shot up. "Anyone I know? Or should I guess?"

Not wanting to add fuel to a fire that may have already burned itself out, Deidre responded nonchalantly, "Let's just say for now that I'm not even really sure I know him."

"Sounds cryptic," Agatha said.

"Isn't that the case with all men?"

TWENTY-NINE

Spencer had timed it just right. Within two minutes of arriving at Deidre's house, he watched her drive up. Now came the hard part: convincing her that the worst of it with Gayle was over and they could pick up where they left off.

He waited for Deidre to exit her car before he got out of his and walked up to meet her.

"Are you stalking me now?" she asked half jokingly, and immediately thought about the homeless man who may have been stalking her and could have been a serial killer to boot.

"Actually, I just happened to be in the neighborhood . . ." Spencer began, and dropped this pretense. "Oh, hell, I missed you, so thought I'd take a chance that you might be around."

"And what if I hadn't come back for another two hours?" Deidre asked.

"Then I would have been one very lonely, depressed man," he said with a straight face. "Once I got over that, I would've left you a little note, texted, or simply tried calling the next time."

"I see." Deidre looked around as if they might be expecting company. "So where's *your* stalker?"

Spencer sighed. "Hopefully she won't bother either of us again."

Deidre sensed his hesitancy. "That doesn't sound very reassuring."

He had to admit that he was far from certain Gayle would stay away, in spite of his stern warning. "I'm pretty sure she got the message loud and clear," he said anyway, trying to convince himself of that.

Deidre decided to give him the benefit of the doubt for now. "Would you like to come in and tell me about it?"

Spencer grinned. "You won't have to ask twice."

"Then I won't." She flashed him a teasing, toothy smile.

Damn, she's incredibly attractive and too sexy for her own good. Spencer undressed Deidre with his eyes. Just as he had with his hands yesterday. But as much as he would love to go down that road again, right now he had to regain her trust, hard as that may be.

"Have you had dinner yet?" Deidre asked, hoping to keep busy instead of thinking about Spencer in very erotic ways.

"No, I haven't." He had held back from feeding himself for this very reason and it looked like it had been a smart move.

"Then why don't I whip up something for us?"

"Mind if I help?"

"Be my guest," she agreed.

There's just no getting far enough away from this man, whether I want to or not. Deidre realized that she really didn't want to when she was honest with herself.

Together they made a salad and Deidre heated up some leftover chicken and grabbed half a bottle of wine.

They ate in the breakfast nook.

"So tell me what happened with Gayle?" Deidre didn't want to sound too eager, but after last night's scary confrontation, she was not prepared to take a wait and hear attitude.

Spencer sipped his wine musingly. "I told her again that it was *totally* over between us and that if she ever came near you again—"

"You would what?" For some reason, the thought of him being violent, even with an unbalanced ex–romantic partner, frightened Deidre. Much as it had when she saw him in her dream. Or when she was thinking about the violence experienced by those poor women victimized by a serial killer.

Spencer could see that Deidre was hanging on his every word, wanting to see how far he was prepared to go to protect her. And, if he read her right, she was dreading the notion of him being overly aggressive, no matter the danger.

He took a breath and said equably, "I threatened to have the court issue a restraining order forcing Gayle to stay away from us both—or risk going to jail."

"And how did she react?" Deidre locked in on his eyes.

"She wasn't very happy about it, of course. But I believe Gayle begrudgingly came to terms with the fact that this was serious business and, if she kept it up, she'd only be hurting herself and jeopardizing her graduate studies. Not to mention her freedom."

Deidre smiled with relief. She never wanted to fight over a man, especially with someone from his past. But she also didn't want to fear getting involved with someone because of a previous relationship.

"Well, I hope she will respect your wishes from this point on," Deidre stressed.

"Oh, I think she got the picture," he voiced confidently.

Spencer wanted to keep the courts out of this, if possible. He'd made a mistake with Gayle and probably should have handled things a little differently. He didn't want to compound matters by taking a restraining order out against her. She obviously had trouble dealing with rejection before. But so did he, in his own way. For that reason, he wanted to just let this go and part on polite, if not amicable, terms. Whether or not that happened was up to Gayle.

Spencer focused his attention on Deidre. He could see that something was weighing on her mind. Was she still uncertain that he had cut all ties with Gayle?

"Deidre . . . ?"

She snapped out of her reverie. "Sorry, did you say something?"

"I was just wondering how things went with the sketch artist?" Spencer asked, not having had the chance to watch the news or go on the Internet. He saw fear in her eyes and a chilling image of Judith Carpenter's swollen face popped into Spencer's head.

Deidre paused and steadied herself. "I think I might have seen the same man the witness described was loitering around the car of the latest victim in the park. . . ."

Spencer's eyes widened. "Where?"

She told him. "I think he might have even followed me once or twice off the train, but I can't be sure."

"And you told the police this?"

She nodded. "Yes. They're putting the sketch out there everywhere in hopes of identifying the man."

This unexpected news gave Spencer a start. It was bad enough that Gayle had threatened Deidre and that he was loosely acquainted with all the victims of this serial killer. Now Deidre had to contend with possibly being in direct danger from the so-called Park Killer?

Not lost on Spencer was the fact that one of the victims had been left in the creek behind Deidre's house. Could the killer have seen her then—and targeted her as a future victim?

"I know what you're thinking," Deidre said pensively, studying his face.

"You do?" Spencer asked.

"You're wondering if there could be a connection between this and the creek behind my house where you and Sky discovered the body of Rebecca London."

He looked at her. "Yeah, I admit, the thought did cross my mind."

"Mine too. But I don't think one has anything to do with the other," Deidre said, trying to convince herself. "The man I saw on the train couldn't have followed me home, since I doubt he had a car to do so. And since he was on the train before I got on each time, there's no way he could have come on just for me."

"Makes sense," Spencer said. "But that doesn't mean he might not have seen you at home when the killer dumped the body, if he truly is the serial killer."

"I doubt that he could've seen me inside," she scoffed. "My house is on a hill and it's hard to see much from the vantage point of the creek. And since the police believe the body was dumped there between midnight and four A.M., I was fast asleep by then, having never been outside after five P.M. that day."

Spencer drank more wine contemplatively. "You're probably right." But she could be wrong. With a killer on the prowl, it left no room for error or taking dangerous chances.

Deidre smiled, tasting her wine. "Nice to know you're worried about me, anyway." She knew Spencer was also thinking about the other women who had fallen prey to the killer. Did he think she might be next because of their connection?

"Can't help myself," he stressed in a serious tone. "And, no, I'm not superstitious and feel that your knowing me puts you in more danger than you would be otherwise. After all if, as you say, this man is the killer, then my knowing you would be entirely happenstance in this case."

"You're right." Deidre felt better when she looked at it from that perspective. Not that she was superstitious either, no matter what anyone else thought. Her real fears were more about the killer being at large and essentially holding them all captive.

Spencer sat back and cast his eyes across the table. "I wouldn't want you harmed by a serial killer under any circumstances, or anyone else for that matter."

She knew the latter was in reference to his stalker ex–lady wacko friend, prompting Deidre to assure him and maybe herself as well. "I'll be fine, Spencer. My guess is that if this bearded, and possibly homeless, man I saw is really the Park Killer, it won't take long for the police to pick him up, now that they have a good description and where he apparently hangs out. And since you've assured me that Gayle will no longer be a problem, I should be home free." At least it sounded good to her in theory.

"Yeah, you should be," Spencer said, all things considered, while wishing he could be as confident that they'd heard the last of Gayle. But he wasn't about to reopen this can of worms if he didn't have to.

Deidre gazed at him thoughtfully. "If that isn't enough, Hal has promised to have someone check on me from time to time."

Spencer rolled his eyes. "Well, that's a comfort to know anyway that good old Hal has your back—at last."

"I think he always has since I started working for the police."

"Seems to me that he's much more interesting in rubbing your back," Spencer said.

"Oh really?" She eyed him with a brow raised. "Sounds like you're jealous."

"Not a jealous bone in my body," he said with something less than conviction. The truth was, Spencer had never been with anyone who filled him with such emotions. 'Til now. But they had come too far too soon to let insecurities ruin things between them.

Deidre might have liked to hear that there was maybe a tiny jealous bone somewhere in that magnificent body, but preferred the contrary overall. "That's good to know, because Hal is not only a friend and neighbor, but my boss, and he's obligated to protect *anyone* the police bureau employs. And it's particularly true if they're potentially in harm's way."

"I understand and agree." Spencer felt a trifle foolish in making his feelings so transparent. He was sure that Hal was still attracted to her. What straight man in his right mind wouldn't be? But that didn't mean they were in competition for Deidre. After all, she had a say about who she chose to be with.

From where Spencer sat, he was strictly in the driver's seat and had no immediate plans to relinquish it. As far as he was concerned, things with Deidre were just getting started.

"Did you enjoy the meal?" Deidre asked, wiping her mouth with a napkin. She noted his plate was clean.

"As a matter of fact, I did." Spencer stood up and moved to her. He leaned down so their faces nearly touched. "So what's for dessert?"

She playfully fluttered her lashes. "I don't know. Any suggestions? . . ."

He pretended to think about it. "Well, one or two come to mind . . . All right, make that just *one*. . . ."

Deidre had no doubt what that was, especially since she felt the same way. They were of a one-track mind in this instance and there seemed to be nothing or no one that could deprive them of experiencing their own style of dessert.

THIRTY

They couldn't get upstairs fast enough, kissing and fondling each other every step of the way. Each stripped the other naked and resumed where they had left off with unbridled yearning and heated anticipation.

Deidre did not hide her raw attraction to this man, even if she began the day by thinking that what had happened last night could not possibly ever be repeated. But that was then and this was now. Things had a way of turning with the tide and a most powerful and persuasive presence.

Deidre got down on her knees and admired Spencer's splendid erection. Wanting to pleasure him as he deserved, she took him in her mouth and gently coaxed him farther and farther inside. She heard his sharp intake of breath and felt his body quaver to her touch.

"Oh, baby, that feels so damned good," Spencer mumbled. *Too good to be enjoyed alone.* He lifted her up, wanting to return the favor, and then to enjoy together. "Let me give you something. . . ."

Spencer scooped Deidre into his arms and carried her to the bed, setting her down in just the right spot. After spreading her legs and getting turned on even more by her, this time Spencer dropped to his knees and began to kiss Deidre there. He felt her tremble as his lips touched her, exciting him even more. Her moans were music to his ears.

Deidre heard herself crying out his name as Spencer brought her to the brink of a climax with his mouth and expert use of his tongue. Feeling it coming, she greedily grabbed his head and shamelessly held it in place while Spencer went to work feverishly as a wave of sustained delight swept over Deidre. Only after it had subsided did she release him.

But now an even greater need throbbed within her and Deidre knew she needed this man inside her like never before. "Spencer . . . please, don't wait any longer—"

"Wouldn't dream of it," he groaned, aware that his willpower to hold back was starting to crumble like an imploded building.

Spencer lifted up and put on protection in the blink of an eye before fitting between Deidre's soft thighs, ready and waiting for him. He entered her wetness. Deidre was tight and getting tighter by the moment, agreeing with him completely.

Spencer nibbled at Deidre's breasts and nipples, loving every moment and her natural response. Then he began to kiss her lips and their tongues went after one another's in all-out abandon. Spencer felt his orgasm building to a frenzy. He wanted to experience it while deep inside Deidre, and wanted her to enjoy the same internal explosion.

Deidre suspected he was holding back just a bit, not wanting to go first. But, as Spencer went deeper inside her, the more excited she got and was sure she would come at any moment.

"Go ahead, honey," she whispered. "Let's come together."

Spencer groaned, happy to be thought of as her honey, even in this moment of sexual urgency. "Yeah, I'm with you every step of the way."

Her body slick with sweat, Deidre arched her back and desperately latched on to Spencer's mouth for hard kisses. Draping one leg around his buttocks, she moved with his frenetic and potent thrusts 'til the splendid waves of orgasm overcame her. She felt Spencer do the same as they climbed the mountain of ecstasy together.

The sounds and scent of sex and erratic breaths filled the air like a melody, and Spencer held on to Deidre tightly while the moment came with a flurry and slowly began to wane. He gave her a hearty kiss before rolling off, spent and perspiring, but happier than he could remember.

And still very much turned on by the incredible lady.

"I think this is something I could really get used to," he said with a sigh.

"Oh you do, do you?" she asked playfully.

Spencer dribbled his thumb across her still erect nipple. "Yes, I do."

Deidre felt a burst of fresh desire in that moment. "So does that mean you're going to stay for the night? Or do you need to go home and babysit your dog?"

Can't believe I'm asking him that. Do I sound desperate or what?

Deidre colored with embarrassment at practically throwing herself at Spencer for all-night sex. While she would love to spend more time in his arms and touching each other all over, inside and out, she couldn't very well expect him to cancel his other plans for her.

Could she?

Spencer kissed the nipple he had caressed, and then smiled devilishly. "I'd love to stay the night," he declared without further thought.

Even though I believe Gayle fully understands I meant business in my warning to stay away from Deidre, it's probably a good idea to err on the side

of caution by standing guard, in case she decides to
come around again.

A small part of Spencer was also worried that the
Park Killer might have latched on to Deidre as a target,
independent of him, though Spencer obviously still
knew her. Just like the others. Keeping Deidre within
his sight for at least this night would make him feel a
hell of a lot better.

"As it is, I took Sky over to my old man's house—just
in case I was, uh, too preoccupied to take care of his
needs tonight." He kissed her other nipple and Deidre
bit her lip. "Especially when I'd much rather take care
of your needs. . . ."

Spencer kissed her neck, causing Deidre to nearly
rise satisfyingly. She lowered her hand down to below
his waist. "How about if we take care of each other's
needs?"

Spencer felt his libido once again coming to life.
"You'll get absolutely no complaint from me there."

"Didn't think so." Deidre giggled, and was silenced
by a kiss, which she returned enthusiastically.

She had forgotten what it was like to look forward to
each and every intimate moment with someone. Now,
given the opportunity to experience fresh and special
memories, Deidre was prepared to fully embrace them
for as long as she and Spencer were together. Even if
she hesitated to look too far ahead, knowing that the
future was not guaranteed for anyone, let alone being
happily coupled.

The following day, after teaching two classes, Spencer went to pick up Sky. All he could think of was the
immense pleasure he'd gotten when he made love to
Deidre practically the whole night through and cher-

ished every aspect of her. Gayle had not shown her face like she had the night before, giving Spencer a feeling of relief and allowing him to focus all of his energy on the beautiful lady he was now seeing.

Spencer really liked Deidre, more than he had anyone in a very long time. He also knew that no woman in his life had lasted very long since his divorce, and he didn't want to read too much too soon into the amazing chemistry that existed between him and Deidre. The last thing he wanted was for either of them to get hurt, knowing they both had more than their fair share of that already.

Sky practically bowled him over the moment Spencer entered the house. He laughed, playing with the dog. "Calm down, boy. It's only been since yesterday that we last saw each other."

Sky licked his hands, as if that had still been too long.

"Guess he's just not as comfortable being over here as his own home," Evan said, an unlit cigar dangling from his mouth.

"Did you take him out to . . . ?" Spencer asked.

His father's brows knitted. "Course I did. You think I'm going to let him do his thing right there on the floor?"

Spencer twisted his lips. *Stupid question.* And definitely getting off on the wrong foot with his father, who had taken in Sky with no questions asked, as usual.

"Forget I asked that." He studied his old man, who looked a bit worn down. *Or is it only my imagination?* Maybe the arthritis was taking even more of a toll on him than Spencer realized. "How are you doing, Pops?"

"Hangin' in there. Not like I have any other choice."

"True." Spencer paused, his mind working, and decided to go for it. "You know, you could always move in with me if you wanted. My place is big enough for the two of us."

Evan chewed on the cigar. "I don't think so. This is where I belong."

"Maybe you belong with family, Dad. Someone who can look after you." Spencer was not sure where this was coming from, but believed it was the right thing to say.

His father grimaced. "I can look after myself. And I've got the memories of your mother and brother to keep me going in this old house."

Spencer stiffened. "I'm not suggesting I could begin to take their place. But I'm here now for you."

"I know that and I'm grateful," Evan said. "Just don't ask me to give up what little independence I've got left. I'm too damned old to want to be anywhere else. Besides, maybe one of these days that house you live in will be filled with a new family of your own."

For some reason, this made Spencer think about Deidre and the family she'd lost. Would she be able to love again? Perhaps have another child? A second husband?

Spencer wondered if he could put his own baggage behind him to even think about something long-term in a relationship—including giving Charity a new sister or brother.

"Here," he heard his father say and saw that Evan was handing him a beer. Spencer hadn't even realized he'd left the room, taking the bottle. "Thanks."

"Looks like you could use it."

Spencer was thoughtful. He hadn't meant to shift gears from his father to himself. But then, maybe he hadn't given his old man credit for being able to read him like a book.

"So tell me about this latest gal you're seeing," Evan said.

Spencer took a swig of the beer. "Name's Deidre. She's an artist and also a spokeswoman for the Sinclair Heights Police Bureau."

"Yeah?" Evan seemed intrigued. "Never married? Divorced?"

"Widowed. Lost her husband and son in a carjacking three years ago."

Evan frowned. "Sorry to hear it." He paused. "She know about Wesley?"

"Yeah, she knows," Spencer said lowly.

His father lit the cigar. "Looks like you two have somethin' in common."

"Yeah, unfortunately." Spencer preferred to think about the positive aspects of their relationship and how Deidre made him feel alive again, instead of just living.

"So when do I get to meet her?" Evan asked.

Spencer met his gaze. "How about Saturday? I'm throwing a little birthday party for Charity, and Deidre agreed to come. I hope you will too?"

Smoke streamed from his father's nostrils. "Yeah, I'll be there."

"Good." That was at least one way to get him over to his house. Spencer felt good knowing that his old man loved Charity almost as much as he did. Being a grandfather suited him, especially with Wesley no longer around to keep him company.

"No more troubles with that other gal you were seeing?" Evan asked.

Spencer had kept him abreast of his seeming inability to get Gayle out of his life, but had not mentioned that she had stooped to a new low in harassing Deidre.

"I think she's moved on now," he answered, hoping it was true.

"Maybe you need to be more careful how you pick 'em," his father said bluntly.

Spencer could hardly contradict that. Maybe he should have known how obsessed Gayle would become. Or maybe he'd found that attractive in her early on, only to regret it later.

Deidre was much more to his liking as a beautiful and vivacious woman.

"You're right, Pops. I think I've learned my lesson."

Evan tasted his beer. "It's called life, son. If you're lucky enough, you'll get to live a lot more of it, with all its lessons."

"Yeah, I guess so," Spencer said. "Well, I'd better get going." He called out to Sky. The dog came running in. "You ready to head home, boy?"

"He's been ready," Evan said.

"Well, we'll get out of your hair for a while. Thanks for watching him."

His father dismissed it with a sweep of his hand. "I do what I can. All you have to do is ask."

Spencer nodded appreciatively. "That goes both ways, Dad."

He sensed that his father got the message.

THIRTY-ONE

Deidre sat on the train tentatively. She almost expected to come face to face with the bearded man, who may have doubled as a stalker and ruthless serial killer. But there was no sign of him among the passengers that Deidre could see. Did that mean he wasn't on the train? Could he have seen the sketch and was now on the run?

She noted the undercover cops who occupied some of the seats. They were hoping to bring the man the witness had described and Deidre had fingered in for questioning.

Could I have been wrong believing they were one and the same man? Maybe the man I saw was perfectly harmless and innocent and had just been dealt a bad hand in life to put him on the streets.

It was better to eliminate him as a suspect than to disregard him, only to learn later that more women had been battered, raped, and murdered by him.

Deidre calmed her nerves, realizing it did her no good to over think this. She had done the right thing, no matter how it turned out. Everyone in the city was on edge right now with a serial killer on the loose. If there was any chance to stop him from killing again, no one could afford to pass it up.

Deidre managed to turn her mind to something less frightening and much more pleasing: Spencer Berry. Her skin still tingled at the thought of him touching it. His scent continued to register excitingly in her nostrils, as if he were sitting right beside her. She had never before found sex to be so exhausting, yet utterly passionate.

It had been nearly two days since they'd seen each other. They had both decided that they weren't ready to move too fast, partly out of paranoia regarding something that they had little control over—the reality that a serial killer was on the prowl, targeting women Spencer knew. Why take chances, even if Deidre felt confident that Spencer was as much a victim of chance as the dead women?

Besides, they were busy with their everyday lives, which could not be ignored in spite of their strong attraction to each other.

Neither had made any promises they might not be able to keep, but both felt that this could be going somewhere. Deidre allowed herself to imagine where it might go, while staying grounded for what was still something new and unpredictable territory right now.

No reason to get my hopes up too much only to wind up hurt and lonely again.

Yet hope was the one thing Deidre did have for finding true and lasting love again with an equal. It was not too much to ask, even if such a candidate out there was someone other than Spencer.

When her stop came, Deidre exited the train. At least one undercover detective discreetly did the same, following her from a distance in case the bearded homeless man was on board and decided to get off and come after her.

But when she got to work, it had become clear to Deidre that the authorities would have to look elsewhere for this person of interest.

***

After keeping a low profile for a few days, he felt in need of some fresh air and exercise. Bypassing the light rail, he went on foot, walking around downtown Sinclair Heights. There were a fair amount of shoppers and strollers about, whom he managed to blend in with quite easily. None could imagine that a cold-blooded killer was in their midst.

He stopped in front of a donut shop, the aroma of fresh coffee filling his nostrils. Entering the shop, he walked up to the counter.

A woman with a burgundy bouffant barely looked at him while saying routinely, "What can I get you this morning?"

He looked at the display filled with donuts and pointed to a glazed twirl. "I'll take two of those along with a black coffee."

"You got it," she said tonelessly.

He waited for the order to be filled and noted the folded newspaper someone had left on the counter. Opening it, his eyes landed on the headline: POSSIBLE PARK SERIAL KILLER?

For an instant, fear swept over him that he'd been made. Only after he assessed the sketch of the suspect did he realize that the authorities were barking up the wrong tree.

He breathed a sigh of relief and grinned. *So you think you found me. Think and think again. Not quite.*

He studied the drawing. The bearded, rumpled-looking man with dreadlocks looked familiar. Then it came to him. The homeless man on the train.

He had seen him loitering around in the park too. Apparently, someone else had as well, and linked him to the last victim of the Park Killer.

This annoyed him for some reason. Not that he had a big issue with the police being thrown off in their investigation. But he'd rather they gave credit where credit was due. He was sure that would be the case at the end of the day.

'Til then, he would continue doing what needed to be done—and enjoying it to his heart and soul's content.

THIRTY-TWO

On Friday evening, Spencer arrived at his ex-wife's doorstep, expecting to be greeted by his daughter. Or Fiona herself. Only when the door opened, a man was standing there. He was maybe a few years older than Spencer and around his height and size, with closely cut brown hair.

The man grinned from the corner of his mouth. "You must be Spencer?"

He blinked once at the man. "Uh, yeah, that would be me. Who are you?"

"I'm Clint Winston." He stuck out a large hand.

Spencer felt obliged to shake it. "Nice to meet you, Clint." *Not really.* But Spencer also felt that his ex was more than free to date anyone she wanted. Just as he was.

"You, too, man," Clint said. "Come on in. . . ."

Spencer followed him inside. What was once his home was suddenly becoming more and more alien with another man dictating whether or not he could enter.

Clint looked at him. "Fiona will be right down."

"Actually, I'm here for my daughter," Spencer said.

"Yeah, right," Clint said, as if it had only now occurred to him.

"Hi, Daddy."

Spencer heard Charity's voice and then turned to watch her spring down the stairs and fly into his arms. He kissed the top of her head.

"Hey, sweetheart. You ready to go?"

"Yeah. Mommy's bringing my suitcase down."

"All right." *The sooner, the better.* Spencer didn't want to be there any longer than he had to. He sensed Fiona felt the same way.

"Did you meet Clint?" his daughter asked.

Spencer kept his focus on her. "Sure did."

"He's Mommy's new boyfriend." Charity grinned innocently.

"Yeah, I gathered that." Spencer eyed the man curiously. "So what is it you do, Clint?" He recalled Charity saying that he worked with her mother.

"I'm a senior analyst at Brookman and Teyrod Associates," he said proudly. "And I understand you're teaching at Sinclair Heights College?"

Spencer wondered if that was somehow a putdown. "That's right."

"I got my BA from the University of Oregon, so I can respect anyone who can put up with us rowdy students."

Clint chuckled, but Spencer didn't. *Hope you're not still rowdy. Not around my daughter anyway.*

Spencer turned to see Fiona coming down the steps with Charity's bag. "You're early," she said as if it were a sin.

"Yeah, by about fifteen minutes," he acknowledged, eager to see Charity. "So sue me."

Fiona sneered. "Don't tempt me. Here." She handed him the bag.

Spencer clutched the handles and glanced at Clint, who put his arm protectively around Fiona. She looked slightly uncomfortable.

"Did you two—"

"Yes, we met," Spencer finished for her and glanced at the boyfriend.

Clint grinned. "Yeah, baby. It's all good between us. Ain't that right, Spencer?"

He looked at his restless daughter, and gazed at Fiona. "Yeah, we're cool."

Fiona smiled, as though relieved.

Spencer didn't want his ex to get the wrong idea that he planned to become friends with the new man in her life, even if he was happy for her. As long as Charity approved, and she seemed to, he had no grounds for complaint. But he still preferred to draw the line between acceptance and bonding between them.

"Are you ready?" he asked Charity.

"Yes, let's go, Daddy!" she said anxiously.

"Give me a kiss good-bye," Fiona demanded of her, bending down.

Spencer watched Charity kiss her mother's cheek and finish with a big hug. "I'll have her back on time Sunday as always," he said before his ex could get the words out herself.

Deidre drove to the mall, not sure what to get Spencer's daughter for her eighth birthday. *I wish I'd had a little girl to dote over.*

It made Deidre think about her own little boy who would be nine today had he lived. How cruel life could be to take away one so young and precious, depriving him of what may have been a productive and blessed future. While no one could ever take the place of Marshall and Adam, Deidre believed that maybe with Spencer and his daughter, she really was being given a second chance at life, happiness, and a possibly a new family.

Or, at the very least, she was sure they would have an opportunity to bond, even if only as good friends.

Deidre pulled into the parking lot. Once she turned the car off, she got out her cell phone and called Sabrina. With several nieces she spoiled rotten, if anyone would have some ideas, she would.

"Why hello there." Sabrina's voice was jubilant. "I was just thinking about you."

"Liar!" Deidre laughed, sure that she was way too busy with artwork and socializing to give her much thought.

"No, really! I was working on a painting—but my mind was elsewhere as usual—and I was wondering if things had worked out with you and that good-looking Spencer Berry."

Did they ever. At least in certain areas. "There's been some progress," she said, downplaying it.

"I see...." Sabrina hummed. "After the gallery showing, I wasn't sure. So, just how much progress are we talking about?"

Deidre felt a tingle, remembering the sensations of Spencer's strong hands, delicate fingers, and wandering mouth in action all over her body. But she wasn't ready to share the explicit details, for fear of jinxing the promise of more to come.

"Enough progress that I'm on my way to the mall to buy his daughter a birthday present or two."

"Oh, really?"

Deidre exited the car, locking it. "That's where you come in, girlfriend. I need your help in a *major* way, as I seem to be at a loss on buying something meaningful for an eight-year-old cutie."

"Say no more," Sabrina told her. "Help is on the way. . . ."

Deidre breathed easier, already imagining the look on Charity's face when she handed her the gifts.

***

They went to eat ice cream at the mall. Spencer watched with joy and a bit of uneasiness as his little girl was growing up right before his very eyes. In ten years, they would celebrate her eighteenth birthday— meaning adulthood, college, and *boys*. Spencer didn't even want to think about Charity dating, much less getting married and having children of her own. Not yet anyway. Right now, he intended to enjoy her sweet innocence and making a mess of a brownie sundae she could eat with her hands.

"So how's school these days?" Spencer asked, realizing with regret that he played almost no role in this part of her life.

"Fine," Charity answered in an elongated voice. "I'm taking an art class."

He lifted a brow, immediately thinking of the sexiest, finest artist he knew. "Is that right?"

"Yeah. It's really fun drawing things. Maybe someday I'll be really good just like Deidre was at the Cinco de Mayo Fiesta."

Spencer smiled and scooped up some of his banana split. "I wouldn't doubt it. You can be good at anything you choose to do, honey, as long as you put your heart and soul into it."

"You mean like a psychology professor? Or a senior analyst?" She giggled.

He chuckled. "Yeah, like those." Truthfully, Spencer wasn't sure just how much of his heart went into teaching psychology, but he knew that he definitely put a lot of soul into the job.

"Do you ever think about Uncle Wesley?" Charity looked up at him with squinty eyes.

"All the time," Spencer said wistfully. "He was my only brother and my twin at that. Why? Do you think about him?"

She licked her lips. "Sometimes. Mommy thinks about him too."

"Does she?" He looked into Charity's eyes with surprise.

"Yeah. She tells me stories sometimes about when she first met you and Uncle Wesley, and how you hit it off right away."

It was more like they hit it off right away. Spencer felt a twinge of envy as he recalled how close Fiona and Wesley were, seemingly from day one. It took longer for him and Fiona to begin to like each other, much less start dating. And even longer for at least one of them to fall in love. He wondered if, in retrospect, Fiona should have married Wesley. Maybe they were the ones who truly belonged together. Had it worked out that way, maybe his brother would still be alive.

And I would be looking at his child instead of my own beautiful soon-to-be eight-year-old.

The thought was sobering to Spencer. He knew he wouldn't give up his daughter for anything. Even if he would give anything to have his brother back, too.

THIRTY-THREE

Deidre hoped she hadn't overdone it, but the more she saw, the more she liked. It had been three years since she'd had a child to buy anything for and maybe she was making up for lost time. Or daydreaming that it was Adam who was the recipient of her gifts.

Deidre held on to her bags while zigzagging between other shoppers. She was about to leave the mall when she noticed Spencer and Charity inside the ice cream parlor. Her first thought was to pretend that she hadn't seen them. But it was clear that Spencer had spotted her and was beckoning her to come in.

Problem was, Deidre had Charity's gifts and they weren't wrapped. *What do I do?* She tried not to panic. *Think fast.*

After taking a deep breath, Deidre gathered herself, and headed into the parlor.

"Why are you smiling, Daddy?" Charity asked curiously. She followed the flight of his eyes looking over her.

"I see someone I know," he said happily. "Er, that *we* know."

"It's Deidre, the artist!" Charity squealed. "And she's coming in here—with *lots* of bags!"

Spencer cocked a brow. "Hmm . . . I can see that." Another chance meeting between lovers? Or maybe it had nothing at all to do with chance and was simply the magnetism of their mutual charms and sizzling sex appeal that drew them together time and time again. Along with something called destiny, were he actually to believe in such. "Be right back," he told Charity.

Spencer stood and met Deidre halfway. Grabbing a few of her bags, he said amusingly, "Looks like you could use some help."

"Very funny." She saw Charity still seated, eating ice cream. "These bags happen to contain gifts for *your* daughter's birthday party."

Spencer's eyes widened. "All of them?"

Deidre blushed. "So maybe I got a little carried away."

He chuckled. "Just a little. Though I doubt Charity would complain one bit."

And neither would he, at the risk of spoiling his daughter more than she already was. Quite the contrary, this was another side to Deidre that Spencer found quite endearing. Obviously, she had maternal instincts that had not gone away with the death of her son.

"The gifts aren't wrapped, though," Deidre warned. "What if Charity gets a tiny bit nosey?"

"She won't," Spencer said, and then reconsidered. "Maybe we can have a pre-birthday celebration, right here and now."

"You think so?" Deidre gazed at him.

"If we have to. All I know is that neither Charity nor I want to see you go just yet—"

"Then I won't." Deidre felt happy to be wanted. And even happier to want someone such as Spencer. With Charity being a bonus.

As if by design, Spencer's daughter stood up, eager to see what was going on.

Deidre gazed up at her father. "Uh-oh, looks like we've got company."

"I'll handle this," Spencer said, and hoped he could back up his words.

"Hi, Deidre." Charity flashed her teeth.

"Hi back to you, Charity." Deidre smiled.

"So what's in all the bags?" Charity asked.

Spencer held several of them with one hand and put the other on Charity's shoulder. "Just some things Deidre bought for herself. Maybe she'll show you later. Right now, let's get back and finish our ice cream."

This seemed to pacify Charity for now. Looking up at Deidre, she asked, "Do you want to have some ice cream with us?"

Deidre swallowed enthusiastically. "I'd love to."

Gayle looked into the window of the ice cream parlor. She spied Spencer there with Charity and Deidre, careful not to be seen herself. Gayle had followed Spencer from the time he left his ex-wife's house to pick up Charity and the long drive to the mall. Gayle could not get him out of her head and the way he made her feel inside. She'd wanted desperately to talk to him, try to convince him that they belonged together. But he'd made it perfectly clear that it wasn't going to happen.

And all because of that bitch he had fallen for.

It should be me sitting there with him and Charity, enjoying ice cream, and loving companionship. Not her!

Spencer would live to regret dumping her. And so would his whore!

You can both rot in hell. You'll find out what happens, Spencer, when you decide to toss away my love like soiled diapers.

When Gayle saw Spencer look up, she quickly ducked out of sight. She didn't want to be seen by him. Not now. Not until the moment of truth had arrived and he paid the ultimate price for his stark betrayal.

THIRTY-FOUR

On Saturday, Spencer was up bright and early to take Sky out to do his business. He used the time to think about what a pleasure it had been to run into Deidre yesterday at the mall and how creative they had been to keep Charity preoccupied and therefore away from the bags of birthday gifts for her. He felt a bit guilty that Deidre had gone to such lengths for his daughter, but could tell that it truly made her happy. It would make Charity even happier. And if Deidre and Charity were happy, then he was happy too.

Before they left the mall, Spencer and Deidre had managed to sneak in a long kiss without Charity being the wiser. Not that Spencer wished to keep his romance a secret from his daughter. After all, her mother seemed to be fully ensconced in a romance of her own. But he was wary of getting Charity's hopes up too much that he had found someone for the long term. Especially after he had let Gayle meet her and now deeply regretted it.

This time, he'd rather take things slowly where it concerned his daughter. Even if Spencer would just as soon prefer that things moved at warp speed between him and Deidre. Certainly in bed anyway, where they seemed wholly compatible and burned up the sheets each time they were together.

Charity was still sleeping when Spencer and Sky went back inside, giving Spencer time to shower and make breakfast. By the time she woke up, he'd made pancakes and turkey bacon for her.

"Morning, sweetheart."

"Morning, Daddy." She smiled and rubbed her weary eyes, still wearing her pajamas. "Where's Sky?"

"He's around here somewhere."

"I'll go find him," Charity said. "He's probably hungry too."

"Sky's always hungry," Spencer said with a laugh, tossing pancakes on a plate.

The doorbell rang and he heard Charity heading toward the door with Sky. A moment later, Spencer heard his father say, "How's my birthday girl?"

"Hi, Gramps."

Sky barked.

"Hey, boy," Evan said.

Spencer set out another plate. When his father came into the kitchen, Spencer said, "You're right on time, Pops."

"You've got that right," Evan said, eyeing the pancakes and bacon.

"Glad you could make it."

"How could I not? Charity's my only granddaughter—at the moment."

Moment? Spencer wondered if he was somehow disappointed in him for not fathering more children.

It's not my fault that Fiona fell out of love with me before we could have any more children. Or that Wesley died before he could become a father.

But there was still hope. Spencer could well imagine having another child or two someday. And having someone like Deidre as their mother.

"Have a seat, Dad. Breakfast is about to be served. . . ."

Deidre had no trouble locating the house. It was newer than hers was and had some great views of the city. She wondered if Spencer had lived there long, and if he had purchased it with the idea of adding a family someday.

Deidre wasn't quite sure what to expect in attending a family gathering in which she was not part of the family. Her relationship with Spencer had not yet been defined. Was she his girlfriend? An occasional sex partner? Or perhaps what it entailed would still have to be worked out between them.

I'll just play along and when one of us knows for sure what we want out of this, we'll know it.

She rang the doorbell and immediately heard Sky barking.

The man who opened the door was not Spencer, but an older, frailer version of him.

"You must be Deidre," he said. "I'm Evan, Spencer's dad."

"Hi." She smiled and watched his eyes crinkle as they shook hands.

"Come on in. The party's already started."

Indeed, Deidre could hear music, song, and laughter. She went inside, just hoping not to do or say anything stupid.

"I'll take those for you and put them with the rest 'til the big moment," Evan offered, eyeing her load of gifts. "Looks like you've got more than the rest of us combined."

Deidre blushed. "Hope you don't hold that against me."

"Are you kiddin'? It's a real plus in my book that you like Spencer enough to want to bring a great big smile to my granddaughter's face."

"Well, it's not every day that one turns eight," Deidre said, deflecting attention away from herself. Even if it was true that she really had begun to grow fond of Spencer and Charity.

"You've got that right." Evan grinned and winked at her. "Or even nine, ten, or eleven."

"Very true." Deidre knew that all too well, but promised herself that she wouldn't dwell on the past, and would enjoy the occasion instead.

They went into the great room. Deidre marveled at its openness and architecture and imagined the work Spencer had put into it.

Children were gathered around Charity, singing. Nearby Spencer was at a piano, playing like a professional, surprising Deidre. She knew he played, but hadn't realized that he was that good.

"More company," announced Evan.

"Hi, Deidre!" Charity cooed, running up to hug her.

"Happy birthday, Charity!" Deidre gave her a big kiss on the cheek.

"Thanks." Charity proceeded to introduce Deidre to her friends.

When Spencer saw Deidre, he could barely take his eyes off her. Wearing a cami shirt and capri pants, she looked great and fit right in. He could see that she had no trouble interacting with Charity's buddies. Or his father. Which, in Spencer's book, made her even more of a catch.

Deidre walked over to Spencer, and he stood up. "You didn't tell me you were a concert pianist."

He laughed, appreciating the compliment. "Well, I wouldn't go quite that far. Just a little hobby I developed in college to help relieve the boredom and studying. I doubt I'd ever be invited to Carnegie Hall or anything, but I'm good enough to play a few appropriate tunes at an eight-year-old's birthday party."

Deidre had always wanted to play the piano, but had never gotten around to taking lessons. Perhaps she could coax a few lessons out of Spencer sometime. Right now, she would settle for an inconspicuous kiss.

Spencer seemed to be reading her mind as he planted an open-mouthed kiss on Deidre, surprising her somewhat, and practically sweeping her off her feet. When he pulled away, Charity and her friends giggled.

"Oops, looks like you caught us," Spencer said jokingly, but felt good in making it clear that Deidre was much more than just a birthday party friend.

"I think they can keep a secret," Evan said, amused. "Ain't that right, girls?"

They giggled again.

"I see you met my father," Spencer said to Deidre.

"Yes, and he seems like a nice man," she said.

"He is, when he's not grouchy."

She smiled. "Spoken like a true son."

Spencer chuckled. "Or someone looking to blame his own foibles on inherited genes."

Deidre fluttered her lashes at him. "So do you want to give me the grand tour of your home before or after the cake and ice cream?"

Spencer looked at the girls, who seemed preoccupied, and his father, playing with Sky, and decided they would not be missed for a few minutes. He took Deidre's hand. "Now seems like as good a time as any."

THIRTY-FIVE

Spencer was shocked to see his ex-wife standing at the door. Her new boyfriend was not with her.

"What are you doing here, Fiona?" he was afraid to ask.

"I came to see *my* daughter on her birthday—and to give her a present."

Only then did Spencer notice the small wrapped box in Fiona's hand.

"Can't that wait?" he asked. "I'll be bringing her back tomorrow and you can see Charity all you want for the next two weeks."

Fiona frowned. "But her birthday will have come and gone by then, won't it? This is a special day and I want to spend a little part of it with Charity. Is that so bad?"

Spencer swallowed. It wasn't bad. But it sure as hell wasn't good either. The last thing he needed was for Deidre to think that he was still somehow pining for his ex, when that couldn't be further from the truth. But it was Charity's birthday and Fiona did have a right to share it with her whether Spencer liked it or not.

"Come in," he relented. "But I won't have you upsetting any of my guests, Fiona. Is that understood?"

She sighed theatrically. "Now why would I want to do that, Spencer? We're not married anymore, remember? You're entitled to have your fun with your *guest*. Just like I can with Clint."

Spencer stepped aside and hoped it wasn't a decision he would soon regret.

"I heard you lost your husband and son in a carjacking incident," Evan said to Deidre in the kitchen. She was busy filling paper cups with fruit punch.

"Yes," she said sadly. "The worst moment of my life."

"Yeah, I can only imagine." He poured some potato chips into a bowl. "None of us can ever be prepared for somethin' that traumatic and senseless."

She knew that Evan was also thinking about Spencer's brother. "I'm so sorry about your son's death."

Evan nodded. "Yeah, me too. There was a time when I could hardly tell Wesley and Spencer apart. Never thought the day would come when one of 'em would leave this planet before me. Guess it was just Wesley's time to go or somethin'."

Deidre took exception to that. "Not sure it's ever really anyone's time to go when it happens by unnatural causes."

"Good point you got there. Nothing natural about Wesley's death, or your son and husband." Evan's face sagged with emotion. "Looks like we both lost people that we loved too damn soon . . . The pain never goes away either, does it?"

"No, it doesn't." Deidre felt a connection with the elder Berry, much as she did with her own father. She wondered if Wesley's dying could have caused a rift between Spencer and his father in being the one who had to live in the shadow of his brother's death.

"There you are." She heard Spencer's voice.

Turning, Deidre saw him enter the kitchen with a tall and attractive woman. She glanced at Evan, who cocked a brow and looked uncomfortable.

"Deidre, this is my ex-wife, Fiona," Spencer reluctantly introduced them. "She dropped by for Charity's birthday party. Fiona, this is Deidre. . . ."

"Hello." Deidre smiled brightly, hiding her discomfort.

"Hi," Fiona said tonelessly to her and then quickly turned her attention to Evan. "Nice to see you, Evan."

"Yeah, you too." He grabbed a couple of potato chips and tossed them in his mouth.

Spencer felt the awkwardness of the moment, as surely as if it were a wall of ice he needed to chop his way through or risk ruining the whole day.

"Can I take that?" He looked at the tray of cups filled with punch, then faced Deidre.

She met his eyes, feeling comfort in them. "Yes, I think I'm done for this round."

"Thanks." Spencer grabbed the tray. "Well, why don't we go join the others?"

"Good idea," Evan said, lifting the bowl of chips and leading the way.

"She's very pretty," Deidre said of Fiona as she watched her dote over her daughter.

"Not as pretty as you are," Spencer told her honestly.

"You sure about that?" Deidre batted her eyes with uncertainty.

"Positive," he said, hating to think that she felt she was in some type of competition with Fiona in the looks department or otherwise. "It wasn't my idea for Fiona to be here."

"It's all right, Spencer," Deidre tried to reassure him. Well, maybe not in the ideal world. But this was reality. An ex-wife came with the territory, particularly when there was a child involved. If she and Spencer were going to make this work, Deidre knew she'd have to get used to Fiona being in the picture to one degree or another.

"Thanks for being so understanding," Spencer said. He suspected that Deidre was just taking the high road rather than whining and complaining, as he imagined Fiona would have done had the shoe been on the other foot. This was yet another feather in Deidre's cap, making Spencer like her all the more.

"Well maybe you can reward me for it later," Deidre whispered in his ear.

Spencer felt a swell of desire at the mere thought. "Name the time and place."

It was something Deidre was only too happy to do. But, for now, they had to keep their eye on the ball. Or the birthday girl and everyone who had come to celebrate it with her.

"So how long have you two been seeing each other?" Fiona asked Deidre when they had a moment alone.

Deidre really did not want to discuss this with Spencer's ex-wife any more than talking about why on earth Fiona had let such a good man get away. But she wanted to keep it all friendly for Charity.

"Not long," she said evenly.

"My daughter tells me that you're an artist?"

"Yes, I do sketches and paintings," Deidre responded.

"Good for you. I don't really have an artistic bone in my body," Fiona said unapologetically. "But I am great at interior design and helping people invest their money properly."

"We all have our talents," Deidre allowed and sipped punch. She had no problem recognizing what Fiona brought to the table professionally and as the mother of Spencer's child. Deidre wondered what Fiona thought of Spencer as a psychology professor. Or, for that matter, when he was with the FBI.

For some reason, I have the feeling that she wasn't totally supportive. Or am I just grasping at straws here?

"That we do," Fiona said. "I also heard that you're a police spokeswoman."

"Yes, I am," Deidre acknowledged.

"Yeah, I thought I saw you on TV." Fiona wrinkled her nose. "It must be kind of hard to share that depressing news all the time."

"It can be," Deidre said. "But keeping the public informed is important for everyone, including the families of the victims."

Fiona shook her head and frowned. "Well, better that you have to deal with it than me. I don't think I could do it."

"Someone has to," Deidre pointed out. "It's not always depressing news."

"I'm sure you're right." Fiona took a breath. "Anyway, I just want you to know that I'm cool with you dating my ex, especially since my daughter seems to really like you. Not that I have any say in it one way or the other."

Deidre was thankful for that. "I like Charity too. And Spencer." She locked eyes with Fiona, and couldn't resist adding, so she wouldn't think that she had a problem with Spencer having an ex-wife, "And I'm cool with you, too."

Deidre guessed that this was probably as close to friendship as they could expect to get. But she would take even that to keep the peace and give things between her and Spencer a fair chance to play themselves out.

It was time for Charity to open her gifts, so they all gathered around her. Deidre watched as she opened boxes and gift bags containing clothes, toys, DVDs, and books. Then it was time for her to open Deidre's gifts. She held her breath as Charity ripped open the wrapping paper on the first box to find a princess costume, including a tiara. That was followed by a beginner cross-stitch kit, miniature dolls, and more books.

"Thank you, Deidre," Charity said, and hugged her.

"You're very welcome," Deidre said. The joy on Charity's face had made it all worthwhile for Deidre. As did the grin spread across Spencer's face.

"Okay, there's one more gift here," Spencer said. It was an unwrapped shoebox. He picked the box up. "Who's the gift giver?" No one spoke up. "Oh, well, I guess we'll see." He handed it to Charity.

She jiggled it, trying to guess what might be inside. Finally giving up, Charity lifted the lid.

Inside was a dead rat.

"What the . . . ?" Spencer yelled as Charity let out a piercing scream, dropping the box. The rat flopped onto the floor, ending up at Deidre's feet. Suddenly Charity's friends all started screaming and Deidre fought hard to hold back her own scream.

"Is this someone's idea of a sick joke?" Evan asked as he scooped the dead rodent back into the box.

"Not anyone here," Spencer said with certainty.

"Then who?" Deidre was aghast at the horrible thing someone had done at a young girl's birthday party, even as a person she felt was more than capable of such suddenly entered her mind.

Spencer fixed Deidre with a sour look. "I've got a pretty good idea. . . ."

The doorbell rang and everyone jumped.

"I'll get it," Spencer said, fearful that it might just be the one he suspected of being responsible for this despicable act.

He opened the door. Instead of seeing Gayle standing there, it was a lanky man in his thirties, wearing a dark suit.

"Are you Spencer Berry?"

Spencer eyed him warily. "Yes. Who the hell are you?"

The man met his gaze head-on, and then handed him some papers. "You've been served. Have a nice day."

Before Spencer could utter a word of protest, the man had vacated the premises like his pants were on fire.

Spencer opened the document and saw that it was a temporary restraining order, barring him from any communication or contact with Gayle Kincaid pending an order to show cause hearing.

THIRTY-SIX

"Damn her! If I get my hands on that bitch—" Spencer said furiously.

"That's exactly how she wants you to feel," Deidre told him.

"Yeah, and that's what bothers the hell out of me. It's working. . . ."

They were in his bed after all the guests had gone home. Charity had gone home too. She was so shaken up by the dead rat as a birthday present that Fiona had insisted she return home a day early. Under the circumstances, Spencer could hardly refuse. Lucky for him that Deidre was there as a calming influence, otherwise there was no telling what he might have done, restraining order or not.

Deidre kissed his chest, then his mouth. "Then make it stop," she implored him. "If you let Gayle get under your skin with this, then she'll just end up winning, at least psychologically. Besides, I doubt she left any fingerprints to tie her to the rat or shoebox. And since nobody saw Gayle in or outside the house—"

"I don't have much of a case," Spencer said sourly.

"Those are my thoughts." Deidre put her breasts in Spencer's face and trembled as his tongue ran across one nipple, then the next. "Maybe now that she thinks she's gotten a little payback, she'll go away for good."

"Yeah, maybe," Spencer said, but somehow didn't believe it for a second. Gayle was obviously hell-bent on getting revenge for being dumped, even as she sought legal protection from any retaliation. At this point, Spencer felt his best bet was to be extra diligent and await his day in court.

Spencer's mind switched gears to Deidre, who was driving him crazy with her constant movement and intoxicatingly sweet smell. She was on top, and it turned him on as she rode him like a prized stallion. But he wanted more control. Easily turning Deidre onto her back, Spencer gripped her buttocks and moved inside her with overwhelming desire. Deidre urged him on with her melodic murmurs.

She heard Spencer's grunts even as she clawed at his sturdy back and cried out his name. She was surprised at how comfortable she felt with him and their burgeoning sexuality. It was as if Spencer had awakened the dormant woman in her, and now she could hardly get enough of him. And, apparently, he felt the same way about her.

She met him halfway as they moved in synchronized rhythm, each desperate in their intimacy to reach the ultimate height of passion.

When Deidre felt her orgasm coming, Spencer came as well with a powerful shudder that literally lifted them both off the bed and back down with a frenzied finish. His loud moaning blended in with Deidre's uncontrollable gasps, waning when their bodies finally relaxed, still joined together.

Spencer took a deep breath and kissed Deidre. "What a way to turn frustration into triumph."

"Can't think of a better way." She laughed, enjoying the feel of his body on her.

He kissed Deidre again, lingering on her tasty mouth. "Just more of this."

Deidre ran her hand across Spencer's smooth head. "Be careful what you wish for."

"I always am." Spencer kissed one of Deidre's nipples, feeling it rise. "I only wish for things that are money in the bank. Or something every bit as valuable. . . ." He felt his erection growing again inside her.

After another round, Deidre wondered if this truly was the beginning of something special. Something that not even Gayle or Fiona could derail.

Gayle could barely hide her delight over killing a nasty rat and boxing it for Spencer's daughter to open at her party, which Gayle had overheard Spencer talking about at the mall. Her intent had not been so much to scare the girl, but to get back at her father. And it had been so easy to pull it off. Gayle had borrowed Spencer's spare key after they'd slept together one night and had a copy made. She'd used it to sneak in to his house last night and quietly placed the gift among some others, hoping to get the maximum effect. She was sure she had achieved just that.

Gayle suspected that Spencer would want to come after her for the rat gift, which was why she had cleverly gotten the temporary restraining order against him, beating him to the punch. But she had no intention of staying away from Spencer.

Or that bitch he was in his house sleeping with right now.

Gayle stared at Spencer's bedroom window from her car. She had watched as the light went off and the sex began, no doubt.

Spencer and his whore would be sorry for what they did to her.

If she couldn't have Spencer, no other woman would have him either. She would make him wish he hadn't hurt her by tossing away her love as if she was nothing more than another notch on his belt.

Gayle gritted her teeth, started up the engine, and quietly drove away.

Hal stopped off at a club after work for a drink. It sure as hell beat hanging around his place, alone and lonely. It hadn't always been that way. He was in love once and thought marriage would follow. Instead, she decided things were moving too quickly and slowed down to a crawl before the relationship disintegrated altogether.

More recently, any chance he had of romancing Deidre was squelched by her, leaving him once again on the outside looking in. Fortunately, most of the time he had his work to occupy his thoughts and take away the need for some female companionship. But even that could only go so far, especially when trying to keep gang members from killing each other and a serial killer from taking liberties against women in the city were hardly things one looked forward to getting up in the morning to deal with.

Hal was immediately taken by the good-looking woman sitting at the bar. Her dark hair was in sexy long braids and she was dressed to kill in a low-cut black cocktail dress and stilettos.

Damn, she's smokin' hot! He also noted that she appeared to be alone, just like him. Perhaps he could change that.

He walked up to her and pointed to the empty seat beside her. "This seat taken?"

She batted her eyes at him. "Does it look like it?"

Hal cracked a smile. "In that case, I hope you don't mind if I join you?"

"Whatever," she said with disinterest.

Hal figured she just needed to be softened up a bit. He called the bartender over and ordered a drink. "And get another for the lady too, whatever her pleasure." She appeared to be drinking Scotch on the rocks. A hard drinker did not mean she had a hard body. Not from where he was sitting.

But it was her face that Hal honed in on, as there was something familiar about it. Or was that only in his dreams?

"Have we met before?" he asked, realizing it sounded like the oldest line in the book.

She gave him the once-over, showing no sign of recognition. "I don't think so."

He grinned. "My name's Hal."

Gayle studied the man who was coming on to her. In fact, she had seen him before. At the art gallery, when he was talking to Spencer and that bitch he was sleeping with. Gayle wasn't interested in anyone other than Spencer. But maybe this one would do as a substitute 'til she got her man back.

"I'm Gigi," she lied, using the name of an old friend. She didn't want this man to connect her in any way to Spencer, which could possibly interfere with her plans for him.

"Nice meeting you, Gigi." Hal flashed a smile, extending a hand, which she shook.

"You too," she told him, offering her own sweet—though deceptive—smile.

They went back to Hal's house, where they barely made it to his bedroom before ripping each other's clothes off. Hal put on a condom and joined Gigi in bed, highly aroused by her and a bit tipsy. Though he would have preferred that it was Deidre he was about to make love to, Gigi was nearly as good-looking and probably every bit as sexy.

They sucked on each other's mouths and made lustful noises while their hands explored each other's bodies, before Hal put his penis inside the lady. She was wet and tight, just as he liked it, clearly ready to play. He moved fluidly between Gigi's legs, hoping he would be able to last for more than a few minutes. But it had been too damned long and his need to have an orgasm too great.

Hal sucked in a deep breath and trembled mightily while exploding inside her. Gigi sucked his lips and moaned loudly, telling him that she too was about to climax and wanted him just as badly.

Gayle spread her legs wider and clutched Hal's buttocks, pressing him hard against her. She concentrated, imagining that it was Spencer taking her to bed, wedged inside her, wanting to pleasure her as only he could.

When she came, the moment was electrifying and her love grew stronger as Spencer thrust himself into her time and time again, needing her body to relieve himself with the same degree of satisfaction.

It was only after it ended that Gayle came back down to earth and realized that it wasn't Spencer she had just had hot sex with, but some other asshole she'd picked up in a bar. She slithered away from his sweaty body and off the bed.

"Where you going?" Hal asked, still caught in the throes of a most powerful orgasm.

"Home," she said simply.

"Stay the night," he pleaded, not ready to see this end just yet.

"I prefer to sleep in my own bed—alone." Except when Spencer was in it with her.

Hal could see that she had made up her mind. She had followed him home in her car, so she could leave just as easily, much to his chagrin.

"When can I see you again?" he asked.

"This was a onetime deal," Gayle told him tersely. "I have a man."

Hal cocked a brow in surprise. On the other hand, why should he be shocked that a woman who looked like her and performed like her would have someone in her life—if not this night?

"So why did you come home with me?" he asked, feeling a little irritated.

Gayle gazed at him lying naked atop the comforter. "Because you asked me to and it seemed like a good thing at the time."

"Well if you ever need a good thing in the future, give me a call," Hal said, realizing they had never even exchanged numbers, but figured it was probably best that way, all things considered.

"Thanks, but I think from now on I'll be true to my man," she said, wishing Spencer could say the same instead of cheating on her with another woman.

Gayle got dressed and grabbed her purse. "I'll see myself out," she told Hal, and left him in the room. Part of her would've been happy to have him walk her to her car, what with a serial killer on the loose and targeting attractive women. But that might be sending the wrong signals, so she decided to take her chances.

It was only when she was downstairs that Gayle noticed a framed picture on the wall of Hal in full uniform. He was a cop. The notion gave her a bit of a start. He could easily become her worst enemy. But just as quickly, she recognized that having him on her side could become an asset down the line, even if playing with fire.

She grinned slyly. Looked as though the man hadn't seen the last of her after all.

THIRTY-SEVEN

Bright and early on Monday morning, the Park Killer task force assembled to discuss the case. Deidre was asked to sit in, to take notes for the press conference scheduled for this afternoon. She sat next to Hal at the long table. Zack Hernandez stood at the head of the table, talking.

"We'll get this son of a bitch sooner or later . . . one way or the other. . . ." Hal whispered to her in a measured voice.

"I know," Deidre said softly, though wondering if it would be later than sooner. So far, the police had found no sign of the man she believed to be the person the witness described to Roland. Did that mean he'd gone underground? Would Deidre's less–than-positive identification of a homeless man as a suspect blow up in her face, possibly throwing the investigation off track by shifting attention away from the true killer?

Hal said to her reassuringly, "I trust your eyes and instincts. We may not have a name, but we're ratcheting up the pressure to find this man—assuming he's the killer—and making it that much more difficult for him to go about his business as usual."

Deidre crinkled her eyes at Hal hopefully, even as she and every other woman in Sinclair Heights remained on edge as long as a serial killer was free to continue to attack those he set his sights on with seeming impunity.

"The Park Killer is getting more confident," Hernandez pointed out. "Instead of essentially letting the victims come to him, he's now going after them. He's even willing to steal their vehicles as part of his boldness to go along with his desire to break women's jaws and spirits, and rape and murder them. He left behind DNA in the latest victim's car that will prove to be valuable as soon as we catch his ass. When that will be is anyone's guess. But something tells me it won't be long now. We've got a physical description of the man we're looking for and we have a pretty good idea where he's been spending his time. We're going over it with a fine-tooth comb."

The detective paused. "What we don't have is enough information on the man's psyche. For that, we've brought in a profiler from the FBI to assist us in developing a psychological profile, over and beyond what our own people have been telling us."

Hernandez nodded at an officer standing by the door. A moment later, a tall thirty-something African American man walked to the front of the room.

"This is FBI Agent Jeremy Haskell," Hernandez said. "He'll be joining our team. Hopefully, he can give us some valuable info that we can use to help catch our killer. . . ."

Deidre gazed at the handsome profiler with a 360 waves hairstyle as he said some opening remarks. She wondered if he and Spencer had crossed paths when Spencer was with the FBI. Maybe Jeremy could contribute something that might tell them what their killer was thinking. And where he was hiding.

Hal listened intently to Jeremy Haskell give what amounted to a pep talk, before glancing at Deidre, who seemed to be hanging on to the profiler's every word. Much like Hal suspected, Haskell's former colleague,

Spencer Berry, had entranced her. He knew Deidre was seeing Berry, in spite of her best efforts to keep it under wraps. One of his officers checking up on Deidre, as instructed, had spotted Berry leaving her house early one morning.

Hal was not about to tell Deidre who she should or shouldn't date. Even if he felt she could do better than the former FBI psychologist turned professor. But Deidre had made her choice—and it wasn't him. He would have to live with that and would continue to respect her as a police spokeswoman, artist, and female friend, of which Hal had too few in his life.

He might have been able to start a friendship with Gigi, but Hal suspected she was not interested in going down that path now that she had used him to cheat on her boyfriend. For his part, Hal was trying to put Gigi behind him, even if their one-night stand had been much needed and unforgettable.

Hal turned his thoughts back to Deidre choosing Spencer Berry over him as her love interest. *If that prick ever steps out of line with Deidre, he'll have to deal with me.*

When Haskell had finished, it was Hal's turn to brief the task force and take questions.

He drove toward his destination, listening to some contemporary jazz music while reflecting on the double life he led. There was the side that played by all the rules and put on a damned good show for everyone to see. Then there was his very dark side that made up his own rules as he went along. Unfortunately, for the women who happened to capture his attention when the mood hit him, it was the dark side that always prevailed.

Maybe destiny had a way of catching up to you one way or the other. It was his destiny to kill; it was theirs to be killed. And neither side could change the inevitable, only accept it and suffer the consequences.

He was prepared to do that whether his chosen ones were or not.

I can't help myself, so why even try. I just go along for the ride and enjoy every step of the way.

He intended to do just that without looking back.

That included going after the woman from the train who now had a name to go with the face. Deidre Lawrence. He'd gotten wind of who she was quite by accident. There was a small article in the paper about the artist who'd gotten rave reviews for a showing she'd done. The article had a photograph of Ms. Lawrence, whom he would recognize anywhere.

Thanks for saving me the trouble of finding you. Soon, when you least expect it, I'll have you right where I want you. And you'll have nowhere to escape—except in death. But not 'til I've had my fun and oh so much more with you, Deidre.

He brought the car to a stop, took a deep breath, and readied himself for the appointment he had.

THIRTY-EIGHT

Deidre stared at the girl who looked very familiar. She was sitting in the back seat of a red Honda Accord in the next aisle over at the gas station. The driver, a chunky African American man of medium height with a shaved head, was standing by the driver's side door, cleaning his windshield.

Once again, Deidre looked at the African American girl of eight or nine with short dark hair, and she looked back at her with a blank stare. Suddenly, Deidre could picture the girl with pigtails and it began to sink in.

It was Keaare Sanchez—the girl who had been abducted in front of her house earlier in the month. In spite of the Amber Alert, she seemed to have disappeared into thin air with no leads as to her whereabouts.

Until now.

Deidre turned her head quickly when the driver looked her way suspiciously. She put on some lipstick to make it appear that she was oblivious to him and who she was sure was the kidnapped girl in his car that had replaced the dark van the kidnapper had used.

Only after the man got back into the car did Deidre take a breath. She abandoned her plans to get gas 'til later, knowing that what she did next could very well be the difference between life and death for what had to be a very frightened girl.

She grabbed her cell phone and punched in Hal's direct line at the police bureau.

"Yeah, Iverson."

"Hi, Hal. It's Deidre. I think I may have found our missing girl. . . ."

"You think?"

"I'm pretty sure," she said, going out on a limb, figuring she'd rather be wrong than to let the real girl slip through her fingers.

"Where is she?" he asked.

"She's in the back seat of a red Honda Accord at a gas station on 133rd Avenue." Deidre noticed that the car was on the move. "The driver's leaving now, headed east—"

"Did you happen to get a plate number?"

"I wasn't in a position to," she said, pulling out of the station. "But I'll see if I can follow them and get it."

"Not a smart move, Deidre," Hal grumbled. "You're *not* a cop, remember? If he is our kidnapper, we don't want to put the girl at greater risk. Not to mention yourself."

Deidre frowned. "Isn't she at risk right now while the kidnapper has her in his custody? What if he melts into the woodwork again or changes cars again? I couldn't live with myself if something happened to her and I never tried to do anything to help her." Deidre thought about her son, and the things she might have done differently to prevent him from being a crime victim. Maybe in some strange way she was meant to discover Keaare Sanchez, to honor Adam and his life that was cut short.

"Good point," Hal said. "See if you can get all or part of his plate number, without being made."

"I'll be careful," she promised, grateful that he was allowing her to do this.

"In the meantime, I'll dispatch officers in the vicinity to see if we can catch up with the vehicle you've described."

Deidre realized that a car had slipped between her and the Accord, which was probably a good thing, in case the kidnapper had noticed that she was tailing him.

It wasn't 'til the other vehicle turned that she was behind the Accord, but at a safe distance. She was still able to make out the license plate number and relay it to Hal. "BJF 572."

"All right, you're done," he ordered her. "Now get out of there and leave the rest up to us."

"Yes, sir," she said sarcastically.

"I'll let you know what happens."

Deidre hung up and was about to drive away and let the police do their job when the Honda turned onto a side street. Against her better judgment, she decided impromptu to follow it.

The car drove above the speed limit another three blocks before pulling into the driveway of a detached bungalow with a courtyard. Deidre slowed down and parked alongside the curb several residences away. She watched the man and girl go up some steps. The man looked back toward the street and, instinctively, Deidre ducked her head as if he was zeroing in on her.

After a moment, she lifted up and saw no sign of him or girl.

Deidre cringed. *Now what do I do? I'm not a detective and blatantly went against Hal's orders. I hope I don't get fired for this.*

It was a chance she decided was worth taking. She had no intention of confronting the man, but thought it was her duty as a concerned citizen to do the right thing.

She phoned Hal and told him where the suspect and girl were located.

If he was pissed, Hal didn't indicate such. "The car's registered to Jason Foxx. He's a known sex offender and ex-con. We had him downtown on this case, but his alibi checked out and he doesn't own a van. Turns out his aunt does. As such, we didn't have enough to hold him. Now I wish to hell we had, as it looks like he's our man."

"I hope so." Deidre hated to think about what he might have done to the girl. Right now, the girl's survival was most important, then they could assess her other needs.

"Just sit tight," Hal said, surprising her. "We'll be there in a minute."

Deidre hung up. She considered calling Spencer for moral support, but didn't want to get him involved in another police matter. He already had enough to deal with.

She glanced at the house again. The occupants were seemingly staying put for the moment, apparently feeling secure from detection or apprehension.

While keeping watch, Deidre allowed her mind to drift off again to Spencer. They had been seeing each other a lot of late. She couldn't remember sex being as fun and fulfilling as it was with him. Had she forgotten what it was like with Marshall? Or had Spencer simply raised the bar, making it hard to compare him with anyone else?

The knock on the driver's side window nearly gave Deidre a heart attack. She was sure it was the kidnapper, who had figured out she followed him and was prepared to make her pay for it.

But when Deidre looked, she saw that it was Hal. She took a breath and let down the window tentatively.

"You don't follow orders very well, do you?" Hal's eyes narrowed sharply at her.

"I usually try to," she said, knowing how lame that sounded.

"I believe you." He glanced over at the house. "Good job, Deidre. I guess working for the police has rubbed off on you—in a good way."

She smiled, accepting the compliment. "So what happens now?"

"Now we go rescue a little girl and reunite her with her mother, while taking down a man who doesn't deserve to be on the streets anymore."

Deidre watched the police and SWAT team move into position.

"You've done your job, Deidre," Hal said. "Now go home."

"Okay, I'm leaving," she said, even though she wanted to be present to see how it all played out. But she wasn't going to push the envelope any further, content to let the police take it from here while saying a little prayer for Keaare Sanchez.

THIRTY-NINE

Spencer stood in front of his class wondering if his students were absorbing everything he was saying. Or were they drifting off from time to time, as he was, caught up in thoughts about his daughter, her scary episode with the rat, and playing footsies in bed with Deidre.

He noted a tall dark-skinned man in his late thirties come in the back door and take a seat. At first glance, Spencer thought it was a freeloader looking for some psychological wisdom. But as he honed in on the face staring back at him, Spencer realized the man was no stranger. He was someone from his past, paying him an unexpected visit.

Jeremy Haskell.

Somehow, the notion unnerved Spencer, as if he were seeing his brother again. Jeremy had more or less died in Spencer's life in direct correlation to Wesley's death.

'Til now.

Spencer went through the motions before letting the class go ten minutes early. The only one left seated was his former FBI colleague.

Spencer walked toward him. "Is the FBI doing surveillance in my classroom now?"

Jeremy chuckled. "Something like that." He got to his feet, which made him about two inches taller than Spencer. "Looks like this classroom stuff really suits you, man."

"Yeah," Spencer agreed. "It's probably where I belong right now."

Jeremy gazed at him, sticking out his hand. "So does
that mean you aren't ruling out returning to the FBI at
some point?"

Spencer shook Jeremy's hand warily. The two had
come up through the FBI ranks together and been
pretty much inseparable for a time. This in spite of
being essentially in competition every step of the way.
But things went south once Spencer left the agency, as
if they had never been tight. He took part of the blame
for that, being too absorbed in his own life and times
to keep the lines of communication open. So what was
Jeremy's excuse?

It made Spencer all the more curious as to why the
man was in his classroom on this day in particular,
given that he could have contacted him at any time, but
obviously chose otherwise. "Don't tell me that this is
what brings my old buddy around for the first time in
ages—some misguided attempt to lure me out of early
retirement?"

Jeremy laughed. "You've been watching too many of
those TV law enforcement shows. Far be it for me to
try to talk you out of anything. Especially if this is what
makes you happy—"

"I've been happier," Spencer muttered, thinking
about a time before his brother's death and failed marriage. Then he thought about the sheer joy he got from
his daughter and Deidre of late. Neither of which he
took for granted. "But that's another story. I'm much
more interested in *yours*. What the hell are you doing
here, Jeremy?" he decided to ask bluntly, sensing there
was more to it than mere happenstance.

Jeremy grinned. "Thought I might buy you a drink,
buddy—for old times' sake. Anything wrong with that?"

"Not at all, if I believed for one second that's what brought you my way. But something tells me it isn't."

"You're too damn suspicious for your own good," Jeremy said with a straight face.

"I doubt that." Spencer was only mildly curious, which was enough to go along for the ride. "Where did you have in mind for that drink?"

"There's a watering hole just outside of campus—the Oasis Brewpub."

Spencer had been there once or twice. "You're on. Let me just gather my stuff."

The place was packed, but they managed to get a table. Jeremy ordered a pitcher of beer.

"So how's the wife?" Spencer asked, knowing that Jeremy had married his longtime girlfriend last year. He hadn't been invited to the wedding, which seemed to go along with the distance that had built between them.

"She's expecting—four months along now."

"Congratulations." Spencer thought back to when Fiona was pregnant with Charity and how beautiful she had looked. He imagined Deidre would look even better pregnant and be every bit the mother she had been to her son.

"That may be a bit premature. Connie's been pretty bitchy lately and I'm not sure it has anything to do with being pregnant. I think she's still trying to figure out what she wants to do with her life, besides being a mom. Unfortunately, I can't help much because she wants to do things her way and in her own time."

Spencer tasted his beer. "I wouldn't worry about it. Probably just first-year marriage jitters. I'm sure it'll work out."

"You think?" Jeremy titled his head. "Just like your marriage, right?"

"Ouch." Spencer winced as if he'd punched him in the stomach. "Let's not even go there."

"Sorry. I guess going down memory lane has its drawbacks."

"Yeah, in more ways than one." Spencer paused. "So why don't you tell me what the hell this is really about, Jeremy?"

He took a swig of beer and regarded Spencer. "Okay, I won't drag it out any longer. I've been assigned to the task force investigating the park serial killer."

Spencer was not too surprised to hear this, knowing that the local police often called upon the FBI to assist them whenever a case got too hot to handle alone. And this one certainly qualified.

"So what does that have to do with me?" he was almost afraid to ask.

Jeremy wiped his mouth with his sleeve. "As the best damned forensic psychologist I know, I was hoping to pick your brain a bit on what you think about this guy. I know you've been following the case. Unfortunately, I haven't. I've been too busy shuttling between here and Quantico for the past few months."

Indeed, Spencer had been keeping up with the police investigation, especially since he had known every victim thus far. Whether he liked it or not, catching this killer had become personal for him, even if he was not directly involved in the case.

Spencer collected his thoughts. "From what I've heard about the killer, I'd say he's pretty much a loner who gets his kicks out of catching women off guard, brutalizing them, and then killing them. He's probably either divorced, never married, or wishes he weren't; hates his mother, is unemployed or dissatisfied with his job, and lives on the edge—even while presenting a far different picture to everyone else."

"Yeah, I've gathered that much," Jeremy said and hesitated, looking Spencer in the eye. "I understand that you've been acquainted with *all* of the victims. What's your take on that, *professor?*"

Spencer's temperature rose a few notches. "Are you accusing me of having something to do with these murders?"

Jeremy shook his head. "Not at all. I don't believe for one minute that you're involved in this, regardless of your familiarity with these women. You wouldn't do something so heinous. Besides, you have solid alibis for your whereabouts for each of the murders that have checked out."

"So what are we talking about then?" Spencer knitted his brows, waiting for the punch line, if there was one.

"I'm just trying to make some sense of this peculiarity, that's all," Jeremy said, shrugging. "I mean, what are the odds that one man would be indirectly tied to all of the victims, but not be the one who's killing them?"

"Maybe better than you think," Spencer suggested flatly. "Yeah, I've known all of the victims, but not equally. I never dated any of them, and barely knew some other than by association, such as working at the college or seeing them at the grocery store. My point is, I'm sure there are others who are also at least loosely linked to the victims."

"None that the police are aware of," Jeremy pointed out.

"So the police may not have done their homework right," Spencer countered. "We both know they're far from infallible."

"That's true," Jeremy said. "Which is why they've brought me in."

Spencer leaned forward. "I think the killer probably has no direct ties to the victims, as is often the case with serial killers, aside from being the common denominator in their deaths."

Jeremy drummed his fingers on the table. "You don't think someone could have it out for you?"

Spencer had considered this at one point, but ruled it out. He had no enemies that he knew of. Not to mention, since he was not a bona fide suspect or closely involved with any of the victims, the killer gained nothing by murdering people he happened to be acquainted with.

He thought about Gayle and the rat episode—she was a stalker with an obsessive and mean-spirited personality. Could she have anything to do with the serial murders? Spencer ruled it out. Since they were going out while the murders were occurring, she had no reason to express such homicidal rage. Even then, this was clearly the work of a male and there was no evidence to indicate he had a female partner.

He eyed his old FBI comrade. "Unless the killer is you, Jeremy, I doubt there's someone out there who would take all these lives just to get under my skin."

Jeremy cocked a brow. "You think I want to get under your skin?"

Spencer drank more beer. "Never said that."

"What are you saying?"

"I'm saying that we were friends once. But, as soon as I called it quits with the Bureau, you called it quits with me. So, yeah, I guess that did get under my skin a long time ago."

Jeremy stared at him. "It's a two-way street. You left the FBI, not me. I thought you wanted to be left alone, to be cut off from that whole world, including someone who was supposed to be your damned friend."

"You thought wrong," Spencer said, sucking in a deep breath. "My beef was against the bureaucracy and my own inner demons—not my friends at the FBI. And certainly never you." He scratched his pate. "I suppose I felt sorry for myself and, in the process, cut myself off from people I never meant to."

"So we're both to blame," Jeremy said. "I guess I can live with that."

"Yeah, me too." Spencer wondered if it was too late to make up for lost time. Or maybe that was the point of this little get-together.

Jeremy finished his beer. "If the killer doesn't have a grudge against you, who do you think his anger is vented at, aside from the women themselves?"

Spencer knew that this time Jeremy was asking for his help as a criminal psychologist and not an adversary. He considered the question for a moment before responding. "Based on what I've heard about the killings and the method used, I'd have to say that he's using these poor women as tools to express his rage for everything that's gone wrong in his life."

"Such as?"

"Such as maybe being abused or mistreated as a child, being singled out unfairly—in his mind—for taunting, bullying, or disrespect, always seeming to come in second when it comes to women, if they pay attention to him at all, and he probably has trouble holding on to a job and blames everyone else for it." Spencer paused. "My guess is the killer is as much an opportunist as he is clever in pinpointing his targets, seeing it as payback for whatever beef he has with society or maybe women in particular."

"So you don't have any doubt that he'll just keep kill-ing 'til he's either caught or killed himself?" Jeremy wondered.

"Do you?" Spencer asked straightforwardly. "Why would he stop, when it seems like the bastard can do whatever he damn well pleases without anyone stand-ing in his way?"

"Yeah, I see your point," Jeremy said as he refilled his mug. "But there has to be a line drawn somewhere in the sand—even if he's gone totally berserk."

"I agree, there probably is. But only he knows where that line begins and ends." Spencer grabbed the pitcher. "Unfortunately, I doubt he'll volunteer the information 'til he's good and ready. And by then—unless you guys stop him—I'm afraid there's no telling how many more women will fall prey to his homicidal tendencies."

The thought didn't sit well with Spencer, though he knew it was even more burdensome for Jeremy and the rest of the task force who were being called upon to catch the Park Killer before any more lives were merci-lessly snuffed out. Jeremy, in particular, had his work cut out for him. He had to somehow strike a delicate balance between being a team player and using his FBI acumen in going after a brutal serial killer. Even if it meant stepping outside the line drawn by Lieutenant Iverson and his team. That included picking the brains of an ex–FBI comrade who was best equipped to see things as he did.

Spencer took that as a compliment, though he still wondered if Jeremy was over his head on this one. Or did he have an angle that could tear this case wide open?

FORTY

"Are you settling in pretty well there, honey?" Deidre's father asked her over the phone.

"Yes, Daddy, things are going great."

She saw no reason to worry him or her mother unnecessarily about things that had not been so great. Like dead bodies, rats, and stalkers. All part of life in the big city. Or so Deidre tried to convince herself, glancing at the painting she'd recently begun.

"That's good to hear. I figured as much, but you know your momma. She's always worried that you can't handle being on your own so far away from home."

"This is home for me now," she reminded him.

"I know and I'm proud of you for being able to get back on your feet. Marshall would be proud too."

Would he? Deidre had always depended on him, and he relished the hold he had over her. How would he really feel now about her newfound independence? Not to mention another wonderful man who was now part of her life.

"How are you doing, Daddy?" she asked, remembering his issues with high blood pressure and cholesterol. "You're taking good care of yourself, aren't you?"

"I see you've been talking to your momma about me."

"Hey, if we have to conspire to keep you healthy for years to come, so be it."

He gave a raspy chuckle, which Deidre had always loved when she was young. "Guess it's two against one, and I'm stuck in the middle."

"We wouldn't have it any other way."

"Neither would I," he admitted.

"So are you following doctor's orders and keeping your cholesterol and blood pressure in check?"

"Yeah, I'm doing what I have to, honey," he said. "Otherwise, you and your momma will never let me hear the end of it."

"That's right, we won't." Deidre smiled, and noted that another caller was on the line. "Hang on just a moment, Daddy." She connected to the second caller and saw on the caller ID that it was Spencer. Her heart skipped a beat. "Hello. I see you got my message."

"Message? . . ."

"I left it on your voice mail."

"Oh," he said. "Haven't listened to it today. I'm just leaving the college. Is something wrong?"

"Only missing you," she cooed warmly.

"I think I can rectify that." Spencer hummed. "What do you like on your pizza?"

"Pepperoni . . . and anchovies."

"Consider it done. I should be at your place in half an hour."

Deidre felt like kissing him that very minute, but would have to wait. "I'll see you then."

"You bet. Bye."

She allowed herself a moment of reverie and intimate thoughts before remembering that her father was still on the other line. "Daddy . . . ?"

"It's your mother, dear. Daddy got a bit restless and went out to do some work in the garage."

"Sorry about that," Deidre said guiltily.

"Don't be. You know your father, he has to be doing something with his hands all the time."

"Don't remind me," she said good-naturedly.

"You're just like him, you know," her mother said. "Only you're more comfortable with art supplies than a set of tools."

Deidre smiled and studied her latest artwork in the upstairs room that she had turned into a studio. "You know me too well."

"It's called being a mother with too much time on her hands."

Deidre glanced at the clock. "I really hate to cut this short, Momma, but I've got a pizza date to get ready for."

"Oh really?" Her mother's tone perked up. "What's his name?"

"Spencer Berry." It felt strange admitting that she was dating someone other than Marshall. But Deidre also saw it as liberating in living for today and not the past.

"Handsome name. Where did you meet?"

"Actually, right on my front porch," Deidre said.

"He's not a door-to-door salesman, is he?" Deidre detected the concern in her mother's voice, as if salesmen were somehow beneath her.

He did have to sell me on a dead body, but we won't go there. "Spencer teaches psychology at Sinclair Heights College. And he used to work for the FBI," Deidre added to impress her.

"That's a good, stable profession—and an interesting former career," her mother said.

Deidre could tell that she was at least halfway sold on Spencer. And she would be even more when and if she ever met him. "He seems to like it."

"And how well does he like you?"

"Well enough for now, I think." Deidre again peeked at the clock, giving her a perfect excuse to leave it there, before her mother could ask more prying questions. "I really have to go now. I'll talk to you later. Love you."

"I love you, too, sweetheart. Enjoy your pizza date with the professor."

Deidre disconnected and felt a little badly that she couldn't satisfy more of her mother's raging curiosity. But it was probably best for now that she not get her hopes up. At least not until Deidre knew if this was really going somewhere over the long haul or if it would end up being short and sweet, if not a bit sour, at the end of the day.

"I just wanted you to know I've been thinking about you a lot. Call me when you get the chance. Bye."

Spencer smiled after listening to his voice mail. He loved hearing Deidre's voice, even in a recorded message. He'd been thinking about her a lot too. How could he not? After a rough patch or two along the road, they seemed to be hitting it off nicely. He wondered if this could truly be the start of something wonderful. He wanted nothing more than to be in a long-term relationship, with the right woman. Deidre seemed to fit the bill in every way he could think of. All that was left was to let it happen naturally.

He parked behind her car in the driveway and grabbed the still hot pizza box.

Before he could ring the bell, Deidre opened the door. She was barefoot, wearing a tight-fitting T-shirt and cutoff jeans, making her look even more appetizing than the pizza.

"Right on time." Deidre flashed a smile and noticed how fine Spencer looked, as usual. She kissed his lips, enjoying their taste as the smell of pizza infiltrated her nose. "That smells yummy."

"So do you, baby."

She batted her eyes teasingly. "Flattery can only get you so far."

"I'm counting on it being just far enough."

"Oh you are, are you?" Deidre felt an electric jolt run up and down her body. "We'll just have to see about that."

"Indeed." Spencer grinned amorously and snuck in another kiss before setting the pizza on the table that had already been set. A bottle of white wine sat beside two wineglasses.

"Hope your day was at least half as interesting as mine," Deidre said, grabbing a slice of pizza.

"It probably was." Spencer poured the wine thoughtfully. "Why don't you tell me about yours first."

"Well, I helped locate an abducted girl."

"The one that caused the recent Amber Alert?"

"Yes," Deidre said. "Believe it or not, I spotted her in a car at a gas station and recognized her, then followed them to a house. From there on, it was a matter of the police closing in on the suspect."

Spencer gazed at her. "Congratulations on being at the right place, right time, and making it stand up."

"Thanks." She smiled. "I'm just glad that the girl— who will need medical and mental health treatment after her ordeal—was reunited with her mother and is home, safe and sound."

"I agree, knowing how often the outcome is much worse."

"Tell me about it." Deidre had certainly heard about many missing kids who never came home.

"So is Iverson ready to hire you for the force?" Spencer joked.

She chuckled. "Not quite. In fact, he chided me for getting involved in police work, but seemed to get over it quickly with a satisfying result."

"I'd say Iverson and I agree on this one." Spencer didn't want to see her get hurt. "I think in the future, you're better off leaving police work to the people who get paid to go after criminals."

"You mean like you did when you went after a gang member *twice,* not knowing if he had a gun the second time?" Deidre challenged him.

Spencer cleared his throat. "Point taken. Guess we've both been bitten by the adventurous bug, making us use our hearts sometimes instead of our heads."

"Is that so bad?" she asked. "Using our hearts?"

He met her gaze. "Depends on if we're using our hearts for the right reasons."

"And what if we are?"

"Then I'd say let's jump right in and see what happens." Spencer hoped he hadn't just locked himself into something he couldn't get out of, though maybe he didn't want to.

"Might be a good idea," Deidre agreed. Or a bad idea, if both parties weren't on the same page when the book was finished.

"We'll see about that," Spencer said, reaching for another slice of pizza.

Deidre was thoughtful. Yes, they would. All that they really needed was willingness to open up their hearts to each other honestly without being afraid to fail. Whether they both had that in them remained to be seen.

"So tell me about your interesting day," she said. "And please don't say that more dead rats showed up at your house."

Spencer shook his head. "No more rats, thank goodness." He washed down the pizza with more wine. "Well, I ran into an old friend. Or more like he ran into me."

Deidre dabbed a napkin at the corners of her lips. "His name wouldn't happen to be Jeremy Haskell, would it?"

Spencer's head snapped back in surprise. "Do your considerable talents also include mind reading?"

She laughed. "Not quite. I sat in on the meeting yesterday when they introduced Jeremy to the task force as an FBI profiler. Something told me that your paths might have crossed."

Spencer's eyes twinkled. "Yeah, a few times."

"Is he the friend you spoke of from Clarksdale, Mississippi?"

"One and the same," he said.

"I take it Jeremy wanted to solicit your opinion about the Park Killer case?" she guessed.

"Right again. Including questioning me about how I happened to know all the victims of the killer."

Deidre's eyes widened. "He doesn't think you had anything to do with the murders, does he?" She recalled that Hal and Zack had their own suspicions at one stage; and she herself had been no less guilty of uncertainty, 'til she'd gotten to know Spencer. So why would Jeremy Haskell be suspicious, unless he'd forgotten the character of his former FBI comrade?

"No, I don't think so," Spencer said. "At least not after we agreed that I could account for my whereabouts during the time of each murder . . . not to mention had no motive for wanting these women dead. Mainly, he just wanted to compare thoughts on the psychological profile of the killer."

"Were you able to help him?"

"Don't know if it helped or not, quite honestly, but I gave him my candid assessment of the serial murderer and his possible motivations for the killings. Whether he chooses to use it in developing his profile of the killer is up to him."

"So what happened between you two?" Deidre asked curiously.

Spencer's eyebrows arched. "What makes you think anything happened?"

"Well you originally mentioned Jeremy as a friend in past tense. If I'm overstepping my bounds, just say so."

Spencer supposed he was being a little oversensitive about water under the bridge. Also, he wanted an open relationship with Deidre. Meaning no suppressed memories.

"You're not," he said softly. "Jeremy and I had what you could call a mix-up in communication at a time when feelings were easily hurt and misunderstood both ways. I think it's behind us now."

"I see." Deidre wanted to know as much about Spencer as he was willing to share and was happy to see him open up some. She was sure that more would come in time—both ways.

Meanwhile, they had a connection that was already working in ways that made her happier than she had been in a long time.

FORTY-ONE

"Sounds to me like Spencer's someone you could easily fall in love with," Sabrina said. "If you allowed yourself to. . . ."

They were lying on tables at the Crystal Spa being worked on by massage therapists, who Deidre hoped weren't listening to their discussion.

"If I allowed myself to?" she repeated. "I think it's a bit soon for that." Or was it? Deidre meandered back and forth on the subject, afraid to feel anything that wasn't reciprocated.

"Love doesn't have a timetable, Deidre. When it happens, it just does."

Deidre didn't doubt that for one minute. She quickly turned the spotlight on Sabrina. "What about you, girl-friend? When is this love of your life going to material-ize?"

Sabrina hummed. "I couldn't say, honestly. I haven't been as lucky as you have to nail down a gorgeous hunk of a man who really does it for me. But that doesn't mean I won't keep trying to find Mr. Terrific In Every Way."

Deidre felt the therapist digging her strong fingers into her back and shoulder muscles. She closed her eyes to enjoy it, which allowed her the time to consider the prospect of falling in love with Spencer or anyone else. Was she ready for this big step? Or was she just lusting after someone along with great sex? Had she gotten sufficiently past her marriage to begin to move into even more uncharted territory?

Deidre suspected that what she felt for Spencer was something bordering on love. She needed more time to assess her feelings and ascertain if what he felt for her measured up or if, when the dust settled, they would be like two ships passing in the night, destined to never connect on an emotional level.

Gayle had followed Deidre's car to the spa, waiting for her and the other woman to go inside. After the lot had emptied, Gayle decided this was a good time for some payback. Armed with a six-inch knife, she stayed down low to avoid detection.

Reaching the car, Gayle dug the knife into a tire 'til air began to hiss out. She completed the task with the other three tires. Then she ran the knife liberally and randomly across the top and sides of the car, relishing seeing its finish hideously tarnished.

Finally, Gayle removed a can of white spray paint from her pocket and spelled out the word "BITCH" on the hood and "ROT IN HELL" on the trunk.

Gayle smiled crookedly at her handiwork. She wished she could see the look on the face of Spencer's whore when getting a load of the damage done to her car.

No free rides, bitch. When you go after my man, you have to be prepared to pay the piper.

And I'm not through with you yet.

She lowered herself again and crept away, staying close to some tall bushes 'til she'd left the parking lot. Her car was waiting a block away.

Gayle put the knife and spray paint in a plastic bag, and put it in her trunk. She drove to a nearby apartment complex garbage Dumpster and tossed the bag in among the other rubbish.

On the way to class, Gayle contemplated what her next move would be in making sure Spencer regretted the day he ever walked out on her and their relationship.

"How's my little girl today?" Spencer asked over his cell phone, set on speaker, en route to the store.

"I have a tummy ache," Charity moaned. "Mommy thinks it was something I ate."

"Oh, I'm sorry about that, sweetheart." It pained him to think that his daughter could ever be in discomfort. "I'm sure you'll get over it soon."

"Yeah, I think so too."

"I have someone here who might cheer you up a bit."

"Who, Daddy?"

Spencer could hear the anticipation in her voice. He looked to the back seat, where Sky was sitting, and put the phone toward him. "Say hello to Charity, boy."

As though on cue, Sky barked loudly into the phone. When Spencer got back on, Charity was giggling. "See, told you that would do the trick."

"You're right, Daddy. I love Sky."

"He loves you too, just as I do, with all my heart."

"I know. Love you too."

"Well, put your mother back on the phone. And get some rest, Charity."

"I will. Bye, Daddy."

Spencer made a left turn at the light.

"Hey," Fiona said.

"You didn't tell me Charity was sick."

"No reason to. Children get stomachaches all the time. It's part of growing up and discovering what foods work and which ones don't."

"Yeah, I suppose." He was pensive. "Is she still hav-ing nightmares about the dead rat?"

"I think she's gotten over it," Fiona said. "But I haven't. If you're going to give Charity a party in the future, you'd better get your act together as far as the people you choose to associate with who would do such a horrible thing."

"You know I feel terrible about what happened," Spencer muttered guiltily. "But I can't change the past. And I damn well can't read people's minds insofar as what they may be capable of." Maybe he should have been able to where it concerned Gayle.

"I thought that's what you were supposed to be good at to be a good criminal psychologist." Fiona snorted.

Spencer knew she'd hit a soft spot. "I'm not perfect, Fiona, and never claimed to be. I messed up here and I'm sorry for it."

"I knew Gayle was trouble from the moment I saw her," his ex-wife said almost gloatingly. "Too bad your mind was obviously elsewhere."

"Get off my case, Fiona." Spencer gritted his teeth, hating that he'd misread Gayle's psychological state, given her clingy behavior early on. This had caused his daughter unnecessary trauma. But that didn't excuse Fiona in using it as an excuse to bitch at him. "Who I date is my business."

"It becomes my business when that person tries to hurt my daughter!"

"She's *my* daughter too!" Spencer reminded her, as if she'd forgotten. "No one got hurt—except the rat." He drew in a deep breath. "In any event, I've had the locks changed so this shouldn't be a problem anymore." He could only hope that was true, assuming Gayle had got in with a key she had made. But at this point he wouldn't put much past her, in spite of the restraining order she'd instituted supposedly to keep them apart.

"Too little, too late," Fiona scoffed. "The damage has already been done to Charity. One can only hope your latest lady doesn't turn out to be a nutcase too."

Spencer fumed, wishing she hadn't drawn Deidre into this conversation, if you could call it that. "Deidre's nothing like Gayle, okay?"

"If you say so."

"Why the hell are we having this conversation anyway?" he questioned, frowning. "We're divorced, *remember?* Maybe it's time you focused more on your dating life and stay out of mine."

Fiona sighed noisily into the phone. "Yeah, whatever."

Spencer approached the giant supermarket. "I have to go. If Charity needs me for anything, let me know."

"Fine." She hung up without so much as a good-bye.

What's her problem? Spencer could only hazard a guess. *Are things not going well between her and Clint, so she needs to blow things out of proportion regarding someone I used to date?*

In spite of that, Spencer could not afford to underestimate Gayle and what she was capable of doing beyond what she'd already done. He hoped she'd satisfied her thirst for vengeance and moved on, yet didn't feel very secure about that. For now, he just wanted to focus on the present and what could turn into a bright future with Deidre.

Spencer parked the car and let down the back window a bit. "Be right back, Sky," he told the dog. "Try not to miss me too much."

Deidre felt the heat soaking away her impurities as she lay in an herbal wrap. Across from her was Sabrina, who looked as though she would die from perspiration and the steaming sheets wound tightly around her body.

"Hope you can survive this," Deidre teased her. *Hope I can too.*

Sabrina cracked a smile. "Hey, if we can survive in this city with a serial killer on the loose, we can survive almost anything."

"I agree." Deidre closed her eyes and breathed in the fragrant blend of lavender, orange peel, and peppermint. She imagined for a moment making love to Spencer and sweating up a storm in another erotic way. She luxuriated in the fantasy.

Her thoughts returned to survival in Sinclair Heights where a killer bent on debasing, sexual assault, and murder was targeting women. No one was safe, no matter where they lived. Not while he was out there. Somewhere.

"Maybe we need to form a neighborhood watch group or something," suggested Sabrina. "That way, we could all keep an eye on each other while this madman is creeping around."

"I think that's an excellent idea," said Deidre in complete agreement. In fact, such groups had already formed in the neighborhood, though only loosely organized and inconsistent in practice. "I can talk to Hal about it."

"Good. And I'll speak to Sam." Samuel Arness was a Sinclair Heights City Council member, a poet, and one of Sabrina's past boyfriends. "Even though we're not dating anymore, we're still friends and want what's best for the community."

"Yeah, like reclaiming our streets again," Deidre declared.

"Not to mention making the park a place where runners like me no longer have to be afraid to do our thing."

"Even we non-runners could use a break." Deidre turned over in her cocoon. These days she actually felt safest in the park when accompanied by Spencer and Sky. Not a bad twosome when a woman needed to feel at ease, even under the toughest of circumstances, from killers and gangbangers.

They left the spa at 3:30 P.M. and headed across the lot. Deidre felt as if the massage and wrap treatments were just what she needed to be reinvigorated while also relaxing her mind. She was still on this high when she saw the horror-stricken look on Sabrina's face.

"What happened to your car?" she shrieked.

Deidre looked at her car ahead of them and could see that the tires on one side had been flattened and the finish was scarred like someone had deliberately taken a knife or razor to it.

"What on earth . . . ?" Deidre raced to the car and saw that the damage was even worse than she thought. All four tires were flat with slash marks, the exterior was badly scratched, and spray paint had been used to write in capital letters "BITCH" and "ROT IN HELL" on the hood and trunk, respectively.

"Who would've done such a thing?" Sabrina asked.

Deidre was trembling as she faced her friend and thought of the dead rat episode at Charity's birthday party. "I can only think of one person. . . ."

FORTY-TWO

Spencer had just left the store with a bag of dog food and some groceries when his cell phone rang. Freeing up a hand, he lifted the phone from his pocket and saw that it was Deidre. He lit up immediately and answered.

"Been thinking about you too, baby," Spencer began.

"I'm sort of stranded at the moment," Deidre said in a shaky voice, dismissing his charm. "We were wondering if you could pick us up."

"We?" He sensed that something was going on beyond her words.

"Sabrina and I are at the Crystal Spa on Broadway and Appoline Street." Deidre sighed. "My car was vandalized to the point of being rendered unusable right now. . . ."

"I'll be there in ten minutes."

Spencer tossed the groceries in the trunk and got behind the wheel. "Prepare yourself for some company, boy." Sky barked and Spencer drove off, wondering exactly what—or who—was behind this vandalism.

He pulled into the spa parking lot and spotted Deidre and Sabrina talking with a couple of uniformed officers. He glanced at Deidre's vehicle. Spencer could tell that someone had worked it over pretty good. The first person to come to mind was Gayle.

Deidre practically ran into Spencer's arms when she saw him approaching. She was crying. "I'm sorry. I know it's just a car . . . but seeing this senseless destruction is just . . ."

Spencer held her, sharing her distress and wishing he could make it go away. "Don't apologize for what someone else did, Deidre. You have every right to be pissed." He looked over at the officers, who were talking to Sabrina. "Did anyone see who did this?"

"Apparently there were no witnesses."

Meaning no one saw Gayle add yet another crazy thing to her stalking of Deidre and him. A vein bulged in Spencer's temple.

Deidre wiped her eyes. The car vandalism brought her back in time to the attempted carjacking that led to the deaths of her husband and son, while leaving her slightly wounded. She wondered if she was cursed for some reason. Or was this incident entirely avoidable?

She favored Spencer's hardened face. "I know what you're thinking: that Gayle is behind this—"

"Should I be thinking otherwise?" he asked doubtfully. That woman would obviously stop at nothing to make their lives miserable.

Before Deidre could answer, the police officers joined them, along with Sabrina. Spencer was introduced as Deidre's boyfriend.

The older, heavier officer looked at him. "As we were telling Ms. Lawrence and Ms. Murray, we have every reason to believe that some local vandals are responsible for the destruction of Ms. Lawrence's vehicle."

Spencer frowned. "Every reason?"

"Yeah," said the younger, thinner cop. "There's been a rash of these types of crimes in the neighborhood recently. With kids getting restless for summer break, this is how some of them choose to get their kicks."

"Why couldn't they have chosen someone else's car?" Deidre asked with irritation.

"It's usually a random thing, ma'am. They tend to go after any car they find, with the intent to do major damage with minimal risk of being seen."

"So what are you doing to put a stop to it?" Spencer demanded, though still not convinced they were on the right track.

The older officer jutted his chin. "We've got some extra patrols out, and actively investigate every incident and file a report. But I'd be lying if I told you we could catch all of these vandals in the act. We're too understaffed with budget cuts and all. . . ." He looked at Deidre. "Real sorry about your car. Maybe we'll get lucky and find the punks who did it."

"I hope so," Deidre said with a sneer. "They don't deserve to get away with this. It's bad enough that we have to contend with muggers and serial killers. Now we can't even enjoy a day at the spa without someone trashing the car!"

"Believe me, we understand how you feel," the younger officer claimed, and glanced at his partner.

Spencer doubted they did, but knew their hands were tied. So were his, short of any solid evidence to link this to Gayle.

The older officer handed Deidre his card. "If you need to speak with us about this or have any further questions, feel free to call."

"Thanks," Deidre said, knowing they were doing the best they could, given so little to work with. Unfortunately, no matter how she sliced it, her car was in for some major repair work. Thank goodness her insurance would cover it. Healing the emotional wounds inflicted upon her would not be quite as simple.

Deidre's back was flat against the wall and her legs were wrapped tightly around Spencer's waist as he made his way into her. She winced for an instant as he moved inside and it quickly turned to sheer pleasure.

They were in the hallway between his bedroom and a spare room, never making it to the bed after she'd had her car towed and they dropped Sabrina off at home.

"Maybe this isn't such a good idea," Deidre said between smothering kisses, feeling guilty that she should turn to sex after her car had been all but ruined.

"Can you think of a better idea?" Spencer brushed his fingertips across her breasts, hoping to take their minds off more troubling things.

She moaned. "Maybe not."

"Neither can I." He held her buttocks and brought their bodies closer together. "Besides, why deny ourselves because of things that are beyond our control?"

"You're right." Deidre held the back of Spencer's head firmly to keep his mouth from getting away. She kissed him with a burning passion, musing that this seemed to be the one thing that was absolutely right in her life at this time. She brought her legs farther up Spencer's back, feeling the heat sizzling between them. Deidre wanted—needed—him so badly that she could think of nothing else but the moment at hand.

"We're right—for each other," Spencer whispered, his orgasm about to come. He tasted the wine of Deidre's tongue and thrust harder and faster, as her body demanded, and his was more than willing to accommodate.

"Oh yes, most definitely!" Deidre practically shouted for the world to hear. The throbbing between her legs intensified and she needed it to be relieved more than ever.

With a guttural sound escaping his lips, Deidre clung to Spencer, absorbing his powerful, spasmodic climax even as she experienced one equally potent as it rippled throughout her entire body. When it was over, both were spent and neither apologetic.

Spencer kissed Deidre generously. "That was wonderful . . . and getting hotter every time."

She kissed him back. "Then I guess we'd better be extra careful. Wouldn't want anyone to get burned."

"Afraid it's too late for that. Every time I'm with you, I feel on fire." He kissed her again, probing with his tongue.

"Same here," Deidre admitted, which concerned her as much as it enthralled her. She didn't want the feeling to go away only to be replaced by emptiness. She pulled back, exercising some self-restraint. "I think I could use a shower right about now to cool off."

Even if he wished they could forget about the rest of the world and just concentrate on each other from now on, Spencer knew that wasn't possible. But he could still dream and enjoy every moment they had together as though it were their last. He gave Deidre one more kiss, savoring the feel of her soft lips on his, before separating from her.

"I think we could both use a cool shower now," Spencer said, the perspiration of intimacy coating his body like armor.

Beneath the brim of his cap, he watched as she jogged through the park. Even though she stuck to the lighted pathways, he could tell that she was being extra cautious, as if sensing danger.

With good reason. He knew that her time on this earth was about to run out.

He kept his distance, aware that she was not a lone runner this night—perhaps making her more courageous, if not wary.

He kept the cap down low over his head so as not to show his face to anyone who might be able to identify him and thwart his plans. Jogging at a steady pace, he was easily able to keep her in sight without attracting attention. Soon it would be time to put the woman out of her misery. But not until he'd had his fun with her.

FORTY-THREE

Deidre was back at home, curled up on the couch, reading a book. She tried not to think about what happened to her car, and found it almost impossible not to think about making love to Spencer this afternoon and wishing it could have gone on forever. But that wasn't very realistic. Was it? Could what they had really go on forever—unlike either of their marriages?

Whoa, now. Who said anything about a second marriage? First, they had to establish a *serious* relationship before crossing that path. Or were they doing just that?

Let's just keep a proper perspective and not get in too deep too soon, so you end up getting hurt, despite your best intentions.

Deidre flipped the page just as the phone rang. She grabbed it off the coffee table. Sabrina was the caller.

Deidre uncurled her legs. "Hi there."

"Hey, girl. Sorry again about your car," Sabrina said, sounding a bit winded.

"So am I, but what can you do, except curse the ones responsible and move on."

"You're right," Sabrina said. "But it still pisses me off just thinking about it. Talk about spoiling one's day."

"Tell me about it." Deidre heard what sounded like shuffling. "Where are you?"

"Pelle Park. I thought after all that excitement today, I needed a release. Nothing beats a good run. So here I am."

"Alone?" Deidre asked with alarm.

"Not really. There's lots of people around. Also, my current Ugandan beau, Kwame, is supposed to join me any minute now. Then what happens is anyone's guess. . . ."

"Hmm . . . I can only imagine," Deidre teased, glowing with more thoughts about hot sex with Spencer.

More shuffling noise, then Sabrina said, "You know, my mind may be playing tricks on me, but I could almost swear that someone's following me."

"What?" Fear rose in Deidre's throat.

"Well, it's just that I think I saw this man wearing a cap when I first started running and I've seen him here and there several times since. But I don't see him now." Sabrina gave a nervous chuckle. "Guess I must have been more freaked out than I realized from talking about the Park Killer earlier, not to mention the hatchet job on your car. Don't mind me. . . ."

Deidre stood up as if she'd sat on a pin, sensing more to this than Sabrina may have even realized. "Listen to me, Sabrina, *trust* your instincts. If you think this man with the cap has been following you, he probably is—and for all the wrong reasons."

Sabrina breathed into the phone. "Now who's getting paranoid? This man looks nothing like the one in the sketch, although admittedly I haven't seen much of his face. I know he definitely doesn't have a beard. Which makes him safe, I suppose. . . ."

Deidre was suspicious. "So the person, if he is a killer, and the man in the sketch, could have shaved his face."

"Are you trying to scare me?" Sabrina asked unevenly.

"Yes, I am!" Deidre made no bones about it. "I want you to get out of there *now*, Sabrina, please!"

"All right, all right, I'm going. I'll call Kwame and tell him to come to my place instead."

"Good idea. And call me when you get home, so I'll know you made it in one piece."

"I will." Sabrina's voice drifted in and out. "Glad you moved to Sinclair Heights, because I really like having you as a dear friend and someone to look out for my welfare."

"Same here." More than once Sabrina had expressed concern about her living in that big house alone and within a stone's throw of where a dead body had been found.

As far as Deidre was concerned, it was far better for them to look after each other when alive than dead.

Feeling unsettled about the whole thing, she dialed Spencer's number after saying good-bye to Sabrina. He picked up on the third ring.

"I hate to bother you again today . . ." she began.

"Never a bother when you call, Deidre," Spencer insisted. "I certainly can't complain about the first time today. What's up?"

Deidre explained her anxiety about Sabrina running in the park and possibly being pursued. "It may be absolutely nothing to worry about, but—"

"You will worry anyway 'til you know she's safe and sound," Spencer finished.

"Exactly."

"Have you called Hal about this?"

"No, because there's been no crime yet," Deidre uttered meekly. "And, according to Sabrina, the man she saw looks quite a bit different than the one the police are currently looking for."

Deidre was hesitant to phone Hal prematurely every time she had an inkling. It was bad enough that they had yet to locate the bearded man, calling into question whether or not he really was the Park Killer or just some homeless person looking for food or money who vanished into the streets.

"So maybe they're looking for the wrong man," Spencer said, reading her mind. "Or he could easily have changed his appearance if he felt the authorities were on to him. I say you should call it in, just to be on the safe side. I'm sure Hal would appreciate it."

Deidre found his logic hard to ignore, especially with the stakes being so high for Sabrina and every woman living in Sinclair Heights. "I'll do it right now."

"Good. I'll stop by so we can see this through."

"You don't have to do that," Deidre said, not wanting him to think she needed him to come running every time she called. Or did she?

"I *want* to." Spencer's voice was resolute. "Sabrina's my friend now too. Let's just be sure she's not in trouble. See you shortly."

Deidre disconnected, grateful to have such a virile and compassionate man in her life. She thought about how odd it had been that they had literally met over a dead body and now couldn't seem to stay away from each other.

She called Hal.

Sabrina took a short cut that would lead her out of the park and practically right to her doorstep. She had looked several times for the man wearing a cap and had not seen him. Maybe she had gotten carried away over the whole thing. That was what this damned serial killer was doing to independent, strong women like her: turning them to mush, afraid of their own shadow.

Well she refused to live in a state of fear. But, in keeping her promise to a friend, Sabrina would not continue to run. Not tonight, anyway. Maybe she could talk Deidre into the sport and they could buddy up in the future. Right now, she just wanted Kwame to hold her in his arms and they could discuss the rest.

Sabrina jogged through the red cedar trees and suddenly became aware of footsteps behind her. Or were they in front of her? The forest had a way of distorting sounds. But then the footsteps became heavier and definitely sounded like they were coming from behind her.

Terrified, Sabrina looked over her shoulder. She saw the man wearing the cap. He was moving rapidly toward her. While she wanted to believe that he was merely another runner and not the Park Killer, her instincts told her otherwise. He had been following her and set his sights on her.

What was she to do?

I can't freak out. I can't let myself become another victim of this madman.

Sabrina dug into her reserve of courage and picked up her speed considerably, knowing she would reach the clearing soon. Looking back again, she saw that the killer had veered off in that direction, as though to cut her off. Not wanting to confront him, she ran back farther into the woods, hoping to find another way out or run into someone who would help.

She darted this way and that, trying to keep him off balance. In the process, the sounds all around her seemed to blend together.

Sabrina stumbled upon an opening in the woods and slowed down. She was surprised to see a tent, sleeping bag, cooking utensils, and other evidence that someone was apparently camping out there. Perhaps it was someone out for a wilderness experience. Or, more likely, a homeless person.

There was some movement in front of her. Seizing the opportunity, Sabrina yelled, "Help me, please. . . ."

The person came upon her so quickly that it took her a moment to realize that it was the man wearing the cap. Where had he come from when he had been behind her? How did he know . . . ?

This is his camp, Sabrina guessed, putting a hand to her mouth in shock.

"Don't hurt me," she entreated, backing up.

"Don't be afraid," he said to her in a calm voice.

The voice had a familiar ring to it. Indeed, the closer he came, the more Sabrina believed she recognized the man. He had tried to hit on her once at a bar, but she'd turned him down, which didn't seem to set too well with him. It had never occurred to her that behind the handsome façade and persistence was a serial killer.

"You . . ." she gasped. "Stay away—"

"No can do," he said in a smug voice. "It's time we finished what you and I started. . . ."

He watched with excitement as she backpedaled, trying hard to overcome her disbelief. But he couldn't afford to take pity or give her a pass, not with so much at stake.

He raised his fist and struck the woman hard on the jaw, hearing the crunch that broke it and sent her reeling. She bit back the pain and tried make a run for it. He easily closed the distance, grabbing her from behind. He turned her around and put his fist hard into her nose, bloodying it instantly.

This time she went out like a light. He caught her before she hit the ground.

Now the fun was about to begin. Sabrina Murray would awaken only to wish she hadn't.

FORTY-FOUR

Hal had no choice but to take Deidre's concerns regarding her friend seriously. He had met Sabrina at the art gallery. Nice-looking lady. Maybe they all were a little paranoid these days when it came to a serial killer in their midst and every male in the city a suspect. But to ignore the mere possibility that the killer could be out on the prowl tonight with the intent to do bodily harm to Sabrina or any other woman, as the lieutenant overseeing this investigation Hal would be derelict in his duty were he to look the other way.

Not to mention, he could hardly quibble with Deidre's instincts, which had been responsible for nabbing a kidnapper and possibly linking a homeless man to the Park Killer investigation.

With this in mind, Hal dispatched some extra officers to the park in hopes of averting a tragedy before it happened. Even if it proved to be a false alarm that Sabrina Murray was in trouble, it would be welcome, given the alternative. In the meantime, they could not afford to leave any stone unturned in going after this psychopath who had made a habit of brutalizing the women of Sinclair Heights in the worst way imaginable.

Not on my watch. Not this time. Hal was en route to the park where Ms. Murray had last been in contact with Deidre.

***

Having been unable to reach Sabrina, Deidre became worried that something was wrong. Why wasn't she picking up? What if she'd never made it home? Could the man in the cap have truly been after Sabrina—and killed her?

"I'm really scared something happened to her, Spencer." Deidre looked up at him, glad he was there.

"I know you are," Spencer told her. He'd been at her house for nearly an hour and much of it had been spent trying to reach Sabrina by cell phone or at her house, leaving messages on her voice mail. "Maybe she's with her boyfriend."

Deidre thought about that. Sabrina had mentioned phoning Kwame to meet her at her place. Maybe they had decided to go out to dinner or had gone to his house.

"That's possible," she allowed, but her gut feelings suggested there was more to it.

"I don't suppose you have his number?" Spencer chewed his lip, gazing at her.

Deidre shook her head. "There was never any reason for me to have it, especially since Sabrina seems to go through boyfriends like some people do hairstyles."

Spencer could relate. Since his divorce, there never seemed a reason to settle on one woman. 'Til now, when he had every reason to.

"On the other hand, Sabrina did promise me she'd call when she got home," Deidre said with trepidation.

Spencer frowned. "What if she never actually went home, but went directly to her boyfriend's house or somewhere else with him?"

"All the more reason for her to call and let me know. Particularly since she knew I'd be worried silly after her fear about being followed."

"So I guess our first step should be to go over to her place and make sure she's not there or otherwise pre-occupied."

Deidre blushed as she thought about her friend being *preoccupied,* something she and Spencer were beginning to know all too well. But something told her this was not the case with Sabrina tonight. She feared her absence was due to something far more sinister.

"Let's go," she prompted Spencer.

Sabrina lived two blocks away in a rented Victorian house. Her car was not parked in the driveway and there were no lights on inside.

"Doesn't look like anyone's home," Spencer said as he drove up to the house. "We'd better check anyway."

Deidre agreed. They got out of the car and went up to the door, ringing the bell. There was no answer.

"What if she's inside . . . hurt or something?"

"I doubt an attacker would have brought her back home afterward," Spencer reasoned.

"You're probably right." Deidre knew she was grasping at straws. That didn't stop her from fearing that something was wrong. But what?

Just then, a dark Mercedes pulled into the driveway behind Spencer's car. Stepping out was a well-dressed, tall and slender dark-skinned man with long brown dreadlocks. Deidre guessed him to be in his midthirties.

"Hello," he said. "Are you friends of Sabrina?"

"Who's asking?" Spencer said, peering at him suspiciously.

"My name's Kwame Oboe. I was supposed to meet Sabrina an hour ago, but ran late. She didn't answer her phone, so thought I'd come over." He glanced at Deidre and Spencer. "What's going on anyway?"

Deidre knew that the homeless man the police were looking for had dreadlocks. But the man before her looked anything but homeless. Nor did he look like the man she had seen on the train or described by Marina Elkins. Moreover, he certainly wasn't the man wearing a cap who had scared Sabrina in the park. Was he?

Feeling somewhat confident that Kwame was not the Park Killer who had targeted his own girlfriend, Deidre told him about her conversation with Sabrina when she was at the park and how they reached this point.

"So you think she might have been abducted by this killer?" Kwame narrowed soot-colored eyes at her alarmingly.

"I don't know," Deidre admitted. "But Sabrina isn't here and hasn't called me or you to tell us why. That tells me she's probably in trouble."

"I'm inclined to agree with that." Spencer gazed at the boyfriend, wondering if Kwame could possibly know more than he was letting on. Or was he just as befuddled as they were?

"Well, did you call the police?" asked Kwame.

"Yes, and they're probably combing the park right now," Deidre said hopefully.

"Then maybe we should join them?" he suggested.

"Someone needs to stay here in case Sabrina does show up," Spencer said. He looked at Deidre and then decided he didn't want her waiting here alone, so he turned to Kwame. "I think that should be you, man. We'll go to the park and see if the police have found out anything and keep in touch by cell phone."

Kwame gave a thoughtful nod and lifted the cell phone from his pocket to be sure. "Yeah, all right." He sighed and exchanged numbers. "I just hope Sabrina's not out there hurt somewhere—needing me. I hope this whole thing just turns out to be nothing."

"Don't we all." Spencer got a chill when imagining that it could just have easily been Deidre missing, leaving him to deal with the worst possibilities.

"We just have to keep thinking positively," Deidre tried to reassure them, even as she had a sinking feeling to the contrary.

"What do you think?" Hal asked Hernandez as they directed the search in the park for the missing woman.

"I'd say it doesn't look good," the detective responded bluntly. "Several people thought they heard a woman scream, but couldn't tell where it was coming from. Then there's the fact that Ms. Murray dropped her cell phone—presumably in the process of an assault . . . or trying to get away from an attacker."

"Damn." Hal touched the bridge of his nose. He feared that Deidre had hit this one dead on the money. And it may have already been too late to save her friend. But, until they knew one way or the other, they had to give it their best shot. "We have to find her!"

Hernandez's brows came together over his nose. "We will . . . one way or the other."

"Yeah, that's what scares the hell out of me: not knowing which way it will be."

The search was expanded to outside the park with the knowledge that time was of the essence in locating Sabrina Murray.

Deidre and Spencer joined in the park search for Sabrina after getting an update from Hal that there was still no sign of her.

"Do you think she could still be inside the park?" Deidre asked Spencer.

"The police seem to think so," he said. "Apparently there were people who saw her jogging, but no one seems to remember her leaving the park, voluntarily or otherwise."

"Then Sabrina could be hurt somewhere." Deidre felt weak in the knees at the thought, but hoped her friend was still alive.

Or she could be dead. Spencer looked at the prospect squarely. "We don't know that for sure. This park is so damned big that it's possible she could be anywhere and unaware that anyone's even looking for her."

Deidre knew that Spencer was trying to be optimistic. So was she. But there came a point when optimism had to give way to pessimism.

Where are you, Sabrina? Deidre felt more than a little frustrated. *Please don't be dead. Or a rape and assault victim.*

Deidre prayed that her friend was not hurt through an accidental fall or an animal attack, which would be no less painful. And potentially fatal.

Using flashlights the police had given them, they searched high and low, hoping against hope for any clue that could lead to Sabrina's whereabouts.

"With the park overrun with cops, where could someone have taken her?" Deidre decided that Sabrina likely had been abducted, probably by the Park Killer. If so, how long would he keep her alive?

"It's a question I've been asking myself," Spencer said pensively. He remembered a few weeks ago when he and Sky stumbled upon the body in the creek. Could the killer have killed Sabrina and disposed of her body there too?

Grabbing Deidre's hand, he uttered, "Come with me. . . ."

"Where?" Deidre asked.

"You'll see." Spencer hoped to hell he was wrong, but his gut told him he wasn't.

The moment they approached the clearing that led to the creek, Deidre recognized the area as not far from the back of her house. They walked onto the grass and started to look around past a clump of bushes.

Spencer drew a deep breath and felt he had to explain. "I know this is outside of the parameters of where the police think Sabrina may have been taken, but given the fact that a body was already left here with an open means for the killer to escape . . . ."

Before Deidre even had a chance to digest the eerie parallels to when she first met Spencer, they saw the nude and discolored body lying face up in shallow water.

Deidre gasped and clutched Spencer's arm tightly. It was undeniably Sabrina Murray. And, by all accounts, she wasn't alive.

FORTY-FIVE

Three days after Sabrina's death, Deidre was still in a state of shock. She couldn't have expected that her dear friend would fall prey to the Park Killer. Or that he had succeeded once more in evading the police net and was still on the loose.

In spite of this, Deidre had declined Spencer's offer to move in with him 'til this killer was caught. She felt secure in his company, but did not wish to become a victim again in her life through fear. Besides, Deidre didn't see herself as a target of the serial killer, per se, simply because she lived near the spot where two bodies had been found. Virtually all the victims had apparently been preyed upon around one of the city's parks or the university's campus, not at their homes. And since she had no intention of being in either place alone, Deidre felt relatively safe.

But safe was one thing, invulnerable was another. As far as Deidre was concerned, every woman in Sinclair Heights was susceptible to bodily harm and death as long as a relentless and seemingly chameleon killer was at large.

Her friend Agatha Gray agreed as they had tea in Deidre's living room. "Girl, we all just need to keep our doors locked, lights on, and pepper Mace handy. If someone even looks at me funny, I'm going to scream my head off and run for the hills."

Deidre lifted her cup. "That didn't seem to help Sabrina any." She choked back the words. It was extra depressing to think that Sabrina was a runner in the best shape of her life. But, at the end of the day, it did nothing to help her survive against a determined and apparently faster killer.

"Yeah, you're right," Agatha conceded. "Maybe we all can learn from Sabrina's death. People just need to be careful and not do things like running alone in the park that can attract weirdos out there like serial killers. Not that I'm blaming your friend for what happened . . ."

Even though she wanted to object to the notion that Sabrina was somehow at fault for what happened to her, Deidre wished she hadn't tempted fate by making herself a target where women were most at risk while this killer was on the loose. It made Deidre sick to think of what that psychopath had done to Sabrina. Along with breaking her jaw and nose, he'd raped and strangled her before tossing her body into the creek like yesterday's trash.

No one deserved to die that way. Certainly not one who had everything to live for at this time in her life.

"Sabrina had so much talent and was going places," Deidre said sorrowfully. "Why is it that so many good people die before their time?" Her husband and son came to mind, along with Spencer's brother.

"I wish I knew." Agatha looked down at her cup of tea. "That's how life is, or seems to be. All we can do is try to keep it from happening to us. And count our blessings in the meantime."

Deidre did just that, even if the losses she'd endured had been almost too much to bear. She could only hope that those blessings could somehow compensate for the tragedies. One such blessing was that Spencer had come into her life, giving her renewed enthusiasm for having companionship and possibly a bright future.

They finished up their tea and carpooled to work. It seemed a smart idea to Deidre to avoid taking light rail for the time being while she plied her trade as a spokeswoman for the Sinclair Heights Police Bureau.

Spencer took Sky out for some exercise. He hated that this park he'd enjoyed for much of his life had suddenly turned into a haven for gangbangers, muggers, and a serial killer. But it had also been the source of many good things, such as Spencer bonding with his brother, family barbecues, and providing a place for recreation. Then there was the fact that the park had turned a negative into a positive when he'd met Deidre. If she wasn't the best thing to happen to him thus far in life, apart from the birth of his daughter, he sure as hell didn't know what was.

Spencer wanted to protect Deidre from harm. Especially the type Sabrina had endured. But his hands were tied as far as keeping tabs on her twenty-four hours a day. Deidre wanted, and needed, her space. And so did he. The worst thing he could do was crowd her, such as insisting that they live in the same house, at least while as a killer was out there. Maybe this type of smothering was what had ended his marriage. Or maybe it had been doomed from the start. He wouldn't let that happen with Deidre. If this was to be a second chance for both of them, he wasn't going to screw it up.

That didn't mean he wouldn't use every opportunity to check on Deidre, or be there at a moment's notice if she ever needed him.

When Spencer arrived back home, he was surprised to find Lieutenant Iverson sitting on the porch. Sky barked, as though he were their nemesis.

Maybe the lieutenant was. Spencer cocked a brow at him.

"To what do I owe this pleasure, Iverson?" he asked with something less than cordiality.

Hal stood, dusting off his pants. "Your neighbor told me you'd taken your dog out for a run or whatever."

"Is that against the law?"

"Not the last I knew."

"Good because Sky gets really antsy when he can't go running *or whatever*."

Hal grimaced. "Look, I just want to talk to you for a few minutes, Berry. Why don't you put that beast away? I'll wait."

Spencer smiled, holding the leash tightly as Sky growled at Hal. "Whatever you say, Lieutenant."

Hal stepped aside with room to spare as Spencer took the dog into the house, giving him something to eat. "Enjoy it, boy. Be back in a few. Have to see what's on Iverson's mind, as if I can't guess."

Stepping outside, Spencer could see that the lieutenant was deep in thought. He could only imagine what Hal was thinking, even as Spencer empathized with the pressure the man must be under these days, having gone down that path himself when he was with the FBI and dealing with elusive killers.

"Let me guess, you want to hang me because I happened to be acquainted with yet another victim of the so-called Park Killer?" Spencer tossed out sarcastically. "Or maybe because I outsmarted the Sinclair Heights Police Bureau and figured out first where to find her body?"

Hal studied Spencer. Cool and calm as usual. And definitely a smartass. But not a killer. Though Hal would have loved nothing more than to tie this murder to Berry in one neat package and give himself another crack at winning Deidre over, it wasn't happening. Besides, he had Gigi in his life now and wasn't complaining one bit—certainly not in bed. As it was, Hal didn't believe Spencer was guilty of anything other than being maybe too clever for his own good and luckless when it came to the women he befriended these days.

Except for Deidre.

It was as clear as day to Hal that Berry was in love with her. He sure as hell couldn't blame him for that, given the pure quality oozing from the lady's pores, along with beauty, intelligence, and sex appeal. The truth was Hal had known from the start that there was something between Deidre and Berry, probably even before they knew it themselves. Once upon a time, he'd been hoping that it would pass, as least from Deidre's point of view. But that hadn't been the case. Any chance Deidre might pull away from the criminal psychology professor had vanished when Hal saw the way she looked at Berry during and after the search for Sabrina Murray. She was as much in love with Spencer Berry as he was with her.

"I'm not here to arrest you, Berry," Hal said sourly.

Spencer feigned a sigh of relief. "That's good to know, I think."

Hal gave him a half smile. "Relax. I'm not your adversary."

"Could've fooled me."

"I have a job to do. And if I have to step on a few toes to do it, my suggestion would be that you move your big feet out of the way to keep them from getting hurt."

Spencer laughed, but was not amused. "Am I being warned off of something? Or maybe *someone?*"

"Neither." Hal scratched his chin thoughtfully. "It's cool with me that you're involved with Deidre, as long as she's happy."

"I think she is," Spencer said confidently.

"Then I'm happy." At least he tried to be happy for
her. Hal changed tracks. "I'm not too thrilled that we
lost another beautiful young woman to this killer."

"Who is?" Spencer widened his eyes. "She was a good
friend of Deidre's."

"I know. I also know that we probably came *this*
close"—Hal held his hands about two inches apart—"to
nailing the bastard, but somehow he managed to get
away."

"So how can I help?" Spencer wasn't sure he wanted
to find out. Especially if it had anything to do with
backing off from seeing Deidre. Or protecting her to
the best of his ability.

Hal exhaled. "That's just it. I'm not quite sure. You've
known every one of the victims in one respect or another—no small feat. Yet the connection is too choppy to really feel there is a connection, if you know what I mean?"

"I think I do."

Hal tugged at his chin. "I guess what I'm trying to
say is, until we figure out if there's anything to this, I'd
watch my back if I were you."

Spencer batted his lashes in astonishment. "You think
I could be the target of this asshole?"

"Could be in a roundabout way," the lieutenant suggested.

Spencer gave a mirthless chuckle. "Seems to me he
doesn't have the balls to go after a man. Much less one
who would kick his ass from here to kingdom come if
the opportunity ever presented itself."

"Yeah, maybe you're right about that," Hal conceded, "unless in his warped mind, he was going after you
through the back door, so to speak."

Spencer scratched his head. "That doesn't make a
hell of a lot of sense, Iverson."

"Neither does murdering women whose *only* connection appears to be crossing paths with you in one manner or another." Hal pressed his lips together. "Don't get yourself worked up, Berry. It's just a theory right now, in the absence of any others that can be considered credible at this point."

"I'll keep that in mind."

"You do that." In fact, Hal had really just concocted this theory off the top of his head. Now he wondered if maybe it was something they should seriously look into. Maybe Berry had quit the FBI not because of being broken up over his brother's death, but to escape the enemies he'd built up over the years. One of whom may be out for blood, if not Berry's. "Well, I've said what I had to. I'll let you get back to your day and your dog."

Spencer smirked. "Thanks. I'm sure Sky would be happy to thank you himself."

"I'll pass." Hal snorted. "Me and dogs don't seem to mix too well."

"Yeah, I noticed."

Spencer went inside and pondered the lieutenant's warning. He didn't believe for a moment that there was anyone out there who had enough of a grudge against him to kill women he knew. This seemed particularly unlikely, given that he was not being set up to take the fall for the murders.

Unless the killer had an unknown agenda. . . .

FORTY-SIX

Spencer met Jeremy at the Oasis Brew pub that evening. He told him about Hal Iverson's theory that that the serial murders might be somehow tied to him.

Jeremy put the mug of beer to his lips. "That's news to me."

"Figured Iverson might have made it up along the way," Spencer said. "But it got me to thinking: what if the lieutenant was doing more than blowing smoke?"

"You think it could be true?"

"Doesn't seem likely," Spencer said. "But I was a forensic psychologist with the FBI for the better part of seven years. More than enough time to have made an enemy or two along the way."

"Yeah, but you've been out of the loop for over a year now, more or less," Jeremy pointed out. "A bit long to carry a grudge, don't you think?"

"I suppose so, relatively speaking," Spencer agreed. "Especially to carry out a vendetta that's only indirectly tied to me in killing these women, were that the case. On the other hand, that's no time at all for someone who's been stewing in a penitentiary for years, waiting for the chance to get back at the person believed to be responsible for putting him there."

Jeremy ran a hand across his face. "Hmm, doesn't add up to me. If this killer is hell-bent on revenge against *you*, he has a very strange way of showing it."

Spencer drank beer. "You know as well as I do that serial killers often are *strange*. In that sense, nothing would surprise me about their irrational thinking."

"I can't argue with you there, buddy, but I still say it's a bit farfetched to think that murdering all these women—none who even knew each other, as far as I understand—somehow comes back to you."

Spencer stared at the notion. "But you were wondering yourself about the odds of my acquaintance with the victims. Maybe this is the answer: I'm acquainted more with the *offender* rather than the victims. Only I have no idea who the hell he is."

"Nice try, but I'm still not buying it," Jeremy said dismissively. "And neither should you. Yeah, the odds that you knew *all* the victims are staggering, I'll grant you that. However, the pieces of the puzzle still don't fit, insofar as anything more than a superficial correlation. My guess is that Iverson is just getting desperate trying to find answers—even if they are long shots at best—before the powers that be bring someone else in to head the investigation into these murders."

"You're probably right," Spencer said, not wanting to believe that he could have been responsible in any way for so many deaths through no direct fault of his own.

But the longer this went on, the more Spencer would wonder if, by romancing Deidre, he could be putting her in danger well beyond Gayle's wrath.

Hal played with Gigi's breasts and nipples as she galloped atop him feverishly like a woman on a mission. His erect penis met her halfway each time she came down, impaling herself deeply. She ran her fingernails across his chest, giving him painful pleasure in combination with the sex, which had him moaning with delight.

Indeed, he had been surprised when the sexy lady actually showed up at his door. Short on words, all she wanted was to get him in bed. He was more than happy to oblige, considering there was no one in his life and no prospects other than her.

He turned them around and took over, propping her long legs onto his shoulders and thrusting himself well inside her time and again. It was music to his ears when Gigi cried out each time they connected. He brought his head down and attacked her lips with kisses, sliding his tongue between her teeth.

"I'm just about there . . . I'm coming . . ." Gayle murmured. She had to bite her tongue for she nearly called out Spencer's name, just as she imagined it was him lodged inside her, making love to her as only he could. It was the only way she could get off with another man who didn't do it for her the same way as Spencer, her true lover.

"Go with it, baby," Hal moaned as he continued to propel himself into her, his own orgasm fast approaching. But he didn't want to get there 'til she had reached hers, knowing it would make his that much more fulfilling.

Gayle started to tremble as the sensations came in waves that quickly spread throughout her body. She wrapped her legs around Hal to hold him close while she went through the motions of dual climaxing. She was slick with sweat, as was he, and their mouths were locked in passion as the sex reached its height and the stimulation's intensity waned.

When it was over, she wanted him off of her as reality once again set in that she was not with Spencer, who was instead sticking his penis between another woman's legs.

"Wow!" Hal uttered, catching his breath. "That was incredible."

Gayle eyed him, unwilling to concur, as she'd been caught up in her own little world during the sex.

"So I take it things still aren't right with your boyfriend?" he asked.

She sneered at him. "What do you think?"

Hal didn't mind being a substitute lover, especially with such a hot lady. But since they seemed to be a good match, he had a better idea. "Maybe you should consider getting a new man in your life?"

Her lashes fluttered. "Like you?"

"Have anyone better in mind?"

She did, in fact. There could only be one Spencer, but he didn't need to know that. At least not while her man was being an ass, cheating on her with that bitch artist.

"No one I can think of," Gayle lied.

"Good."

Hal went for a kiss and Gayle blocked him with her hand. "Why didn't you tell me you were a cop?"

Hal met her gaze. Some women were turned on by the revelation; others were turned off. He tried to read her, beyond her body's response to their sexuality. "Never got around to it," he said. "We haven't exactly spent much time making small talk."

Gayle didn't deny that. It just made her a little nervous that he carried a badge and gun. On the other hand, she felt it didn't hurt to have a cop in her corner, in case Spencer or his bitch tried to go to the cops and accuse her of something where they had no proof. She might even be able to use Hal as her alibi, if it came down to it.

"You know, I think a man with a gun is sort of exciting," she suggested.

Hal grinned lasciviously. "Yeah?"

She nodded and ran her fingernail down his chest. "Especially if he knows just where to stick it."

"I think he does," Hal said, aroused by a woman who talked dirty and could more than hold her own in bed.

He kissed her, feeling this was the start of something good that could help take his mind off work and the quest to apprehend a vicious serial killer in Sinclair Heights who had just added another notch to his murderous belt.

FORTY-SEVEN

Clint Winston left the office at 7:00 P.M. He thrived on work and making money, but had still meant to be out of there a couple of hours earlier. Especially since he had a hot date with Fiona tonight. She was one fine lady and great in the sack. He had no idea where this relationship was going, but fully intended to enjoy the ride as long as possible. The fact that her kid thought the world of him was a definite plus. The key to most women's hearts was being nice to their children. In this case, it was working like a charm as Fiona had really opened up to him and seemed to want this to work out as much as he wanted it to.

Clint rode down the elevator to the underground parking garage and took out his cell phone. He called Fiona, enjoying hearing her voice.

"Baby, I'm running a little late."

"Yeah, I can see that," Fiona complained.

"Things were crazy today," he offered guiltily, knowing she could relate all too well. "But I'm leaving now. I should be there in say . . . half an hour—"

"I'll be expecting you," she said evenly.

Clint got off the elevator and headed toward his silver Cadillac.

"I've been fantasizing about you every chance I got," he cajoled her.

Fiona hummed sexily. "Well, you had better not be thinking about anyone else."

Clint laughed lasciviously. "There are no other wom-
en out there, as far as I am concerned, baby."

"Music to my ears," she sang.

He neared his car and heard footsteps rapidly coming
up from behind. Turning around in what Clint thought
was an empty garage, he saw a man wielding a knife.

"What the hell . . . ?" he stammered, assuming the
man was out to rob him.

"What's going on?" Fiona asked worriedly.

Clint dropped the phone and tried to cover his face
when the assailant lifted the knife, but he was too late
to prevent it from slicing deeply across his throat. Making a gurgling sound, Clint fell to his knees, clutching
his throat as blood spurted out thickly. He watched the
man, whom Clint recognized as someone whose path
he'd crossed, glare at him for a moment before taking
the wallet out of his pocket and running off.

Slumping over beside the phone, the last thing
Clint heard before everything went black for good was
Fiona's sweet voice say, "Honey, you're scaring me. Are
you all right? Clint? . . ."

Detective Ronald LeCarre was called to the scene of
an apparent homicide in the Lakeridge District. The
victim was located in the parking garage of a building
that housed several financial firms. LeCarre showed
his badge to the police officer guarding the crime scene
and made his way inside. He approached another officer, who was standing near the deceased, and LeCarre
routinely identified himself.

"So what do we have here?" LeCarre asked, though
he could plainly see that it wasn't pretty.

The young female officer winced. "The victim has been identified as Clint Winston. He's an analyst at Brookman and Teyrod Associates. His girlfriend—a Fiona Berry—called 911 after she heard him scream during their phone conversation. Looks like his throat was slit during a robbery, sir."

LeCarre looked at the pool of blood around the decedent's head and streaming away from it toward a sewer. "Robbery, huh?"

"Yeah. The victim's wallet is missing."

"Hmm, that would seem to indicate robbery as the motive. Probably an addict looking for a quick fix. Though I wouldn't rule out that it could be gang related, or something else."

LeCarre more or less nixed the gang-associated homicide theory. Judging by the designer suit the decedent wore, which must have gone for several hundred dollars, he didn't strike the detective as someone who was involved with gang activity.

The officer looked as if she wanted to run somewhere and throw up. LeCarre couldn't blame her. Unfortunately, murder scenes like this came with the job for both of them.

He glanced at the silver Cadillac near the body. "Does this belong to Winston?"

She nodded. "He still had the keys on his person."

"Guy kills the man for a couple hundred bucks probably and a credit card or two that can only go so far, but doesn't take a fifty thousand dollar car. Or that expensive Rolex he's wearing? Go figure."

"Maybe the robber was spooked when he heard someone else entering the garage," the officer suggested.

"Yeah, maybe." LeCarre took out a stick of gum and stuffed it in his mouth. This homicide was definitely suspicious as far as he was concerned. There must have been more to Clint Winston—or his assailant—than met the eye. And the deceased was certainly no longer able to provide any clues.

FORTY-EIGHT

Spencer ran a wet towel over his head after shaving it. He was looking forward to spending the evening with Deidre, having already dropped Sky off at his father's. Indeed, Spencer found himself wanting to spend more and more time in Deidre's company. The idea of needing someone again scared him some, but was far more appealing than scary.

He quickly dressed in some slacks and a button-down shirt, dabbing on some new cologne. In the back of Spencer's mind were still some lingering thoughts that the Park Killer could be violating and murdering women to get to him. It made no sense and he could not find a real connection here or believe that someone from his past FBI days had resurfaced with a serious vendetta against him. But he owed it to Deidre to warn her about the mere possibility that she could be a target of this killer—not because she was involved with him, but as some sort of measure of revenge aimed at Spencer—assuming Iverson hadn't already briefed her on his off-the-wall theory.

Which may not necessarily be that off the wall.

Spencer was nearly out the door when his cell phone rang. He frowned when he saw it was Fiona and not Deidre.

"Look, you caught me at a bad time. Unless there's a problem with—"

"Clint's dead," Fiona sobbed.

"What?" Spencer put the phone up closer to his ear.
"He was killed tonight."

"How?"

"The police say he was stabbed to death during a robbery . . ." Fiona began bawling. "I heard it happening
over the phone . . ."

Spencer exhaled breath. He wasn't sure what to say.
Winston dead. Unbelievable. He didn't know the man
very well and didn't particularly like what little he did
know. But Clint was someone Fiona liked and a potential stepfather to his daughter, both of which Spencer
had to respect.

"I know you're hurting right now, Fiona. And I'm
sorry about Clint. He was a—"

"I haven't told Charity yet," she cut in, sniffling. "I'd
like to do it with you."

"Why me?" Spencer raised a brow, perhaps sounding a little more coldhearted than he meant for it to. "I
mean, she needs to hear the truth from you."

"But you're her father, Spencer. I just think it would
be better for her if we were both there to deliver the sad
news."

"Charity's a strong girl," he voiced in opposition.
"Hell, she went through Wesley's death and dealt with
it as well as could be expected. My being there with you
might send the wrong message."

"Damn you, Spencer!" Fiona spat. "This isn't some
attempt to get us back together, I promise you. Charity was just starting to become attached to Clint. I'm
simply not strong enough right now to handle this all
by myself." She started to sob again.

Selfish as it sounded, Spencer had no desire to go
to his ex-wife's house to console her. Not when he
was expected at Deidre's. He certainly did not want to
be a substitute for Clint or any other man, if that was
Fiona's intent, in spite of her denial to the contrary.

But helping his daughter get through yet another tragedy in her young life was a different story altogether.
Charity needed him and he always wanted to be there
for her. Spencer only hoped Deidre would understand
and not hold it against him.

"I'll be right over," he told his ex-wife glumly.

Deidre fried some chicken to go with mashed po-
tatoes, gravy, and corn muffins. Her mother firmly
believed in the adage that the key to a man's heart was
his stomach. She didn't necessarily buy into that, but
Deidre enjoyed cooking for a man, tapping into her
culinary skills that had, until recently, been underused.
Especially a man who wanted her company beyond the
kitchen. And vice versa. Her toes curled at the thought
of Spencer caressing them, before going up her legs
and farther . . .

Deidre wore a black embroidered slip dress for the
occasion, hoping Spencer would find it sexy. She had
also bought a bottle of wine and planned to put on
some romantic music. She wanted the night to begin
and end perfectly, being in Spencer's comforting arms.
Maybe they could even talk about what they hoped to
find in this relationship beyond their obvious strong
sexual attraction and great companionship.

Deidre had no intention of putting the cart ahead of
the horse. Yet, knowing how precarious life could be,
she wanted to embrace the one she had and do more
with it. Having a man in her life that she could count on
and spoil rotten was something Deidre was definitely
ready for. But was Spencer prepared to step into those
shoes?

Her reverie was snapped when the phone rang. She
answered it in the kitchen, welcoming the deep tones of
Spencer's voice.

"I was just thinking about you," she admitted. "I hope you're hungry for dinner *and* dessert . . . ?"

More than I can say—especially dessert. Spencer didn't know quite how to tell her that their evening plans had to be put on hold, if not canceled altogether. But, under the circumstances, he didn't see where there was any other choice.

"Fiona's boyfriend was stabbed to death tonight," he said somberly.

"Oh, I'm so sorry," Deidre said in disbelief, coming off of Sabrina's death just days ago. While she hadn't met the boyfriend, Deidre felt for Fiona, having known what it was like to lose a man in her life.

"The police think it was a robbery-homicide."

"Oh no. . . ." Deidre put a hand to her mouth, thinking back to the carjacking that cost Marshall and Adam their lives.

Spencer hated telling her this, knowing it would remind Deidre of her own tragedy. He sighed miserably. "Look, I need to go over to Fiona's for a little while. Charity will be torn up over this—"

"I understand." How could she not, even if part of Deidre saw this as Spencer being unable to completely break away from his ex-wife. Or was it the other way around? Was Fiona hoping that they might be able to pick right back up now that she was on her own again, albeit under heartbreaking conditions? "Do what you need to do."

"What I need is to be with you," Spencer said frankly. To some degree, he felt that by going to be with Fiona, he was betraying Deidre. But then he realized that made no sense, when he looked at it squarely. It still didn't make him feel any better.

"No, Spencer, you need to be with your daughter *and* Fiona right now," Deidre forced herself to say in being the bigger person over her own interests. She held back tears.

Why did she have to be so damned accepting? Spencer admired that and so much more in Deidre. Including being the most gorgeous and super sexy lady he knew.

"Thanks for saying that," he told her sincerely.

"I meant it," she replied sympathetically.

"I know you did." He paused. "Well, I'd better go now. I'll try to get there as soon as I can. I'm sure you went through a lot of trouble to—"

"Don't worry about it," Deidre said, wiping tears from her eyes. "This is something that can't be helped. Stay with your daughter and your ex as long as they need you. If necessary, I can always use the excess food as leftovers. You go ahead. Bye."

"Bye." Spencer heard her disconnect, grateful for her words, though almost feeling as if she were saying good-bye. He had no intention of letting that be the case.

He headed out for what promised to be a depressing night.

In more ways than one.

Deidre stood there unmoving for a moment, the phone still in hand. She felt as if the wind had been knocked out of her. One moment she had this fantastic evening planned. The next, it had been ruined by circumstances no one wanted. Certainly not her. But what could she do other than cry about life's cruelties?

After willing herself to budge, Deidre took the chicken off the stove and cut off the oven. Suddenly she was no longer in the mood to eat. Not alone. All she wanted to do now was clean up and pretend tonight had not happened.

As if.

FORTY-NINE

Spencer went inside the house he used to call his own. He looked at Fiona's tear-stained face and, feeling her pain, gave her a hug.

"You'll get through this in time," he told her, fully aware that it was easier said than done.

"I'm not sure I want to," she wept. "Not again."

He knew she was referring to Wesley. "Yeah, I know. But you have to be strong for Charity. We both do."

Fiona pulled back, wiping her nose. "Thanks for coming."

"No problem." Actually, it was a big problem, but he'd have to deal with that later. "Have you talked to the police yet?"

She nodded. "They were here just a little while ago."

"What did they tell you about Clint's death?"

"Just what I told you: someone stole his wallet and killed him for it."

Spencer gazed at Fiona's red eyes. "And they're sure about that?"

She peered back. "Why wouldn't they be? His wallet was missing and . . . Clint's throat was slit."

"Okay," he said thoughtfully. "Just wondering why it had to happen now."

And if it could be related in any way to the serial killer murder by association, since Clint was the boyfriend of my ex-wife.

Had the Park Killer suddenly decided to begin targeting males that Spencer knew, too? Or was that getting a bit carried away?

Fiona wiped at the tears on her cheeks. "Why does
it ever have to happen? People just do crazy things all
the time."

"Yeah, you're right." Spencer had to believe this was
just another random or targeted act of violence in town
that had nothing to do with him or anyone he was acquainted with, per se. "Is Charity in her room?"

Fiona nodded. "She's asleep."

"Well, I hate to wake her up, especially for something like this." Maybe he could still get out of this yet
and head over to Deidre's with time to spare, though
feeling for his ex and her grief.

"Charity *has* to be told, Spencer," Fiona insisted.
"Better not to keep it from her any longer than we have
to."

"All right," he relented, figuring it was best to get it
over with and hope it didn't unnerve Charity too much
so that she believed they might be next.

"Daddy . . ." Spencer saw Charity standing there in
her pajamas. "Thought I heard your voice."

"Hi, sweetheart. Did we wake you?"

"Yeah," she admitted, rubbing her eyes. "But I'm
glad you did. What are you doing here?"

Spencer looked at Fiona and back. "Your mother
asked me to come."

"Why?" Charity gazed at her parents.

Spencer waited for Fiona to say something, but when
she seemed reluctant to, he did. "Honey, something really bad happened tonight."

Charity's eyes widened. "What?"

He sighed. "Clint is dead. Someone robbed him and
he was killed as a result."

She looked shocked. "Clint's really dead, Mommy?"
Fiona began to cry. "Yes, baby. I'm sorry."

Charity started bawling. "Why does everybody have to die?"

Spencer almost wondered the same thing, but said gingerly, "Not everyone, sweetheart. Your mother and I are still very much alive and we plan to stay that way for a long time."

"Promise?" she asked intently.

Spencer hesitated, wishing he could guarantee what no man could. But looking at the fear in his little girl's eyes, he had to do just that. "Yeah, I promise."

He put his arms around Charity for a long embrace and looked at Fiona.

Once Charity was put to bed, Spencer considered his work done, believing that his ex-wife would do well to follow their daughter's lead in taking a breather from her tragedy. With any luck, Deidre would still be up, if not eating, and waiting for him.

"I should go," he told Fiona.

"Stay," she said softly.

"What?" He met her eyes.

"You heard me. Stay with me tonight, Spencer." Fiona wrapped her arms around his waist. "I *need* you. We were once good together. And we could be again. . . ."

She tried to kiss him, but Spencer averted his mouth and then held her at bay.

"I waited a long time to hear you say that, Fiona, but you never did when it might have counted. It's way too late for us to go back down that road. I know you're hurting right now, but it won't dull the pain to go where neither of us really wants to." He kissed the top of her head. "Try to get some sleep. You'll feel better in the morning."

"And what if I don't?" Fiona challenged him.

Spencer weighed the question. "Then make it happen. Clint's dead just like Wesley and nothing's going to change that, no matter how much either of us wants it to. You've got a daughter up there who's depending on you. Don't let her down."

Spencer left on that note, his mind squarely on Deidre, hoping they could still salvage the night.

And beyond.

FIFTY

Deidre tossed and turned restlessly as the nightmare came back in full force.

The carjacker now looked like the bearded home-less man she had seen on the train. He held the gun to Marshall's head and yelled, "Get out of the damned car!"

"Like hell I will!" Marshall was defiant and grabbed hold of the gun as the two men struggled.

"Stop it, Marshall!" Deidre screamed in desperation. She peeked at her son in the back seat. He looked terrified. "Give him the car, Marshall—please!"

Deidre's husband rejected her pleas. "I'll give him something all right," he retorted. "I'll make this bas-tard wish he'd never been born."

Helplessly, Deidre watched as two shots rang out in the scuffle. One hit Marshall squarely in the chest and ricocheted, grazing Deidre's arm. The other went through the seat, hitting her son Adam in the head.

Deidre screamed over and over again as the shooter began to laugh hysterically. When she looked at him, she saw that he was now smoothly shaven and wear-ing a cap.

Deidre screamed again when he aimed the gun at her face and fired. . . .

Deidre awoke in a cold sweat, though she felt hot. A low moan resonated in her ears as though she were still caught up in the nightmare. It had been so vivid, yet surreal. And horrifying. She took a moment to adjust to her surroundings.

I hate that nightmare. Will it ever end?

Or was it going to continue to evolve and take on a life of its own as a real serial killer haunted the female residents of Sinclair Heights?

Deidre sat up when she realized the doorbell was ringing. Glancing at the clock, she saw that it was nearly eleven o'clock. She had visions of Gayle returning to attack her after disregarding her warnings to stay away from Spencer. Or maybe the Park Killer had tracked her down and would do the same thing to her that he'd done to Sabrina.

When the bell rang again, Deidre thought she heard, "It's me . . . Spencer."

She felt herself able to breathe. *Guess my imagination got carried away with itself again, coupled with that bizarre nightmare.*

Slipping on a robe, Deidre went downstairs. At the door, she hesitated. What if it wasn't really Spencer, but someone pretending to be him?

"Spencer . . . ?" she asked tentatively without looking through the door window.

"Yeah, it's me."

Recognizing his voice, Deidre cut on the porch light and looked out just to be sure. Spencer stood there with an unreadable expression on his face.

After opening the door, Deidre stared at him, unsure why he was there.

"It's late," she said.

"Not in my book," he said huskily. "Sorry if I woke you, and sorrier that I wasn't able to come sooner."

Deidre thought about her ruined dinner, but had to admit that she was happy to see him now.

She invited Spencer in. "You hungry . . . or did you—"

"Yes, hungry for you," Spencer said succinctly. "I'm hoping we have the whole night ahead of us to satisfy my hunger pangs . . . and the morning, too."

"Oh really?" Deidre batted her eyes, a fresh wave of desire sweeping over her. "And what about *my* hunger pangs, Mr. Berry?"

Spencer grinned lasciviously. "Those will be satisfied too, I promise."

Deidre needed no more convincing. Even if she wanted to be angry at Spencer for not coming earlier, she couldn't. He had a good reason, and Deidre actually applauded him for wanting to be there with his daughter to break the terrible news to her. The fact that Spencer cared enough was another endearing quality Deidre truly appreciated in the man.

Right along with his undeniable sex appeal and sheer masculinity.

Deidre held Spencer's cheeks and kissed him on the mouth. He quickly took over the kiss, putting his tongue in Deidre's mouth probingly. She felt her heartbeat quicken and her legs go limp.

Fortunately, Spencer was there to keep her from falling, easily scooping her up in his arms. He carried her straight to the bedroom where he easily removed Deidre's robe and nightshirt, wanting only to feel and taste her bare skin.

Spencer began to kiss every inch of Deidre that his fingers weren't caressing. Small arousal bumps formed on Deidre's body wherever he touched, making him want her even more.

Deidre swallowed with delight as Spencer put her on the bed and put his face between her legs. The moment his tongue found its way to her most tender possession, she felt a mini explosion within, biting her lip to keep from screaming with erotic pleasure. Grasping

Spencer's sturdy shoulders, Deidre felt him trembling and knew he was holding back for her. But tonight, she wanted no prolonged sex.

She needed all of him right now.

"Let's make love now, darling," she murmured.

"Are you sure?" Spencer asked, trying not to let go prematurely, so strong was his desire to be inside her.

"Yes, more than ever!" Deidre gasped boldly. "Please . . . !"

Eager to oblige, Spencer lifted up, undressed, and put on a condom, before moving front and center and taking her. His thrusts were fluid and powerful and Deidre took him in willingly. They kissed enthusiastically and their close bodies molded together as if they were glued.

Deidre constricted around him as he went deeper inside her, not wanting to let him go. Her legs were wrapped high around his back as they kissed passionately. Deidre was totally caught up in everything about Spencer and their lovemaking. When the surge began to take hold of her body, she didn't fight it, wanting to savor every tiny moment as though nothing else in the world mattered.

Spencer grunted as his climax came, enhanced by the prolonged sounds of satisfaction coming from Deidre's mouth. When it was over, their naked bodies lay side by side moist with perspiration; neither saying a word as the ripple of lovemaking slowly subsided.

After she'd come back down to earth, Deidre thought about Clint being murdered and Spencer going to be with his ex-wife and daughter, but ending up in her bed.

Deidre lifted her eyes to Spencer's face. "So how did things go with Fiona and Charity?"

Spencer thought about Fiona's halfhearted attempt to seduce him. He was willing to overlook it because of the trauma she'd experienced with her boyfriend's murder and for the sake of their daughter.

"Fiona's still in a state of shock that Clint's dead," Spencer said, meeting Deidre's gaze. "It'll take some time . . ."

Deidre imagined that time would be forever, having been down that road and knowing that one never quite got over such a senseless loss of life.

Spencer sighed. "Charity took it hard, of course, but I think she understands as much as an eight-year-old can that this is a dangerous, often unpredictable, world we live in and bad things happen that we often can't control."

"That's almost asking too much of a child," Deidre said sadly.

"Tell me about it. But what can you do?"

"Exactly what you did, Spencer," she replied. "Be there to support your daughter." *And your ex-wife.*

Spencer frowned. "Doesn't seem like that's really enough sometimes."

Deidre thought about the unwavering support her parents had given her when Marshall and Adam died that was still present to this day. "Even in the face of death, showing your love and devotion can mean the world to Charity. Trust me."

"I do." Spencer kissed her shoulder. "More than I have anyone in a long time."

Deidre felt good hearing this. "I trust you too, Spencer." She said it in spite of knowing that there was still a lot for them to learn about each other and no more guarantees about tomorrow than yesterday.

Spencer wanted nothing more than to earn Deidre's trust. As such, he didn't want to hold back anything that she had a right to know.

"Hal came to see me yesterday afternoon," he told her.

"Oh?" Deidre cocked a brow. "What for?" She hoped Hal wasn't still badgering Spencer or harboring any notions that they might someday get romantically involved.

"He wanted to toss out a theory that the Park Killer might somehow be targeting these women as a way to get back at me," Spencer said.

Deidre reacted. "You mean Hal thinks someone has a vendetta against you and they're taking it out on women you're acquainted with?"

"Yes, that's pretty much the gist of it." Spencer cleared his throat. "It doesn't seem to stack up in my book, though. I can't think of anyone who fits the bill and would go after innocent women. And since I don't have much of a personal investment with any of the victims, aside from knowing who they were and regretting that they had to die, I don't see anything to be gained there if someone is out to hurt me. But on the small chance that Iverson could be right, I wanted to tell you, if he hasn't already."

"No, Hal hasn't mentioned any of this to me," Deidre said. "He probably didn't want to scare me half to death or scare me more with something that may have no legs to stand on at the end of the day."

"More likely, Iverson was counting on me to warn you," Spencer said. "So I am. Deidre, you're the last woman in the world I'd want to see hurt by this monster. If you feel for any reason that we should stay away from each other 'til—"

Deidre put a finger to his lips. "I don't. As you've said, the killer seems to be going after women you know casually, not lovers. So I should be safe. Even if we were to stop seeing each other, does that mean I'd be in less danger or more? After all, I could be seen as simply another woman you're merely acquainted with."

This made sense to Spencer in an uneasy way. How the hell could he know exactly what might set this psychopath off? Maybe not seeing Deidre anymore would put her directly in the killer's path more than if they continued to pursue a relationship. Spencer also liked the idea of being around to protect Deidre should anyone come after her.

"I think you might be right," he told her. "Still, I want you to be extra careful and pay attention to the people around you and places you go. And please keep your doors and windows locked while you're inside, just to be on the safe side, 'til this guy is caught."

"I promise I'll do that," Deidre said to all of his requests. "Believe me, I don't want to become a victim of a crazed killer any more than any other woman."

Spencer smiled faintly. "Then we understand each other?"

"Perfectly." She dribbled her fingers down his chest, resisting going down farther for the moment. "But I also won't live like a woman afraid of her own shadow. Been there, done that, thank you. If something's going to happen, it probably will, no matter what."

Not if I have anything to do with it. Spencer steeled himself to the notion of not letting one hair on Deidre's head be harmed. Over his dead body.

Even if it meant going over his history backward and forward to eliminate any possible connection to the serial murders. Spencer would be damned if he let Deidre become another victim, though he greatly admired her strength and courage under fire.

FIFTY-ONE

Slipping through a back window, Gayle made her way inside the house. She wore gloves, aware that fingerprints could give her away and lead to that bitch having her arrested. She looked around, not particularly impressed with what she saw, and pissed off that Spencer was probably hooked on the old place and its occupant.

Gayle went upstairs to the master bedroom, where her man and that cunt were doing the nasty probably every night. The mere thought of it caused her to fly into a rage. She tossed pillows off the bed, fragrances off the dresser, and pictures off the walls; knocking over a plant as well.

That's what you get for stealing my man!

After yanking out a drawer in a nightstand, Gayle noticed the gun. She grabbed it and tucked it in her pocket. *Might come in handy.*

She made her way to a room that had lots of art and art supplies, and went to work on it, destroying paintings and turning over paint cans and brushes.

Downstairs, Gayle did much of the same, making a mess in one room after another 'til she was exhausted. Imagining she heard someone coming, she panicked and decided to get the hell out of there, satisfied with her handiwork.

Leaving the way she came, Gayle crept out behind the house and into the woods, making her way to the park, where her car was waiting.

After a mostly uneventful day, during which she assisted as police spokeswoman on two minor cases with no updates on the Park Killer investigation, Deidre dropped Agatha off at home in her newly repaired car before heading to the grocery store to pick up a few items. She was making Spencer dinner, just as she had a few days ago. Only this time she hoped it could be served hot, straight from the oven, rather than in the wee hours of the morning as leftovers.

Driving home, Deidre found herself checking the rearview mirror periodically to make sure she wasn't being followed. She saw no indication of such, making her wonder if she was being a bit too paranoid. If the Park Killer was after her, he probably wouldn't follow her around like a lovesick puppy.

Instead, he would try to catch her off guard, just as he apparently had most of the other victims. Deidre was determined not to let that happen. As if to bolster her confidence, she pulled the pepper Mace from her purse, looked at, and put it back in.

Deidre thought about the pistol Marshall had left behind. It was something she never wanted to use, but would not hesitate to if it meant saving her life.

In any event, she was glad to know that Spencer would be around tonight—all night, if Deidre had her way. The thought of more wonderful and erotic sexcapades with him excited her.

The moment Deidre stepped onto her porch, she knew that something was wrong. Call it intuition, but warning bells seemed to go off in her head nonstop. Removing her pepper Mace, she unlocked the front door.

Hesitantly, Deidre went inside. . . .

The place was trashed. It looked like a hurricane had blown through. Or a tornado had left behind its calling card. Deidre was stunned. And frightened. Her first thought was to see if anything had been stolen and further assess the damage. But then she heard a sound that seemed like it was coming from upstairs. Or was it downstairs?

The person was still in the house! Deidre was petrified.

I have to get out of here. Now!

Backpedaling, she went out the front door, ran to her car, and locked the door. She started the car, half expecting the home invader—whoever it was—to come storming out, planning to attack her. But when no one came, Deidre took a moment to catch her breath before backing out of the driveway and taking off.

Only when she felt safe from the intruder did Deidre pull over and reach for her cell phone to call Spencer. *Please let him be there.*

He picked up on the first ring.

"What . . . ?" Spencer asked as if he hadn't heard clearly the first time.

"Someone broke into my house." Deidre's voice was controlled, but raised an octave. "The place is a disaster. And worse, I think I walked in on the home invader at work. . . ."

Spencer's heart skipped a beat as he imagined how frightening that would be. "Where are you now?" He hoped to hell she wasn't still in that house.

"In my car . . . on my way to your place—"

"Good," he said with relief. "We'll deal with it together."

"I was counting on it," Deidre uttered, still shaking at the thought of someone actually breaking into her house. But who? And what were they looking for? "I'm going to call the police now. Maybe they can get there before the intruder leaves."

"Good idea," Spencer said. "See you in a bit."

Spencer wondered why someone would pick Deidre's house in particular to break into, apart from the location, which made for a quick getaway into the park. What had they been after? Did it have anything to do with a serial killer out for more blood? Or an unstable stalker who couldn't or wouldn't seem to leave them alone?

Hal was en route to Deidre's house after she'd called to say that she had been burglarized. He wondered if it was a coincidence, in light of her romance with Spencer Berry and the series of deaths that could indirectly lead to his doorstep. Or was there some connection? Had someone been sending Deidre or Berry a message? And, if so, would either of them even realize it?

It was something Hal did not wish to leave to chance, even if he more or less discounted the notion. He knew that break-ins in the area had risen twofold this year from last. Meaning it was likely that Deidre's house had been targeted for some time now and had been broken into when the opportunity best presented itself.

But the person or persons responsible obviously hadn't counted on Deidre getting home when she did. Thank goodness she had gotten the hell out of there before confronting them. Even if she had run to Spencer Berry for comfort. Hal was past pining for the pretty lady now with his new romantic interest, Gigi, more than enough to occupy his bed and time away from the job. He was more concerned with getting to the bottom of this, while making sure it was indeed a burglary they were dealing with and not something more.

Hal got on the phone. "I want that house gone over from A to Z for any evidence that can point us in the right direction here," he ordered after being told that there was no sign of the intruder. He didn't want a misstep here.

But Hal was also determined not to jump to the wrong conclusions one way or the other.

FIFTY-TWO

When Spencer and Deidre arrived at her house, the place was crawling with cops. More than Spencer would've thought necessary for what was supposed to be a relatively simple case. He didn't doubt that Hal Iverson was behind the extra detail, looking for any signs that it could have been connected in any way to the Park Killer investigation.

"Are you going to be all right?" Spencer turned to Deidre in the passenger seat. He'd decided that she was a bit too shaken up to drive.

"I'm not sure," Deidre said, hating that her private space had been violated. It was bad enough that her car had been wrecked recently. Now someone had gone after her house. Was it the same vandals? Could this be the work of Gayle? Or someone else? Whatever the case, Deidre was determined not to fall apart now. She needed to be strong to get through this and hopefully help the police get to the bottom of it. "I'll be fine," she told Spencer. Thanks in large part to his protective and comforting presence.

He smiled, but Deidre knew Spencer was just as concerned as she was that this might be something bigger than a standard break-in.

Hal greeted them inside. "How are you holding up?" he asked Deidre.

"Pretty well, all things considered," she answered evenly.

"Looks like someone really went to town on your place."

"Tell us something we don't know," Spencer said, gazing at the crime scene and destruction of property.

Hal regarded him beneath knitted brows. "We're on the same side here, Berry. I'm just trying to get some answers."

Spencer gave him that much. "Yeah. So what've you got so far?"

Hal ran a hand down the side of his face. "Not much, to tell you the truth. Whoever did this was long gone by the time police arrived. So far, it looks like a typical burglary." In truth, it seemed more like a personal vendetta, but he didn't want to say that until he had more to go on.

"What are the alternatives?" As if Spencer didn't already know.

Hal rolled his eyes. "You tell me. Do either of you know anyone who could've done this?"

Deidre looked at Spencer, who seemed to read her mind and nodded to that effect. Her gaze returned to Hal. "I've been the victim of a stalker," she admitted.

"Oh?" Hal raised an eyebrow. "You mean that man from the train . . . ?"

"Actually she means a woman named Gayle Kincaid," Spencer spoke up, thinking he should have reported this a long time ago. "I used to date her, but she's had trouble accepting that it's over. She's stalking me . . . and threatened Deidre . . ."

Hal cast hard eyes on one, then the other. "And neither of you thought it was important enough to mention until now?"

"I'll take responsibility for that," Spencer said, pursing his lips. "I was hoping that Gayle would back off without legal intervention."

"You're really starting to scare me, Berry." Hal snorted. "Women you know are either stalkers or victims of a serial killer. Kind of makes you wonder if any woman is safe if she happens to cross paths with you." He gazed at Deidre with uncertainty.

"That's not fair, Hal," Deidre said, feeling compelled to come to Spencer's aide. Especially since she knew that Hal was essentially placing the blame for her house being trashed squarely on Spencer's shoulders. "You know as well as I do that Spencer is *not* the Park Killer. And anyone can be a stalker. It usually doesn't have anything to do with the person being stalked. Just sick, fixated individuals."

Spencer was surprised at Deidre's strong words on his behalf. Not to mention her acumen on stalking in general. It made him appreciate just what type of woman she was that much more. But he wouldn't sit back and allow her to fight his fights for him.

He gave Hal the benefit of a stern look "Look, Iverson, whatever you may think of me isn't important. Why don't we just forget our personal issues and focus on what happened in this house and who may be behind it?"

Hal held his gaze for a moment or two before relenting. "Yeah, okay."

"I, for one, have my doubts that Gayle is behind this," Spencer said, realizing he might not be giving her enough credit for what she was capable of doing.

"And why is that?" Hal wondered.

Spencer gave the disheveled room a sweeping glance. "Well, if the rest of the house looks like this, it seems more like the work of an army than one woman."

"So she had help to settle some scores with the woman who stole you from her," Hal surmised, glancing at Deidre with something akin to resentment.

"That's not her style," Spencer said, brushing it off. "The Gayle I knew was pretty much a loner. I doubt that's changed."

"We'll have to see about that. Give me her address and we'll question her." Hal turned to Deidre. "The Park Killer may very well be on to you . . . and this could be his calling card. . . ."

Deidre was afraid Hal would think that, as the thought had also crossed her mind. But she remained skeptical. "So why would he trash my house as a warning sign instead of just killing me, like he did the other women?"

Hal set his jaw. "That's a great question that I don't have an answer to at the moment."

"Well, when you do, will you please let me know?" Deidre didn't mean to sound flippant, but she was more interested in facts than possibilities where it concerned her property and life.

Hal gingerly put his hand on her shoulder. "I will," he said evenly. "In the meantime, we're going to need you to take a look around and see if anything has been stolen. If so, whoever did this might try to sell it, which could lead to an arrest."

Deidre felt her stomach churn at the prospect of going through her entire house and surveying what the intruder or intruders had left behind or taken. But she knew that it was the only way to proceed if she wanted answers.

"I'll be happy to do whatever I can to help in the investigation, Hal," she said, and eyed Spencer, who clearly supported her decision.

"The only thing that seems to be missing is a gun," Deidre said, after she had completed her trip through the house. Being nervous and upset in seeing the vandalism everywhere, including her beloved art room, she admittedly couldn't be sure if there was anything else missing. "It belonged to Marshall, my husband," she told Hal, Spencer, and a detective on the case. "I was keeping it for protection from . . . a break-in. Looks like it didn't do much good."

"It was better that you weren't home when this happened," Hal said. "Much too often it's the homeowner who ends up getting hurt with their own damned gun."

Spencer was inclined to agree, but was still troubled. "Any idea why they only took a firearm?" He faced the lieutenant. "If that's the case, it wasn't much of a burglary."

Hal shifted his feet. "First of all, we don't know for sure that it was just the gun they took, even if that was Deidre's assessment at first glance. Who knows what else could be missing? Also, the thief or thieves, if that was the case, may have been scared off by Deidre or the police before they could take anything else. But, to answer your question, illegal firearms are a hot commodity these days on the streets of Sinclair Heights. It wouldn't be unheard of for thieves to go after guns when they break in, and leave behind other valuables that may be easier to trace. We'll just have to see where the investigation leads us."

It was something Spencer could only hope did not lead back to him, even if circuitously.

A little later, when they were alone, Deidre told Spencer what he had probably already figured out: "I don't think I want to stay here tonight."

"I don't want you to either," he said. "Let the police do what they need to do and you can stay at my place for as long as you like."

Deidre gazed at him. She was hoping he would say that, but she needed a bit more reassurance that she wouldn't be imposing on his space. "Are you sure?"

Spencer looked her in the eye. "Believe me, I'd love to have your company any way I can get it. And Sky will be glad too, as he's really warming up to the thought of having to compete for attention with someone other than Charity."

"So I have to compete with a dog for your attention, huh?" Deidre's eyes twinkled playfully.

"Not in a million years," Spencer declared. "In this case, Sky definitely has to take a back seat to you."

Deidre was happy to hear that. "Well then, it looks like you have yourself a temporary roommate."

FIFTY-THREE

Deidre arched her back and relished the feel of Spencer's gentle hands caressing her nipples and breasts as she lowered herself onto him. She involuntarily contracted once he was inside her and watched the satisfaction light Spencer's face. Deidre began to move up and down him slowly, her body trembling ever so slightly while her knees pressed against the sides of his nakedness. Spencer began to stroke her, driving Deidre mad with delight.

"Come to me, baby," Spencer urged, wanting to feel Deidre's beautiful body on his . . . their skin touching as if one.

Deidre lowered herself and Spencer wrapped his arms around her slender waist and brought their lips together. He loved the taste of Deidre and kissed her hungrily, and she greedily kissed him back.

"Spencer . . ." whispered Deidre through held breath as they made love to each other. He'd made her forget that she had come over there to escape the work of vandals, thieves, or worse. All that mattered right now was her need to have him and give herself to him in every way. "Take me . . . I'm yours. . . ."

"With pleasure," Spencer murmured, holding Deidre's buttocks as he guided her body onto him.

A few minutes later, Spencer turned them over on the bed and propelled himself inside Deidre again and again while she kissed his chest and ran her fingernails haphazardly across his back, arousing him even more.

With her legs spread wide and elevated from the bed, Deidre brought Spencer deeper and deeper within, burning up inside with his passion. Unable to hold back, she freely let go and cried out loud when she came like thunder, electrifying every fiber in her.

Spencer held on to her firmly and Deidre to him as they both shook as if from a mini earthquake and moaned in harmonic sounds of ecstasy.

When the quivering subsided and noise quieted, they continued to cling to each other's sweaty body, content to enjoy the togetherness after the fact.

"I can't think of a better way to pass the time," Spencer said lightly.

"Neither can I," Deidre cooed in a tired but very contented voice.

"This arrangement of living together definitely has its perks." Spencer climbed halfway off her and imagined it being a permanent thing.

"You'll get no argument from me." Deidre licked her lips. While this was true enough, she still didn't want to be forced out of her house. Which someone had managed to accomplish. She dribbled her fingers down Spencer's hard stomach. "But it has to be done right. Meaning that the police need to get to figure out who was behind the burglary and vandalism, so we can see where it is we want to go from there."

"I agree." Spencer caressed her feet with his, while pondering the latest round of trouble that one or the other had encountered. Until they were out of the woods in dealing with break-ins, stalkers, and serial killers, their future remained uncertain at best. "In the meantime, let's just bask in the moment, Deidre."

"I thought we just did that." Deidre smiled at him, surprised at how playful and at ease she had become with him, as their emotional attachment grew stronger.

Spencer kissed her shoulder. "So we did at that. But, last I knew, we still had the whole night ahead of us. Tomorrow will take care of itself."

Deidre turned his face to hers. "And the day after that, and the one to follow," she said, kissing him and putting the darkness of the day away for now.

The following morning, Spencer let Deidre enjoy her beauty sleep while he picked up Sky at his father's house and took him to the park. After being cooped up all night, Spencer decided to give the dog a treat and let him run loose in the no-leash area, mindful of other dog owners and their pets.

Spencer sat on a bench, reflecting on his life and its ups and downs. On the down side, he thought about anyone he'd come into contact with as a forensic psychologist who might be crazy enough to do these women bodily harm as a way to get back at him. He'd been allowed to keep records of offenders he had profiled or otherwise came into contact with for possible use in further profiling, research, or even a book. As of now, no one in his past seemed to fit the profile of the Park Killer, assuming his motivation to beat, rape, and kill was directed toward Spencer. He would continue to dig.

On the positive side was Spencer's warm and exciting relationship with Deidre. She had single-handedly made him more or less forget about every woman who had come before her—including Fiona. He didn't want to run away from Deidre or try to make her someone she wasn't. He was more than ready for a committed relationship and he was pretty sure that Deidre was too.

Now they just needed to get past this serial killer who was casting a long shadow over their community,

and the residual effects of a stalker, break-in, and vandalism. If they could do that, then there would be no
mountain that Spencer and Deidre could not climb.

Gayle watched the dog roaming freely on the grass,
seemingly in no hurry to socialize with other dogs.
That was what she had counted on. She had followed
Spencer from his house, careful to keep her distance,
and then watched as he retrieved Sky from his father's
place and brought the dog to Pelle Park. Gayle was
about to carry out another plan to further make Spencer pay dearly for cutting her out of his life, as though
he'd never truly given a damn about her.

Hidden amid some thick bushes, Gayle took the raw
chicken that she'd laced with rat poison out of a plastic
bag and put it on the dirt. She glanced at Spencer who
was sitting on a bench talking on his cell phone. Probably to that bitch of his. Well that was perfect to keep
him preoccupied.

In a soft voice, Gayle called out, "Sky . . . Sky . . .
Come here, boy." The dog heard her and sauntered toward Gayle. *Good dog. Keep coming . . .*

The dog stopped for a moment, as though sensing
danger. But then Gayle held up the raw meat, tempting him. "Come on, Sky," she whispered. "Time for a
breakfast you'll never forget."

The dog did a three-sixty and then came bounding
her way. Gayle smiled, realizing that her latest plan of
revenge was about to come to fruition. What better way
to hurt Spencer than to poison his stupid precious dog?

Sky stepped cautiously into the bushes, licking Gayle's hands. "Yeah, you remember me, don't you, boy?
We were good together once. Just like me and Spencer,
'til he conveniently chose to forget that. Well, I have a
treat for you, Sky, and it'll be your last. . . ."

She pushed the chicken toward the dog. Sky sniffed
it and seemed reluctant to taste it, before his canine

nature kicked in and he began to devour the raw meat as if he hadn't eaten for days.

Gayle watched for a moment with utter satisfaction, then quietly moved backward and slipped out of the bushes, disappearing into the woods. She grinned wickedly as she envisioned the look on Spencer's face when he discovered what had happened to the mutt.

"Trust me when I tell you that everything looks sexy on you, baby," Spencer uttered sweetly into the phone after Deidre called him to ask what type of lingerie he liked best.

"Why did I figure you would say that?" she cooed.

"Because it's true," he declared. "Of course, sexiest of all is when you're wearing *nothing* on that gorgeous body, except me."

The mere thought of seeing Deidre naked last night and making love to her was playing with Spencer's libido.

"Ditto, Mr. Berry." Deidre hummed.

"I'll remember that, Ms. Lawrence." Spencer chuckled and glanced in the direction where he'd last seen Sky, having only taken his eyes off the dog for a few moments. He didn't see him. Swiveling around, Spencer looked behind the bench and saw other dogs running around aimlessly, but not Sky.

"Spencer . . ." He honed in on Deidre's voice, having missed whatever she said.

Then Spencer heard a horrible yowl coming from a cluster of bushes not far away. It was clearly the sound of a dog in obvious distress.

Sky.

"I think Sky's in trouble," he told Deidre. "I'll call you back."

Spencer cut off the phone and raced toward the bushes where the terrible sounds grew louder.

"Sky," Spencer called out, his heart thumping. Stepping inside the bushes, he saw Sky writhing and howling in pain before suddenly collapsing.

Spencer nearly tripped over something as he came to his dog's aid. He saw some raw chicken that appeared to be coated with something.

Deidre drove to meet Spencer at the vet. When she'd heard that Sky had apparently been poisoned, the news horrified her. She knew how much Spencer loved that dog, and she had begun to love him too. Who would do such a wicked thing? Would Gayle actually stoop to this level to get back at Spencer? Could this horrendous act be tied in any way to the vandalism of her car or the break-in at her house?

The thoughts left Deidre unsettled and fearful as to what was next.

She found Spencer in the reception area, looking as though he had already lost his best friend.

Deidre gave him a hug, then met Spencer's eyes and asked tentatively, "How's Sky . . . ?"

Spencer's forehead creased. "I don't know. They're working on him now. He was in pretty bad shape when I brought him in, so . . ." Spencer couldn't bring himself to say that Sky might actually die from this, but he knew it was more than a real possibility, given the poison he'd ingested and the suffering he had endured as a result.

"I'm so sorry, Spencer," Deidre said, wishing she could somehow ease his pain.

"Yeah, I know you are. Thanks for coming." Spencer gazed at Deidre, glad to have her support.

"You said Sky ate some chicken? . . ."

He nodded. "Someone left it in the bushes . . . or lured him to it."

Deidre frowned. "You think Gayle was behind it?"

Spencer twisted his mouth angrily. "I don't know, but I sure as hell intend to find out."

At that moment, the vet came out. Her expression was unreadable. Spencer was afraid to hear what she had to say, but knew he had to for better or worse.

"Mr. Berry, after some shaky moments, it looks like your dog will pull through."

Spencer was elated with this news, taking Deidre's hand. "That's wonderful." He sighed. "What about the chicken?"

"We're not sure, but we think it was laced with some kind of poison," the vet responded, touching her glasses. "It's being sent to the lab for further analysis."

"Have you had any other recent report of dogs being poisoned?" Deidre asked, trying to figure out if this could have been a case of someone who hated dogs in general and was systematically attempting to eliminate them, as opposed to specifically targeting Sky.

The vet wrinkled her nose. "Not too recently, and definitely not with raw chicken."

"When can I take Sky home?" Spencer asked, having already decided who the culprit was.

"We'd like to keep your dog for a few days of observation, just to be on the safe side. But you can see him if you want—"

"Yes, I'd like to." Spencer put his arm around Deidre's shoulders. "We both would."

"Why don't we go out to dinner tonight at a nice restaurant," Spencer suggested to Deidre in the parking lot. "It'll help take my mind off other things." *And keep it more on us.*

"Sounds good," Deidre agreed, while wondering if either of them would be in much of a mood to eat then with everything going on.

"Right now, I have something I need to take care of—"

"You mean *someone.*" She raised her eyes to his. "You're going after Gayle, aren't you?"

Spencer didn't try to deny it. "I want to hear it from her that she poisoned my dog—and maybe even vandalized your car and house. . . ."

Deidre's brows knitted. "If Gayle admits to being responsible for those awful things, what then?"

He stiffened, reading the concern in her face that he might do something foolish. "I don't know. I haven't thought that far ahead."

"I'm going with you," Deidre announced flatly.

"I don't think that's a very good idea," Spencer said.

"Well, I think it's a *great* idea." She looked at him, fearful as to what he might do when confronting Gayle. Or vice versa. "I was once with a man who allowed his temper and machismo to get in the way of common sense and intelligence. Now he's dead. I don't need another man in my life who acts impulsively, only to regret it. If we're going to make this work, Spencer, we need to be able to trust each other to do the right thing—then do it together."

As much as Spencer wanted to do the wrong thing, he knew that violating a restraining order, and worse with no witnesses, would not change what had already happened. But it could do irreparable damage to the burgeoning relationship he was building with Deidre. He wouldn't let that happen, no matter what.

Spencer eyed her softly. "Okay, let's go," he said. "We'll take my car and pick up yours on the way back."

"That works for me." Deidre was satisfied that she had talked some sense into Spencer. Now came the hard part.

Confronting Gayle and her inner demons.

FIFTY-FOUR

Gayle left the college library and walked across the campus to her nearby apartment. She thought about the last moments of Sky's life and how painful it must have been for Spencer to witness it. It was the same kind of pain Gayle felt in falling in love with him, only to have that love rejected once she'd given the man what he wanted.

Well, I hope you're happy that you made me kill your dog. I hope that bitch you're banging was worth seeing your daughter's birthday party ruined with the rat, and then your dog suffering horribly from rat poisoning. Not to mention the job I did on your whore's car and house.

Gayle reached her apartment and unlocked the door. She went inside and poured herself a glass of wine, drinking it triumphantly, while recalling an unexpected visit she'd had yesterday from Hal. He'd come to see her not as a lover, for he knew her only as Gigi, but in an official police capacity. She had pretended not to be home, but suspected he was investigating the break-in and vandalism at the house where Spencer's lover lived. Spencer and that bitch had probably pointed the finger at her.

Hal left his card with a note for her to call him. Maybe she would and maybe she wouldn't. Better yet, maybe she would come clean about her true identity while he had his dick inside her. She would profess her innocence about everything, certain he would believe every word she said.

In the meantime, she had some unfinished business with Spencer. She fully expected him to pay her a visit anytime now. If he tried to get rough with her, she would be ready.

But would he be ready for what she had in store for him and his lover?

He had watched with interest as the woman poisoned the dog, leaving it to suffer in excruciating pain. He might well have done the same thing, had he thought of it. It would certainly give the dog's owner something to think about.

He'd followed Gayle Kincaid to the library and even pretended to browse through books, all the while keeping his sights set on her.

He trailed her for the short walk to the apartment building, observing as she entered an apartment on the ground floor. His guess was that she lived alone, despondent over being jilted by the dog owner.

Well, maybe he could alleviate her pain some, while at the same time dishing out a whole lot more.

He kept the cap low over his brow and made his way to the front door. Knocking once, he thought about his plan of action and the satisfaction he'd receive when the deed was done.

Gayle heard the knock on the door. She looked at the gleaming pistol in her hand that she had stolen from the house she'd ransacked, admiring it for a moment before putting it back in her pocket. Calmly, she peeked through the peephole, expecting to see Spencer's angry face. Instead, there was another man standing there, wearing a cap. He looked innocent enough. Could he be a cop? Someone Hal had sent over to question her about the break-in?

The man didn't look like a cop, though. Not that she knew what one looked like, except for Hal. Gayle wondered if it was possible that Spencer had sent someone else to do his dirty work for him. If so, he would meet the same fate, and she would deal with Spencer later.

"Can I help you?" she asked through the door.

"Yeah, I think so," the man said. "I work at the Sinclair Heights College library. Looks like you dropped your student ID there. I told my boss I'd be happy to bring it to you on my way home."

Gayle was suspicious. She distinctly remembered putting her ID back in her purse after she'd checked out a book. Could she have actually dropped it without knowing? Or was this a line the man was giving her to get her to open the door for whatever purpose he had in mind?

"Just a minute. . . ." Gayle went to check her purse and was surprised to find that her student ID was not in her wallet. *Guess I made a boo-boo.* She was disappointed in herself, since she made few mistakes these days, other than letting Spencer get away.

The expected confrontation with him would have to wait a little longer.

She unlocked the door and opened it, smiling with embarrassment at the man. "I appreciate your dropping by with my ID."

"No problem, since I was in the neighborhood," he said in a voice that sounded strangely familiar to Gayle, though she didn't recognize him right off the bat.

The man held the ID out to her, and Gayle reached for it, all the while studying his face, obscured somewhat by the way he wore the cap. Then, as familiarity came to her, Gayle sensed peril. She backed away and went for the gun.

He watched as Gayle dug into the deep pocket of her skirt for something. Taking no chances, he dropped the ID on the floor and immediately went on the attack.

"Sorry," he lied, and in the split second that her eyes lowered, he swung his long arm so his fist landed solidly on her jaw.

Gayle went reeling backward. He stepped inside the apartment, kicked the door shut, and came after her. She removed a gun and was attempting to aim it at him. But before she could steady herself, he slammed his fist into her jaw again, this time hearing the unmistakable crunch of it breaking.

She went down in a heap and the gun went off, the bullet landing in the stucco ceiling. He climbed atop her and took possession of the gun, putting it in his pocket.

He sucked in a deep breath and gazed down at the semiconscious woman beneath him. She had been prepared to shoot someone. Undoubtedly the owner of the poisoned dog.

Spencer Berry.

Instead, Gayle Kincaid was about to face an even worse nightmare before breathing her last breath.

FIFTY-FIVE

Hal got the call that a woman named Gayle Kincaid was found dead in her apartment by a neighbor. Hal figured that it was the work of the Park Killer. Equally disturbing was that he recognized the name of the victim as the person Deidre and Spencer had accused of being a stalker, and someone who Deidre believed might be responsible for the burglary and vandalism in her home. Further investigation had uncovered that Gayle Kincaid had taken out a restraining order against Spencer, something he had failed to mention.

Pondering these issues while trying to keep an open mind, Hal stepped past the officer at the door and went inside the apartment where Detective Zack Hernandez stood over the body.

"What have we got?" Hal asked routinely without zeroing in on the victim.

"Definitely the work of the Park Killer," Hernandez said. "The lady didn't stand a chance. Worked her over good before carrying out the rest of his MO."

Hal stepped closer to the nude body. It wasn't 'til he looked at the face, which was badly swollen and almost unrecognizable, that he gasped with disbelief.

It was his Gigi.

Gayle Kincaid was the woman he had started getting serious about with no clue as to her alter ego.

Now she'd been reduced to a battered, beaten, raped, and strangled victim of a serial killer?

And she was yet another female that Spencer Berry was acquainted with.

"What is it?" Hernandez asked the lieutenant. "Do you know this woman?"

Hal regained his equilibrium, even if this was one of the hardest things he'd ever had to see and deal with. "No," he said glumly. "She just reminded me of someone I used to know."

Spencer and Deidre arrived at the apartment complex and found police cars there, lights flashing. More importantly, they were being blocked from entering the parking lot.

"What's going on?" Deidre asked.

"Not sure." Spencer looked in the direction of Gayle's apartment and saw the familiar crime scene tape. "Think we'd better find out." He parked outside the complex and they walked across the street.

"Afraid we can't let you in," said a burly uniformed officer.

"You have to," Deidre said impulsively. "I'm a spokesperson with the Sinclair Heights Police Bureau—here on official business." She showed her credentials.

The officer studied them, and then looked at Spencer. "And who are you?"

Spencer considered using the FBI as his front, but thought better. "I'm with her," he said simply, hoping it would be enough.

It was. The officer let them through.

"Good thinking, Ms. Lawrence," Spencer said with a slight smile.

"Seemed like quick action was necessary," she said, hoping it wouldn't get her into trouble later.

He concurred. "Now let's see what the police are up to over there."

When they reached Gayle's apartment, they saw Hal conferring with Hernandez just inside the door. Both men stopped talking after looking their way, before Hal said lowly, "I'll handle this."

Hernandez nodded, stone-faced. "Good luck."

Hal stepped outside and Deidre immediately got a sinking feeling.

"What the hell are you two doing here?" he asked suspiciously.

"Suppose you tell us what's happened?" Spencer decided to put the onus on him first, suspecting the worst.

"Gayle Kincaid was murdered in her apartment. A neighbor heard a shot and called 911. The telltale signs indicate that the Park Killer has struck again."

Spencer gulped. In spite of his firm belief that Gayle had sent his daughter a rat and poisoned his dog, among other things, he'd never wanted her life to end like this. "I'm sorry to hear that."

"Are you?" Hal drew his brows together. "Since it was only a day ago that you accused Ms. Kincaid of stalking you, I would think you'd be glad to have her out of your hair, figuratively speaking."

"I'm not that coldhearted, Lieutenant," Spencer replied, curling his lip.

"Neither of us wanted this to happen," Deidre spoke up, still reeling from the news that Gayle had become yet another victim of the serial killer. How did they go from confronting Gayle to discovering a murderer had gotten there first? Would this madness ever end?

"That doesn't change the facts any," Hal said, hating that she had to be caught smack dab in the middle of this latest investigation. "Again, I'd like to know how you just happened to show up at this apartment complex." Hal peered at Spencer, needing to vent against someone. "Especially since the victim had a restraining order out against you."

"That was just a clever ploy on her part to do whatever the hell she wanted and keep me from legally being able to respond," Spencer snapped.

"Doesn't seem like it did a hell lot of good, since here you are, violating her space." Hal glared at him and then looked at Deidre. "You both better have a damned good reason for that, under the circumstances."

It seemed to Spencer that Iverson was taking this much more personally than he should have. *Wonder why?* Maybe the case and his inability to catch this guy was starting to get to him. Or was there something else about Gayle's murder that bothered the lieutenant?

"If you're suggesting either of us had anything to do with this—" Spencer began.

"Never suggested anything of the sort," Hal said, sucking in a deep breath as he thought about Gigi and the horrible way she had died. The last thing he wanted was to tip his hand about being romantically involved with Gayle Kincaid and all the questions sure to follow, including questioning his own judgment and objectivity with this case. "But even you have to admit that this latest coincidence, if we can call it that, between you and a Park Killer victim, is unsettling at the very least."

"Maybe," Spencer allowed, "but we've just spent the last three hours at the vet—in case we need an alibi." He glanced at Deidre, and could only imagine how this latest twist was playing with her mind and her lack of safety from a killer who seemed like he could target anyone, at any time, with no one able to stop him.

"And now you walk right into a murder investigation." Hal narrowed his eyes at him. "Again, why?"

Spencer swallowed. "We were on our way to see Gayle."

"I gathered that much," the lieutenant snapped. "What for?"

Deidre spoke up. "Spencer's dog was poisoned this morning at Pelle Park, Hal. Someone left raw chicken in the bushes."

"And you think it was Ms. Kincaid?" *Would Gigi really do such a cruel thing to an animal?* Hal turned to Spencer.

"Well, she was certainly the first person to come to mind, given her behavior of late," Spencer said, making no bones about it. "I also strongly believe Gayle sent my daughter a dead rat and may have vandalized Deidre's car." Even the damage to her property now seemed like something Gayle could have carried out on her own.

Hal studied Deidre, still trying to wrap his mind around this side of Gigi that he apparently never knew. "That true?"

Deidre nodded. "There wasn't any solid proof that Gayle was behind it. But I did file a police report and had a good feeling about it."

Hal was disappointed that he'd been kept out of the loop on this. Maybe if he'd known sooner, he could have gotten Gigi the help she needed to turn her obsession around, possibly preventing her from being murdered. He glared at Spencer. "And you came here to do what exactly?"

"Talk to her, that's all," Spencer assured him. "I thought that maybe I could get her to either admit to what she'd done or convince her to back off and leave us the hell alone once and for all."

"We only wanted to see if Gayle committed this despicable act of poisoning a dog," Deidre added. "And, if so, report it to the authorities."

Hal chewed on his lip sadly. "Well, you're too late for that. Someone else got here before you could. Witnesses have reported seeing a man wearing a cap, matching the description of the person of interest we're looking for in the murder of Sabrina Murray, among others."

Deidre's stomach lurched when she thought of Sabrina dying at the hands of a vicious serial killer. And now apparently Gayle had met the same fate. Was she bound to become a victim too, sooner or later, as someone in Spencer's life?

Spencer frowned. "Believe me, Lieutenant, when I tell you that I wouldn't have wished what happened to Gayle on my worst enemy, if I had one that I was aware of."

Hal believed him, given that there was nothing to indicate otherwise. But the question of whether or not he had any enemies capable of these murders was still up for debate." Looks like the killer also stole Ms. Kincaid's car," he said. "We've got an APB out on it right now. If we're lucky—and we haven't been thus far—we'll find the car and the person behind the wheel."

Spencer had to wonder again if Gayle's murder could be more about him than her. Was this part of a pattern that included the death of Clint Winston? Or simply the work of a maniacal serial killer who just happened to target someone else Spencer knew?

"Did you happen to find anything in the apartment that would indicate Gayle was behind poisoning my dog?" he had to ask the lieutenant.

Hal paused, hating that the facts were beginning to add up against the woman he wanted to have a long relationship with. "I believe we did," he answered evenly. "There was half a raw chicken and a box of rat poison on the kitchen counter. Looks like you *really* got on the bad side of this woman, Berry." Might she have turned on him next had things turned sour between them?

Spencer eyed Deidre and wished he had met her before ever laying eyes on the likes of Gayle. "Yeah, my mistake, I'm afraid. I take full responsibility for that—but nothing that's happened since."

"Ms. Kincaid was targeting the wrong man," Hal suggested. "Maybe if she'd fed a bit of that rat poison to her killer, she could've beat him to the punch and made all our lives a little easier."

"I'm beginning to wonder if that's more of a pipe dream than anything," Spencer said despairingly. "Looks like this killer is determined to make all our lives as miserable as possible."

Deidre agreed, feeling a bit lightheaded. She sensed that as long as the killer kept killing, any hope that she and Spencer had for a normal relationship would be hindered at best and dubious at worst.

FIFTY-SIX

The following day, the rain came down in buckets as Spencer awaited word in his office at the college on whether the police had a suspect in custody after Gayle's car was found abandoned less than two miles from her apartment. He could only hope this nightmare would soon be over and he could focus on spending more time with his dog, daughter, and girlfriend. It was easy for Spencer to think of Deidre as his girl, given that he thought the world of her and that she was really into him.

For the first time since his divorce, Spencer actually believed that he had met his match in Deidre, and she was everything he could ask for in a partner. Maybe even a wife . . . and mother of more children in the future, if things continued to move in the right direction.

At the moment, Spencer would settle for just having Deidre under his roof so he could always be there to protect her. At least as long as there was danger in the air and a killer on the loose. But Deidre had other ideas, insisting that she go back to her place this morning to clean up and get her life back in order. Especially now that at least one threat to her safety, Gayle, was no longer in the picture. Spencer had gone along with it, knowing he had little say in the matter and not wanting to complicate things any further in their relationship by being too demanding . . . like a husband-to-be—

When the phone rang, Spencer broke from his contemplation and the essays he was supposed to be grading. He assumed it was Deidre calling, as they had agreed to check in with each other frequently.

Instead, his father was on the line. Probably ready to give Spencer another earful about allowing Sky to wander in the park unattended, damned near costing the dog his life. Spencer cursed himself for that almost fatal error in judgment, though he knew the blame ultimately fell on Gayle's shoulders, even if misguided in her dangerous and deadly obsession.

"Hey, Pops." He wanted to sound cheerful, even though he felt anything but.

"I need to talk you about somethin', Spencer." His father's voice shook.

"Sure, I'm listening."

"Not on the phone."

Spencer sat up, alarmed. "What's the matter?"

"Just come over—please. I'll be waitin'."

The phone went dead.

Spencer's heart skipped a beat. Something was wrong, even by his father's standards of often being overly cryptic. He grabbed his keys and umbrella, and headed out the door.

Deidre watched the rain pelting the ground from her living room window. The house was still in disarray, though she had made some progress in reclaiming what was hers. After the police had completed their investigation, Hal now seemed convinced that, with circumstantial evidence, the home and car vandalism, along with the gun theft, were most likely the work of Gayle Kincaid, as part of her pattern of misconduct due to her grudge against Spencer.

This was good enough for Deidre to want to return home and not be defeated by fear of being accosted in her own home by a serial killer, even against the strong protestations of Spencer. Though Deidre had started to feel as if she truly belonged in his home as a partner, she wanted to be there for the right reasons and not the wrong ones. She didn't want to confuse the two in the process of being in Spencer's warm and sturdy arms.

Deidre's thoughts turned to the phone conversation she'd had earlier with her parents. Not wanting to worry them needlessly, she had neglected to mention what Gayle had put her through, to say nothing of the terror a serial killer had brought to the community. Instead, the talk had centered on her parents' plans for a September visit. It would be their first since Deidre moved to Sinclair Heights. She prayed that by then the Park Killer would be long since apprehended and they could all get on with their lives in a relatively safe atmosphere. And Sabrina and the other victims could rest in peace.

Deidre looked forward to having her parents meet Spencer without the drama and danger that existed in their present lives. She was sure Spencer and her parents would get along great. What Deidre wasn't so sure about was what the future held for a widow and a divorced man with a daughter he shared custody of.

At the end of the day, all Deidre wanted was to love, be loved, and live happily ever after. She was realistic enough to know that dreams did not always come true. And that they could die a quick death, as evidenced by the loss of Marshall, Adam, and Sabrina. But that would never stop her from believing in good things happening, even in the midst of so many bad things.

The phone ringing gave Deidre a start. She picked up on the second ring and a half.

"Hi, baby," Spencer said.

"Hi, sweetie. Where are you?" She could tell that he was in his car.

"I'm on my way to my dad's house. He sounded really strange. Hope he's not having a heart attack or something."

"Oh, dear." Deidre thought about her father and his battle with high cholesterol and blood pressure, either of which could trigger a heart attack. Surely this couldn't happen on top of everything else Spencer had endured of late?

"Or it could be nothing at all but a major case of loneliness," he suggested. "In any event, I'll swing by your place afterwards . . . help you get it back in shape. If that's all right?"

"It's more than all right," she assured him. *I could certainly use a helping hand. Especially yours.* "Kind of creepy being here alone on a rainy, dreary day."

"Yeah, I know what you mean," Spencer said. "We'll see if we can do something about that."

"I'm counting on it."

Deidre hung up and watched the rain again, hoping that everything was all right with Spencer's father, and anticipating her man's arrival.

Spencer parked in the driveway, feeling the absence of his beloved dog.

Doesn't feel quite the same not having Sky with me when visiting dad. Thank goodness he'll be fine soon and back to himself and home where he belongs.

But, right now, Spencer needed to find out what was going on with his father.

When he reached the door, Evan had already opened it and stood there stoically.

"What's wrong, Dad?" Spencer asked, stepping inside.

Evan hesitated. "I think I know who the Park Killer is. . . ."

Spencer's eyes widened. For some reason, a thought went through his mind that Wesley's name might be mentioned. Except for the fact that Spencer's brother was dead.

"Who . . . ?"

Evan peered at him. "Jeremy Haskell."

"Jeremy . . . ?" The mere allegation took Spencer totally by surprise.

"Yeah. Your old FBI pal."

Spencer found that hard to accept. He wondered if his father had any real basis for such an outlandish suspicion. Or if it had anything to do with the fact that his old man had never gotten along well with Jeremy. Evan had always felt that Jeremy resented Spencer and his accomplishments.

"Where did you come up with that?" Spencer asked skeptically.

Evan's mouth pursed. "I was visitin' my friend, Maurice, a little bit ago. After I left his place, I heard on the radio about Gayle and her car missin'—a brown Chevrolet. I happened to see one on the road just a little ways in front of me. The license plate matched, so I decided to follow." He sighed, gazing at Spencer. "The car was abandoned about a mile later. I'm the one who called it in to that hotline number. I saw a man get out of the car. He was wearing a cap that he took off and tossed in the back of another car. I'm sure it was Jeremy."

Spencer was stunned, still finding it difficult to accept. "Could your eyes have been playing tricks on you?"

Evan grimaced. "I can't see as good as I used to, but good enough to know who I'm lookin' at. It was him, son."

"Well, did he see you?" Spencer asked, still trying to come to terms with it and concerned for his father's safety.

"No. I stayed just far enough away to make him think he was all by his lonesome."

"Did you call the police?"

"No, I wanted to talk to you first." He paused. "Jeremy was your pal and former colleague, operating a double life and taking aim at you, for some reason. I wanted you to be the one to bring him down, Spencer."

Jeremy—the Park Killer? Spencer didn't want to believe it but, all things considered, it made sense. Sort of. The history was there between them, and Jeremy certainly had the means and ability to commit the crimes while staying under the radar as a profiler on the case.

But that still didn't explain why.

At this point, pending a police inquiry, Spencer had no choice but to accept his father fingering Jeremy Haskell as a vicious rapist and serial killer.

Spencer believed that his father could be in danger, whether he thought Jeremy had seen him or not.

"Do me a favor, Dad, lock your doors, and get your rifle and load it," Spencer insisted. "If Jeremy saw you, he could come after you."

"I can do that." Evan's face tightened. "If he shows up here, I'll be ready for 'im."

"Good. I'll be back in a while."

"Where you goin'?" Evan asked.

Spencer met his gaze. "To try to prevent Haskell from killing anyone else."

FIFTY-SEVEN

In his car, Spencer phoned Lieutenant Iverson, not because he wanted to, but he had no other choice. He wasn't willing to take any chances that Jeremy might somehow be able to worm his way out of this one. The hard part was convincing Hal that there was a very bad apple among his task force.

"What can I do for you, Berry, on this miserable day?" Hal asked.

"I know who the Park Killer is," Spencer said unevenly.

"This I have to hear," the lieutenant responded sarcastically.

"It's Jeremy Haskell."

"What . . . ? Is this a joke or what?"

"No one's laughing, Iverson," Spencer said brusquely. "My father was the one who found Gayle's car. He also happened to see who was driving it. Haskell's your man."

"And how would your father know this?" Hal asked unbelievingly.

"I worked with Jeremy when I was with the FBI. We had dinner with my father on more than one occasion."

"That may be, but to make such a serious allegation against a member of—"

Spencer cut him off. "Dammit, Hal, this isn't about protecting one of your own—which Jeremy sure as hell isn't, last I knew. It's about catching a demented serial killer. Now I suggest you bring him in before he can cover his tracks—or kill again. . . ."

Hal took a deep breath. "If you're wrong about this—"

"Then sue me or whatever the hell you want to do. If I'm right, you'll get all the credit." *Most of it anyway.*

"I'll be in touch."

"So will I," Spencer said. "And, to be on the safe side, I'd like you to send someone over to my ex-wife Fiona's place, and also Deidre's house. Since these murders are obviously directed toward women I know, Jeremy just might go after them next."

"Will do," Hal said, getting Fiona's address. "Anything else?"

"Just get the son of a bitch!" Spencer said with a definite edge to his voice.

That was all he could hope for at this point. Only then could this deep feeling of trepidation escape him.

Spencer called Deidre, but there was no answer.

Then he called Fiona, fearing that her life and Charity's could be in jeopardy. She answered the phone on the third ring.

"Where's Charity?"

"Hello to you too," Fiona huffed. "She's in her room. Why?"

"I need you to make sure all the doors and windows are locked."

"Now you're scaring me, Spencer. What's going on?"

"Jeremy Haskell is the Park Killer," Spencer said bluntly. "It's a possibility he may show up at your door, pretending to be anything but. If he does, do not let him in, no matter what! The police are on their way."

"Did he kill Clint, too?" Fiona's voice shook.

Spencer stared at the notion. "I honestly don't know. But somehow I wouldn't put it past the bastard."

"But why would Jeremy go after Clint? You and I have been divorced for some time."

"I'll be sure to ask him if I get the chance," Spencer said, just as befuddled about his motives for the killings. "I have to go."

"Where?"

"To try to keep Deidre out of harm's way."

Spencer focused on the wet road through the windshield wipers moving at full speed. He tried calling Deidre again. When all he got was a weird noise, Spencer's anxiety increased. He pressed down on the accelerator to get to her house faster. Now that Jeremy Haskell had gone from murdering female acquaintances to Gayle, whom Spencer had once been intimate with, Deidre was surely next on his hit list.

Worrying Spencer even more was the fact that he'd been unable to reach Deidre by phone. He feared that the cell phone signals were out due to the weather.

Or maybe someone was preventing Deidre from answering her phone. . . .

Deidre winced when the power went out. She'd feared that might happen with the way the rain was coming down and the wind blowing like crazy. Fortunately, it was still light enough inside that she had no trouble navigating through the house. She would be glad when Spencer arrived so they could sit this one out together.

When she heard the knock on the door, Deidre felt as though her prayers were answered. Or at least one of them.

She looked through the window in the door and saw Jeremy Haskell standing there. What was he doing here? Had someone else been killed?

Assuming he may have tried to reach her by phone, and knowing the signal was dead, Deidre unlocked the newly installed deadbolt and opened the door.

"Jeremy . . ."

"Hi, Deidre," he said smoothly. "Bad day to pay anyone a visit. But duty calls, so here I am. Mind if I come in?"

"Please do," she told him, praying that the Park Killer had not struck again, leaving a body behind her house.

"Thanks," he said.

"So what happened?" she asked, assuming that her role as police spokesperson would be needed.

Jeremy studied her for a moment, liking what he saw, as he knew his ex-chum Spencer obviously did.

"Too bad they never caught the bearded guy from the train," he said abruptly.

"I don't think he's the Park Killer anymore," Deidre decided, knowing the man did not fit the description of Sabrina's killer or one that was being mentioned in connection with Gayle's murder.

"Neither do I. In fact, I could've told you a long time ago that the man you thought was following you off the train was just another homeless person, riding the light rail as a break from the streets."

There was something about the profiler's demeanor that unnerved Deidre. "Did Hal send you over?"

"Not exactly. In fact, he has no idea that I'm here."

Deidre took an involuntary step backward. "Why are you here, Jeremy?"

He grinned crookedly. "Well, since you asked, I'm here to kill you. But not before I get a taste of what Spencer's been getting."

Deidre backpedaled, realizing too late that she had just let in the Park Killer.

Hal issued an APB on Jeremy Haskell, who had not responded to messages left on his cell phone. Though finding it hard to fathom that the serial rapist and killer was one of them, the more Hal studied the sketch Roland Vesper had drawn of the suspect in Sabrina Murray's murder, the more it began to look like Jeremy Haskell. When he put that together with the circumstantial evidence that seemed to fit, Hal came to terms with the reality that Spencer Berry's father had indeed fingered their killer.

Now where the hell was Haskell? And would they be able to take him alive before he killed another woman associated with Spencer.

Such as Deidre?

Phoning Zack Hernandez, Hal said in a low voice, "We've got our man within our grasp, and you won't believe who he is—"

"Don't leave me hanging, Hal," Hernandez said dubiously. "Who the hell are we talking about? And if you say Spencer Berry, then we've got some real problems."

"No, it's not him." Hal was already on the way out of his office, wanting to be in on the action when they put this case to rest. "But you're damned closer than you would have ever imagined in your wildest nightmares. . . ."

Spencer cursed as some traffic accidents and the slick roads slowed him down. Again, he tried Deidre's cell phone and got nothing.

Dammit. Spencer pounded his fist on the steering wheel, fearful that time wasn't on his side to avert another tragedy of the worst kind.

Let me be wrong about my feelings that Jeremy plans to go after Deidre—the woman I love and want to spend the rest of my life with.

Spencer didn't even want to begin to speculate about what had turned his onetime friend and colleague into a rapist and killing machine, though he imagined it would make an interesting case study.

Right now, the only important thing was to get to Deidre and make sure she was safe.

Then he would deal with Jeremy Haskell.

Something inside told Spencer that the two went hand in hand.

FIFTY-EIGHT

Jeremy Haskell is the Park Killer . . . and obviously a madman.

Deidre tried to stay calm, though she was scared to death. She prayed that help was on the way, but knew with the stormy weather they would likely be delayed. Meaning she was pretty much on her own.

"Why, Jeremy?" she asked him tonelessly, after he had backed her into a corner. "Why kill those innocent women?" *And why come after me?*

Jeremy chuckled derisively. "Inquiring artists want to know, huh? Well, that's between Spencer and me. Maybe I'll let him in on the secret sometime. But I'm afraid by then, you'll already be dead and probably buried."

He approached her, and Deidre raised her hands defensively. "Stay away from me!"

"Or what? You'll scream? Go ahead. The rain and wind will just drown out the sounds."

I've got to stop him and find a way to buy some time.

Deidre flickered something resembling a smile. "You're right, Jeremy. I won't scream. I won't even fight you. If this is the way it has to be, at least let's do it in bed."

Jeremy wondered if this was some sort of trick on her part to make him lower his guard. It wouldn't work, for he was much too clever for that. But he was intrigued that she appeared resigned to her fate and didn't want him to force himself upon her.

It might be fun to have sex with her as a willing participant, unlike the others, before killing her and leaving Spencer to wonder.

"All right, Deidre, you've got yourself a deal. Why don't we go up to your bedroom and get better acquainted. But, I warn you, try any tricks and I'll make you regret it. Now lead the way. . . ."

Jeremy grabbed Deidre's arm and shoved her toward the stairs. She knew she had little time to do something before he had her in an even more vulnerable position. But what? And when did she make her move?

Spencer recognized Jeremy's white BMW. It was parked a little ways from Deidre's house. There was no sign that the police had arrived. Spencer's pulse raced. The son of a bitch had targeted Deidre and had gotten sloppy at the same time, perhaps hoping that the rotten weather would make a good cover for a killer to come and go.

Parking his car on the street, Spencer rushed toward the house and onto the porch. He noted that the front door was open a crack. Had this been by accident? Or perhaps it was Deidre's way of letting him know she had unwanted company and was in trouble?

Stepping inside carefully, Spencer saw that the power was out. His eyes adjusted to the darkness, but saw no sign of Deidre. He wanted to call out her name, so she could tell him where she was and if she was hurt, but Spencer realized that would play right into Jeremy's bloody hands.

Instead, Spencer relied on his instincts in searching for Deidre, while praying that he wasn't too late to prevent Jeremy from doing to her what he had done to the other women.

***

Deidre wished her gun hadn't been stolen from the nightstand in her bedroom. She could certainly use it right now. Instead, she was at the mercy of a maniacal man who fully intended to brutalize and kill her.

Oh where are you, Spencer? Do you even know that your old sicko friend is a serial rapist and murderer with his hateful eyes firmly planted on me as his next intended victim?

Deidre reached the foot of the bed and turned to face her assailant. "How many more women will you kill before enough is enough, Jeremy?"

"Guess I won't know 'til I do," he responded wryly. "Take off your clothes, Deidre. Now!"

Deidre had no intention of giving in to a rapist and killer, compliantly or otherwise. She also didn't want to die a horrible death.

I have to fight him any way I can.

"Whatever you say, Jeremy."

She unbuttoned a couple of buttons of her blouse. While Jeremy looked on lasciviously, Deidre made her move.

With lightning quick speed, she kneed him in the groin as hard as she could. Jeremy doubled over in pain and Deidre tried to hit him in the face, but he somehow recovered and managed to grab hold of her wrist.

"So you want to play rough, do you?" he spat. "Have it your way, Deidre. The result will still be the same."

"Not this time, Jeremy," the authoritative voice said.

Deidre looked through the darkness to see Spencer standing there. Her heart warmed at the sight, though they were both still very much in danger.

"Let her go!" Spencer demanded.

Ignoring the pain between his legs, Jeremy tightened his grip on Deidre's arm and removed a gun from his jacket.

"Afraid I can't do that, old buddy," Jeremy said, and held the gun to Deidre's head. "I might've known you would somehow show up to try to be a hero in saving your girlfriend's neck. Well, it ain't gonna happen!"

Spencer's ire caused his temperature to rise a few notches as he thought about Gayle being murdered, as well as the other victims of the Park Killer. "You sick bastard."

"I've been called worse." Jeremy kept Deidre between them. "Indulge me, Spencer. How on earth did you manage to put two and two together so quickly?"

Spencer had no interest in feeding his curiosity. At least not while he had Deidre in his grip.

"I saw you ditch Gayle's car," he lied. "The rest was pretty easy to figure out."

Jeremy frowned. "So you got lucky. But then I guess that's how most cases are solved when you get right down to it. Pity neither you nor Ms. Artist and Police Spokeswoman will ever get the chance to spill the beans." He cackled, pressing the gun barrel against Deidre's temple. "By the way, I borrowed this baby from your dog-poisoning ex-girlfriend after I broke her jaw, raped, and strangled her. The stupid bitch planned to shoot you. Imagine that. Now I'm going to shoot your latest lady with it, and then you—"

Spencer inched a little closer. "First, tell me why, Jeremy. Obviously, this has been about you and me from the beginning. Why kill women I knew?"

"Because I knew it would piss you off and make me look good at the same time," Jeremy said acerbically. "I was tired of living in your large shadow with the FBI. Even after you left, it was clear that many there still worshipped the ground you walked on. I wanted you to bleed a little at a time, so you could see how I felt being snubbed by the Bureau for promotions I damn well deserved. You were a tough act to follow as far as the brass was concerned. But you weren't smart enough to figure this one out. Not 'til it was too late to stop it."

Spencer was stunned at everything he'd just heard. Clearly, Jeremy's resentment of him had crossed over into madness. That was his problem. Spencer had to make sure he and Deidre came out of this alive.

Deidre felt the cold steel of the gun barrel against her skin and did not dare make a move. She remembered when Marshall chose to fight the carjacker for control of the gun, only to end up dead, along with their little boy. She couldn't act impulsively only to have the same fate.

But I can't just sit back and do nothing, either, or Jeremy will surely kill us both and probably get away with it.

"You don't have to do this, Jeremy," she said desperately.

"Oh, I think I do," he said.

Deidre winced. "You'll never get away with it."

Jeremy laughed. "I have so far. With the only living witnesses dead, I'll be home free."

Spencer was now within reach of Jeremy, but had no intention of risking Deidre's life by being reckless. *Just keep him talking.* "I suppose you killed Clint Winston, too?" Spencer guessed.

Jeremy saw no reason to deny it at this point. "He was strictly a diversion to shift attention elsewhere. I figured a good old-fashioned robbery-homicide might give the cops something more to think about. Didn't exactly put a dent in the task force investigation, but what the hell? Just another bastard put out to pasture. Like you two will be shortly." He pushed the barrel of the gun into the soft skin at the side of Deidre's head. "Say bye-bye to your sweetheart, Spencer . . ."

Deidre suddenly saw what Marshall must have seen in refusing to give in to the carjacker as a matter of survival and maybe a healthy dose of stubbornness. When Jeremy turned his eyes to look at Spencer for an instant, Deidre knew it was now or never. She grabbed the gun and turned it away from her face, pointing it up as a shot rang out. It echoed in the air, blending with the sound of rain pelting the roof.

Before Jeremy could redirect the gun, Spencer used the opening to attack him, pushing Deidre aside. He wrestled the killer to the floor, causing the gun to fly across the room. The two men fought. A determined Spencer gained the upper hand with two solid blows to Jeremy's jaw, one of which may have broken it, rendering him unconscious.

Deidre quickly scampered in the darkness for the gun, not knowing if she would need to use it. By the time she had retrieved the weapon, the nightmare was over with Spencer in full control atop the Park Killer.

"Are you all right, Deidre?" Spencer asked worriedly.

"I am now," she said with a deep sigh.

"I'm glad to hear that, because if anything had happened to you—"

"You would've been devastated," she finished.

Spencer smiled. "Something like that."

Deidre smiled too. "Well, I couldn't let that happen. Not when we both have so much more to live for."

"My sentiments exactly, baby."

The lights suddenly came back on, as if to reiterate that the force of darkness had been successfully repelled.

EPILOGUE

Charity tossed the Frisbee and Sky galloped after it, jumping at the precise moment to catch it in midair.

"Good going, Sky!" she exclaimed.

"Just be sure to stay in the leash-free zone with that Frisbee," Spencer called out.

"We will, Daddy."

Spencer beamed and turned to his fiancée, as they walked hand in hand in Pelle Park on a sunny afternoon, keeping one eye on Charity and Sky and the other on each other.

"Looks like Sky is pretty much back to his old self," Spencer said thankfully, the poison now completely out of the dog's system three weeks after the incident.

"I never imagined he wouldn't be," Deidre said. "Like Sky's owner, he's hard to keep down for long."

Spencer grinned. "You've got that right."

He thought about Jeremy Haskell. The former profiler had been arrested and charged with multiple counts of aggravated assault, rape, and murder, among other offenses. He had made a full confession and promised to be some aspiring true crime writer's dream, not to mention clinical psychologists.

"Think you'll ever know what really made Jeremy snap like that?" Deidre asked, gazing up at the man she planned to marry this fall. She assumed there had to be some underlying issues, mental or otherwise, to cause

Jeremy to become a homicidal psychopath over and beyond his resentful hatred of Spencer.

It was a question Spencer had pondered as both a criminal psychologist and a man who had once considered Jeremy a friend. Spencer suspected that it might take years to come up with an answer. This made his decision easier, with Deidre's approval, to rejoin the FBI as a means to try to do just that, as well as assess and profile other future psychotic and violent individuals.

"Not sure any psychologist—forensic, clinical, educational, or otherwise—will be able to unravel that mystery," Spencer said honestly. "But I'm certainly willing to try. All I can say for now is that Jeremy must have gone off the deep end after his wife left him, unbeknownst to me. It didn't help when his problems on the job seemed to magnify. I suppose I was a convenient scapegoat for all his troubles, even if I had a few of my own along the way."

"Haven't we all," Deidre said thoughtfully.

"But at least two people, in particular, have found a way to turn those troubles into something very constructive."

She smiled genuinely. "I agree."

"I thought you would." Spencer smiled back, putting a protective arm around her shoulders.

Deidre looped her arm around his lower back. In spite of the joy she felt in her life right now, there were still some anxieties, such as becoming a mother again to a wonderful little girl. She looked at Charity, who was giggling and running around in circles with Sky.

"How do you think Charity will feel having two mothers to cope with?" Deidre raised her eyes to Spencer.

He stared at his daughter, believing Charity was a well-adjusted little girl, smart beyond her years, and coping with every trauma that came her way. She also happened to adore Deidre almost as much as Spencer did.

"I think she'll love being doted on by *both* of you—meaning twice the love and devotion."

Deidre flashed her teeth. "I was thinking the very same thing." She rested her head against his chest. "You know my parents are really excited about this wedding and, of course, meeting Charity, Sky, and Evan."

Spencer thought of how his father had turned out to be a hero by being in the right place at the right time to provide the tip needed to nail the Park Killer, even collecting reward money as a result of it leading to Jeremy's capture.

Gripping Deidre a little more firmly, Spencer felt warmth envelope him. "They couldn't be nearly as excited as I am. This time I plan to make the wedding bells last a lifetime." He had at last met his soul mate in a woman who had shown him the meaning of true love. They had both been tested more than once and used this to elevate themselves beyond to discover the best in each other. For that he would always be grateful and planned to show this to his beloved time and time again, so she never questioned it or his devotion to her and what they had together.

"You'd better." Deidre refused to think about just how short such a lifetime could be, preferring instead to think that the second time around would be the charm, blessing her and Spencer for years to come. She was sure that destiny was smiling upon her, along with Marshall and Adam, who could only be comforted in knowing she had found a way to move on and someone very special to share her life with. She cherished everything that Spencer brought to the table and knew there was even more he would give as a husband and loving partner. He had gained her trust and undying commitment to making this a marriage that would combine their collective experiences in making each a better person. Together, there would be no stopping them from achieving the ultimate in happiness.

"Maybe Charity will have a little sister or brother to play with someday when Sky gets too old or cranky," Spencer suggested wistfully.

"That sounds like a wonderful idea to me," Deidre said, thrilled at the notion of having a child or two of their own, with Adam's spirit ever present and rooting them on.

"You're wonderful, Deidre," Spencer stated unequivocally.

"Oh, really?" she gushed. "So prove it, Mr. Berry."

"It would be my pleasure."

Spencer turned Deidre into his arms and gave her a mouth-watering kiss, determined to convince her beyond a shadow of a doubt that he was a man every bit as good as his words. Of course, he understood that the true measure of his feelings and deep love for this woman could only come over time, when they could grow old together and make good use of the golden years. He very much looked forward to the journey and had the perfect woman in Deidre to share it with.

But for the moment, his attention was devoted toward enjoying the sweetness of her lips beneath his. From the penetrating kiss that was being returned, it was clear to Spencer that Deidre was of precisely the same mind.